TENDING TO VIRGINIA

"Miss McCorkle's sense of pacing and restraint imbues the novel with the best kind of suspense. It's almost as if the story were being told on a front porch on one of those rare Southern summer nights, with a breeze stirring and the promise of early-morning rain. She makes the reader want to know what happens next, and in so doing, she inextricably binds the reader's heart."

The Richmond News Leader

"A profound picture of the legacies of families, one that will stay in the reader's mind."

The [Memphis] Commercial Appeal

"An immensely enjoyable book. Every family has its secret and unknown personalities, and *Tending to Virginia* just might get you thinking about where you came from."

Milwaukee Journal

"It is [the]...talking — the perfect dialogue, the vivid recollections, the memories and emotions... that make *Tending to Virginia* so rewarding."

The New York Times Book Review

Also by Jill McCorkle:

THE CHEER LEADER

JULY 7TH

TENDING TO VIRGINIA

A Novel by

Jill McCorkle

FAWCETT CREST • NEW YORK

A Fawcett Crest Book
Published by Ballantine Books
Copyright © 1987 by Jill McCorkle

Library of Congress Catalog Card Number 87-1481

ISBN 0-449-21624-1

This edition published by arrangement with Algonquin Books of Chapel Hill.

Manufactured in the United States of America

First Ballantine Books Edition: October 1988
Third Printing: October 1991

IN MEMORY OF *Claudia Meares Bullington*

With love for:

Margaret Ann (Annie) Meares Collins
Melba Collins McCorkle
Jan McCorkle Gane
and
Margaret Ann (Annie) Gane

Thus strangely are our souls constructed and by such slight ligaments are we bound to prosperity or ruin.

Mary Shelley, *Frankenstein*

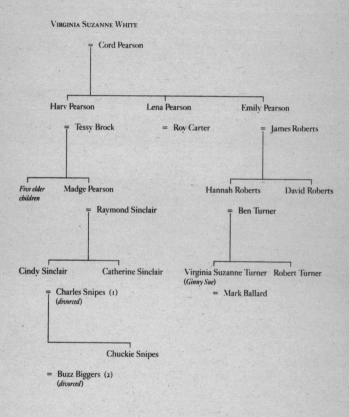

PART I

VIRGINIA WAKES TO THE GENTLE PRESSURE OF MARK'S hand, there, the baby, distended abdomen like a moonlit mountain in the pale glare of the streetlight. She lies dark beneath it as though there is no connection to this mound of flesh, no connection to the man whose hand has found its way to her. She turns her face to a cool spot on the pillow; aware that his hand has fallen beside her, touching her thigh; but, she is heavy with sleep, with eyelids that won't open, at that fine line between the two worlds, and turning back to a scene so clear in her mind. Perhaps there was a photograph, somewhere, in some box, or maybe it is a picture that she has made up herself, outlined by words and memories, and then colored:

Gram is sitting in the front porch swing, her hair dark then, the calm heartshaped face, pale green eyes, a wide placid stare and when the movement begins, she pushes lightly off the gray planked floor, swing gently rocking, her fingers running down the split husk while peas fall into the colander in her lap. Gram moves freely in this scene, up and down the garden, while her little sister, Lena, sits on the porch railing, one foot propped up while she paints her toenails bright red. Lena's loose white skirt billows with a slight breeze, showing her thigh; her dark auburn hair, frizzy and bobbed. She is waiting for Roy Carter to pick her up in his fancy car with the convertible top.

"Lena thought I needed her company the summer my baby died," Gram said. "I didn't have the heart to tell her there was nothing anybody could do."

Lena said, "Emily needed me all that summer. I couldn't

3

go back to New York with her that way. It was like I was her
mama." And Lena stayed the summer, Roy Carter driving
down from New York to see her, while Gramps sat in the
side yard and whittled pointed ends on tomato stakes and
stared at the chicken-wire dog pen built years before.

* * *

It is going to be another beautiful day, no clouds, might
hit a hundred, rain not in sight for a week, better water
those lawns. Virginia could kill the weatherman, kill Mark
for not turning off the radio alarm and the sun not even up.
Barefoot and pregnant. That is the line that stays in her
mind this summer. Barefoot and pregnant and hot as hell.
She stretches her legs flat against the sheet, so cool where
the sweat has gathered behind her knees, and focuses on the
sound of the window unit as it spits and gurgles and stirs
the humid air. She would kill for central air, kill for a cigarette, to be on a beach towel, the ocean roaring, that
breeze, hipbones visible while the radio plays old songs.
When I was a single girl used to go to the store and buy.
Now I am a married girl, just rock that baby and cry. That's
what she sings in her head but it clashes with Nat King
Cole's "Lazy Hazy Crazy Days of Summer," Mark whistling, whistling "Lazy Hazy Crazy Days of Summer" when
he is the one that complains about the North Carolina summers even though he goes and sits in an air-conditioned
library all day to study, even though he can put on clothes
that he wore seven and a half months ago, even though she
is ready to explode like a bottle rocket.
    The dull morning light, framed by the window, clouds when
Mark opens the bathroom door and stands there, towel around
his waist, thick curly hair slicked back. He steps into the
darkness of the room and just stands there, a dark shadow at
the foot of the bed, a faceless creature who tiptoes, slowly
opens drawers in a way that prolongs every creak and whine.
She feels the bed slope, hears him pulling up his socks. *One
hundred dollars to the fourth caller who can name the song
that we played to wake you up this morning. If you're heading
to the beach, better take sunscreen. We're talking heat wave,
folks, and here's Linda Ronstadt. . . .* Too late for sunscreen,
got a brown patch, just above the right cheekbone, symbol
of fertility. She turns and tosses, writhes as if she is asleep

when Mark's mouth, fresh with Colgate brushes her lips. "I love you," he whispers, and though there is an impulse to respond, she continues to act, a deep sigh as she turns away from him. She wishes she could place her face into the cool pillow, hide, but there is an obstacle, a large round obstacle which houses a mutant-looking creature with tiny ears and arms, and the creature just hides there, waiting. As soon as its baby pink lungs become independent, it will bust out and take control of her life. And for those of you students taking off for a wild season, just remember . . . See You in September.

She will see it before September. She will see it in August, a month and a half and she will see it; she will be up on that table like the women in the films, her knees bent and parted, while she stares at the mirror on the opposite wall. She will see her face, white and drawn, a hand on her arm, and she will breathe, breathe, scream as it fights its way out for air, scream when she sees it, small and bloody.

Barefoot and pregnant. It is a growth the size of a pumpkin that makes her pee incessantly, makes her sit with her legs splayed like a woman she once saw at a bus station—brown polyester, plastic bubble beads, a child with Nab crumbs all over its mouth. "I told you to sit in that chair and be still," the woman snapped and he obeyed, one little tennis shoe going back and forth like a windshield wiper until the woman slapped his leg. Now, she can't get that dirty little face off of her mind, the small solemn girl who always sat at the back when Virginia went on Tuesday mornings to give the first graders their art lesson; the girl would never look her in the eye, would never smile and lean close as the other children did when she squatted by their desks. Screams echo through Rose Dime Store every time she goes to buy more Formby's refinisher. Everywhere she goes there are children that need to blow their noses, need to tie their shoes, sitting in grocery carts, grunting with their little arms outstretched for Smurfberry Crunch or Lucky Charms.

When she hears Mark's car door slam, she makes her way into the bathroom. The fluorescent glare of porcelain makes her squint as she bends to pick up wet towels, dirty socks and underwear, stops the shower from leaking, puts the cap back on the toothpaste. And this is only the beginning, the beginning of another long boring day, the beginning of another six weeks, and then what? God, then what? "Today is the first day of the rest of your life," a girl with straight orange hair used to tell everyone in junior high. The girl would say, "Smile, God loves you!" and once she had made her way over to Virginia after Sunday school. "God would like for us to be friends," the girl said. "God and I know that you're a believer but what good is it if you won't tell others? What good is it if you act like you're too good? Today is the first day of the rest of your life!" And Virginia had frozen, hoping that someone, something would intervene. She finally smiled noncommittally and said that she had to be excused, had to hurry, had to go meet her cousin.

"Why don't you just tell her you know all that already?" her cousin Cindy had asked. "Why don't you say 'yeah and I ain't going to spend the rest of my life listening to you. Dye your hair. It would make the rest of mine and everybody else's life better.' " Cindy had laughed, leaning up against the back of the church building, smoking a cigarette, planning how she was going to skip church. The thought of the orange-haired girl placed next to Cindy was sad, Cindy with her thick blonde hair streaked by the sun, and those pale blue eyes made bluer by her tan.

"I can't say that!" Virginia said, worried that Cindy was going to get caught, though Cindy didn't seem the least bit worried.

"Then live with it. Live the rest of your life with it," Cindy said and made herself comfortable on the large root of a shade tree. She pulled a worn copy of *Peyton Place* from her pocketbook and opened it. "See you after church."

Now, that girl with the orange hair has an illegitimate baby and bartends in Clemmonsville. She wore tight black jeans and a halter top to Virginia's high school reunion. And what happened to her? What shaped that shy, orange-haired born-again girl who could add and subtract so well in the first grade into that? And to Cindy? Cindy, now married, divorced, married, divorced, and still ticking along like a little windup toy, still talking about *Peyton Place* whenever book reading is a topic of conversation. Cindy's daddy killed himself and nobody has ever been exactly sure why; Cindy's own sister won't have anything to do with her, and she just keeps right on going to Ramada Inn every Friday night hoping to meet a man. Cindy does not get along with her mama, which is sad since Madge is all by herself now. It would be hard enough to have Cindy for a daughter, petite and cute and full of herself, while Madge is as big and lifeless as a rock, long ago given up on fashionable clothes; she wears drab dark pantsuits when she's not in her hygienist uniform.

"Having a baby is nothing," Cindy said. "Just go in, lie flat on your back, say 'I'm in terrific pain! I don't think I can live!' They'll give you some drugs, prop your feet up, tell you to count a little and when you wake up you're still on six and they tell you if it's a boy or a girl."

"Mark and I are doing natural."

"Well, then don't complain about it!"

Pregnant. Barefoot and pregnant. A derogatory connotation, a picture of a female clad in a gunnysack with a brood of runny-nosed children and a distended belly just like her own.

"Grandma Tessy had nine babies," Cindy told her. "Good God what her stomach must've looked like. Now I can still wear a bikini. Of course I Fonda to keep myself this way."

"Tessy had herself a terrible time," Gram told once. "Had herself three miscarriages. I didn't have but one."

"I was in J.C. Penney's buying your daddy some socks when my water broke," her mother said. "I just drove on to the hospital."

"I didn't have a child because I never wanted a child," her great aunt Lena said and lit a cigarette. "Who had time?"

* * *

There are times like right now when she doesn't believe it, when she gets this odd sense that nothing is happening and that she will be this way forever with her navel turned inside out and poking up through the orange nightshirt that she has worn until it makes her sick. "The Great Pumpkin," Mark likes to say when she's getting ready for bed, rubbing his hand over her navel, the growth on the growth. Sometimes it makes her mad for him to touch it that way, to look at it; sometimes she doesn't want to touch it herself and there are people that she barely knows who think they have some right to walk up and pat her stomach like it might be a dog.

"Wait until it comes out!" she had snapped at one of Mark's tennis buddies the other day. "You can pat it all you want then."

The man's wife who was standing beside her laughed, halfway, her teeth clenched together. But women will do it, too; that same wife had already patted her stomach and called her "little mommy" and gone on and on with "when *we* had our baby, when we had *our* baby, blah blah blah," until Virginia wanted to throw up which she's been doing quite often anyway. "Then go have mine," she felt her mouth shaping the words. "If you know all about it, then go have mine," but Mark was making his embarrassing moment apologies, laughing like it was no big deal and dragging her to the car.

"That was uncalled for." Mark turned halfway toward her on the seat as they were leaving the tennis courts, his hand suspended like he had been about to pat and caught himself, his mind really on this case or that case, the legalities of life, innocent until proven guilty.

"It *was* uncalled for." She clasped her hand protectively around her stomach. "He can pat his own wife. She loves having babies and is the specialist on it all so she can just get pregnant and he can pat her. People have babies all over the world, every minute. You can just about grow one in a bottle, keep it on your windowsill. It's not big deal." She laughed a sarcastic mimic of the tennis player, loud and obnoxious, and then fell silent, first staring at her stomach and then at Mark's profile, straight nose, jaw clenched.

"It is a big deal," he said quietly, eyes on the road. "He didn't mean anything by it."

"But what if I wasn't pregnant?" she asked, suddenly ready to prove her point. "What if I wasn't and men kept walking up to me and rubbing and patting my abdomen, women, too. What if everywhere we went, somebody wanted to feel my stomach, would that make you mad?"

"It's different," he said calmly.

"No it isn't, it's still *my* stomach. It's like renting an apartment, I still own the building."

"Let's not argue," he said and reached his open palm across the front seat. "Please."

"I just don't like him at all," she said, a fact stated, calmness coming to her voice as she took Mark's hand, loosely cupping her own around it. "It's something about the way that his head is so flat and wide. I bet his mama had a hell of a time with that head." She lifted up the bottom of her

yellow sack dress and angled the air conditioning vent so that
it would blow up her body and maybe cool her off.

"Let's not argue." It seems that Mark has said that a lot
these days and she hates that yellow dress. She loathes it and
there it is right now hanging on the door, waiting for her to
get in it again, transforming her from the Great Pumpkin into
a giant squash like one she saw in her hometown paper once—
a squash just about as big as its grower who was a farmer
in a neighboring county. She was a teenager then, a thin, lean
teenager who never questioned that she had ribs and hip
bones, and everyone in the county, including her father,
had spent the summers since tending their squash in hopes
that one morning there would be one the size of a Volks-
wagen.

"I'm going to shred this dress into dust cloths," she had
told Mark when they got home from the tennis court. He just
nodded and stretched his legs out on the coffee table, one
foot going back and forth like a windshield wiper. *You sit in
that chair and be still.* "It'll make good ones, cheerful bright
dust cloths," he said and she went out in the yard and pulled
up every weed she could find; she even pulled a few out of
her neighbor's yard, the ones that looked like they would pole
through the fence if they didn't cut their grass soon.

"We got a boy coming to cut it today," Mrs. Short's voice
startled her and she pulled her hand back through the wire
and stood up. "Can't keep it cut often enough," she said and
swatted at a gnat with her hand. "Grow like weeds, that's
what people say about children, grow like weeds. One of
mine's a wild weed for sure."

Virginia let the weed in her hand slip to her own rented
grass that came with the rented house, temporary, temporary,
a temporary life; pregnancy is temporary. Breast-feeding,
kindergarten, junior high, college, all temporary. Birth de-
fects, reform schools, jail sentences, could be permanent.
She knew Mrs. Short's wild weed all right; he drives an old
souped up Corvette and spends every weekend washing and
waxing it, all kinds of things hanging on the rearview mirror,
and then he goes off and does who knows what with his tee
shirt cut up to show his navel and black spike arm bands.
Virginia moved slowly to her flower bed and began weeding
there, all temporary flowers, one shot. She won't be here next
spring; she won't be here in three months. She will be in

Richmond in another temporary place with a temporary job and temporary day care.

"Gonna have yourself your own weed pretty soon," Mrs. Short said. "Hope it turns out all right." She screamed something into the kitchen and Virginia caught herself staring at Mrs. Short, her full breasts under a polyester tank top, the disbelief that there was a time when that boy with his spikey hair and greasy hands had curled there. "You just tend to your own weeds now, I'll get mine cut directly," she snapped and went into the house. Virginia stood there, hands pressed into her back, dirt on the front of that yellow dress, first feeling her cheeks flame with the reprimand and then feeling so angry that she wanted to dump all of the weeds she had pulled over the fence. "You tend to yours," she murmured, bending to pick up the one she had dropped.

"If we had to stay here forever, I'd build an eight-foot fence," she told Mark, who had not moved the entire time that she had been outside working like a dog. "When we move to Richmond, I want to live somewhere where I can come and go and never see another person."

"Don't count on it," he said solemnly, the same voice, same tone as when he said "let's not argue."

And she won't count on it, can't count on anything except what she already knows, the future so unknown, looming like a big dead-end billboard, temporarily blank white with no clue of the end result. And what she does know—the quiet coolness of her grandmother's old house, Lena's laughter, the rhythmic whirr of her mother's sewing machine—makes her so homesick. Hell, she'd settle for riding around with Cindy with the radio going full blast, and Cindy lighting one cigarette after another while she told with soap opera drama about her latest fling. Virginia wishes she had kept working; she bets her sixth grade art students have ruined their projects over the past two weeks. She bets that substitute knows nothing about putting papier-mâché on a balloon to make a puppet head. Well, that's all right. Let them screw up their puppets. Another week and they'll be singing "Put Away Your Books and Papers" and dashing from that cafeteria like a band of dwarfed devils on the verge of acne, to have bike wrecks and bust their heads on diving boards, and she can't help that.

She rubs her hand over her stomach and feels so detached

from it all, this house, this room, that man that eats, sleeps, reads, and showers here. She has to think of things familiar, things that keep her busy, things that can put it all in perspective. She has stripped down to bare oak four chairs that once belonged to her Great Aunt Lena and is working now on the table where Lena and Roy Carter ate every day for thirty-five years. The table had been a permanent part of Lena's life; it lived with her and Roy in New York, Florida, Detroit, right back to Saxapaw. It had always been in the kitchen when she got up. It never made Lena cry or feel sick.

She has read a crock of Spock and every *Southern Living* she can get her hands on just so she can salivate when she sees what people do to walls that they own and do not rent. *Glamour* is too depressing at this stage with her dark frizzy hair still frizzier. And she has this dark patch, a dark patch just above the cheek. And, she hates yellow. She wishes there was absolutely nothing yellow in the entire world. "Yellow is perfect for a nursery because it can go either way—boy or girl, yellow," the tennis guy's wife had said. Screw here, impregnate her, paint her life yellow. But, hadn't Virginia said thank you? Yellow, a good idea. And she had gotten permission from the landlord to paint that small spare room yellow, and the woman had arrived with rollers and cans and the two of them, Virginia and this friendly stranger, had painted and laughed and talked about how exciting it all was.

* * *

Virginia's own nursery had been half of her brother's room, pale blue walls and white curtains with blue ball fringe. Her crib was in one corner, Little Bo Beep and Jack and Jill cutouts on the wall beside her. There are pictures of her sitting there, propped up and baldheaded, while Robert reached his arms inside the bars to touch her. The rest of the room was cluttered with cars and trucks, his kindergarten paintings decorating the walls of his half. He had his "big boy" bed with the blue and white striped spread that their mother had made, George, the big stuffed monkey that sat on the bed while Robert wasn't there. Though Virginia's mother is not the kind to hold onto everything that has some sentimental value, she has never been able to part with George, or with

Virginia's equivalent, Pinky, a large pink rabbit that in the pictures is bigger than Virginia. George and Pinky have been wrapped in plastic and sitting in the attic for years now.

When Virginia was old enough for a bed, and Robert complained that she broke his crayons and touched his things when he had told her not to, Virginia was moved into the sewing room where her mother sat and worked most of the day, the hum of her machine nonstop, bolts of cloth piled in the corner at the foot of the "big girl" bed, which had a pink polka-dot spread that her mother had made. "Don't sit on the cloth," her mother would say, her words garbled by the straight pins that she held between her lips.

"It just isn't fair is it?" her mother asked one day after she had told Virginia that she couldn't take her shoes off until the room had been swept free of pins. They had already started having to keep that headless black mannequin in the living room at night because Virginia couldn't sleep with her in the same room. "It isn't fair to either one of us."

Soon after that, her mother rented a part of a small building downtown. It was a green cinderblock building that had been attached like some kind of afterthought to the long line of tall stores and offices on Main Street. Two men came to their house in a pickup truck and loaded the sewing machine, floor lamps, bolts of cloth, and headless woman and took them to the building where Virginia stood and watched the backwards letters as her mother stood outside and carefully stenciled "The Busy Bee" on the large plate glass window.

"It's all yours now," her mother had said, and in came the maple dresser and mirror that Lena had grown tired of, up went the white curtains with the pink ball fringe. "Now you have your very own room just like Robert."

She had always had her own room at Gram's house, at least that's what Gram said. Gram had two bedrooms that no one ever even used unless she had company. Virginia's room there had a big high double bed that sank when she got in the middle, the feather mattress fluffing up all around her so that if she got up very carefully, she could see where she had been, her shape like a snow angel, left there until Gram came in and fluffed it back up. It was a corner room that got the late afternoon light that made everything look golden, the specks of dust riding the thin planes of light that came through the venetian blinds. There was a large wardrobe, the inside piled with quilts, and a big overstuffed chair positioned such that whoever sat there could see out into the side yard and into Gram's garden.

Virginia loved to spend the night with Gram, and she would go first thing and place her clothes in the top drawer of the big dark dresser, put Pinky in the center of that bed. But when it started getting dark, she would have to go get Pinky and bring him into Gram's room. Virginia only slept in her room in the daytime, at nap time, when she could raise the blinds and see Gram out working in the garden or picking up pecans in the side yard. When night came, she slept with Gram, a secret which Gram promised never to tell. "This is my room," she would tell Cindy whenever Cindy went with her to spend the night. "This is where I keep my clothes," and she would show Cindy her drawer and then offer the one beside it.

"It's not *really* your room," Cindy would say and flop down on the soft bed which Virginia would then fluff back up. "It's your grandmother's room. It used to be your uncle's room and he's dead. He might even come back at night and want to sleep here and then what are you going to do?"

"That is nonsense," Gram said, when it was just the two of them. "If David did come back, which he isn't, he wouldn't hurt a hair on your head."

When Virginia turned thirteen, her mother said that she could decorate her room any way that she wanted, within reason, of course. Getting a set of French provincial furniture like Cindy had with a canopy bed and little velvet-seated vanity was not within reason, so they painted Virginia's furniture white. She had in her mind that she could then get some gold paint and edge around all of the drawers and her headboard; her mother said that she didn't think that was a good idea so they compromised on a trip to Sherwin-Williams, where Virginia was allowed to pick out her wall paint. Her mother liked the pale, iced pink and Virginia liked the flamingo pink, a color that would have matched a piece of Bazooka bubblegum. They finally settled on lavender and waited while the man mixed the colors to match the little card that Virginia held.

"And look what I just happen to have," her mother said when they got home with the cans of paint, and she pulled a bolt of cloth from under the living room sofa; it was a bolt of thick shiny cotton, stripes in pastel colors. "The lavender is a perfect match," she said and held the card against the cloth; the pale iced pink would've matched it, too. "I can make curtains and a bedspread." But Virginia wanted the white eyelet one that she had seen in the J.C. Penney's catalog; she didn't want a pastel baby room, and had already imagined the white spread with lots of velvet pillows in a deep purple.

"Isn't that beautiful?" her mother asked when Virginia showed her the picture. "I could never make one like that I'm afraid." And while Virginia waited, trying to imagine what she could do with the room if it had those pastel stripes, her mother went to the phone and called J.C. Penney's to place the order.

Now, she goes into *its* room, its pale yellow room, where she has halfway painted a large canvas, her version of The Animal Kingdom, a cross between Noah and the Ark and Mutual of Omaha, a clear hot blue sky and the yellow eyes of a tiger. She bought that canvas with such a nice picture in her mind, tame gentle animals with cute little faces like Care Bears and Peppi Le Peu, but she has done the opposite.

"Maybe if you didn't use the encyclopedia," Mark had said last night when he finally came home from the library, dark circles under those big blue eyes. She didn't feel sorry for that, a little sleep or an erase stick will cover that; his fate is not in a jar of Porcelana. The library is where he said he had been but he could have been anywhere at all and how would she know? *Don't believe everything you hear.* Whole truths, half truths, believing in something only to find that there's more to it. "You know, maybe you could use the Frosted Flakes box for a tiger, Kix for a rabbit." He leaned against the doorway and smiled, tired, earnest eyes.

"Look," she said, her paint brush dipped in serpent-tongue pink. "Am I going to tell you how to run a divorce when somebody comes to you wanting one? Am I going to tell you how to divide and separate somebody's life like an egg?"

"You might," he said and shook his head. "I wish you'd get off the divorce thing; it's not like that's all I'll be doing. I mean people get divorced and occasionally I'll probably be handling one. Somebody has to do it."

"Somebody has to collect trash," she said and drew that

long serpent tongue out further than she'd intended. "Why don't you do that? You can start with your first wife." Eat this fly, and she dabbed a blob of black just short of the tongue. She watched him leaning there, his eyes staring into a borrowed crib, blanket and tiny quilts that Gram had made years ago, stacked there. His shoulders curved forward, head shaking slowly.

"Look," he said. "I never lied to you about being divorced. You knew from the very beginning. You're the one that wanted to keep it a secret from your family. I'm not ashamed that I made a mistake."

"But I didn't know you had other secrets," she said, glancing away from his stare. "I was afraid my family might get the wrong idea about you if I told them in the very beginning."

"And what's the excuse now?"

"Because now, I see that I had the wrong idea about you," she said. "I mean, divorce I could handle; I lived with someone. I almost got married myself. You told me your divorce was mutual, a joint mistake."

"And I should have left it at that," he said. "I never should have tried to explain. I just wish you could leave it back where it belongs."

"Leave it?" She painted spiky hair on the camel's hump because that's how it really is, not soft like a stuffed one but sharp and coarse, a thin bony face with bared teeth. "You lied to me. You said you were both so unhappy, both wanted out. You saved the other part; you didn't want out. Let me get big as a horse and then tell me all about it. If Sheila hadn't gotten an abortion, if Sheila hadn't made that big decision, you would have stayed with her."

"Yes," he said, still staring in the crib. "But I knew it wouldn't have worked. It would not have worked."

"But you cared enough to try," she said, bending her knees to reach another brush. "I don't know why you felt the sudden urge to confess unless it's that now I'm well beyond the point of Sheila's decision. I mean, I have no choice. Here's your baby." She stood and patted her stomach, paint from the brush dripping to the floor. "After all these years, here's your baby."

"What do you want, Virginia? Would it make you feel better if I was the kind of person who didn't take marriage seriously, the kind who would look at his wife and say, 'sure, get an abortion, I don't care.' ''

"I don't like being the substitute. At least before I didn't know that I was just filling in where Sheila decided to spread her wings and fly away."

"I shouldn't have said anything, or I should have said everything sooner, I realize that now." He stepped closer, his voice attempting softness. "I just wanted you to know how important it all is to me, how very lucky I feel. I guess I wanted to be reassured that you feel that way, too."

"Yeah." Give that rhino a long sharp blood-spearing horn. "It's on your mind, been on your mind since you got that offer in Richmond—home to Richmond, Sheila's hometown. She might even decide to move back there one day, you know?"

"She might," he said with an edge like she might be a child, like she might be a sixth grader putting papier-mâché on a balloon. "And then, she probably won't; she lives in New York, has for years, married. She might even have a child."

"Might even have a child, well." She stood, her hands pressing the small of her back, every ounce of blood draining to those puffy flounder-looking feet. "What do you mean might? You know. You keep in touch with some of the same old friends. You hear everything about Sheila and I guarantee she hears what she wants to hear about you."

"Okay, she has a child. She's an interior designer, married to a banker. I can probably find out more information if you need it." He slapped his hand against the side of the crib, a little stack of blankets falling to the side. "Can't we leave it alone? Please?"

"I can. I had forgotten all about Sheila. You're the one that started feeling like your life was repeating itself, started questioning. Ask me if I'm sure that I want a baby. Look at me! Come touch it now." She watched the paint make another drop on the floor. "I mean it's a little late to change my mind." She started a big black could in the corner just above that elephant's eye. He never asked her questions about how she almost married Bryan Parker; he said it was in the past and didn't matter. No damn wonder. It was a part of her life wasn't it? "I don't even know why you married me," she said, attempting to choke back whatever emotion was rising in her throat. "Except to have a baby, somebody to work so there would be a salary and health insurance so that this baby could be born in a hospital instead of the backyard."

"Might as well be the backyard if that's what he's going to grow up looking at." He pointed at her vulture circling the sky. "I mean look, a vulture? A *vulture* in a baby's room?" She reached up, magenta, a drop of magenta on the vulture's beak. "Oh, that's good," he said. "How about a carcass? A collie's maybe? Let's put Lassie's skeleton right here." And he pointed to the olive-green swamp where the alligators live. "How about a big bulge in the snake here and then you can tell all about how snakes eat rabbits, little bunnies like the Easter Bunny, and the Lord God made them all."

"This vulture up here is your daddy," she said in a story-telling voice. "And this is you." She dotted a dot of brown in the swamp. "You are the little baby parasite here in the water."

"Good," he said. "Funny."

"It's a shame you didn't handle your own divorce." she said. "Maybe Sheila would have paid alimony."

"Maybe I'll handle ours," he said and she had not turned from the jungle until she heard the front door slam and the car crank and she outlined a fat pregnant monkey and started crying. She had faked sleep when he came back, crawling up beside her, whispered murmurs of sorry and love and everything will be fine, all of the things that she wanted to hear and believe. And just like this morning, she wanted to turn and say it all back to him, but she couldn't. She couldn't pretend nothing had happened.

Virginia goes and plugs in the Mr. Coffee, her mind still on last night, still on the night a month ago when Mark, in the darkness when she was almost asleep, began talking, leaving her first silent, then hurt, then angrily separated from him as if Sheila had found her way into their home and into their bed. And it comes and goes, silence, anger, fatigue, thoughts of Gram and Lena and her mother, all of them carrying on their days so quiet and simply, thoughts of leaving it all behind, everything here, and going home where the history and knowledge is solid.

Too much caffeine is not good, not good for the two of you. She makes an eight-cup pot and goes to sit on the screened porch, first reaching up to that rotted rented rafter to find two stale Virginia Slims all wrapped up in a baggie, given to her by Cindy just last weekend, one of the quiet days when she had returned Mark's morning hug and clung to him with a brief feeling of hopefulness that she could put it all behind.

"He isn't going to know if you smoke one little cigarette," Cindy said, reaching into her Kenya bag, interrupting Virginia's thoughts of the wonderful mural she would paint for the nursery, friendly pastels. "I hate this fucking purse," Cindy said while pulling out tube after tube of lipstick. "I wouldn't even carry it if everybody else wasn't. Here." She handed Virginia the mashed up pack. "It's got your name written right there on the pack," Cindy laughed. "I hope you don't mind that I still call you Ginny Sue. I mean if I suddenly up and went to college and switched off to Cynthia, you'd have a hard as hell time changing." Cindy shook her head, those short mousse-spiked bangs not even moving. "I don't know why you changed it to begin with. Go on, smoke up. Beats the hell out of having a fit." Cindy plopped down on the door stoop. "I didn't smoke during the Smoke-Out except two right before I went to bed. I sat there at the clinic and honest to God I got to feeling like I wanted to bite somebody. You know how it is to go without a cigarette till you want to bite somebody? I mean hard, leave teeth marks and everything. I smoked all the way through my pregnancy and look at my Chuckie, full of air, talks on the phone the tee-total time these days, runs track—and Lordy, baseball, there ain't a thing up in his head but a soggy baseball."

"Chuckie's fine," Virginia said and Cindy laughed, her thin eyebrows arched and Virginia thought how young Cindy looked sitting there in her cut-off jeans and fashionable cropped, paint-splashed-looking tee shirt. It could have been one of those days when they were teenagers and their families went to the beach, Cindy whistling and waving out of car windows to boys they passed while Virginia bent over and fumbled with the radio, painfully aware of her flat chest behind an oversized shirt and her hair too frizzy for a cute pixie cut like Cindy's, her hair too dark for Sun-In.

"Chuckie is fine. That's what I'm telling you," Cindy said. "I probably could've smoked even more. They say it'll make the baby smaller but that's good, I mean, look at my stomach." Cindy lifted her shirt, stood and patted her flat, tan stomach. "Smoke." Cindy fumbled through her bag again and finally gave up and took one of the three that Virginia had removed from the pack.

"I'm going to save these."

"Shoot," Cindy said, blowing a short puff of smoke. "You think what everybody did before Columbus was so great, well think now, my Grandma Tessy smoked a pipe, for years she smoked a pipe and every now and then would flat out chew tobacco. Look at your grandma, for godssakes, Emily dips snuff with her lips like this." Cindy put her tongue down to make her chin stick out and kept talking that way. "Lena smokes more than I do."

"But they didn't know what it could do to them."

"And now they do. In their eighties and they know. Grandma Tessy would know, too, if she was living but tobacco didn't kill her; she lost her mind is what killed her."

"Will you stop talking like that?" Virginia breathed a sigh of relief when Cindy lifted her tongue up towards her nose as if stretching it back in shape.

"Getting a little testy these days, Ginny Sue, better smoke up. Think about it, you say you love Saxapaw, over and over you talk of how much you love home which we all know is because you don't live there, but aside from that, think about it. If it weren't for tobacco we wouldn't have public schools, that new shopping center they're building which is going to have a Nautilus Center and a Baskin Robbins; we wouldn't have the Duplex Cinema or the Putt-Putt range."

"That's not true," Virginia laughed. "Aunt Tessy did not lose her mind. Gram talked to Tessy the day that she died; Gram said she was sharp as ever. And Mama saw her that day and Tessy . . ."

"I know, I know, that dogwood tree story. You have told it so many times that I can say it by heart."

"Well, it's true," Virginia stated, the same tone in her voice that she has always used when Cindy doubted the stories.

"Maybe Emily talked to Grandma Tessy and Emily said, 'Hannah is going to plant herself a dogwood tree today,' and then when your mama got to the hospital, Grandma said, 'Hannah, I sure hope that dogwood lives.' "

"But it didn't happen that way," Virginia said adamantly.

Cindy could get to her so easily, had always been able to get to her. "My mother hadn't told anyone that she had bought that tree. She was at Roses and for some reason she felt the urge to buy a dogwood tree and it was sitting right there in the back of that old Chevrolet station wagon of ours when Mama went in the hospital."

"And Grandma Tessy died and turned into a tree," Cindy said, fumbling again in her bag and this time finding a cigarette.

"I have never said she turned into a tree!" Virginia said, enunciating each word and feeling her face go hot with each wide-eyed lift of Cindy's eyebrows. "We just like to think that it was a sign that her spirit would go on." Virginia was sorry as soon as the words got out.

"Well, I say that if Grandma Tessy wanted to be a tree during eternal life that she would have been a tree in our yard. I mean if I was going to be a tree, I'd be a tree in Chuckie's yard so I could see what he was up to rather than being a tree in your baby's yard."

"Let's stop." Virginia stood, her hands pressed to her back. "Come see if you can wear these dresses of mine."

"Now, if I had a husband when I died, I'd probably want to be planted in his yard so I'd know what he was up to." Cindy brushed off the seat of her pants and followed Virginia inside. "Of course, Grandma Tessy wouldn't have wanted to be in Granddaddy's yard even if he had been living. You know there was that other man that Lena says Grandma had the hots for all those years."

"You don't know that," Virginia said and pulled two sundresses from her closet. She hated seeing them there, size sevens that were snug last summer. "Try these on."

"That's a story, a family story." Cindy lifted her shirt over her head. "Grandma got the hots for this young traveling man, traveling man, isn't it sad about Ricky Nelson?" Virginia nodded and watched Cindy pull the first dress over her head without even taking off her shorts. "I can't say that I blame her with my granddaddy old as the hills."

"Gram says nothing every happened between Tessy and that man."

"Emily ain't God. Besides, Lena says something *did* happen so who knows? My mama doesn't. The whole world is going to pass her by while she plays solitaire and gets bigger.'' Cindy reached back and pulled the zipper up. ''I'm not going to wear a bra with this, waist is a little big, but I'll just wear a belt.'' It made Virginia sick to see that material so loose and full around Cindy's little wasp waist. ''My mama might be a love child. How 'bout that?''

''Your grandma knew that man long before your mama was born. Besides, nothing happened. Here,'' Virginia handed Cindy the other dress, ''they're the same size, I'm sure it'll fit.''

''Well, I want to try it anyway. This material is kind of cute looking, you know prissy and out of date. I might not like it.''

''Beggars can't be choosey.''

''Beggars? Beggars? My whole life I tossed clothes your way until you got so much taller. Good clothes, expensive clothes.'' Cindy stood in the center of the room in her bra and shorts, hands on those thin hips. Just four inches taller, Virginia is only 5'5", was a normal size 7/8 before pregnancy, but Cindy could make her feel like Paul Bunyan's ox. Cindy could make Audrey Hepburn feel fat. ''I happen to know that you never even wore that red crushed leather miniskirt that I wore all through the sixth grade.''

''It was way out of style by the time I got it.''

''I never noticed you were in style,'' Cindy said and pulled the other dress up from her feet. ''You went to college and lived in blue jeans for four years; my life and wardrobe weren't so easy. I wouldn't care if my mama was a love child, a product of lust, Lord God it would be nice to know somebody in the family was hot-blooded.'' Cindy went and stood in front of the mirror, turned side to side, smoothing her hands down her stomach. ''Don't shake your head like that. You've got all those ideas of how everything was or should be and it doesn't make it right. I could be right. Look at my mama some time why don't you? Me and that slut sister of mine, who I don't speak to and so can't recall her name, are the only signs that my mama ever did the act. If I didn't know that Tessy had been as petite as me and hair just as blonde, I'd think I was adopted.''

''Do you want that dress?''

''I'll take it, wouldn't wear it to Ramada but I might wear it around the house.'' She pulled off the dress and put back on her tee shirt. ''I mean I hope that baby of yours is the product of a little lust, 'cause if it isn't then your marriage might be on shaky turf.''

"Just take the dresses,'' Virginia said and thrust the other one at Cindy.

"What is bugging you?'' Cindy took the dress and crammed in into her purse. "Did I hit a raw spot or are you just in need of some nicotine? Mark won't know. I say play while the tomcat's away.''

"He's not the reason I've quit smoking.'' Virginia fluffed up the pillows on the bed, wadded up that orange nightshirt and stuffed it in a drawer.

"Shit. That is the reason, scared he'll get upset with you. I learned from Charles Snipes and then with Buzz Biggers that you can't please 'em all the time so you might as well do what you take in your head to do.''

"Well, I needed to quit. It's not good for me, not good for either of us.''

"Mark is not perfect. God knows that no man is perfect.'' Cindy pulled her car keys out of her back pocket. "I mean he's divorced, not perfect I'll tell you, now I know you hate to think about it but it's the truth, the God's truth. Your husband is divorced.''

"He made a mistake. Look at you, you've made two mistakes.''

"And I might make a third but I don't pretend like I never made them. I don't pretend that none of that ever happened.''

"Mark doesn't pretend.'' Virginia felt her face getting hot again and she wished suddenly that Cindy would get the hell out, take those skimpy-looking dresses and get out.

"No, but *you* do,'' Cindy said. "You can't stand to think that there was somebody before you.''

"Of course I can. I mean there were people before him. I almost got married myself one time, remember?''

"Do I ever?'' Cindy bit her bottom lip and then came over and slung her arm around Virginia's shoulders. "I'm just picking is all. All I'm saying is that he made a mistake so if he says, 'Ginny Sue,' ''

"He calls me Virginia.''

"See? I always forget how you went off to college and changed your name. When he says, 'Virginia, where there's smoke there's fire. I smell smoke on your breath and in your hair' well, then you say, 'Marcus,' ''

"His name is not Marcus."

" 'Mark, I made a mistake just like you made a mistake and I can't take that smoke out of my lungs just like you can't get back all the sperm you lost with what's-her-name.' "

"You're gross."

"But I'm your favorite cousin."

"You're not even a first cousin!"

"It's like we're first cousins, though. It always has been and I see no reason to get into removal shit or second this or that. The fact is we're cousins which makes me your favorite cousin due to the fact that my sister is a slut and so you wouldn't choose her over me." Cindy tightened her arm around Virginia and squeezed once, then abruptly moved away. "C'mon, Ginny, admit it. You're pregnant and that's okay; you aren't going to die like they used to do back in those old days that you think were so perfect. Women had a baby and dropped dead, some of 'em right in the middle of a push with that baby half in and half out. I'm telling you there's nothing to be afraid of. I work in a medical clinic so I know these things. You're pregnant and it's okay. Your husband was married once before, got her pregnant and that's okay, too."

"Cindy," Virginia said. "I asked you never to mention that."

"I haven't told anybody. I'm telling you. I don't know what the big damn secret is any way. I've been married twice and I had a baby and I've still *got* that money-eating baby all grown into a scrawny teenager who thinks he's something."

"Please don't ever tell." Virginia grabbed her arm and held it. "Please don't ever."

"Relax, Ginny Sue. Who would I tell, the old folks? Emily and Lena don't even know who they are half the time."

"Yes, they do."

"Well, I'm not even going to argue that one. But really, who am I going to tell? Your mama?" Cindy laughed. "Hannah would say I was lying because 'Ginny Sue would have told something like that' and I sure as hell wouldn't tell my mama who would say I had made it up just to make you look like you'd picked a wrong number like I've done twice. I wish I did have somebody to tell but I don't."

"Please, just don't tell." Virginia caught herself begging just like all the other times she had confided in Cindy. Cindy

wouldn't really tell; she would just mention it every chance
she got to let Virginia know that she was over a barrel.

"Okay. Thanks for the dresses. Don't *ever* tell that you
gave them to me. I don't want Mama or anybody to know
that you gave me these." Cindy laughed and looked like a
little imp with that punk hairdo and upturned nose.

* * *

Virginia strikes a match and breathes in on that dried-out
Virginia Slims and feels sick. But she's going to smoke it, sit
right on that porch and smoke it to the filter just like Lena
does. She wishes Cindy could see her now. Cindy can get
away with murder: married, divorced, married, divorced,
looking for a third and all anybody ever says is "doesn't
surprise me," whereas Virginia can't get away with anything,
never has been able to. It isn't envy that she feels for Cindy
because certainly she would not trade places for that soap
opera life and she wouldn't want that streak of wildness Cindy
has that came from God only knows where. As children the
difference had been easy enough to pinpoint: Cindy had that
French provincial room and the Madame Alexander dolls;
she had that vanity table covered with perfumes and makeup
before she was old enough to wear it. On her sixteenth birthday, Cindy's father bought her that baby blue Mustang convertible which Cindy drove to Clemmonsville every Friday
night to buy beer while Madge and Raymond thought she
was at the movies or at the library. "Goody two shoes,"
Cindy always said to her. "Won't even ride to Clemmonsville
with your own cousin."

What? What is it about Cindy that makes her feel so lifeless, so predictable? They'd all be surprised if they could see
Virginia right now, puffing away on that Virginia Slims with
her nightshirt hiked up and her legs spread apart the way that
Cindy always sits and it doesn't surprise a soul when Cindy
sits that way. She wishes she could name her baby Latoya
Montreal Canada Ballard if she wanted to, because Cindy
could. Cindy could have named Chuckie, Dirt Britches Snipes
and no one would have batted an eye. If Mark was Cindy's
husband and had told her all about Sheila, Cindy would have
said, "Thank God, I'd hate to have to think that *it* was going
to visit me over the summer because that first wife of yours,
slut that she is, would have ruined a child." And maybe that's

what she envies about Cindy, saying whatever pops into her mind, though it is still a mystery where Cindy got that—Madge, so quiet and withdrawn and Uncle Raymond so methodical and calculated and crazy right down to killing himself. It makes Virginia squinch her eyes just to think of Uncle Raymond, to think of how crazy he must have been. She didn't cry at the funeral or afterwards while Cindy was putting on a spectacle, which surprised no one, and Cindy's sister, Catherine, was talking to a woman about getting her tubes tied and Madge was standing out in the backyard as stiff and silent as the huge oak tree where Chuckie was digging a hole.

Virginia tosses the filter to the concrete and loosens her grip on that rocking chair, a red Kennedy rocker which she has painted so many times that she can't count. For years she has painted that chair. If she felt good, she painted it red or blue or pink; if she felt bad she painted it black. Now, she doesn't give a damn. She'd like to toss it to the side with a lot of other junk and forget about it. She'd like to be able to do the same with her brain, pick and choose what she wanted to know and toss the rest aside, to feel that everything was clean like that yellow room the day it was painted, like a fresh canvas, and then she could start over, carefully applying what would someday be observed by someone who would say, "this is my mom." She doesn't even know what time it is; cars still parked in driveways down the street, some people probably still sleeping. If she tried to paint something representative of herself for the sake of posterity right now it would be a smeary blob of nothing, scene after scene carved on top of another with nothing unique about any of it. It would be nothing like the soft pastels, soft as baby powder, that Gram would have, a strong dark background that holds the softness in place. Or Lena who would be a bright splash of color that, though opposite, would blend with Gram, or her mother who would be strong sharp lines that all connect and round at the corners. Even Cindy, though wildly abstract, would be appealing in the same way that someone says, "It's really interesting but I wouldn't want it on my wall." If somebody did her it would be so typical like a bed of jonquils, sunny yellow jonquils on stiff stems, so stiff they'd stand as long as they could and then crack off to one side and she hates yellow right now, that jaundiced jealousy.

* * *

"We painted the chair the university color," Madge had said the day before Virginia was to leave for college. "Cindy bought the university symbol decal for me to put on the back there."

"I love it," Virginia lied, her eyes still focused on the chair so as not to meet eyes with Cindy. "But you've done too much. You already gave me sheets and towels."

"Well, it's special," Madge said, somehow lighter than her usual deep sighs. "Not everybody goes to college. Not everybody comes out second in the class." It was obvious that Madge was avoiding Cindy who was standing there in cutoffs with Chuckie perched on her hip like a grocery bag. "Not everybody gets to graduate," Madge said and Cindy sighed and shifted Chuckie.

"You hate it don't you?" Cindy asked later when they were alone in the yard, Chuckie inside with Virginia's mother and Madge. "I told her you'd think it was tacky."

"I don't hate it, though," Virginia said and finally looked at Cindy who was perched on the hood of Madge's car and they both laughed. Cindy laughed until she started crying and then she sat staring down at her key ring, which was shaped like a Coke bottle.

"Oh shit," she mumbled and shook her head, those pale eyes filling with tears. "This makes me so goddamned mad."

"What is it?" Virginia asked, surprised to see Cindy that way, her shoulders shaking and those long-nailed fingers spread over her eyes. "Cindy?" Virginia stepped closer expecting Cindy to turn on her any minute, to burst into that raucous laugh of hers.

"Hate to see you leave," she said, wiped her eyes and then looked up with the most serious expression that Virginia had ever seen on her face. "You'll never be back," she said. "I mean for good. I'm stuck here, me and my one friend, Constance Ann Henshaw, and Charles Snipes and Chuckie the snot factory and Earl Conners." She stopped and laughed quietly after saying Earl Conners, who was a man that for years sat out in front of Endicott Johnson's and sold boiled peanuts, a man with one eye and no teeth who was given clothes by the Jaycees; for years, it had made Virginia cry every time she bought peanuts from Earl Conners, which is why her mama stopped taking her to Endicott Johnson's even though they had the cheapest shoes. "Yeah, Earl and all the rest of us will be right here, but not you."

"Stop, I'll be back," Virginia said and hugged Cindy close, the scent of Ambush cologne filling her head.

"You're lucky," Cindy pushed her away. "Not that I'd want to go, I mean why in the hell would I want to go when I've got a husband and a baby. I mean I'll read *Peyton Place* or *Valley of the Dolls*, but really I think books are used best for mashing flat a corsage or stacking them up so you can reach something if you're small like me."

"You are lucky," Virginia told her.

"Well, learn something other than school, Ginny Sue," she said, then no trace that she had cried except that her mascara, midnight blue then, was clumped in the corner of her right eye. "You've got a hell of a lot to learn." She shook her head from side to side. "And I mean the important stuff, none of that what so and so who's been dead forever said about the moon or the pope, you know? And don't let them tell you stuff about Jesus that isn't true, and don't you tell that I brought Jesus up because I don't want Mama or anybody else asking me to go to their Sunday school class."

"I won't." Virginia took hold of Cindy's hand and squeezed that plastic Coke bottle key chain which Virginia thought was so tacky, even the day she saw Cindy pick it out and buy it in the check-out line at Roses, Virginia thought it was tacky.

"God, toughen up. Stop acting like such a queer," Cindy said. "You ain't going to the moon."

"No."

"Jesus, God, two hours from home and you'd think you were moving to Russia." Cindy jumped off the car, readjusted her little gold anklet. "I hope you'll mature a little."

"You started it," Virginia said, the blood flooding her face. "You cried about it."

"Shit, I cried for something else. Something a hell of a lot bigger than school, real things you know?"

"What? Tell me." Virginia had pleaded but Cindy only laughed and looked away. "You can tell *me*. I'm your cousin, remember?"

"You wouldn't understand," she said. "Maybe someday when you're all grown up and married with a baby like me,

I'll tell you or I won't have to tell you 'cause you'll see for yourself."

"I'd probably understand right now."

"Oh come on. Now why would I spill my gut to somebody that has a chair with a school decal on it? Why would I trust somebody with such a queer and tacky chair?"

"You fixed that chair!" Virginia screamed. "I have nothing to do with that chair. I didn't pick out that damn decal. I would never have . . ." Virginia caught herself and looked away from Cindy.

"Damn, ooh, ohh, Emily would be surprised to hear her little grandbaby said 'damn' and that Ginny Sue played technical-virgin sex with a boy so dumb he can't write his name in a rented cottage at the beach while her mama thought that she was chaperoned all hours of the day and night."

"Cindy!" Virginia screamed. "I know things about you, too."

"Honey, I don't care what you say about me because I've got enough stored right up here that could shock the earth." She got in Madge's car and blew the horn several short times. "I knew you hated the chair. Admit the truth, let the skeletons out of the closet."

"You've got some, too, and I'd never tell, never."

"What, that I got pregnant and then got married, me and the Virgin Mary, tell it, ain't news to a soul. Tell how I got pulled and had to walk a line on I-95 coming back from Clemmonsville. My daddy paid the ticket." She blew the horn again. "Tell how much I hate my sister Catherine and call her a slutbucket. Shit, I wrote that down on a piece of paper, signed my name to it and gave it to her. You can't tell a thing on me that isn't known."

"Your dad," Virginia said and was sorry she had let it slip, sorry when she saw Cindy's eyes narrow and her face go as pale as the white eyeshadow that was right under her brows.

"What do you mean?" She lowered her voice, took her hand off the steering wheel. "My dad isn't well. He has cancer."

"He doesn't have cancer." Virginia's voice was slow and deliberate.

"Well, Miss doctor know-it-all, what is it then?"

"You know." Virginia stared down at the grass, feeling Cindy's glare the whole time.

"No, no I don't know but I'll tell you this much, he wouldn't care if he knew you told people something other than the truth about him because he's never really liked you, Ginny Sue. He is forever saying how strange acting and plain looking you are and how you'll never amount to anything. He says you are so unfriendly and that all you've ever been is jealous of me and what I had. He says you'll be lucky if you *ever* get a husband."

"That's not true."

"He told me about that time he caught you in my room going through my things and I remember, I remember coming in with my tap shoes still on and you were crying because you got caught going through my things, and Mama said, 'oh poor little Ginny Sue she didn't mean any harm. She didn't mean to break the vanity mirror.' "

"But I didn't break it."

"I know, I know, you were reaching up to get my best doll off of the cornice and almost fell off the vanity and in the process broke the mirror. All my daddy even said to you was 'seven years bad luck.' He didn't even yell at you and you sat right there and wouldn't say the words 'I broke it,' just sat there and cried until my daddy drove you over to Emily's house where you'd be treated like a little baby, that's what my daddy did for you." Cindy took a deep breath. "He paid for your summer camp that one year that you got to go. Did you know that? Did you know that your parents couldn't afford Camp Tonawanda like we could every summer and you pitched a fit to go until my daddy had to pay for it."

"That's not true."

"Ask Aunt Hannah, just ask her, and then you tell things that aren't true about my daddy."

"I will ask her," Virginia said, the anger that had brought a rush of words, things, that broken mirror, to her mind, slowly passing with the dull sick numbness that anger always leaves. "Can we forget it?"

"Sure, sure, just forget it." Cindy, with a sweetly put-on smile, waved her hand out the window when Madge and Chuckie came onto the front porch. "Hey baby!" she yelled and then, "Mama, I wish you'd hurry. Charles Snipes might want to see me a little bit today."

"Cindy," Virginia whispered. "I didn't mean anything about your daddy, I'm sorry that he's not well."

Cindy tooted the horn right when Madge was in front of the car and laughed when she jumped. Virginia laughed too, patted Cindy's arm and tried to get Cindy to look at her in a way that would make things okay again. "I won't tell mother what you just now said," Cindy said and cranked the car, not even looking at Madge who was sitting in the front seat in her burgundy pantsuit.

"Take care, Ginny Sue," Madge said, the heavy sighs returning. "We're proud of you."

"Yes, all of us," Cindy said. "Me and Mama and Daddy. Don't do anything I'd do, you might have fun." She laughed, that hand still out the window as she drove around the corner.

* * *

"Is that the same old shitty chair we gave you?" Cindy had asked last weekend with no mention of the whole scene that followed. "I wonder if that tacky decal is still there?"

"I never took it off," Virginia told her, the thought coming to her that one day this chair would be sitting in some garage for some child of some child to strip through all the layers, down to the decal and on under to bare soft pine.

"Looks better red," Cindy said. "I never really liked that kind of chair anyway, only reason it caught on was because of those Kennedy boys who looked all right if they could get their mouths closed over those teeth and that voice they all have, I mean we ain't talking Magnum P.I." She laughed and patted the chair like it might be alive. "That's some tough car next door to you, though," she said and pointed to the Corvette that raised the hair on Virginia's neck every time she heard it crank and rev and screech and scratch.

"I love it, though," Virginia said, meaning the chair, smiling as if by repeating the same words she had said ten years ago, they could redo that scene, correcting and editing the bad parts, the parts that had worried Virginia all through freshman orientation to the point that she wrote Cindy a long letter. "Your father did pay for my camp," she had written, not going into the explanation that she had gotten from her mother.

"I can't believe she told you or that they told her," her mother had said. "Ben's garage hadn't done very well that year. It was his idea. He wanted you to go to that same camp because he knew you wanted to and he went and asked Raymond for a loan.'' Her mother had paused and stared hard as if she was reading the fine print of a document. ''It was done real formallike because Ben wouldn't do it any other way and we paid back every cent.''

''Why didn't you tell me?''

''You would have felt bad; a child shouldn't worry over money, that comes soon enough.''

She didn't tell Cindy that part of the story, didn't tell how Raymond had pulled her father aside at every family gathering and whispered. ''Don't worry about it, Ben. You may never be able to repay me.'' No, she just wrote that what Cindy had said was true and she apologized and then continued to send cute little funny cards to Cindy and to Chuckie, always mentioning Charles and Madge and Raymond, and Cindy never responded once.

''Why don't you ever write?'' Virginia had asked over Thanksgiving.

''Write? I've got a baby and a husband, a sick daddy and a mama that gets on my nerves the tee-total time.'' They were eating at Gram's house—the old house before she had to move to the duplex—as they had done every year; Gram, bustling around the kitchen where she had a ham, a turkey with all the trimmings, vegetables that she had frozen from her garden, fried apple pies. Lena, standing in the kitchen chain smoking, talking and pacing so that it seemed like she was doing something even though she wasn't while her husband, Roy Carter, sat with a newspaper spread over his lap and puffed a cigar, leather driving gloves still on his hands, a flat tweed cap on his head.

''Take off that cap you look like a clown,'' Lena yelled.

''Ah, ya, ya, ya, *RO*lena.'' He looked up, their eyes meeting and staring, never blinking, the room going silent as it always did during their momentary outbursts. ''Just shut up and do something other than pace and act like you're doing something.''

''I do more in a damn hour than you've done in your life!''

''I hope Charles and I never get like that,'' Cindy said to Virginia. ''Charles and I will never be like that, and I won't be like my mama either. God, I don't know why Daddy married her.''

"Write?" Cindy had asked just four months after Thanksgiving. "How could I write a letter back about what little dip shit fraternity party you went to when I'm getting a divorce and have a dead daddy?"

* * *

Virginia rocks faster, her legs feeling so full and heavy; all those years, the bits and pieces that she can't get off her mind, and then it started changing, one thing after another; Gram's move to the duplex, a Piggly Wiggly replacing Gram's old house, Raymond's suicide, Roy dying, Lena having to move to a home, Cindy divorced remarried and divorced again, and Gram's hair turning so white, her mind wandering back and forth over the years. Gram, the one person who could always say where she was and what she was doing and why she was doing it, suddenly roaming through her mind, here, there, places she's never in her life really been.

Virginia has what Gram would call "the budgies"; can't keep still, can't stay in one place, so wishy-washy restless and uncomfortable. "Lena was born with the budgies," Gram used to say on those Sunday afternoons when Roy and Lena would climb in that Lincoln and head back down to Florida.

"Drop a rusty nail in a bottle of vinegar, shake it up and then, rub your legs down good," Gram has said countless times. "That's what'll cure the budgies. Then a body can relax."

* * *

"Relax? Relax?" Lena screamed when she was being moved to the rest home, her hand on the car door as if she was preparing to jump out. "How can I relax with Roy dead and doing what he's doing?" All that was left of Lena's life was in a Samsonite bag and a pasteboard box.

* * *

"I believe in love at first sight," Gram said. "That's how it was when I met your granddaddy. I no sooner met him but what he said, 'Emily, I'd like to call on you right regular' and I said, 'very well.' "

* * *

"Your daddy and I knew each other our whole life," her

mother said. "We just up and one day realized it was a whole lot more. That's a good feeling to know it's a whole lot more."

* * *

"Fireworks," Lena said. "I met Roy Carter and it was fireworks—a man—I was tired of those silly boys and Roy Carter was a man."

* * *

Their voices, their lives and words and stories are so clear, so familiar as if there have been no changes at all; and this house and Mark, the things that should be familiar and are so foreign, becoming more so with each slow passing day while an image of Sheila lingers like a caution sign. Was Mark the same person when he was with Sheila? The same person that she met and fell for so quickly? And what made him different? What made her want to turn and roll into his warmth when the room was dark?

The stone flooring is cold despite the heavy humid air and Virginia pulls her feet up on the rung of the chair, her stomach resting on her thighs—a kick, already it is telling her what to do. *Put your legs together, ladies don't sit that way;* she had always obeyed.

It is easy to picture Gram right: she is sitting in her wheelchair in front of the TV, her hair so white, gum packed with snuff, blank stare. Or Gram twenty years ago; brown cotton "frock," as she bends and works down a row of beans, her hair dark with only slight streaks of gray, voice like a lullaby that teaches how to do things, shell the butterbeans, make a French knot, bake a pound cake. And, she can picture her mother forty years ago in her plaid skirt and saddle oxfords, chestnut hair, smooth and shoulder length. Or now, right this minute, in the kitchen fixing coffee, frying bacon, her hair in a short fluffy perm, whistling or humming. But, she can't picture Mark with Sheila, can't imagine his familiar voice saying all of the words that he must have said, all of the thoughts that he must have thought when he married Sheila, words like forever—words repeated when he married Virginia.

Everything she knows is still there, still at home, just changed and disguised, a scene on a scene, different colors and textures, Gram's hair gone white, but every texture of the new scene interrupted by a bump or a groove beneath the surface. Homesick—twenty-eight and homesick and who would have ever thought. She never imagined herself this way. She always imagined a little lacy apron over a cute little maternity smock with gleaming tile counters in her kitchen, loaf after loaf of home-baked bread cooling, when the front door opened and someone said, "Hey Honey, I'm home," and swept her back in a kiss and told her how beautiful and wonderful she was. But, that was only part of the dream because she was also a professional woman of independent means who toured the country with her paintings, who on a whim would reupholster the furniture in an array of watercolors in the spring and warm rich plaids in the winter when a blazing fire filled the fireplace that she does not have, and she sat in a worn cherry rocker and knitted just as she has imagined her great-grandmother, the other Virginia Suzanne. And people would say, "How have you done it all?" and they would look at Mark, wink and say, "You better hold onto her for life" and he'd say, "don't worry" and all traces of Sheila would float away forever.

Sheila is a design consultant in New York, wealthy Richmond family, northeast girls' school, though Virginia isn't sure which one. Sheila would say, "women's college" and emphasize the point. She has some advanced degree, probably making money hand over fist, probably has a baby named Thurstan Beauregard Something IV, probably would laugh her bony anorexic ass off if she saw Virginia's house. Well laugh! Just goddamn laugh! That's what she'd say. She'd say, "You need to eat meat! You need some bloody beef, good for you, give you color!" It makes her furious just to think of that woman even though she has never met her and never seen her except a small wedding snapshot that Virginia found mixed in with some of Mark's old photos at his mother's house in Pennsylvania. She could have fixed that picture right up with some Flair pens had Mark's mama not been sitting there. The photo was too small, too blurred. She doesn't know that Sheila is thin as a post with long silky blonde hair and blue eyes, at least not the picture that comes to mind with that description of blonde hair and blue eyes. She might be gangly and transparent with buck teeth and thin stringy hair. For all Virginia knows she might even eat meat, though she bets not; it's easy enough to get the whole picture from the bits and pieces that she knows, such as Sheila wanted everything natural, health food store food, which is why Mark hates herbal teas and such. That's the fact: Sheila was into health foods. But, Virginia knows as well as the next what follows that: Perrier and brie, which she thinks tastes like what dirty feet smell like, granola, wine coolers and little spritzers if she drinks at all but no, probably not, and Virginia would love a drink right now; she'd love a shot of bourbon and a beer chaser. The doctor would say. "Have you been drinking?" No, Sheila doesn't drink. A Perrier with a twist, thank you for not smoking, no caffeine, no soda? Why that is a vile filthy liquid; I only wear cotton; I only wear hypoallergenic cosmetics. My shampoo is pH correct and natural, it's all natural. I use tartar-buster toothpaste and floss every single day. Nutra Sweet is poison. I jog and I play tennis and I go to the spa to work out and do aerobics three times a week and I only watch PBS, never anything other than PBS, and I never have PMS, and I only listen to classical radio stations and I would never hang a print on my wall and I would never think of anything but professional stripping for my fine furniture. Yeah, Virginia knows the type, that touchy feely, do it all perfectly, I'm okay you're okay, my child can read at age two and will have a volume of Haiku by the time he's four, type.

Virginia would tell her a thing or two right then and there. She would tell her that she loves bloody beef and coffee and Coke and Budweiser and Formby's and 96 Lite which plays everything from Smoky Robinson to Dolly Parton to Lulu "To Sir With Love," and that she likes to bowl and eat things with preservatives and take a Goody's for a headache. "I'll watch the goddamn 'Brady Bunch' if nothing else is on." That's what she'd like to say. And people standing closeby would applaud and Mark would never ever look back again. If Mark would just say that he hates Sheila and never wants to hear about her again, she would feel better, but he won't.

"She was a nice person," he had explained. "But it was a mistake."

"Nice? Nice?" she asked.

"Yes, but it didn't work. We weren't right for each other. That doesn't make her a bad person."

"I was Junior Rotary Honey," she told him after hearing

the list of Sheila's qualities which she had asked for, not knowing there would be such a list of credits. "I was second in my class. I am pregnant with your baby and my art teacher called me little Monet." That was all true, all of it, the only details left out being that her high school class was very small and that Mrs. Abbott who had called her little Monet all through high school seemed to barely even remember Virginia now.

* * *

"I'm moved into string art," Mrs. Abbott had said when Virginia saw her in the grocery store. "I really love those knots. What did you say your name was again?"

"Virginia," she said while Mrs. Abbott gazed at her with a blank stare; thank God, Mark wasn't there.

"Virginia," Mrs. Abbott repeated and shook her head while the woman pushing the chair stared pitifully down on Mrs. Abbott's head.

"Turner, Ginny Sue Turner."

"Of course," Mrs. Abbott said and clapped her hands. "Ginny Sue Turner, my little Van Gogh."

"I was Monet."

"I saw where you got married, too," Mrs. Abbott said. "It was the second time I saw you were getting married and I told the PTA that my little Van Gogh was married for the second time."

"But I only got married once," Virginia explained. "Two engagements but only one marriage."

"I remember your cousin, too. And she's been married twice I believe, too."

"She has but I haven't."

"Try knots little Manet," Mrs. Abbott called out. "Knots are so knotted."

"Monet!" Virginia insisted, heard only by a woman in barefoot sandals reading a Correctol box. Mrs. Abbott had given everyone a name; everybody's report card had a different name and all that time she thought she was special, thought she was the first, thought she had been given a name because she was good and different from the rest. She probably wouldn't have even majored in art otherwise. She probably would have majored in something else and been a consultant instead of knotting knots and getting frustrated with sixth graders who always drew pictures that came close enough to resembling body parts so that all class control was lost, frustrated that she can't seem to get the ideas that she has in her mind onto the canvas; somewhere in midair they get all twisted and dark and ugly and everything changes too fast, Gram and Lena, and her stomach. There were probably hundreds of Monets over the years and Virginia is certain that her waterlilies looked nothing like the real ones though Mrs. Abbott had clapped her hands and said, oh yes they did. "That woman's so full of shit," Cindy said when Virginia brought up Mrs. Abbott once. "She called me her little Charles Schultz."

Virginia's waterlilies, a gift to Gram, a small watercolor in a cheap frame is still in Gram's bedroom, but it looks nothing like the *real* waterlilies, nothing about it. Mrs. Abbott did not tell the whole truth—a lie, deception. Virginia at that time had never seen the *real* waterlilies, and ignorantly believed Mrs. Abbott, only to later, on a trip during college, find herself in front of a Monet exhibit. Her face flushed with inadequacy while reality burst forth, *you will never in your life do anything that can compare.* "Don't put all your eggs in one basket," Gram always says.

* * *

The sun is in full view now, hot and hazy, the Corvette door slamming as the thug makes his way to God knows where in his loud orange tank top. It is already nine o'clock and here she sits, having done nothing. Her great-grandmother, the other Virginia Suzanne, at her age would have already cooked a huge breakfast and be working on lunch. She would have already fed chickens and washed clothes that would be hanging and blowing in that warm country air. Virginia Suzanne, a familiar name, a name shared, Virginia Suzanne Pearson, she thinks as she gets up and goes to the bathroom. Virginia Suzanne Turner, Ginny Sue Turner, Virginia Turner Ballard, little Monet. Suddenly an image comes to her mind of a tombstone with all of those names listed on it, last of which is Mrs. Ballard, whispered in her mind with the voices of those first graders whose faces are now so sharp in her mind, faces that she may soon forget, faces that will change and perhaps pass her unnoticed. *Virginia Suzanne White, wife of Cord Pearson, devoted mother and child of God.* Virginia had seen that tombstone, had knelt there in what used to be a churchyard and now is the back side of a parking lot, and she read those words over and over while Gram placed a plastic flower arrangement that the two of them had made.

"Mama would be so proud of this arrangement," Gram said and bent the wire stem of a rose down so that it didn't block the word "child." "I know she wouldn't like all these cars pulling in and out, though. It would scare her good, I know."

"Would she have liked me?" Virginia asked and turned to Gram who was shielding her eyes and staring up into the sky, the horizon that she knew as a child, trees and tobacco fields, now cluttered with mobile homes.

"Oh, she would have loved you," Gram said. "She'd have been so proud that you have her name."

"Do you think she can see me?" Virginia asked, followed by a series of beeps from Roy Carter's Lincoln. He and Lena had driven them out there and now were ready to leave. Virginia stood, her eyes level with Gram's waist, and while Roy whistled and clapped and tooted the horn again, Gram knelt, ignoring the parking lot as if it weren't even there.

"Do you see that tree way out yonder?" she asked and pointed to a huge oak, underneath which someone had abandoned an old car. "That's where we had our pump. That's where I'd sit sometimes and wait for my daddy to come in from the field." Gram's voice was low and quiet, like she was telling a secret. "I loved my home."

"Do you think she can see us right this second?" Virginia whispered and moved in closer to Gram, a sudden chill coming over her as if she had been lifted and carried to a place different from anything she knew.

"I hope so, Sweets," Gram said. "I hope she knows."

"Knows what?" Virginia asked and Gram smiled, shook her head, Lena's shadow falling over them.

"Roy is getting fidgety," Lena said and fanned herself with a neat little patent leather clutch bag. "God, it's a blessing Mama don't know she's out here in such a cheap part of town. She'd turn cartwheels there in that grave." Lena waved to Roy and walked ahead of them. "I can't believe we used to *live* here, can you, Emily?" But Gram just smiled and shook her head, turning back once to look at that tree and squeezing

Virginia's hand so tightly that all of it was pressed into her mind.

* * *

Virginia is suddenly so aware of the stillness of the house, the fact that she left the door to the porch open, the fact that she is alone. What would she do if she heard someone come in through the porch right now, footsteps through the house like that time at Cindy's. What if she heard that kitchen drawer open, the fumbling of silverware, while she's here in this bathroom, as pregnant as possible in an orange nightshirt. Barefoot and pregnant. Barefoot and pregnant. She closes the bathroom door, locks it, checks behind the shower curtain. She turns on the bath water and starts to turn on the shower when she realizes that she can't hear anything in the house with the water running, couldn't hear the phone ring if Mark called, if he called to say that he was serious, did want a divorce, or if her mom called with the words that she has dreaded for years, "Gram is dead." No, no, she couldn't hear if someone were fumbling in the silverware right this minute, walking closer and closer, those brown wingtip shoes closer and closer, Anthony Perkins, Sharon Tate, Uncle Raymond. I'm in your door, I'm on your stairs. I'm at your room. I'm at your bed, under the bed, out the window, behind the shower, in your backseat. Now she is holding that orange nightshirt up to her chest, a deep breath. Slowly, she opens the bathroom door and the bright sunlight is coming through the window. The bright sunlight making everything look so much better.

She drops the orange nightshirt onto the bed, quickly pulls the yellow sack over her head, her back to all of the photographs on the dresser. Once, at home, she had a poster on her wall, Paul Newman and Robert Redford as Butch and Sundance, a black and white poster with only their eyes colored bright blue, and she couldn't undress in front of them; it was like anywhere she went in that room, they could see her.

"You can't even put on a bra without turning your back to a dumb piece of paper," Cindy used to say. "You are so crazy, Ginny Sue. I'd take the damn thing off my wall if it kept me from walking around my own room nekked."

Virginia turns slowly and lifts her dress in front of those

photos, catching a side glimpse of herself in the mirror; Mark's parents, her parents, Gram, great-grandmother. "Virginia!" the real Mrs. Ballard would gasp.

She lets the dress fall back around her legs, a sense of dignity coming to her. "We all have bodies, Mrs. Ballard." She puts on her tennis shoes, now just pregnant, and gets her car keys and pocketbook off the dresser, the other Virginia Suzanne staring out of that brown tin photo. *I hope she knows.* Virginia has a Kenya bag, too, only she bought hers because it's big enough to hold everything; she will be able to carry Pampers and rattles and pacifiers. "Shit, you bought it for the same reason I bought mine," Cindy had said. "You bought it because everybody else on earth has one." Everybody else, any and everybody. You ain't the first to have a baby. You ain't the first wife he's had. You ain't the first little Monet. You just ain't the first.

A person with the budgies should not be alone, drop a rusty nail in a bottle of vinegar. A person with the budgies should be where it's cool and quiet, high ceilings and shade trees. She could drive home blindfolded, the road so straight and flat, cornfields and tractors, Gram coming in from the garden with a sack filled with butterbeans that she could finger while shelling them into that tin pan. High ceilings, cool, fans blowing and whirring. "I've come home to stay," she would say. "I made a mistake and now I'm back."

But, she can't do that. *Then live with it. Live the rest of your life with it.* She is going to go to Roses, walk every aisle, spend a hundred dollars in that air-conditioned building, piddle away these long hours where she can be near people that she doesn't know, people who will not take one look at her and say, "Virginia, what's wrong?" Strangers, she wants to be surrounded by strangers who do not notice that she is there, filling her cart up with useless items which Mark will sift through and say, "I'm surprised at you, we can't afford this" and she will say, "I'm glad you're surprised; I'm glad because I can't afford you. I'm at your door, I'm in your bed, Surprise! Tell it to your first. Just go on, leave. Leave me here all by myself, big as a squash, because you wouldn't know a speckled butterbean if you had it in your mouth!"

She sits on the edge of the bed and leans her head as far forward as her stomach will permit. Her face feels so hot, so flushed from the anger, the anger that makes her want to run so fast she'd leave this stomach way behind. "It's hard to go home once you've got a child," Gram said. "I used to go out to the country every single day. I'd let James leave for work and off I'd go home. He didn't know of it half the time, didn't need to know, and it helped to pass the time. Imagine that me and my mama didn't have a better thing to do but to pass the time. That's why I never would have married a man who would carry me from my home." She had looked hard at Virginia, her eyes so clear and honest. "I would have been scared I'd never get back. And those were good days with my mama. I've always been so glad that I was there with her when she died."

Virginia opens her eyes now, her head feeling so heavy that she can't even cry. And she wants to; she feels like she'd like to scream her lungs out because she did marry a man who will take her from her home, already has, slowly, bit by bit, moving further and further from what she knows. And one day it will be Gram and the news will come to her in a long-distance call the same way it did when Roy Carter died, and she will hang up that receiver and turn to face rooms and windows and faces so unfamiliar and she will say: Why? Why am I here this way?

PART II

CINDY SINCLAIR SNIPES SINCLAIR BIGGERS SINCLAIR IS SO pissed off, which isn't unusual given her frustrated state, and that's all it is—frustration with a capital *F*. It is not some personality DEFECT, some disease of the mind like that shrink would have liked for her to believe. "Paranoid," he had said as if that meant one thing to her. "Paironerds," she said to that man and his secretary on her way out. "Masochist" is another word he used and she is dead sure that he was feeling her out to see if she did any kinds of way out stuff. Well, she didn't or doesn't, but she sure as hell knows what's going on, mainly because her best friend, Constance Ann Henshaw, reads all of those magazines that are wrapped in brown paper down at the Quik Pik. Constance Ann swears that she only buys those books for a little humor, that she *never* looks at the pictures. Constance Ann swears that in real life she has never glanced down at a man's covered up privates which Cindy knows is a lie. Everybody has done that whether they know or admit it. Where else are you supposed to look in those underwear ads but *there*.

Well, Jim Palmer ain't the norm and Cindy knows that for sure; she ought to know, been married two times and has every intention of marrying again. She admits that she has checked men out that way; men do it all the time. Men will glance down at your boobs and back up to your mouth the whole time you're trying to talk. Of course, maybe men don't do that to everybody; Cindy has got something for them to see is all, and they can't help it. She'd wonder about a man that *didn't* look. Hell yes, she'll admit all that and it has nothing to do with therapy. It's just the truth. She admitted a

45

lot of truths to that shrink before she realized what he was
up to and he suggested that he might should "admit" her.
You admit the truth and they want to admit you, make com-
mitments that you can't possibly on God's green earth keep
and they want to commit you.

"It sounds like a love/hate situation," that shrink said. It
didn't matter *who* she talked about, her parents, Ginny Sue,
Constance Ann, the old relatives, or Charles Snipes, that's
what he said.

"You sound like a damn parrot," she told him. "I've paid
money to come here and have you say that same thing over
and over, love/hate, love/hate. My daddy is dead and nobody
in his right mind hates a dead person; Ginny Sue is like a
sister to me and that's why she pisses me off. Pissed off is
what sisterhood is all about."

"What about your real sister?" he asked, looking just like
those sea monkeys that grin and wave from the comic books
like they can think when they ain't anything but little midget
shrimp. Give a man a diploma and a desk and he'll sit there
and grin and wave like he's something he isn't.

"Catherine is a slut," Cindy said. "Now, who's going to
love a slut who takes an oath on a King James Bible that she
will never claim me as a sister? Nobody, that's who."

"But that was years ago." Smile and wave now, whoa sea
horse monkey.

"Well, I never forgot it. She can put on a three-piece suit
and shake her Rolex wrist out that dwarfed Yuppie van, point-
ing at which houses she's trying to sell if she wants but she's
still a slut. Give somebody a real estate license and a little
van and a husband that sips on that thick liquor in a glass the
size of a thimble and they think they can smile and wave and
act like they're something they're not." He looked away and
wrote on his little pad because he was probably one of those
thick liquor drinkers himself, likooor as they say. "Catherine
comes home and we kill the calf."

"What do you mean? Kill the calf?" Got a diploma but no
Sunday training.

"Have you ever heard of the Bible?" She waited for him
to nod. "Well, there's a story in there that shouldn't be. A
story of this boy who leaves home and spends all his money
on things he doesn't need while the other boy stays at home
and does stuff like picks things up at the A&P when his mama

needs it or talks to her on the telephone when she's lonesome because her husband is dead and she's too boring to have any friends. He does all that and then when that other boy breezes in 'Just for a sec to check' it's like heaven has come to earth and that mama says things like 'Don't you look so nice all dressed up?'

"That's all. Breeze in and breeze out and she just lives right over there in Clemmonsville, but that's a 'city' mind you. She just 'couldn't live here in this town.' Ginny Sue lives two hours away and she comes to visit."

Cindy is not going back to that man. The only reason she went in the first place was out of curiosity. If you keep up with what's going on and what's in style like Cindy does, then you know that everybody is either going or has gone. Even Ginny Sue had a little therapy way back.

"Curosity killed the cat," Cindy's mama always says and that pisses her off, too. She thinks that if that was the God's truth, we'd all be dead. Constance Ann would be dead for sure because she *does* look at the pictures and she *does* glance at covered up privates whether she knows it or not. Constance Ann is a little on the drab side and would rather stay at home and read about things than to get out and try it. The only reason they're friends is because everybody else from the high school class has moved on and because she and Constance Ann work together down at Southern Point Medical Center. Cindy's picture isn't even in the high school yearbook because that was when they wouldn't let pregnant girls finish. Sometimes it makes her sick to look at all those people smiling and waving out of that yearbook, especially Charles Snipes because they *did* let him graduate even though it was *his* you-know-what that got her that way. It makes her sick during the holidays when she sees some of those people in the grocery store because they like to go on and on about how much everything has changed; not a damn thing has changed, boring as ever; the courthouse hasn't moved and people still get sick and die.

She runs that computer at work like she might have been born right there in front of a Video Display Terminal and all she has is high school equivalency. She can talk about bits and bytes and hemorrhages as good as anybody and does her dull mama think that's as good as Catherine selling a split-level over on Dupont Road? Hell no, and all her mama does when she gets home from work is play solitaire.

"I'm getting a Bernoulli box to back up my data in case there's a thunderstorm," Cindy told her mama a couple of weeks ago and her mama said, "Cindy, you'll have to speak English."

"Well, don't you ever say periodontal nothing to me again," she told her.

It's a trap, all of it. Cindy would lose her mind if it wasn't for Friday afternoons at the Ramada happy hour and the fact that her mama will keep Chuckie, let him spend the night. One night. She gets one night to herself and her mama and Chuckie both acting like it's the end of the world just to give her that one night. Chuckie doesn't want to go over there; who would blame him? But he has to. That's the bottom line. He has never had control over what's done and at age twelve, is not going to start trying. It's times like that when she knows that she needs a man, a big strong hunk of man to look at that wirey pimply child of hers in a way that would make him go back to popping wheelies on his bike in front of the house. Now what he does is sneak in her underwear drawer so he'll know what to imagine those seventh graders are wearing under those ripped up tee shirts and miniskirts. God, Cindy would like some minis herself as hot as it is. She'd look good in a mini and her mama would say, "That's too young-looking for you," like she always says. Her mama was born old and plain.

Cindy is thankful every day that she did not take after her mama. Every day, she thinks at least once, 'Thank you, Jesus, that I ain't huge like my mama." A man could take care of this frustration. She needs a man like Randy Skinner who works as a pharmaceutical salesman out of Raleigh and who for the past three weeks has come into the clinic on Fridays and gone with her to Ramada.

"This might be the next Mr. Cindy," she had told Constance Ann, but Constance Ann has never been married and so doesn't know how important it is. Addicting and habit-forming; sex is just like using the bathroom and eating supper. Just try going without something you did so often you didn't even notice. Ginny Sue ought to count her blessings instead of feeling sorry for herself. Feel sorry for yourself, pout and carry on and that man will leave sure as shit. A little pregnancy shouldn't make everything else stop. God knows, that's when you need to keep his interest up. That is just good common sense. She knew when she was carrying Chuckie that Charles was lying there thinking he had a fat wife. Well, not really because Cindy didn't get enormous like Ginny Sue has. But, still, had to keep that fire burning. If she didn't feel like trying to angle herself some way, then she'd just borrow books from Constance Ann and she'd say, "Here, baby, read a little of this and then I'll come back and take care of things." It kept him off the streets. Ginny Sue ought to wise up; men will leave women and women will leave men just for that reason.

Constance Ann will need to wise up if she ever finds somebody. She can talk up a blue streak and doesn't know a thing about it all. Constance Ann will sit right there and eat a danish which she needs like a hole in the head and talk about the "zipless." *The Zipless Fuck* is the exact title, which Cindy doesn't like to think about because it reminds her of her first date with her second husband, Buzz Biggers, which she'd just as soon not think about. It was a vulnerable time in her life; blame it on frustration. Blame it on that shrink. Blame it on whoever said, "if you fall off a horse you got to get back up and ride." Buzz Biggers was standing at the bar inside Blind Tom's Bar and Grill out in the country. Old Tom ain't really blind because Cindy asked the management. Old Tom just acts blind so people who don't know better will leave big tips. "I'll fuck your eyes out if I get half a chance," Buzz Biggers said after about five minutes of talking.

"Just see if you can," she said, and of course he didn't. Those baby blues are still right up in her head. She rode again, all right, but she had saddled herself with pure trash. It was that scar across the side of that rough hairy face that made him so exciting, made her mama look white as a sheet and say, "What kind of man is he?"

"A wild man," Cindy told her. "A wild raring stud." And Cindy laughed to see that look on her mama's face. Her mama needed that.

Constance Ann got that zipless from an Erica Jong book. Constance Ann thinks that Erica Jong is Jesus Christ Born Again and *Fear of Flying* is her bible. Cindy finally read it just so she'd know what Constance Ann was talking about and she didn't like it near as much as she liked *The Love*

Machine or *Peyton Place*. The worst part of *Fear of Flying* was that man that didn't wipe himself well. That was so dumb. Chuckie at age three could wipe himself and she could not bear to think of a grown man who could not. Even Buzz Biggers, as filthy as he was, wasn't like that, and if Cindy had been that woman in the book that slept with that man, she sure as hell wouldn't have told it. Constance Ann said it was symbolic and so Cindy just let it go, didn't argue because Constance Ann knows a lot about symbolic things and as a result can quote lines from all of the Jill Clayburgh movies; that's what Constance Ann has over Cindy, that and a copy of *Our Bodies, Ourselves*. Constance Ann says looking at naked *medical* pictures is different from the other.

Paranoid, masochistic—then that shrink had the nerve to bring up her daddy who was a fine man, book smart and deep. It's nobody's business that he got himself all wrapped up in King Tut. A lot of people have hobbies. Cindy's mama plays solitaire, and Cindy collects those little squat Coke bottles that you hardly ever see anymore.

"Why don't you cash these in?" Charles Snipes asked her once. "Then you can buy a whole case."

"Buying is not the same as finding!" she told him, which made good sense to her but did not to Charles Snipes or her mama who said more or less the same thing at Cindy's daddy's funeral.

"Just take the whole crate, Cindy," her mama said. "Don't stand around in the front yard waiting for somebody to lay one down so you can say you found it." God, that pissed her off just like it did when that shrink asked her questions about her daddy and how he was homebound due to a rare paralysis that came and went. The shrink said "psychosomatic," that word which means it's all up in the head. So stupid.

"If it was all upstairs like you say," she told the shrink, "then it would have been his scalp that was paralyzed instead of his legs, an arm from time to time, his eyelids." Cindy couldn't stand the thought of her daddy sitting in that Lazy Boy recliner with his eyes closed, paralyzed that way; it made her ache. It was a rare cancer that overtook him; a man who had an interest in Egypt, an artist of the mind, overtook and struck down by a rare cancer which is why he shot himself in the chest the way that he did, too much of a man to let himself get weak and helpless. That sea monkey asshole, dragging it all up again. It wasn't his daddy that had been stretched out at the funeral home like he'd been starched and pressed. Catherine was studying real estate and thinking of getting her tubes tied and Ginny Sue was going to fraternity parties and making *A*'s on things like African Astronomy, and there Cindy was facing her first divorce and a dead daddy. "Let's stick to the present," Cindy told the shrink. "I know about what has already happened."

Ginny Sue can go right on thinking that therapy is the thing to do if she wants but Cindy ain't buying. Cindy has never even figured out *why* Ginny Sue went to therapy in the first place, a little broken engagement, big deal. Ginny Sue came home from Atlanta in a pure crazy fit just to say the wedding was off. That pissed Cindy off; there she'd already driven to Raleigh to get a bridesmaid's dress that was so god-awful sweet-looking she wouldn't have worn it to a dog fight. The dress couldn't be returned because Cindy's waist is so tiny it had been altered; she gave it to a child down the street to wear for a Halloween suit.

"I started painting a lot when I was depressed," Ginny Sue had said, like Cindy *is* depressed. Of course, that was before Ginny Sue knew that Mark had knocked up his first wife. "That's what you need, Cindy. Something that you do for yourself, something that you do for yourself and enjoy." Ha! A lot of good all that therapy is doing Miss Ginny Sue now.

"Yeah, well I'd like to fly to Greece and buy a string bikini," Cindy said, as if she has the time between a nine-to-five and a girl-crazy adolescent and a slut sister. And why does Ginny Sue think that Cindy *doesn't* have something she does that is as good as coloring pictures and messing in wheat paste? Cindy has ideas; she has the idea that she could write some books, not for godssakes the kind Ginny Sue reads, but the kind you hear about, the kind you see in every grocery store and the lobby of Ramada. She's got all the titles already figured out, a medical series: *How An Anesthesiologist Put Me To Bed, The Virgin Meets a Surgeon,* and *The Series of G.I.s That Led to My GI Series.* She could do it, make big bucks, get up from her VDT (Video Display Terminal) and say she's going to lunch and never come back just like she did at the loan office of Southern Trust one day during the second divorce. She could write country songs, too.

Ginny Sue ought to do that kind of thinking for a change instead of trying to figure out whose eyes she's got, whose nose? She'll sit for hours and ask Emily and Lena questions like that, or questions about people who have been dead so long that there's probably a motel built over their graves. Both of those women are senile as hell but Ginny Sue believes whatever they tell her. Ginny Sue will drive her baby crazy, twisting its head all around to see whose neck it has or whose ears. It has always reminded Cindy of that story she heard in school once about that god man who had all kinds of nekked women, little *tiny* nekked women which have a name that Cindy can't think of, chasing after his bod but he wouldn't touch one with a ten-foot pole because he was so taken with himself that he just sat and stared at himself in some water until his mind was completely eaten up. Now *that's* disease of the mind. Ginny Sue is not in love with *herself*; she's in love with everybody that's lived, died, and been related since Columbus.

Cindy told Ginny Sue the god man story once, hoping to make a point. She told it good, too, as good as old Miss Harris had told it in P.E. class so that the girls wouldn't sit and stare at themselves and boobs, whatever, while dressing out. "Vanity is the root of all evil," Miss Harris said, but of course she had nothing to be vain about; Cindy's mama would probably say the same thing.

"That's because she's never had a root," Cindy had whispered to Constance Ann. They shared a gym locker. They laughed so hard that Cindy popped a snap on her gym suit and when Miss Harris said, "what's so funny?" for the third time, Cindy spoke up and said, "I said that I'd rather have lots of little nekked men chasing me through the woods than to stare at myself." Miss Harris didn't laugh but everybody else did. School was fun that way; she didn't learn much but she sure had some fun.

Ginny Sue was going to therapy that time, sitting and thinking over useless things, when she should have been doing something. She should have been shaving her legs and rolling her hair and going on dates. The Lord helps those that get off their asses and do something. When Cindy left Buzz Biggers, she did all sorts of things that made her feel good. She went in the bathroom of the loan office on that day that she went to lunch and never came back, and she wrote "Fuck

Buzz Biggers in the nose" right there beside where she had written "Fuck Charles Snipes in the ear."

Cindy mousses her bangs and pulls them straight just like that woman on "Knots Landing"; only a petite person can get away with the cockatoo look. Randy Skinner just loves her hair this way. TGIF! She thinks that tonight might be a good time to ask Randy over to her house instead of just kissing in a parked car in the lot of Ramada.

"I can't believe you do that," Constance Ann said just yesterday. "Eating face in the parking lot of Ramada Inn right there in the center of town."

"Some things you never outgrow, Constance Ann," she said. "It's like putting a quarter in one of those machines at the grocery store knowing full well that you don't want that rubber worm or plastic bracelet inside of it. But you do it. You do it every now and then; pay your money and take a chance just to feel that little plastic egg sitting there in your palm and remembering how you never got exactly what you wanted but you played with it anyway."

Cindy goes now and sprays a little Halston in her cleavage, puts on some mascara and tells Chuckie if he eats all those Cadbury Eggs that she bought up right after Easter that his face will look so bad a dermatologist won't touch him. She tells him he's going to spend the night with his grandmama whether he likes it or not, that if he's bored just to go in a different room from the one her mama's in. *How My Dermatologist Makes My Skin Tingle. My Psychiatrist Had A Lobotomy. A Prescription For Love* by Cindy Sinclair Snipes Sinclair Biggers Sinclair (maybe Skinner). *It's The Man Behind The Pills That Makes Me High.* Cindy laughs right out loud there in the front yard of the house that her slutbucket sister would NEVER have wanted to show. Cindy might buy that house from her landlord. She might get a satellite dish so she can pick up the whole wide world. Then again, she might not. They need to make those dishes look like something other than giant-size diaphragms. Good God, it makes her laugh to picture a woman big enough to insert a satellite dish. The sun is shining like her daddy is smiling from heaven, just smiling, but without the gunshot. He'd say, "There's my pretty little Goldilocks."

The day would be perfect if she didn't have to see her mama, but of course she does. Her mama needs a ride to work, a favor, so what else is new? The Prodigal Son's brother got the shit end of the stick. Do this, do that, Cindyrella. If she drives real fast like she did in high school, screeching and revving, she can keep from getting pissed off when she sees her mama. It's a wonder Cindy doesn't die from pissed off. Her mama makes people want to die; that's all there is to it. "Dead due to pissed off," the doctors would say. "Her mama did it to her."

* * *

Emily Pearson Roberts sits in a green Lazy Boy most of the day, a small tin of snuff tucked deep down in the pocket of her pink fluffy robe along with a little cash and a piece of note paper with important phone numbers written in her own tiny scrawl. The days seem to flow by in a winding weary manner much like the Saxapaw River which curved all around this county and then on to who knows where; it still does though she hasn't laid her eyes on that deep, brown water in years, possibly hasn't touched that water since that day in the rowboat all those summers ago when she had let her hand trail down alongside the boat and leave a momentary mark while James sat there with his shirt sleeves rolled up and lifted that oar from side to side, his fishing tackle spread out between their feet, her whole body hidden from the sun by the large straw hat that she wore, the same hat that her sister Lena said made her look like an old country woman. She reckoned she did, an old country woman, especially compared to that piece of animal Lena wore on her own head. An old country woman, wasn't nothing wrong with that. There weren't any fish, at least not that day, and she was glad because she felt that river was nasty and that anything that lived there was probably nasty, too.

"Is this the same woman that loves pigs' feet?" James had asked and laughed. Even in those last years he was as handsome as ever. He'd say, "Look at that would you?" and point to the shore and there would be a bird or a rabbit or an oleander in full bloom. Oh, how she loves those oleanders, filled that side yard there all along the street full of oleanders like a tropical paradise, like Lena wrote telling of Florida all those years ago. Years and years ago, passing on the shore, and she could not take her eyes off of him, that strong dark face, though tired by then and, behind that face and those eyes, the blood that the doctor said could go sky high if he didn't watch it. She watched it for him; she would have crawled inside his body and held that rush of blood back if she could've.

"Look a there," he said and there was an old possum swinging from a tree. She glanced at it and went right back to trailing her finger in the water. "Never in my life have you made possum stew," he said and grinned. "My mama used to make it when I was a boy."

"Your mama was poor, that's why," she said. "And that daddy of yours didn't know what hunting was, so lazy he probably shot the first thing he saw." She said that mostly out of habit; they had talked their possum talk for years. She never even met James's daddy but she knew well enough that he had not been a good provider. "Unlucky," James always said. "Just couldn't get his head above water." James had made himself everything he was, risen way above that part of the county where he was raised, but he never once put it behind him and forgot. "You've no one to thank but God for what you've made of yourself," she told him once, him sitting in the side yard in his old age, feeling so guilty that he had done so much better than his father ever had. "You were just a young man when he died. You worked, did all you could to help."

"Yes," he said. "But I do have him to thank. You should never forget who reared you," and his stare was so solid and strong that she knew he was saying the truth. He never forgot all those boys he grew up with down there, grown men that had houses full of children and no meat on their tables. They'd come to town on Saturday, five or six of them, and waste their money on getting drunk and then they'd be sitting out on her front porch with bottles and banjos trying to sing with their voices sounding like dying alley cats. They'd sing all those old songs with all kinds of filthy talk in between and her slaving in that kitchen and trying her best to keep Hannah and David away from that door. James would let those men come in and take baths, give them a tee shirt or pair of pants or socks which never came back clean if they came back at all, and they'd eat their fill and fall dead asleep wherever they chose to sit after dinner. Come morning and you've never seen such politeness with "Miss Em," this and "Miss Em," that while she poured coffee and asked after their families, pitiful pictures coming to her mind of tired worn women and dirty little children.

She leans forward in her chair now and glances at that screened door, latched tight and nobody there. She would have sworn she heard somebody there. James knew every curve of that river, had trees that served as markers and he always knew right where they were. And he could sing, Lord in heaven knows that man could sing, and that voice would carry she thought across that river like a skipping stone right on down to South Carolina and back. He'd sing "Red River Valley," and it made tears come to her eyes to hear that sweet sadness. He'd always turn and look at her when he sang "We will miss your bright eyes and sweet smile." That shore seemed to go on forever and as it got later the light would come and go from behind those trees, just come and go, and she took off the hat so she could see better, what with it coming and going. They didn't play "Red River Valley" at the funeral; they wouldn't have allowed that there in the church. She asked for "How Great Thou Art" because that was her favorite but she hadn't known his. There were several he'd sing from time to time, "Love Lifted Me" and "Have Thine Own Way" but she didn't know the favorite. All those years and she never knew which one.

"Go early with me, Hannah," Emily had said the day of the funeral. "Let's go be with him before everybody else comes." Nobody was there, not even the preacher. "Play something real quiet," she said and pushed Hannah up toward that altar and then behind it where there was an old organ. Hannah could play by ear, had her whole life, and they sat there side by side, just the two of them and sang so quietlike, "For they say you are taking the sunshine," and Hannah started crying; Hannah could not even press the keys or sing, so Emily finished it out herself. Hannah's mouth quivered so and those big eyes filling, her hand clinging to Emily's arm and Emily had wanted so bad to take Hannah in her arms like she might be a baby and rock her there in front of the church. She wished for a minute that she could grab hold of her own mama and let the tears come. "We've got each other," she told Hannah and patted her hand. "You've got a family all your own and your daddy wouldn't want to see you so upset over him. He'd want you to be strong."

Emily didn't cry, really cry through that whole service because it was too personal and people should not have seen. If she had let herself cry, then they all would have started, Lena and Hannah, and James wouldn't have wanted such a sad day. She sat through that service and concentrated her mind on Ginny Sue, pulled that child up on her lap and held her there, and while the preacher talked of how good James was, she thought of all the things that she'd tell Ginny Sue; she'd tell of when she met James and she'd tell of her own daddy and she'd tell all the funny stories about Lena, how Lena would try to sneak out of the house to go to school with her chest stuffed up great big with socks when she wasn't but nine years old and how their mama grabbed Lena there in the front yard and pulled sock after sock out of that child's dress, said, "There'll be time enough for bosoms, Rolena Pearson. I wouldn't go wishing things on my body before it's time." Emily caught herself wanting to laugh right there in the church. James had laughed for years over the things Lena had done and she knew that Ginny Sue would laugh that same way, that some day the two of them would be right by themselves and she'd tell those stories one right after another.

Emily did not cry until late that night when she sat in that glider all by herself, Hannah and Ben sound asleep in that room she had made up for them, Robert and Ginny Sue on a pallet there on the floor near her bed. Just fifty-nine years old then, a widow and a grandmother, the nights getting longer and cooler, spider lilies blooming, leaves turning, and she tried to feel his hand pressing and squeezing her shoulder.

"Is this the same woman that loves pigs' feet?" he had asked and she scooped up some of that river water and threw it in his face. "My mama told me that possum was colored meat." *My mama told me if I was goodie that she would buy me a rubber dollie/My auntie told her, I kissed a soldier, now she won't buy me a rubber dollie/Three six nine, the goose drank wine, the monkey chewed tobacco on the street car line.* "Tell them old friends of yours to hush with such silliness there on my front porch," she yelled out that front door. "Hannah and David got no business hearing it."

"Is this the same woman that loves pigs' feet?" he asked when she turned up her nose at what he was telling of French people eating snails. He was talking of going to war; he was talking of a long time away from home. Would she wait for him? "Maybe I'll bring you back some snails."

"You can go out in the yard and flip over a rock," she told him. "We got plenty of snails right here in Saxapaw." Of all the silly things to talk about and right there on her mama's front porch. Right there in ear distance of Lena who was pitching a fit to get on a train all by herself and go somewhere.

"You are not but eleven years old, Rolena Pearson," their mama said.

"I'll go see your people," Lena squealed like a little pig. "I just want to go somewhere."

"Will you wait for me?" James asked and took hold of one of her fingers and squeezed it. She was not but sixteen years old. "Promise me that you'll be right here, just like this."

"I hope so," she told him. "But I can't go making promises when I don't know what'll happen. You might like those snails and decide to stay." She had wanted to say, "Yes, yes," but that would've been forward. They were not engaged and she was not going to chase him, a man eight years older, a grown man getting ready to cross the ocean.

She had cried when her shoulder felt so open and uncovered there while she swayed in the glider, Ginny Sue asleep in her arms, those same spider lilies that were there three nights before when her shoulder was covered, that very last night that she had with him, but there were not enough tears in the world to do him justice. There were not enough and the glider swayed back and forth, back and forth, like that swing at her mama's house and her hand in that cold brown river water. "Now you got to wait for me," she whispered and stared down at her hands so tired and calloused, so much needing to reach over and feel him there.

* * *

Her hands would be so tired after doing all that laundry, those towels after all them men had come in and bathed, James's shirts that would be so dirty from hard work by the end of a day. There wasn't time to stop, had to hire that colored woman to come from time to time, Mag Sykes; Mag Sykes could work circles around anybody in the county. "Let's sit a spell," she'd say to Mag and they would while James was at work and the children at school. "Let's have a little dip," Mag would say and she would though no one knew of it. Mag knew and James knew that she'd take a dip, but nobody else needed to know. It was none of their business.

"Mag?" she calls now and this white woman, a white woman in some brown pants and a flowered shirt comes and stands in the doorway. Oh yes, Esther is here. Mag is not here. It seems Esther is related some way, but she can't think of how, way on down the line.

"You needing something, Miss Emily?"

"Did you ever hear of the Saxapaw River?" She takes out that tin of snuff and puts a little in her gum. Everybody knows about that these days. These days, nobody cares if a person takes a dip of snuff what with what's on TV.

"Did I ever hear of it?" Esther sits in the rocking chair closeby and laughs. "I live on it. 'Bout to dry up these days, but let a big rain fall and that river comes right up in my backyard."

"Hush now," Emily says and laughs until the tears come to her eyes. "No telling what comes up out of that river."

"I ain't aiming to go look," Esther says and takes a sip of the iced tea she is holding. "I know a man that found a body washed up once."

"Hush now," Emily puts her hand up to her chest but still can't stop the laughing. "I bet that give him a scare."

"He was crazy drunk, stood there and talked to that body for awhile." Esther drains the iced tea and gets up. "I'll have lunch in a second. I bet you'll have company before too long."

"Company?"

"Well, Hannah will be here, you know," Esther says. Esther doesn't dip, which is good; it's a habit you can fall under. "Hannah said she might see if Lena feels like getting out."

"Lena ain't doing well," Emily says. "Now don't you tell that I said it."

"Oh no, I wouldn't," Esther says and goes back in the kitchen.

Lena doesn't live at her house anymore. Lena lives somewhere that she says is like a hotel and a school. Lena has ridden trains her whole life and she didn't have anything sung when Roy Carter died. Lena was so mad at him when he died that she didn't even go to the funeral. Lena has been spoiled her whole life.

"Did you say it's lunchtime?" Emily calls out but her voice is so quiet that she has to wait until Esther comes back to the doorway to repeat herself. "Lunch did you say?" and Esther nods. "I thought it was closer to suppertime."

"Where on earth have you been this morning?" Esther asks, and she has to think a minute. It seems like she's been everywhere. She has to think real hard like she might be in school.

"Well, the Saxapaw River."

"Lord, I hope you weren't up in my backyard. The back of my house is a plumb sight what with old hubcaps and them trash men haven't been to my house in a month I know."

Esther goes back in the kitchen and Emily is glad, Esther's white face so shiny like it might have been greased in lard. Esther sings a song that Emily has never heard before. It's about somewhere by the name of Butcher's Hollow and it makes Emily laugh until her chest hurts. "You got to wait for me now, James," she says. "You and David has got to promise that you'll wait for me."

"I can't hear you now girl with all that frying," Esther says and leans around the corner; God, to see Mag Sykes, somebody with a little sense give to them. "What are you saying, honey?"

"Children should be seen and not heard is what I'm saying."

"Well, it's been a coon's age since I've been called a child." Esther laughs and goes back to her singing and it makes Emily laugh, just wash those clothes and shell butterbeans and sit down with Mag and have a dip. It makes her laugh until her chest hurts, laugh until she takes a Kleenex from her pocket and holds it up to her eyes. There are not enough tears in the world for it, just not enough.

* * *

Lena Pearson Carter wishes she was dead. Roy is. It's been almost a year since Roy died, her niece Hannah says, but it seems like yesterday or three weeks what with all that hullaballoo going on, making her house like a regular hellhole. And who would've thought? Who would've thought Roy would throw such a wild party there on the night that everybody said he was dead. There was so much noise a policeman came and he was right nice, not a very handsome man but the Lord can't heap up everybody's plate like he did for Roy Carter, and why? Why did the Lord give all that to Roy Carter, brains and looks and her for a wife. "My husband's cutting a shine," she told that policeman. "And he's dead, too." She had no choice but to tell it. She told the policeman and Hannah and that niggra that came and stole the car. "I hurt," she said, but not a one of them could do a thing for her; not a one could tell her where Roy had gone.

Next thing she knew, Hannah had her name stamped in all her underwear and had her here at this school. Old people, God, old and ugly, looking like fools, walk by her door near about all day and some stop and stand there sipping on some old Pepsi-Cola or shit, who knows, like she might ask them to come in and she doesn't; hell no, ain't about to ask some old drooling fool into her house. She's already got one that stays there with her, a woman with the filthiest hair that Lena has ever seen, could fry an egg on a hot day and that woman just walks back and forth. She walks back and forth till it makes Lena dizzy. "Wear out the damn rug!" Lena told her and the fool said, "I will, sister, I will. God willing and I will." Psshh. God don't have a thing to do with it; God ain't at this school and who can blame him? The food makes you sick; they don't put one grain of salt on one grain of nothing. "I'd love to have me some of them butter cookies," her roommate says ten thousand times a day. "I'd love some, yes sister, I would, God willing and I would."

"Tell God about it then," Lena had said one day and that woman stopped her pacing and just grinned at her, nodded and grinned.

"I do, sister, I do." She went right back to pacing and Lena told her, told her she didn't have but one sister still on this earth and that her sister, Emily Pearson Roberts, lived at home where she ought to be and not in this school where men pee on the floor if they take a notion and nobody cares.

"There's pee on the floor," she had told that fat woman in the white suit. "And he did it." She pointed to that old man that chews tobacco all day long without a tooth in his head.

"Now, let's not be ugly, Mrs. Carter," that woman said. God, ugly, ugly and old—all of them are as old as dirt and who in the hell wants to talk to them or to be here at this hotel school where nothing's going on except some niggras that come on Sundays to sing and play bingo games where

you don't get a damn thing but maybe a comb or a sucker
like you might be retarded. "Let's play for money," she said
one day, "or cigarettes," and that nurse teacher said "Now,
Mrs. Carter." Lena said stop with that Mrs. Carter shit 'cause
Mr. Carter is dead and the food makes her sick as a dog,
sick as hell and people pee on the floor for a person like
herself who can still walk to slip and break a neck. She hasn't
learned one goddamned thing, not one, and that's fine, don't
need such a school; live and learn and die and forget it all.
Roy used to say that. Roy said that and he said, "Walk softly
and carry a big stick." He said, "Do unto others before they
do it to you." Damn right. She's worn this same outfit five
days in a row and she don't care if she wears it for the sixth.
They say let's slip off your clothes and take a little bath, little
bath, shit; she ain't taking off her clothes for people who are
all crazy as hell. Can't even get room service in this hotel,
gotta go to the school cafeteria and walk down a line if you're
able and then sit there with people that can't even get a bite
to their lips without dropping it. God, it makes her sick.
"You close your mouth so I can't see," she told one woman
and that woman smiled at her, *smiled* there with food and no
telling what kind of food it was, who the hell knows, hanging
there around her mouth and there's a woman that sits in a
high chair the whole damn day with a baby doll hugged up
to her bosom and screaming for somebody to "Get Billy, Get
Billy." Lena stopped by that woman's chair one day and said,
"You hush your mouth," and that woman said, "Get Billy,"
and she said, "I don't know Billy, you get Billy on the phone
and shut up, now." That woman kept right on so Lena went
up to that nurse teacher and she said, "You go get that damned
Billy and let it stop."

"Billy's dead," the nurse teacher said. "We'll move her
further down the hall."

"Why don't you tell her he's dead so she'll just shut up?
Roy's dead, they say, and you don't catch me setting there
saying, 'Where's Roy? Where's Roy?' "

"Would you like a Pepsi-Cola?" that woman teacher mule-
head tart asked. They think a Pepsi-Cola is next to God.

"No I don't want some damn Pepsi-Cola." She pounded
her fist on that counter and stuck out her tongue. "Get Billy"
that woman said when she passed and she stopped and took
that woman's doll right out of her arms. It was the ugliest

doll baby that she'd ever seen, dirty and ugly; she never in her life kept a baby doll looking so ugly and dirty. That woman stretched her arms to get that doll back, grunting and carrying on like she might be four or five. Lena looked to see if that doll was wearing underwear.

"That is her doll," nurse teacher said and took it. "Do you want one of your own?"

"God, what would I do with it? I never even had babies, real babies, 'cause I didn't see any use to them, cry, cry, cry," she had pointed to the woman who was clutching that doll baby and rocking back and forth.

"Well, we don't take other people's things," fat tart said and them legs of hers the size of a barrel.

"Somebody took my shoes," she said. "I had nine pair of shoes and somebody took them."

"Your niece is keeping them for you."

"Hannah can't wear my shoes so I know that's not the truth." She took off her bedroom shoe and held up her foot. "I have little feet and Hannah can't wear my shoes." She glanced down them barrels to those white shoes, God, she hates white shoes even in the summer she hates white shoes if they ain't Keds. "What do you wear, a 13?"

"Get Billy! Get Billy!"

"Billy is dead! Dead, dead. Billy is in the school for the dead where we all ought to be instead of this here school Holiday Inn." That woman stopped rocking and looked at her, tears in them old eyes that looked like if they could see anything, they shouldn't be able to. "Dead, I say. Billy's dead." She leaned closer to that woman and put her own cheek on the other side of that doll's head. "I wish I was dead," she whispered and that woman didn't say a word, just stared off past that baby's head. Somebody ought to bathe that baby and give it a little milk like she did for Trickie. She'd stand on that back step and without a word Trickie would be there going round and round her legs. Trickie would meow real sweetlike when she filled up that saucer. "That's why we always run out of milk," Roy had said. I been out of milk my whole life she told him once.

"Get Billy," that woman screams right now, but Lena is used to it, get Billy and God willing, get some butter cookies, sister, yeah, get some butter cookies and get Billy and wear that damn rug out.

"Let's clean you up for your visit today," nurse teacher says. "Your niece is coming to take you for a visit. Come on, now." That woman pulls her shirt up over her head and it's cold there to her back. "We'll get you feeling good."

"You can try," she says. "But I'd just as soon be dead."

"Oh, don't you be that way today. You're going to look so pretty."

"Shit, I used to be pretty. Everybody said so. I was on Broadway once and people said I was so pretty. Roy said I was the brightest broad on Broadway, and my baskets used to bring in more money than anybody's at the Saxapaw church socials and I couldn't even cook. I'd have some fruit and cheese in my basket and those other girls with their fried chicken and ham dumplings."

"I bet those men just wanted your company," nurse teacher says and wipes a warm sponge all around her neck and chest.

"They did," she says. "They'd rather eat an apple and be with me."

"Not too many women who can say that."

"Tell it sister!" the roommate says.

"She can't." Lena points to her roommate and laughs because that sponge feels so good in between and around her breasts, up and down her back. "No, not many women that had men falling all over themselves like I did. I had more boyfriends than you could shake a stick at. They'd hang around calling 'Miss Rolena' till it made me sick. I've never gone by Rolena. Whoever heard of a star named Rolena?"

"I would've liked all those boyfriends," nurse says and buttons Lena's clean blouse up, makes Lena pull her britches off.

"Psshhh. You'd have tired of it. I knew if I ever met a man like Roy Carter, that I'd marry him. Roy Carter knew women and I liked that; Roy knew just what to do. He split a beer with me down there at Myrtle Beach and he said 'you're beautiful, Lena.' My stomach felt sick like he might be just like all the others. I drank my beer and I reached in that bucket and got me another one. Those seagulls were squalling so loud I thought I'd go crazy. Then he grabbed me tight, near about as tight as you've got my foot, let go a little. He said, 'goddamnit, Lena, all I'm trying to do is tell you that I love you.' "

"Shhh," that woman whispers and picks up her other foot.

"That's what he said and I fell flat that's how hard I fell. He said that and he squeezed my arm so tight it hurt and I knew he was the man. He said, 'you crazy broad' and I could've died right then and there."

"There now, aren't you feeling better?" Nurse teacher hands her the sponge. "Now you wash yourself and we'll change your underwear, too."

"Yourself. My mama always said 'yourself' when she meant your. . . . " She stops and stares at the woman. "But he died. I can't believe he died and left me like that." She takes that warm sponge and rubs it up between her legs, up and down, while that nurse turns around so she won't have to see. "Seen one, you've seen 'em all," Roy used to say and she told him just remember that then 'cause he'd never see another but hers. "And mine ain't quite like everybody else's," she had added.

"What makes it different?" he asked, pulled her up close to him and pressed in with his hips.

" 'Cause it's mine," she said. "And that makes anything I've got different. What's yours is mine and what's mine is mine." They had laughed and laughed and that sponge is getting a little cool. She gives it back and puts on her underwear; it has her name on it; it says Lena Carter.

"Let's comb your hair and put on some lipstick and you'll be all ready."

"Get Billy! Get Billy!" comes from the hall and the roommate says, "Tell it!"

"I might have me a Pepsi-Cola while I wait," she says and hands her mink hat to the maid.

"Oky doke." The nurse maid pulls Lena's hat in place. "Won't you be hot in this hat?"

"I've been hot my whole life," she says and laughs. Roy used to call her a hot number, *his* hot number. "Did you say Roy is stopping backstage?" she asks, reaches up to feel that silky mink on her head.

"No, Hannah, your niece, is coming *here*, here to *Pinegrove*."

"Oh yeah." She follows the nurse out into the hall by the Pepsi machine. "You're a right cute woman yourself," she says. "I bet you could get a man if you'd change your shoes."

"I'm married," the nurse teacher says and laughs.

"Well, did you ever know that hayseed sister-in-law of mine, Tessy Pearson?"

"No."

"No, I guess not," she says, shakes her head. "Tessy is dead, been dead. Tessy was married to my brother, Harv, and it didn't stop her none from looking for a man. She found one, too. We all knew. Harv didn't know."

"Hmmm." The nurse hands her the Pepsi-Cola and leads her down the hall to the front where the hotel is so pretty with all the flowers left from opening night.

"I never cheated on Roy," Lena says. "I had chances but I didn't do it."

"You sit right here in the sunshine, now," nurse says. "I'll see you tonight." God knows, the nurse maid couldn't get another man but Tessy Pearson did, God bless and rest her soul and keep it wherever it is. Lena called her Messy 'cause she was so filthy to have done that and because her clothes were so bad; she wore such baggy old dresses over those skinny bones that she could have robbed a watermelon patch and nobody would've known.

"Get Billy!" Lena turns to see that old woman in her wheelchair there in the shade, that doll held to her chest like it might be nursing. Lena gets up and walks past some of the others on a bench, sitting and staring like old fools, and she stops beside that woman, bends down close to her. "I'm going after Billy right now," she whispers and that woman looks at her, squints up those old cloudy eyes. "As soon as I find Roy, we'll go to get Billy. Me and Roy got a great big car."

* * *

Hannah went to Merle Norman two months ago and had them do her face. Now all the products that she bought after seeing her new self, her *retired* self, are spread out across the bathroom counter while she tries to remember what each one is for. "Good God, Hannah!" Ben said that first night when he walked into the bedroom and there she was relaxing on the bed while her Miracol Facial did whatever it was supposed to besides making her face look like hot pink rubber. "You scared the hell out of me. Retirement's not looking real good on you."

"We want to accent those big green eyes," the Merle Norman woman said. Hannah picks up her eyeliner and tries to remember which way the woman pulled her lid to apply it. "You've got some slight red tones in your hair, pretty, a little rinse would do wonders to tone down the gray. We'll want to stay away from light pinks though," the woman said and dabbed a damp cloth over Hannah's mouth, removing the color that Hannah has worn for so many years that her lips looked naked.

"I can't believe you got a makeover, Mama," Ginny Sue said on the phone. "I can't wait to see." Makeover, it sounded the same as when Ben talks about overhauling a motor down at the garage.

Lena would know what to do with all of these concoctions, or rather there was a time when she would have. And sure, the Merle Woman knows; it's her job and she gets paid for doing it. What if Hannah was to give that woman a bolt of cloth and a needle and thread and send her home to make christening gowns with tatted edges and smocked tops, or a pair of lined drapes? Everybody cannot know everything. She gives up and puts on her usual dab of mascara and a touch of her own lipstick. Something you have done your whole life can't be all bad and she doesn't have time to sit and match up every color in the rainbow like Ginny Sue would do if she could.

She brushes her short hair back from her face and fluffs it a little. She is not about to start with hair rinses, either. It would be just one more thing to keep up with and who has time? She has always been amazed that you can go to the grocery store at seven-thirty in the morning and there are women fixed and made up like they might be going to church. There was a time when she wanted to be flashy like Lena, but she just could not get herself to go about it. It didn't feel right. You can't sew or wash or do anything with fingernails that are long and pointed. She thinks that growing out and keeping long fingernails is a good excuse not to work. Lena once got her hand in an ad for a dishwashing detergent and Roy Carter said she didn't wash dishes for two months.

Hannah wishes she could just plop down and relax but even retired, she can't. The only times that she has ever relaxed in her adult life have been short little weekend vacations, long enough to relax, but not so long that she had to start worrying over dust that collected or having to get back to her routine. Two or three days is vacation enough and it can't be done at home where the phone's gonna ring or the doorbell or the dirty laundry starts stacking up.

She would like to be on a little vacation right now; she would like to be some place where she could dial room service and get a breakfast tray, sit there and read a magazine. She'd like to be sitting on a balcony somewhere, watching the people go by and not having to say a word to one of them. She would like to kick up her feet and say, "I'm not cooking, cleaning, or talking today." She knows from past experience that that would not last more than a day if that long. And what's wrong with that? What's wrong with staying busy if that's what makes you happy?

She goes into the kitchen and looks out the window and across the backyard where Ben is out in that garden, working away, every bit of his body covered because he sunburns, probably drenched in sweat. He'll probably do that all day long, take a few showers of towels to wash. It seems that he would just give up on growing some gigantic vegetable and be satisfied that he grows enough every summer that they eat fresh vegetables all winter.

She can keep herself busy with full retirement, but sometimes she wishes that Ben had never decided on going semi-retired and would just keep on going down to the garage every day. He might as well the way that he calls those men on the phone ten times a day, wanting to know every car that's come in and what was wrong with it and where was it going. He spends his whole day talking on the phone and walking around in the garden. It wouldn't surprise her if she looked out there and saw him dressed like an Indian and doing a rain dance. "When is it going to rain?" he has asked every night for the past three weeks, waiting for her response like she might know.

No way could she get him to go on a vacation right now, not during this dry spell. They used to always go to the beach in the summer when the children were growing up. They'd rent a big ocean-front house with Madge and Raymond for a week and she and Madge would just sit on the beach, have a drink if they wanted, and watch the children splash around and play. She could always trust Robert to stand there at the edge of the ocean and keep a watch on Ginny Sue and Madge's Catherine and Cindy. He'd stand there at the edge of that ocean with his hands on his hips like a miniature lifeguard and say things like, "Out too far, Ginny," or "Close your mouth when you go under." Hannah will never forget that, Robert's high steady voice like a mimic of a grown man. It made her think of all those times Lena and Roy took David and her down to the Saxapaw River. Hannah was like Robert, standing on the shore and watching over her baby brother while he splashed and went out too far.

Things seemed so easy on those vacations to the beach. She and Madge would drive, just the two of them, up to the shopping center and try on shoes and hats and sunglasses like they might have been teenagers. She misses those times, times when she could dial home and her father would answer. He'd tell Hannah not to worry, to have fun, that her mother was out working in the garden, that they were baking a hen for dinner, might walk down the street to the store once it got cool.

Hannah would like to go right now and pull a yard chair under the shade of that dogwood tree that she named after Aunt Tessy and just sit until the cows come home. The tree shades a large part of the yard now and it seems like no time at all that she got out there and planted it, digging so carefully, every spade of dirt. It was planted on the day that Tessy died, but Hannah had waited months before telling anyone the story, the way that Tessy had awakened in the hospital that day, taken hold of Hannah's arm and said, "I hope that dogwood will live." Tessy said that and then fell back into a deep sleep that never ended. It sent chills through Hannah, then, and the whole ride home in that old station wagon where she had her dogwood waiting, the burlap tucked around its roots. No one, not even Ben, knew that she was going to buy a dogwood tree that day. She didn't even know it herself. Even now it gives her gooseflesh, and yet a good feeling, the hope that Tessy knows even now about that tree, can see how big it is, knows what a fine seamstress Hannah has been all these years. Tessy is the one that got her started sewing all those years ago. Tessy and Hannah's mama, Emily, would sit for hours sewing or quilting and those are some of the best memories of her childhood. She loved sitting in front of the window fan in that high-ceilinged room, where the conversation might lapse into quiet for a bit, but their hands never stopped, shiny silvery needles and brightly colored threads constantly moving.

But that's all water under the bridge and too much to think about when she's got a million and one things to do today. She's got to run by the shop and pick up her payment from those two young girls that are buying her out. Already, the shop doesn't even look like her own; they've brought in two brand new sewing machines and have all these strange-looking mannequins with their blank faces nothing more than a stuffed piece of cloth. "It's not yours anymore," Ben keeps reminding her and that's true. She has moved most all of her belongings into Robert's old room, carefully placing machine, ironing board and her work table in the same position they were in at the shop.

She looks up at the clock and she knows that Lena is sitting and waiting for her to get there—just sitting and waiting and thinking—Hannah can't help but wonder if that's what it takes to be able to sit and rest, getting old and feeble and unable to do anything else like her mother and like Lena. Of course, Madge will sit and play solitaire for hours when there are dishes in her sink. Hannah couldn't stand for that, and she can't understand why *some* of her neatness hadn't rubbed off on Ginny Sue.

"Nobody can see it," Ginny Sue whined her whole childhood when Hannah pointed out the dust under the bed.

"That doesn't make it go away." Hannah had been able to use that answer for years and then Ginny turned it on her.

"There's a man in my closet," Ginny Sue told her one night after screaming bloody murder. "A man with a knife."

"I don't see a thing," Hannah had said, the lights on, closet door open, Ben's snores that could wake up the dead coming from their room.

"That doesn't make it go away," Ginny Sue said. "He'll be back as soon as you leave me." And she had kept on until Hannah had let her make a pallet on the floor of Robert's room. He hadn't minded, so calm and protective; looks just like his father, tall and lean. Hannah misses him, misses that laundry basket full of dirty baseball socks which she knows his wife Susie probably never gets clean. Susie is sweet and cute and gets along with everybody so well the couple of times a year they fly in from California, but she doesn't use bleach. She stood right there in Hannah's kitchen while Ginny Sue was stenciling a heart over the doorway which Hannah didn't particularly want over her doorway but was too tired from fixing the big Christmas dinner to say anything, and said, "I can't ever get Rob's socks clean." *Clorox*, is what Hannah was thinking, *Clorox* and *nobody has ever called him Rob, I didn't name him Rob.* A son is a son until he takes a wife she told herself, wondering why in the Sam Hill Ginny Sue was making that heart green when there's not a thing in her kitchen that is green except for her eyes when she's in it. You have to bite your tongue and be thankful for what you've got, though, and she reminded herself of Madge sitting in that plastic-covered house with Raymond dead and two daughters that fuss all the time.

She could handle that heart over her door, it's still there, and she could handle Ginny Sue's spooky stage that seemed to go on for years. What Hannah could not handle was when Ginny Sue finally, years later, came out of it all and made an about-face and thought things were so lovely, so interesting, and she'd talk about people and music that Hannah had never even heard of. Hannah had to break in and say something like, "I've seen a mimosa tree, Ginny Sue. I know how pink they are."

"One day I'm going to have long blonde hair and be on the front of a magazine," Ginny Sue said one day and Hannah had not been able to take it. Her mama and Lena just feeding right into those tall tales like it might be possible. Some parents may go right along with all of that, telling their daughters that they're the prettiest thing to land on earth, the smartest and so on like Raymond Sinclair did to that Cindy, but Hannah wasn't one of them.

"Ginny Sue," she said. "You may be on the front of a magazine, nobody knows, but you will never have blonde hair unless you bleach it out and look like a streetwalker."

Ginny Sue had cried and pouted a little, wanted to blame Hannah for her dark hair, but it hadn't really changed things, hadn't stopped her from staring off and making up all these wonderful, beautiful things either. She'd go on and on about how her life was going to be, a long list of college courses and types of furniture, how her yard would be landscaped, what colors would be best for a wedding and not even a ring on that hand, and not one thing out of all that Ginny Sue wanted even resembled anything that Hannah had. "No life is perfect," Hannah told her. "If you are happy, then you've got more than a lot."

"Gram's life has been perfect," Ginny Sue said. "I hope I'm like Gram when I get old." And Hannah did manage to bite her tongue on that one, to bite down on the bad times that Ginny chose to ignore. You can't do it for them, got to find out on their own that if you're waiting to catch that falling star and put it in your pocket, you might as well cash in your chips. That's what happened to Raymond Sinclair, couldn't live up to all his big-talking ways. No sir, you keep a little in your pocket at all times, something to simmer on the back burner, something that nobody else can get and then you just get on with it. Hannah always has material on hand and a pattern of some sort to go with it, start it and see it through. If Ginny Sue would do that then she wouldn't have a dozen different things halfway done and if she'd listened to Hannah long ago when she was getting all caught up in planning a wedding that never even took place, she wouldn't have come home from Georgia looking like a toothpick with hairs on her legs long enough to plait and trips to a therapist who had hairs just as long.

Hannah has never once mentioned all that money that was already spent on the wedding that never was. Ginny Sue stood right out there in the backyard and poured lighter fluid on that wedding portrait, lit a match. Hannah stood on the back porch and watched the bits of hard-earned money turning to cinder. "Well? You didn't want it did you?" Ginny Sue asked, barefooted and wearing a cardigan that had belonged to Hannah's mama about a century ago, supposed to be white and soiled gray. Did she say *Clorox*? *Don't play with fire?* "No, I see no sense in keeping it. But it was a pretty picture." The photographer had looked at Hannah and said, "She looks just like you." And they did look alike when Ginny was all dressed in Hannah's wedding dress and had that long dark hair pulled up and back from her face. The real wedding was small, private, and Hannah was a little disappointed that there weren't more people to see the strong resemblance. "Oh, I thought you were my wife," Mark had said at the reception, and hugged her. "Does this mean I'm in the secret club, now?"

"What club?" Hannah asked and laughed because she has never been a joiner, has never gotten over the time that Madge talked her into being a Lady Lion. Ben was going around selling brooms and lightbulbs and having a wonderful time learning what kind of car everybody in town drove, while she was responsible for telling everybody what to fix for the steak dinner, and learning who did not know how to pick out good meat.

"You know," Mark said, "that club that meets at your mother's house. All the women. When a man comes in it gets quiet."

"Didn't used to be that way," Ben said. "You better count your blessings. When Roy was living, it wasn't that way."

"That's because Roy and Lena could barely separate to use the bathroom," Hannah said and looked at Mark. "You can come sit any time you please." Mark just laughed and hugged Ginny Sue tight. Thank God, he seems crazy about her and heaven forbid that anything should happen. And things do, all over this world; you can see it on those daytime shows and made for TV movies and "Phil Donahue."

Ginny Sue told Hannah before she brought Mark home that first time that sometimes he was quiet and they shouldn't take it wrong, that he had grown up in the NORTH, like Hannah couldn't see that for herself. How could she not see it; she cooked butterbeans and he said that he'd never seen that kind of soup before. Philadelphia; certainly she's heard of Philadelphia. "You've heard of the Phillies," Ben said and she shook her head. "You know what W. C. Fields had on his tombstone?" he asked and she said she didn't even know he was dead. You can live and work and you get out of touch with things, but Hannah is catching up. It would spin everybody's head to know how much Hannah *does* know, and it all comes from living day to day and year to year. Ginny Sue will know how it feels one day when this baby wants to spend her time with Hannah, when this baby takes to sewing and smocking and tells Ginny Sue that she wants to grow up to be just like Hannah.

It makes Hannah smile now to think of a baby, a baby to dress up like a little doll. When Ginny Sue came along, Hannah couldn't afford to go out and do a whole lot of buying. Now she can; she and Ben have already bought a stroller and some stuffed animals. She has made a comforter of white eyelet.

She steps out the back door and walks towards the garden. Ben is still working, bending and working. "I'm going to get Lena," she yells, the sun so warm, sinking into her navy sundress while her barefoot sandals swing from one hand. Ben looks up, returns her wave with a squash in each hand and his face red as a beet; even from this distance she can tell that it is. She told him, tells him every day to use that sunscreen but he won't listen and tonight he'll be in her Oil of Olay and saying how he can't believe that he could get his face so burned with his cap on for that short a time in the garden. "Do you need anything from the store?"

He shakes his head and walks closer, circles under the arms of his shirt, and she wishes he wouldn't get so hot. She knows that one day she's going to look out that window like Lena did for Roy and see him having a stroke there in the garden. Keep a little in your pocket, don't think about what hasn't happened, the Lord could take me in an hour right there in the car. She's already passed the year, fifty-nine years old, which is how old her mama was when her daddy died. That's superstitious, any therapist or Phil Donahue would have told her, but she was so glad last month when she turned sixty, so relieved to have made it. "I was going to check your oil," he says and grins. Ginny Sue would never in her life believe that the two of them had such a joke that had gone on all these years.

"Well, you'll have to check it later," she says and shakes her head, so thankful to see him standing there. She will fuss over all those towels like she always did Robert's dirty socks and she will love every minute of it.

"No, Hannah, I really do," he says and tilts his cap back on his head. "Your car sounds a little rough."

"I won't be long," she says. "You better use that sunscreen." She drops her sandals to the ground and slips her feet in, bends to buckle them. "Why don't you go in and cool off?"

"I will," he says, nodding, but she knows he won't unless it's to call the station and find out what's going on. "And I'll check your oil when you get home."

"I'll let you rotate my tires, too," she says and watches him laugh. It's funny how somebody you've known your whole life doesn't change a bit, ever, until somebody pulls out a picture box and points it out to you like Ginny Sue does just about every time she's home.

"I want to look under your hood this evening," Ben used to say at dinner, Ginny Sue and Robert going right on with baseball and watercolors and never even seeing her face flush or his eyebrows lift as he glanced away, a sneaky bashful expression that he had had his whole life. "Just because you have a child doesn't mean you stop being a wife," Hannah tells Ginny Sue every chance she gets. You don't have to read it in a magazine to know that a woman has to learn to be everything at the same time. It's common sense is all it is, good common sense, but the best advice on a pair of ears that don't want to hear isn't worth beans.

"I see how fast you're getting in from the sun," she yells to him when she passes by the edge of the garden in the car, and he just nods and waves an ear of corn, the silks falling over his hand like the blonde hair that Ginny Sue never had.

* * *

Madge writes to her cousin, sits back and stares at the words, "Dear Hannah, I killed Raymond." Her handwriting suddenly looks so unfamiliar, as unfamiliar as those last years with Raymond had been—the little curl at the bottom of her *D*, the way he bathed himself in alcohol morning and night and then lifted his hands to his face to get the smell. "He held the gun but I pulled the trigger. He begged me. He said, 'Madge, I can't even die; I can't do anything.' He held that gun by the barrel and pointed it at his chest. He said, 'Do it, goddamnit. If you love me, you'll do it.' This was not the first time this had happened; it began years before. It began so slowlike that I didn't even notice or must not have noticed from the very start. I figured Raymond was acting strange every now and again because he was getting into middle age. But then when Mama died and Raymond asked that he be let to watch them embalm her body, I knew that something awful had crept into my Raymond and eaten away at him. He came back from the funeral home that day like he felt so pleased, like most men look after a good meal or, uh, relations. Hannah, he told me what mama looked like lying there at a slant and all drained of her life liquids. 'Tessy's skin was so very very white,' he said and it made me sick as a dog, not just because I didn't want to picture mama that way but because it struck me that Raymond was terribly ill. I got him to go to a doctor when all that paralysis that came and went started up and those doctors told me in private that there was a lot of mental disturbance, that Raymond needed long-term treatment, drugs maybe. Raymond said, 'My body is a holy pyramid over which I reign.' It made my flesh crawl all over to hear those words coming out of the mouth of my husband, the man that I had married, the man who dressed up on Halloween to answer the door for the little children; a man who for years could bowl 200 consistently, was forever getting employee of the month down at Chevrolet, the father of Catherine and Cindy; and Hannah, the only man that I have ever in my entire life seen without clothing.

"He pulled out that gun for the first time years ago when Cindy was only thirteen and was over at your house for Ginny Sue's spend the night. I should have told you then, should have told you that morning when I picked Cindy up instead of taking her to J. C. Penney's to buy a pair of red sneakers that she wore all of three times. Every morning when I washed my clothes, I'd reach up over that washing machine to make sure the gun was still there and I did not sleep through a night that I was not expecting to hear that sound, that same sound that had scared me so when I'd follow my daddy out in the woods and watch him practice on liquor bottles that mama knew nothing about. He'd get a look on his face that made you think of death, like that was what he was thinking the whole time and I'd cover up my ears ready for the blast and yet, it made me jump every time just the same. I'm the same way with balloons. Remember when Chuckie used to love to take a straight pin and pop a balloon. I'd say, 'Cindy, don't bring balloons to my house.' Cindy said I was ridiculous; she said what I really meant was 'don't come to my house' which I didn't. My door is always open. Hannah, you know I've always had a open door, my back door and my heart's door.

"If you love me, 'you'll pull that goddamned' (and I quote of course), 'you'll pull that goddamned trigger.' It wasn't love that I was feeling right then. Sometimes I think I was feeling nothing at all. Sometimes I think I was feeling impatient and ready to get it all over with so that I wouldn't have to be ready to put my hands to my ears all the time. He was so weak. It seemed that weakness had covered over or erased every feature on his face. He just wasn't the same man that I fell in love with and met at the end of the River Baptist aisle. I was staring at him there, those eyes like they couldn't focus right, his hand forcing my finger into that hole and up against that cool metal trigger. There was no recollection; I suddenly felt like I might be preparing to kill a bug or a mouse that had frightened me. I was frightened. My hands shook like jelly. 'Do it, do it,' he kept saying over and over. 'Don't be scared to do it.' I did it and it seems to me when I look back that I didn't even hear a noise. For eight years I've tried to make myself hear that noise so that I can know that's how it happened and get on with what's left of my life. Eight years and I've never figured out exactly what it was I was feeling at the time. I thought of my mama on that slanted table; I thought of that look that my daddy had when he popped those bottles and the glass sprayed; I thought of Cindy when she was first born and Raymond said, 'She looks just like me,' and she does, more and more; sometimes it scares me that she looks so much like him because it makes me think that if she's got those body genes, that she may very well have his brain genes, too.

"I turned off the light because I didn't want to see and I went to the bedroom and I called the police and an ambulance. I watched out the window waiting for them to get there and I didn't even remember calling you and Ben but you beat the ambulance and next thing I knew you had your arms around me and had me out of that house on the front porch all wrapped up in a blanket and then in the front seat of the car where you had left the heater running and the radio playing. The moon was full and clearly we were in for some frost and I kept thinking about my bed of asters and how I hoped they would make it. Ben asked, 'Why Madge, why did he do it?' and I couldn't say a word. Ben said, 'HOW did he do it' and I knew he was trying to picture Raymond with those weak sometimes paralyzed arms holding a shotgun on himself. I have nightmares now. His arms weren't really deadened like he told people. He'd grab me hard by the arms and he'd say, 'I never wanted you. Just the smell of you sickens me.' I never said a word, all that time covering for him the best I could. Everybody remembered the time he was caught up on the roof of Kinglee Hardware with his eyes all made up like a woman, blue shadow and long black eyeliner tails. 'Like Tut,' he said. 'Like Cindy,' I said. I know you've noticed all that cheap makeup when I didn't raise her that way; Ginny Sue never did that to her face. 'Don't you see what

you're doing to the girls? To me?' I asked and I told everybody how he was dressed that way to try out a campaign for
Chevrolet knowing full well that nobody would believe it because what does King Tut have to do with cars? But that was
the only big thing prior to the funeral. All the other stuff
happened there at home where only I knew. I tried to get
Cindy to see but she never did and to this day won't hear it;
she blames me for Raymond's illness, she says that Raymond
was a 'artist of the mind.' Now you know and I know that in
his good years Raymond was a whippersnapper of a salesman
and dressed good, too, but he was never a artist of the mind.
I know people saw things at the funeral; I know they couldn't
help but notice that brand new color widescreen TV when
everybody knows that what I'm still looking at is that small
black and white that I bought when Jack Paar was still on the
'Tonight Show.' It doesn't pick up doodle squat these days
and people tell me I'd enjoy these carry over shows that come
on at night now though the Lord Jesus knows there's enough
pain in this world without watching make-believe. If people
have said things, it's never been told to me. I was sorry on
the day of his funeral that I hadn't confessed all of this to
you. Don't you see I was scared? Scared that I'd be put in
prison. I was scared that I'd lose the only people I've got left,
you and Ben and your children, your mama, and my girls. I
don't know that Catherine and especially Cindy could ever
understand or forgive me and I just couldn't face that. I can't
bear the thought that I could lose what little bit's left, can't
bear the thought of prison. I just couldn't face living my life
that way though God knows it hasn't been much better. I
wanted so bad to tell you but everybody wanted me to bounce
back and went out of their way so to help me. There isn't
really a nice widower over in Clemmonsville that I eat out
with. I go to Clemmonsville and I go to the movies at City
Square Mall, eat at Morrison's and then spend the night at
Catherine's where I'm told that Cindy needs to grow up and
then I come home and Cindy tells me that Catherine, and I
quote, is a 'slutbucket' who needed to have more tied up than
her tubes, like her mouth. Cindy says that to hear Catherine
tell it her tubes were macraméd. Sometimes I think what
Cindy says is funny but I don't laugh, not ever; I don't want
to encourage her. I should have been here at home with that
child instead of studying to be a hygienist at Saxon Tech, but

Hannah, there was nothing to do when Raymond got that way but to take up a profession. We didn't really have a lot of money back then like Raymond told everybody; we did all right but I'm still paying for this house and I just finished paying for all that Raymond bought to take with him and that cematary plot big enough to bury every Pearson that ever walked. We would have had money if Raymond hadn't always taken it in his head that he had to buy the biggest and the best. 'Buy the large box of Tide,' he would say, you know that size that'll barely fit in the grocery cart, 'and stop buying Crisco. Oil, vegetable oil and get the biggest size,' and 'have them grind the hamburger for you, watch them grind it, tell them to wear gloves. Go ahead and get twenty pounds, never less than twenty pounds. It should be brown, Madge, not hot pink like when they inject the poisons.' Now, Hannah, who doesn't buy Crisco in the can? Who doesn't do that so that they have the nice can to put their grease in and store it? Raymond wouldn't let me save grease, not even bacon drippings. I bet Ben has never told you what you could and could not buy at the grocery. You don't know how I envied women in that check-out line; I envied the old and young, coloreds and whites alike with their Pop Tarts and normal-size detergents and pretty decorator toilet paper. I had to buy white, only white. 'If something strange is leaking from my body, I want to see it,' he said. He made me buy the largest box of Kotex and now you know that's something you don't want everybody seeing in your cart, those young boys having to bag it up. And God, I envied these women their cans of Crisco. You and your mama both have always used Crisco, Loretta Lynn, too, and look at her; she's done as good as a body could do. We might could have had money way back but that wouldn't have eased my heart. 'I'm freezing vegetables,' I used to tell those women at the check-out when I unloaded box after box of baggies. That's not why I bought all those baggies. I bet you always wondered why I bought all those baggies if you ever looked in my pantry and saw them. Well, now I can tell you. It was for his underclothing and socks, anything that directly touched his privates or feet. Every piece had to be put in a airtight baggie and I wasn't supposed to use the same baggie twice. I did, though, a few times I did like when Cindy had come down with the mumps and I couldn't get to the store to buy some. Thank God he didn't notice or he would've killed me. He had more socks than everybody in Saxon County could wear in a year, black, gray, navy and dark brown—'Never tan, Madge, brown, brown, as close to black as you can get and still be brown.' I've listened time and again to you telling of how you were in J. C. Penney's buying Ben some socks when your water broke with Ginny Sue and you don't know how I've envied that. Raymond wouldn't have put his foot in a sock from Penney's, Ivey's or Belk's. He ordered most of his socks from the North up in New York, underwear too. He wore Gucci socks, fancy little briefs, and Gucci shoes which had to be kept in large broil in the bag baggies. I had to wash his socks by hand so that they didn't get mismatched, pair by pair, then briefs and tee shirts, take them straight from the dryer and put them in a baggie. '*You* should care about losing *your* mate,' I always wanted to tell him but I didn't. I've seen Ben when his socks didn't match; I've seen him standing right there in your kitchen just as barefooted as a yard dog and I'd think to myself, 'Hannah sure is lucky not to have a man so taken with his own feet.' I've always thought of you as a sister and I used to wish that we were; I used to wish that Emily was my mama and I used to hate going home those nights when I had spent the day playing at your house. I've tried to find the right time when I could tell you all of this, tried to think of when I could be with you all by myself. I think of us just packing up and driving down to Myrtle Beach. I picture us sitting on the beach, watching the ocean and sipping a little wine like we used to do and I'd start at the first. I'd start with that night when Raymond asked me to soak in a cool bath and then lay real still on the bed, so that by the time I got to clothing and Crisco and mama's embalming that I could look at you and say, 'Hannah, I killed Raymond,' and that you would say that you were happy for me, that I had never deserved any of that, that you didn't know how I had lived through it all. I'd like to think that's what you'd say; I'd like to think you'd say there's no court of law that would take my life after all that, that there wasn't even reason that anyone should ever know. That's what I want to think because I did love Raymond, my Raymond, the one I married with you standing right there beside me. I love you like a sister, Hannah, and I hope you can go right on loving me after knowing all this.''

Madge tears up the letter in teeny shreds and washes it piece by piece down the garbage disposal, closing her eyes the whole while that disposal is groaning and gurgling like it is trying to breathe, like it is choking on every word.

"Are you coming or not? Call me at the crack of dawn and then not even ready." Cindy lets the back door slam and Madge jumps and clutches one last little scrap of paper that she missed. "I been waiting and tooting and it's hot as pure hell; my hair will be flat as a pancake before I even get to my VDT." Cindy flops down at the kitchen table and jingles her keys back and forth impatiently. Madge can't tell which jingles the loudest, the keys or all those chains wrapped around Cindy's neck and falling where she's about to show her bosoms with that dress cut like one you'd wear to a beach party and not to work where decent people of this town come and go and know that Cindy is Madge's daughter. Cindy's hair is pulled straight up in the front like something just scared her.

"Don't stare at my jewelry!" Cindy snaps. "It's Napier, gold-filled."

"I didn't say anything."

"No, but you thought it. I don't know why you don't say something because you usually do. I got these at the Thalhimers in Clemmonsville; they're Anne Klein and Napier. Good jewelry, not like those old out of style cheap chains you wear."

"I only wear one at a time." Madge gets her purse off the table and goes to the door. "I just think that they are pretty and that's why I say that they'd show up prettier if you'd just wear one at a time."

"Randy Skinner loves them. Randy Skinner says he'd like to see me wrapped in gold." That sounds like something Raymond would have said and it sends a chill down Madge's spine. She just nods; all those men's names come and go out of Cindy's mouth like a faucet turned on and off. "Randy is a pharmaceutical salesman who I meet on Friday nights, like tonight while you keep Chuckie." Madge walks outside and gets in the car; Cindy had left it running, the air full blast, radio full blast, and a cigarette just burning away in that ashtray, making Madge's eyes water. "But of course you could care less about who I meet at the Ramada Inn."

"I care, Cindy."

"Just say if you don't want Chuckie in your house. Just say 'cause I know that's what's on your mind." Cindy backs down the driveway and out into the street without even looking to see if anything's coming.

"Nothing's on my mind." Madge leans back in her seat so that the line of sunlight shines right in her eyes. "I guess I'm just tired."

"Tell me about it!" Cindy says and pulls right up to a red light without even slowing and slams on brakes. "I've got so much on my mind that it makes me tired just thinking about having to think about it. Of course, you don't want to know what's on my mind, you never do, so I'll just keep it to myself. You don't even ask where I got this dress that I'm wearing and I got it from Miss Ginny Sue so know that and think about it before you mention my titties about to show and think that Ginny Sue must've shown her little bit whenever she wore it."

"It's a nice dress, Cindy," Madge says. "What's on your mind?"

"Well," Cindy turns off the radio and stares at Madge all the while driving down Main Street which makes Madge nervous as a cat. "I've heard that Charles Snipes is remarrying."

"Well? You remarried," Madge says and is glad to see that they are almost at the office building.

"That's not why I'm pissed."

"Please don't use that word."

"Please don't use that word," Cindy mimics and slams on brakes right in front of the dental office, the whole car rocking back and forth. "He could've told me first. Chuckie has a right to be the first to know. Chuckie is his son, flesh and blood and sperm."

"Hush," Madge says, not about to open that car door for the world to hear what Cindy has to say.

"I could just kill Charles Snipes. Randy Skinner would never be so thoughtless. I could kill him deader than dead."

"Hmm," Madge says and gets out before she has to hear one more word. "The service station said they'd bring the car to me."

"Thank you, Cindy," Cindy says and messes with her eyelashes in front of the rearview. "Thank you for being the one daughter who can do something for me other than have her tubes woven into a miniature egg basket, thank you prodigal son's brother, thank you child of God and child of Raymond

Sinclair whose tubes are not tied and who caters to her mother's needs.''

Madge looks away from Cindy and stares at the brown nubby grass in front of the building. Things like that don't bother her so much now, her own azaleas brown and curling from lack of rain. Just curl up and die. "Thank you Cindy," she says and slams the door, that blazing sun feeling so good like it's bleaching her all over as she walks into the building where she loves that calm piped-in music and cramming cotton in people's mouths so that they can't say a word, not a solitary word.

* * *

Virginia goes to Roses and puts everything that she wants in her cart; it is a good place to go for a walk, cool, a lot to see. It has always made her feel better to do this. She has made many important decisions while walking the aisles and filling her cart with items that she has no intention of *really* buying. It was in an Atlanta Roses where she decided that she could not marry Bryan Parker before returning to that condo where they were living together and told him. It had taken hours that day, and then she abandoned the cart in the far corner of the store amidst drapes and rugs, bought a Coke and a pack of cigarettes and left. And Bryan Parker *was* a *nice* person; she could say those same words to Mark, "he was a nice person but it didn't work" except Mark doesn't *want* to know anything about Bryan Parker. He doesn't *want* to know the guilt that Virginia felt just living there while her parents and Gram and everyone else in Saxapaw thought she lived alone. Even now, it makes her shudder to think of the look that would have crossed her mother's face, Gram's face, if they had seen the unmarried Bryan Parker stretched full length on that bed in his underwear. Bryan Parker's parents didn't care; they were cosmopolitan. They owned a chain of seafood restaurants, not even calabash style, and never ate before dark even in daylight savings time. They were young and exciting and nice, but something was wrong. It was not a black/white or red/blue decision; it was lilac and lavender, pale apricot and shrimp.

"I lived with a man once," she had confessed to Mark on their third date; she had never even told Cindy that. And he just squeezed her hand while they sat in the theatre waiting for the movie to begin and told her that he was divorced. She felt a brief moment of iciness but it didn't last; he was with *her*, holding *her* hand, everyone makes mistakes. Though now she can't help but wonder *when* he would have told her, if he ever would have told her. "How long were you married?" she whispered as the lights went down, and she felt his whispered "two years" in her ear while the screen filled with a blast of color. She waited two weeks before asking "who," a month before asking "what happened," receiving only what she asked for, never being asked about when she almost got married, never feeling that she got to the root of it all. "It's all in the past," he would say. "None of it matters now. We matter. What we have is what matters." And she would repeat his words in her head, feeling closer and closer, feeling like nothing could ever come between them. So why? Why did he wait until now to fill in the blanks?

She pushes the cart faster and it soothes her; every aisle of Roses soothes her; she could be in a dimestore anywhere. She could be in Saxapaw. There is a rose-colored satiny comforter that can be reversed to deep wine, the eyelet sheet set, redwood bird feeder, twenty pounds of bird seed on sale for $2.99, buy it! Purple leotard, red stockings, a black lacy bra with cups as pointed as darts, take it. Little red plastic shoes like we're off to see the wizard, protect from athlete's foot in public showers and other fungi. Fungi and Fun Guy. "Bryan Parker's not what I'd call a real fun guy," Cindy had said. "But megabucks, and he's big and cute, can't have it all." Virginia wants it all. She wants mascara, dial a lash, very black for herself, anything but midnight blue for Cindy. Calgon take me away! Oriental Garden, Ah so, Oil of Olay for night and day, say Pond's cold cream in Japanese and don't think of anything else like your husband in bed with a long and lithe blonde who has never eaten Beef Jerky or Cheetos. Apricot scrub and cucumber gel, vinegar and water douche, make yourself a salad, make your*self* a salad. Music—Beethoven and Chaka Khan, Marvin Gaye, Tanya Tucker, Disney on Parade. Hammers and screwdrivers, heavy on the vodka. The doctor says, "Have you been drinking?" Little nails, big nails, clamp on nails and nail polish, plumbers' friend, sketch pad and Crayolas, periwinkle blue and burnt sienna, diaphragm jelly to throw people off.

"I'm just fat this way," she would say. "I have a tumor,"

and she would watch their faces turn ten shades of purple. No, no she wouldn't do that and it isn't working. Nothing is working. One day her phone is going to ring; one day her mother will call to tell her that Gram is dead and she will say, "Oh God, why wasn't I there? Why was I here? Here with a person that I don't even know?" She sees her mouth shaping the words.

"Don't you worry, Ginny Sue," Gram whispered long ago, so many times, words so constant. "I'm here with you. I'm not going to leave you here in the dark." Virginia feels her throat closing, her legs aching as she hurries as fast as she can to the back of the store, the draperies, behind the draperies. There's not enough time. She feels urgent as she makes her way back down the aisles, past a salesperson who is glaring at her because he saw what she did, the cart, the merchandise, everything abandoned. She doesn't care. She doesn't care about anything right this second except getting home. "I'm home," she will say. "I made a mistake and now I'm back."

She cranks the car and starts driving, the steering wheel so hot, air so heavy. "Mona Lisa, Mona Lisa, men have named you," Nat King Cole sings, easy listening, good for the budgies as she speeds along, hills and buildings, knowing exactly where she is every minute of the way and she can't get to where it's flat fast enough, flat and wide and hot, cornfields and speckled butterbeans. "I've always been partial to the speckled," she can hear Gram say. "Here in Saxapaw everybody likes the speckled." It seems she can't drive fast enough, the songs can't change fast enough, and she thinks "Saxapaw, Saxapaw" over and over, Gram's voice saying "Saxapaw" the word itself briefly ridding her mind of everything else, and she thinks of Gramps sitting in that side yard, his blue eyes squinting as he does his Brer Rabbit voice. He says, "Do anything, *Any*thing. Just don't throw me in that old briar patch."

* * *

Hannah spots her Aunt Lena as soon as she rounds the corner. Lena is pacing back and forth in front of the home, whirling around every now and then, and talking and laughing as if someone is right behind her. Sometimes Hannah feels like she can't take it. Sadness. There's Lena and her mama so confused and helpless; there's Esther all by herself. The whole world has got problems. There's Alzheimers and mental illness, homosexuality and divorce, you name it. It's all right there on "Phil Donahue"; for years Ginny Sue had talked about what was on "Phil Donahue," but who had time to watch?

"We are paying for you to go to college and not to watch TV," Hannah would say. Though now she sees that you can probably learn everything you might want to know about this world and things you'd just as soon not know right there on "Phil Donahue." She is trying her best to catch up on things and it isn't easy. It isn't easy to get up and face a day where she doesn't have to go down to The Busy Bee and sew all day, that nice soft humming of the machine, fabrics running under her fingers. She'd press her foot on that pedal and she'd forget all about who she was and where she was and how the years were unraveling like a hem so long she could never get it basted back. The Busy Bee was hers, all hers, twenty-five years of her life.

"Give it up," Ben had said. "Now's the time for us to go places, do things." And she had and now what they do is grow, can, and freeze vegetables and where she goes is to the rest home to get Lena and to the duplex to check on her mama. Sometimes she does Esther's grocery shopping while she does her own; it's the least she can do. Esther is somehow related, takes good care of Hannah's mama and only makes minimum wage.

Hannah held interviews for a housekeeper who could sleep in on occasion because it had gotten to where she could not keep two houses clean and run The Busy Bee all at the same time. It had gotten to where her mama couldn't even get to the bathroom by herself. How could she *not* hire Esther with her somehow related?

Lena is laughing now, her head thrown back with that hat tipped off to one side. She used to have thick auburn hair curled and fixed, perfumed, and colored bangled bracelets that she'd let Hannah wear. "I brought you this dress from New York," Lena had said and opened a box with fancy script on the top and pulled out a lacy pink dress with a wide satin sash. "One day you'll be making dresses like this."

"Hannah's not but sixteen," her mama had said. "And that dress cut to the bosom."

"It's a party dress, Emily," Lena said and fluffed the full skirt.

"There are things in life other than parties." Hannah's mama went back to her cooking while Hannah put on the dress and turned around and around on a stool in front of the mirror. Lena clapped her hands, those long glazed nails, while Roy Carter whistled from the next room. She wore it to the high school prom and danced all night with Ben Turner, his thick dark hair combed up off his forehead, his socks matching for once. It was beautiful with those parachutes hanging from that gym ceiling and the Eiffel Tower painted on a huge piece of pasteboard in one corner. Hannah had painted most of it while Madge and some other girls had put little paper flowers in vases which would go on those little café tables with checkered cloths. Madge was wearing a dress that Tessy had made, a dress that could just as easily have gone to church and Madge had fingered the lace on Hannah's skirt when they were in the bathroom, asking over and over "where did you get it?" Hannah had lied; Hannah had said that she borrowed the dress. Madge, after all, was Lena's niece, too. "But you're my favorite, Hannah," Lena has always said.

Madge probably didn't believe that the dress was borrowed; who did Hannah know to borrow it from? And years later when Madge was going through one new Chevrolet after another and ordering clothes from New York, Hannah wondered why she had lied, why she didn't say, "this is *my* dress." Hannah had twirled around and around under those parachutes with her mind spinning and her heart beating so fast with just one look from Ben Turner. "One day we'll really go to France," he had whispered. "One day I'm going to give you everything you've ever wanted."

"Hannah?" Lena leans forward and squints, her polyester pants slipping down to cover the gold slide slippers. "Is that you?"

"It's me." Hannah hugs Lena close, her spine like a little hooked railroad track. "How are you?"

"Bad," Lena says and shakes her head. "Jesus God take me I'm so bad." Lena clings to Hannah's skirt. "You've got to get me out of here. You've got to tell them I can't come back."

"We're going to go to Mama's for a little while." Hannah

pulls Lena away and leads her over to the bench. "Let me tell them that I'm taking you. Sit down and I'll be right back."

"Don't tell them," Lena whispers. "They gave me a little poison this morning."

"I'm taking Lena for a little while," Hannah tells the nurse, quickly, businesslike. That's how she's decided to handle it. That way they will feel like she's up on everything, that she's keeping a close check of the way the place is run. It looks clean here; the people seem nice enough but there is always that shade of doubt when she leaves Lena here. It's like that question Ginny Sue used to sit and think over about if there's a chair in the room is it still there when you close the door or the one Ben says about if a tree falls in the forest. Those are foolish things to think over but not this way, not "are they nice to Lena when I'm not here?" Lena says not. Lena says all kinds of things and it is hard to stop believing someone that you have believed your whole life, someone who had been places and knew things. "You couldn't have a better husband than Ben. You couldn't have finer children. Hannah, the dresses you make could sell in New York City."

The nurse follows Hannah outside, down the long hall where they are all just sitting in a room, a TV going, pipes, cigarettes, thumbs twiddling.

"You have yourself a fun time, Miss Lena," the nurse says and pats Lena's shoulder.

"Oh I will." Lena smiles and nods, her hat more cocked than it was when Hannah left her. "Isn't she a pretty girl, Hannah?"

"Yes." Hannah looks the nurse square in the eye and smiles. "And she's pretty most of all because she takes good care of you." The nurse smiles and looks away. Modesty or guilt? "We'll be back before supper," Hannah says and leads Lena to the car.

"I'm going to bathe you when we get to Mama's," Hannah says when they are on the road.

"I've had a bath. Bathe, bathe, bathe." Lena pulls off her hat and picks at the fur, rubs her palm over it. Hannah would like to perm Lena's hair; it's so thin and gray, flat from wearing that hat all the time. "You can bathe this." Lena shakes the hat and then places it back in her lap. "I do want you to wash my face, though. I don't know when it's been washed."

"Now that's the sort of thing you need to ask them to do for you," Hannah says.

"Them? Them? You think I'd let that fat twat touch my face?" Lena settles back in the seat. "I've always had perfect skin."

"I thought you liked her."

"I hate 'em all," she sighs, her mouth puffing each word. "I wish to God I was dead."

"We're going to have a fun day," Hannah says as cheerfully as she can manage. "We'll ride around later on."

"Ride. I've ridden around my whole life. Roy said, 'let's ride.' Ride asshole. I'm sick of riding."

"Now, don't talk that way," Hannah says, realizing that she sounds just like her mother, years and years of looking at Lena and saying, 'don't talk that way.' Now Mama laughs when Lena talks that way. Now, to see the people that come and go off the "Phil Donahue Show," talking ugly these days is nothing compared to what they're all doing behind closed doors. Sex changes and two women wanting a baby to bring into this world of plane crashes and rape and child abuse and people dragging one another through the mud to get some money when they weren't married to begin with but living and sleeping with one another like they were. It makes Hannah glad that she is where she is and that her children are grown and married. She wishes people wouldn't talk about Rock Hudson so much. She had seen *Pillow Talk* so many times, always thinking how wonderful it would be to be Doris Day and get to kiss him. She had even told Ben that. They told of people in the movies that they thought were beautiful or handsome but they didn't tell of people in real life. "William Holden is a good-looking man," she'd say, and Ben would say, "My favorites are Susan Hayward and Maureen O'Hara, like the redheads. I like Rita Hayworth, too."

Rita and Rock and Donna Reed and the way William Holden died all make her so sad. All of that makes her glad to be where she is and that's unusual because Hannah has always felt a little out of beat. When Madge and everybody else was staying home and tending to their babies, she was working. Work all day and come home and work all night.

"You could quit if you wanted to," Ben would say but she knew better. She could have quit, yes, but then maybe she couldn't have had a washer and dryer when she was going through stack after stack of diapers, or new cheerful-looking furniture instead of that old heavy dark stuff like her mama and Lena had, and there was college to think of, two children who needed everything from braces to the full scout outfits and shoes that if they weren't too small come September had to be replaced with what everybody else at the schoolhouse was wearing.

"I don't know how you do it," Madge would say, her freezer full of meat that she'd fix up into something like you'd see on the front of a book. "It's all I can do to get everything around this house done in a day's time."

"TV dinners," Hannah would tell her and laugh. She'd have to laugh so she wouldn't bite her tongue in two thinking of how she could whirl through Madge's house in a couple of hours and have it all done.

"Raymond says he has to have a meal," Madge would say and shake her head back and forth like preparing a meal was like jumping the Grand Canyon.

"Why aren't you working?" Lena asks, mumbling, her eyes closed.

"I retired, you know that," Hannah says and Lena sits up straight and opens her eyes. "I sold the shop six months ago."

"Ginny Sue bought it I guess." Lena pulls the hat back on her head. "I knew that."

"No, Ginny Sue did not. Ginny Sue is a school teacher and not a seamstress."

"I know you hate her for that."

"Now why would I hate her for that?" Hannah raises her voice. "I'm proud of Ginny Sue."

"And I'm proud of Ginny Sue," Lena says. "She can sew up a storm can't she?"

"She can do a straight stitch and that's it."

"Well, I'm glad," Lena says and Hannah feels the impatience coming. Talking to a brick wall; sometimes she feels like her words aren't worth the air that she gives to anybody.

"And what do *you* do?" people ask nowadays. For the first time in her entire life Hannah can say, "I'm a housewife," and now that's no good.

"I learn something new every day," Madge says over and over. "I never knew so much went into a root canal."

"I watch the 'Phil Donahue Show.' "

"I used to watch 'As The World Turns,' " Madge said. "Way back, you know before I went over to Tech and decided I'd try my hand at doing something." *Doing something!* For years all Hannah has done is *do something* and people felt sorry for her and now finally she is sitting at home and finding out how the other half has lived her whole life only to be told about how they are doing something. She has always been out of step, and by the time it all whirls back around to where it's the thing to be a housewife, she'll either be dead or in a home.

"Where are we?" Lena asks.

"We're right here in town, going to Mama's."

"Whose car is this?"

"It's my car. It's the same car I've driven for five years."

"A Chevrolet," Lena says and Hannah nods, "Yes, a Chevrolet." Hannah turns on the radio to the station Ginny Sue had recommended to her. She hadn't even known what to listen to because all she had at The Busy Bee was an AM and all it picked up was country which she liked fine, still does.

"Roy always said Chevrolets were cheap cars and that Raymond Sinclair or St. Peter couldn't talk him into buying one," Lena says and scratches her hat. "Where are we?"

"In the car."

"Now, don't act like I'm crazy like Messy Pearson. In a car and where's the car?"

"Aunt Tessy was not crazy," Hannah says, "and we're in Saxapaw." She turns down her mama's street. It's a pretty street and thank God her mama is off Carver Street. Her mama's old house was about the last residence left in that part of town; when her mama moved, they tore the house away piece by piece and built a Piggly Wiggly.

"Messy was crazy and she was filthy," Lena says. "I wonder if Madge knows what a filthy mama she had."

"I want you to stop talking about Aunt Tessy, okay?" Hannah parks and waits for Lena to nod, her mouth primping like a punished child.

Felicia Morton is out mowing her half of the duplex yard wearing near about nothing. It's probably too dry to be mowing, but Hannah is not going to offer advice to a grown woman; she wishes Felicia would just mow on over on her mama's side while she's out there. Felicia is about forty-five or so and has never married. People say it's because she favors women. When Hannah owned her shop, she was forever overhearing stories about people in town which she'd just as soon not have heard. That kind of gossip is like inviting yourself to sit down in somebody's bedroom and watch. Felicia has a good job at Southern National Loans and it's nobody's business why she never married.

"Felicia is like that," Madge had said. "About women."

"I don't want to hear it," Hannah said. "She's good to Mama."

"Her *friend* is a nurse," Cindy said. "I work at the Medical Clinic and so I know."

"I don't want to hear Felicia discussed," Hannah's mama said. "She's good as gold and if she's *that way*, she can't help it. Jesus knows she can't."

"Hi there!" Felicia says now and cuts off the mower.

Hannah waves and opens her door. "Don't let her touch me *there*," Lena whispers. "I mean it, so help me God, I'll have a stroke." Hannah just shakes her head and goes to open Lena's door.

"Hot as blazes isn't it?" Felicia calls and Hannah nods, Lena whispering "she's *that* way" in Hannah's ear the whole time. "I'll mow your mama's half if that's okay with you."

"It would be a blessing," Hannah says. "I hate for you to, though."

"Won't take but a jiffy." Felicia brushes the sweat from her forehead, her short frosted hair standing in a cowlick. "Your mama is such a dear."

"Um hmm," Lena breaths into Hannah's neck. "I told you."

"I've been waiting till after it rained," Felicia says. "But I don't think it's coming."

"Well, you'll have to let me know what we can do for you some time," Hannah says.

"God, now you've done it," Lena says when Felicia has gone back to the mower. "She'll be wanting me."

The sound of the mower fills the yard and it is peaceful to Hannah, a gigantic sewing machine is what it sounds like, bolt after bolt of cloth tumbling to the floor. She could sew up the world, drapes and party dresses and it doesn't bother her if all that is true about Felicia. Phil Donahue would defend Felicia in a flash and so would she. She'd stand right up whether Phil was on an old show in Chicago or in New York and she'd take that microphone and she'd say, "what Felicia does behind closed doors is all right by me. Felicia is a human being and she has human feelings and blood and bone," and people would applaud and they'd close the show playing the song "Behind Closed Doors" all because of what she had said and way back here in Saxapaw everyone would be watching the show. Ben would say, "I never knew your mama was so smart. I mean I've always known she had it in her but I guess I never stopped to think about how smart she really is." And Ginny Sue and Mark and Robert and his wife, Susie, would all nod and say how proud they were. Lena and her mama would say, "Look at Hannah on TV all dressed up like she's going to a party way up there in Chicago." Cindy would say, "Taking up for that kind. I'm so embarrassed," and that would be good for Cindy; she should be embarrassed for all her marrying and divorcing. Madge would say, "I don't know how Hannah found the time to get up there in Chicago"; and Madge would be all tired-looking like she had swum some channel instead of changing the channel on that black and white set of hers. Madge mentions her TV every chance she gets as if watching that tiny set can make up for all those Chevrolets and dishwashers she's had all these years.

"This ain't Emily's house," Lena says and stands there at the door, huffing and puffing from the short walk.

"Sure it is," Hannah says and opens the door. "Yoohoo!" she yells and pulls Lena inside where it is eighty-odd degrees. Her mama won't use the air-conditioning. "I'm going to turn on the air and then I'm going to put you in a nice hot bubble bath, Lena."

"Shit," Lena says. "You can try."

"Well, I thought you'd never ever come," Hannah's mama says and Esther comes out of the kitchen carrying an old dishrag.

"She couldn't wait for company," Esther says. "And since you're here I'm going to run home and see if my trash has been collected."

"You look bad, Lena," Emily says and puts a little snuff in her mouth. "Have you been sick?"

"Poisoned," Lena says. "That nigger that stole Roy's car pulled some gum all chewed up out of his mouth and he said to me, he said, 'here, chew on this gum' and I said, 'I don't chew after nobody not white or nigger' and he said, 'chew it or I'll kill you you beautiful bitch, you.' ''

"Well, I wouldn't have done as he said," Hannah's mama says and shakes her head. "You were taught better as a child, taught to say 'colored,' too."

"He would have killed me dead. He had already snuffed Roy."

"Ain't they a pair?" Esther laughs and shakes her head.

"They don't know what they're saying," Hannah says but she knows Esther doesn't know what she's saying either.

"You go on, Esther, and do what you need to do while I'm here." Hannah goes in the bathroom and starts running the water. She'd like to get in that tub herself, lather her legs, shave and lotion. "Okay Lena, come on in here."

"I shouldn't have chewed that gum," Lena says, her teeth gritted, the vein in her forehead buckling.

"Well I told you not to chew it," Hannah's mama calls out, her voice like a breathless whisper compared to Lena. "But you have never listened to anything. Your whole life you have not listened."

"Give me that goddamn washrag." Lena snatches the cloth from Hannah's hand. "I can wash myself."

"Fine," Hannah says and helps Lena into the tub, that sagging old body like a pillow without enough stuffing. "All I want to do is help you and you talk to me like a dog, so ugly." Hannah sits on the commode and watches Lena sling that cloth up and over those old vein-marked breasts. "If it upsets you so to see me and for me to help you get a bath, well, I don't have to do it."

"I don't know what I'd do without you," Lena says and starts to cry. "I'd die if you didn't get me."

"I'd die, too, Hannah," her mama calls out, that voice drowned out by the mower right near the bathroom window. Patience. Patience is a virtue. They don't know what they're saying; they don't know how useless they make her feel sometimes. She gets the Comet out from under the lavatory and starts cleaning.

"I chewed it, though, Hannah, I did. I said, 'um boy, this is some good gum' I said, 'I believe it used to be a stick of Juicy Fruit before you was so kind as to give it to me and so kind to buy this car that I can't drive 'cause they took my license and that Roy can't drive since he's dead and all' and I said, 'people probably call you nigger and I'm sorry for you that they don't have better sense. Some people just don't know to say niggra or colored.' "

"Or *black*," Hannah says the same way that Ginny Sue had corrected her a few years ago.

"I said, 'you and your blacks ride in style now and I like this Juicy Fruit so much that I think I'll chew it tomorrow and right on till I die because I saw that little bit of something you stuck to this gum before you got me to chew it. I saw it but I can't blame you after what you've told me of Jesus telling you to poison me and put me out of my misery the way Roy did that cat that I loved so way back.' "

Hannah laughs now, tears coming to her eyes while she scrubs that toilet clean as a whistle. "I sing because I'm happy, I sing because I'm free," she sings loud, putting on a voice that quivers on the high notes while Lena sits with bubbles all over her and stares. "His eye is on the sparrow and I know he's watching me."

"Yes he is," Lena nods, laughs and leans back in the tub, her knees spread apart.

"Mama, what are you doing in there so quiet?" Hannah calls.

"Swinging on the front porch," her mama says. "I'm cooking some butterbeans."

"Won't that be good?" Lena asks and stretches her arms up and over her head like she's posing for a centerfold.

"It sure will," Hannah says and flushes the toilet.

* * *

It is hot and even pressing the pedal makes Virginia tired. She slows down as she crosses the Saxapaw River. Usually there are old men fishing from the bridge, cane poles and beer cans, but not today. She has never seen the river so low, the huge gnarled roots of the river trees exposed as they cling to the banks. There is a man halfway out where her parents had said that she and Robert were never to go, and the water is only up to his hips. Everything is drying up; the radio says no rain in sight for a week, says to conserve water.

She passes the Hardee's at the edge of town where she once threw a bracelet that Bryan Parker had given her. It had seemed that by getting rid of every reminder, she could rid her mind of the near mistake, rid her mind of the expression on Bryan Parker's face when he left her at the bus station. He carried no blame, an innocent bystander. She never passes the Hardee's that she doesn't remember all of that, remember that sliver of silver on the ground near the drive-through, the thought that one of those young boys, with his brown cap and pointed stick, found the bracelet and slipped it on the wrist of some young girl who stared at it lovingly as Virginia had once done, words like "eternal" and "always" slipping from adolescent lips with no thoughts that it all might end, that so quickly it can end. It makes her feel sick to think about it now, heavy and sick when the radio says that it's a hundred degrees.

"Now what is your married name?" people ask when she's at home. Nobody cares; nobody remembers. They just call her Ginny Sue Turner who "thank God, no matter who she's married to is finally going to start having some babies. We feared that she couldn't, feared that she was gonna dry up before she did like her Great Aunt Lena Pearson Carter, must have got her man to wear boxers instead of briefs, works every time." Virginia had heard that little tip for years, though no one had ever been able to explain it to her. Easy access? Anatomical freedom?

"Charles has always worn boxers," Cindy said, ten weeks married and six months pregnant. "He went right from Buster Browns into boxers and I'm telling you it was like one of those fertilizer spikes that you can stick into your potted plants, thousands of fertile little things making their way to the root. I was helpless I tell you; this baby had took root before I could even get myself back in the front seat of the car. Charles and I were both virgins." Cindy's face was so serious that Virginia didn't even laugh at the "virgin" part. "You better watch out Ginny Sue," Cindy said. "I'd give anything right now to be skinny and wearing hotpants, hanging out at the Texaco station in Clemmonsville drinking beer."

Virginia pulls into her parents' driveway and everything is just the same, always the same, the cool thick ferns hanging on the small front porch, that worn vinyl cover on the glider, the windows sparkling clean both inside and out. It is cool inside, neat and orderly, as she makes her way down the carpet runner in the hall where there are pictures of her and

Robert at every stage of their lives, except now. There is no big fat picture of Virginia. Her most recent is from the wedding, Mark holding the car door while she gets in, waving as if she will never return. She stares at the picture, the suitcase in Mark's hand, and realizes that she has brought absolutely nothing with her, not even a toothbrush.

Now she has the impulse to move, to get out and walk, get some exercise, some air. She'll walk to the duplex, certain that if her mother is not there right now that she soon will be.

"I'm home," she yells into the living room where her father is sunburned and dozing on the couch. "I'm going to Gram's," she adds but he only mumbles and turns. The TV is on, tuned to MTV which her mother says he has watched faithfully since they got cable. The Stray Cats are singing "She's Sexy & Seventeen" and this girl is running around in her bra and underwear. It makes Virginia feel like she's missed out on something; it makes her feel old.

The smell of the hot pavement reaches her and again she feels that odd sense of detachment like her arms and legs all operate separately. *Ginny Sue is pregnant. Virginia Suzanne is with child.* She wishes Gram still lived in the old house, the high ceilings and window fans, the bedroom on the back corner overlooking the garden and side yard. Her grandfather built that house in 1917. It was way out of the city limits then, but closer than the farm where her grandmother grew up and he picked her up in his buggy, rode toward town and when he got to the clearing he stopped, took her hand and said, "That's ours, Emily. It might not look like much but it's ours." Virginia knows that story by heart, every twist and sigh of Gram's voice, "and he proposed right there in the buggy and we went and sat down right in the middle of where our house was gonna be, and then we took sticks and drew just what we wanted there in the dirt."

"We're going to be renting for quite a few years," Mark had told Virginia as she stood in that rented kitchen and surveyed the peeling plaster, all of the boxes that she had to unpack.

She has only gone three blocks and already the sweat has gathered in her thick hair; she wishes she had a rubber band and could yank it into a high ponytail like she used to wear when she played in all of the vacant lots that are now crammed with new houses. She doesn't know who lives in any of them. There is a woman in the front yard of the Peterson's old house fixing a sprinkler while two little girls stand off to the side in their bathing suits. "Hot isn't it?" the woman calls and she nods, loosens the strings on her tennis shoes. Virginia doesn't tell the woman what they said on the radio, doesn't tell her that she is draining the Saxapaw River. The sprinkler begins to twirl and the two girls run close, their faces and outstretched arms catching the spray.

"Don't touch the sprinkler," the woman calls across the yard while one of the girls squats over it. "Did you hear me, young lady?" The girl makes a face at her friend and promptly obeys. "Don't make me have to tell you again."

Don't make me have to tell you again. Virginia has heard it a thousand times. "You let Robert stay out past eleven when he was my age," she had said all through high school. "It's a little different," her mother always replied. "Robert is a *boy*."

A son is a son until he takes a wife, but a daughter is a daughter all of her life. That's what her mother says; that's what Gram says. "I cannot tell Susie how she's ironing Robert's shirts all wrong, the way the collar stands up," her mama says. "Robert is my son but he's a grown man and I can't go telling his wife how to iron." Then there is a pause, a deep breath like a big secret is about to be revealed. "But you are my daughter and I can tell you that a little spray starch is all it takes. A little spray starch will go a long way." Virginia just listens, nods and listens; she takes shirts from the dryer when they're still warm, puts them on a hanger, buttons a couple of buttons.

Virginia should have driven. Her feet feel so heavy, lead, concrete; watching the sprinkler makes her dizzy. One more block. One more block to the duplex.

"Hey Ginny Sue!" She hears the familiar scream, the horn toot, and sees Cindy's car all at the same time. Cindy gets out of the car with the engine still running and props her elbows on the hood. "Look at you now, grown a foot since last week. Like the dress?" She steps around in front of the hood and poses, her hands on her hips, eyes squinted against the sun, five or more chains dangling down the neck of that sundress that Virginia will never squeeze her body into again. "You got no business walking the streets. Hop in." Cindy

gets back in the car and Virginia sinks into the passenger seat,
the air-conditioning vent turned on her. "Ginny Sue how I
saved her from a life of walking the streets." Cindy grinds
out the cigarette that she had left in the ashtray. "You don't
look so good, Ginny Sue. Where you going, the Old Folks
Home?"

"Yes," Virginia nods, leans her head back into the seat,
that vinyl so cool against her back and neck. "Where are you
going?"

"Over to Del Taco for a little lunch for me and Constance
Ann." Cindy turns the radio down a little. "We just got that
new Del Taco and me and Constance Ann are hooked on
nachos."

"Hmmm," Virginia says, the thought of a nacho making
her sick, the thought of anything in her mouth or on her
stomach.

"You are about the biggest knocked-up girl I've ever seen,"
Cindy says and stops in front of the duplex, the sun so hot
on that treeless lawn, yellow brick, storm door. It looks like
it should be an office of some kind. "I can't wait to tell you
about this man I'm dating; he went to Saudi Arabia once and
can shag like hell. If I'd known you were coming to town, I
would have pulled a sick."

"I hadn't planned to come but I ran out of things to do,"
Virginia says, still studying that duplex, Felicia stretched out
in a lawn chair on her half of the yard.

"God, I wish I'd run out of things to do for once." Cindy
picks at her eyelashes in the rearview mirror. "Are you going
to spend the night?"

"I don't know," Virginia says, wondering now what she
is going to do. It doesn't seem as important as getting indoors
where it's cool.

"Spend the night," Cindy says. "I've got plans but I could
see you first thing in the morning while Chuckie's still at
Mama's. I'll tell you all about my date at Ramada Inn that
I've got tonight. . . . " Cindy's voice trails off in a lingering
question as if hearing about her date will make a difference
in the decision. Virginia is thinking now of all of her things
left behind in that house. She did not even make the bed or
wash the dishes from last night. It's not like her to leave an
unmade bed; if you sleep in an unmade bed, it feels like
you've been sick all day. She wants to tell Cindy the real

reason she's here, but she feels short of breath, has to keep swallowing. Cindy doesn't notice.

"I would call in sick but Constance Ann would have a fit if I didn't bring the nachos. I've got so much to tell you. Mama is so on my nerves and Chuckie is a pain in the rectum." Virginia forces a laugh, her hand on the door handle. Cindy's whole vocabulary has changed since she got her job at the medical center, rectum instead of asshole, breasts instead of titties; it's been a positive change.

"I'll talk to you before I leave," Virginia says, lifts her hand to Felicia, who is sitting up, her hand shielding the sun while she looks at them parked there.

"All right," Cindy says and starts singing "We've a Story To Tell To The Nation," which is a song they had to memorize for Girl's Auxiliary. Virginia hated GA's; she dropped out before she even got to be a maiden, just like she dropped out of Brownies before ever being a Girl Scout. Cindy was a Girl Scout, she said because everybody else was one. Cindy got to be a queen in GA's. "It isn't because of the religion," she had told Virginia. "I did it so I could get me a long white dress."

"Have fun," Virginia says and opens the door, the heat hitting her full force. "Thanks for the ride."

"Sure thing," Cindy says. "I'll tell you all about tonight. Well, maybe not ALL of it, not in your condition." Cindy laughs and pulls away from the curb, her arm waving out the window until she rounds the corner.

"Well, aren't you something?" Felicia asks. "You look real good Ginny Sue."

"Thank you." Virginia smiles and waves, though she feels so funny, like the heat has fallen and settled in a cloud around her, a beeping, flashing cloud. "I've got to get where it's cool," she says and Felicia nods and lies back in her chair. Felicia probably wanted to chat, but she can't help that. "I think she's lonely," her mother has said. Her mother is always thinking of how somebody else is feeling. Well, Virginia can't help it; she can't think about Felicia or Cindy's date or anything except getting cool. She turns the knob but it's locked.

"Your mama ran to the grocery," Felicia says. "I told her I'd keep an eye on things."

"Gram?" Virginia knocks on the door and then goes to a window where the drapes are parted and she can see Gram slowly rolling her chair to the door. "It's me, Gram. It's Ginny Sue." She hears her fumbling with the knob and finally the door cracks open.

"Don't tell Hannah I moved," Gram says, her hair so white against that pink fluffy robe. It is not much cooler in the house than it is outside. Virginia closes the door and pushes Gram back into the small living room where Lena is sitting flipping through a magazine, the hood of the old-style hair dryer covering her face. "Lena's been screaming to get that dryer turned off but Hannah said we were not to move."

Virginia goes and lifts the dryer cap and Lena looks up, her eyes so dull against that red face, the hot pink clamp-on curlers.

"Thank God," Lena says. "I thought you'd left me to smother."

"That's Ginny Sue, now," Gram says and rolls herself over beside Lena's chair. She reaches up and feels the curlers on Lena's head. "She's not done. She could take the pneumonia in this weather."

"Weather?" Lena asks. "It's hot as hell. It's a oven."

"Is it, Ginny Sue?" Gram asks and she nods.

"The sign at school says it is June," Lena says and puts her hat on top of her curlers. "It says the weather is hot. Now don't I know it? Step outside and find out, yeah boy, all you got to do is step outside."

"I think she can sit without the dryer," Virginia says and walks toward the bathroom, a short dark hall.

"You've gained some weight, Ginny Sue," Lena says. "I need to use the bathroom, too."

"You are not to leave your chair," Gram says.

The bathroom is cool, that air-conditioning vent blowing onto the white tile floor. Virginia feels sick, dizzy; if she can just get her face against the cool floor, curl up on that cool floor. She feels so strange all over, rolls on her back and tries to lift her legs the way Gram used to tell her to do for cramps.

"That's not real ladylike looking." Gram is in the doorway, leaning forward in her wheelchair. "Lena says she needs to tee tee. Should I let her?"

"Let me go first," Virginia says. "I'm not feeling good, Gram, so let me go first."

"I'll close the door." Gram reaches for the knob.

"No, no, leave it open." Virginia reaches up and holds

onto the counter and pulls herself in a squatted position. "Stay there, Gram," she says, her face so cool and clammy when she puts her head between her knees.

"Lena says she's about to pop." Gram's voice gets loud on "pop" and Virginia opens her eyes, tries to focus before standing.

"Oh God," she whispers. "I'm bleeding." She sits back and stares at Gram. "Gram, I'm bleeding."

"All women bleed, Ginny Sue," Gram says. "Hannah should have told you that before this happened."

"I can't wait." Lena shuffles into the hallway and stops right behind the wheelchair. "You've got to let me in."

"Will you hold your horses," Gram says. "Ginny Sue has got the curse."

"Hush now," Lena laughs, her legs crossed in those baggy polyester pants. "I hadn't thought of that in years."

"Get somebody," Virginia says and lies back on the floor, her cheek turned against the cool tile. "Please Gram, just get somebody."

"It's not the kind of thing to discuss," Gram says.

"I am gonna wet my britches." Lena pushes past the wheelchair and steps over Virginia, fumbles with the zipper on her pants.

"I'm bleeding." Virginia looks up and Lena is leaning forward, gripping the commode bars, staring down at her with those blank olive eyes, yellow flecks like a cat.

"Best get used to it," Lena says. "Can you turn on that spigot 'cause I can't seem to go."

"Didn't you hear me?" Virginia screams and Gram turns her head away, lifts her chin. "Why are you this way?" Virginia is crying now, turning her head from side to side, the steady trickling of urine while Lena wraps the toilet paper around and around her hand. She hears Gram's wheelchair as she backs out of the hall into the other room.

"Have you ever worn Charlie cologne?" Lena asks but Virginia concentrates on the sounds of Gram; she hears the phone receiver lifted, the slow methodical dialing.

"It ain't Chanel but I like it," Lena says, her hand bound in toilet paper, those gold slide slippers right beside Virginia's face.

"Felicia?" Gram says. "This is Miss Emily Roberts. I'm very well, thank you. Yes, I was so surprised that she came to visit. No, no, I didn't know how hot it was until they told me.''

"Gram, please."

"Felicia, this isn't a pleasure call. No, now you might not be able to help out with this because we need to borrow a Kotex. I know what people say about you and so I don't know that you've ever used a Kotex. Ginny Sue has got the curse and she won't get off of the bathroom floor and Lena got out of her chair to tee tee when Hannah told her not to." There is a pause and then the receiver clicks back on the hook. Felicia is in the bathroom before Gram can roll back in.

"What happened to privacy?" Lena asks, wipes and flushes. Felicia bends and lifts Virginia to her feet.

"I got you now," Felicia says, her arms smelling like bananas and coconuts. "I'm afraid I'm getting sunning oil all over your dress."

"I don't care," Virginia mumbles, staring at her feet as they squeeze past the wheelchair, into the bedroom, all daylight blocked by those heavy yellowed window shades. She gets on the feather bed, stretches her legs, and Felicia's cool hand rubs her forehead.

"I'll call somebody," Felicia says. "Do you know of a doctor you want?" Virginia hears her words like a whisper against the rustling of paper, a little prayer book by Gram's bed, fluttering with the air from the vent, her whole body cool now, shaking, and she is being tucked in, a blanket tossed and folded all around her with only the dull ticking of Gram's huge mahogany clock; a sharp pain in her side dulls, and pillows are under her feet, her legs numb and lifeless.

"I got a nurse friend. Says she'll be right over."

"I'm sorry for what Gram said to you," Virginia says without looking at Felicia. "You know, about the Kotex."

"Oh now." Felicia laughs and lifts Virginia's feet for one more pillow. "She didn't mean a thing by it. She just doesn't understand."

I don't understand, either, Virginia wants to confess. Please forgive me, Felicia but I don't really understand, but the words won't come and instead she focuses on a whirring sound, something outside, far away, a whirring sound. "Hold tight now, Ginny Sue," Gram says. "Don't let go of it." They are in the garden and she is staring at the frayed straw belt that holds Gram's brown plaid dress in place, the pockets of that dress filled with radishes and spring onions. "Are you ready?" Gram asks and when she nods, Gram places the twine in her palm, closes her fingers around it and steps back. "Hold tight, Ginny Sue," she says and that june bug whirrs and whirrs as she turns slowly, clutching the string, that shiny blue-black body humming and flying, whirring around and around while Gram bends and works her way down a row of beans.

PART III

Madge plays Las Vegas solitaire, which is something Raymond taught her way back when he was still Raymond. She pays fifty-two dollars for the deck, then gets five dollars for every card up on the board; she keeps up with all of her scores in a little book that she keeps with the cards. Madge has been in Las Vegas for years and intends to keep playing until she can pay her dues. All she wants is to break even and right now, she owes $44,725. In December of 1976 she was up by $550, and she should have quit while she was ahead.

"Is that all you ever do?" Cindy comes in and slams the front door after Chuckie slouches in. His face is starting to get bad and it makes Madge hurt so for him. "It depresses me the way that is all you do."

"I enjoy it, okay?" Madge goes over and hugs Chuckie who slumps his shoulders and twists away from her. God, she misses the way that he used to come straight to her and cling to her dental suits like he loved her to death. "I'm so glad you're going to spend the night, Honey."

"Can I plug your phone in the other room?" he asks, those long legs so bony and awkward-looking under those bright-colored britches that have a little surfboard on the tag.

"Yes, but you can't stay on all night," Madge says and turns to Cindy who is posed in front of the mirror over the mantel, her chest thrown out like the Himalayas. "Ginny Sue got so sick they had to call a doctor. She fainted and her legs have begun to swell like balloons. That's what Hannah said. I haven't been over to Emily's to see her." Madge goes back to her card game while Chuckie carries that phone upstairs to Cindy's old room and closes the door. "I told Hannah I couldn't get by tonight because I was keeping Chuckie but that maybe you could stop by long enough for Hannah to run by Hardee's and pick up some burgers for Ben's dinner."

"Now you know I have plans!" Cindy flops down on the sofa and puts her feet on it even though Madge has asked her not to a hundred times. "You volunteer my services all the time."

"It would take all of five minutes," Madge says and Cindy hates that tone in her voice, that pitiful, sighing, might as well bury my bones voice. It's a goddamned wonder that her daddy wasn't half-crazy after years of solitaire and that drab face of hers.

"Why can't Ben get burgers himself? He can drive," Cindy says. "Aunt Hannah does all but pee for that man. Daddy would have gotten in that Chevrolet and gone for himself. You don't know how lucky you were."

"There's nothing wrong with Hannah giving him some attention. He is her husband." Madge just lost $37,000 and she adds it to her debt.

"Well, you had a husband and I don't recall that he got any attention."

"And you've had two."

"Turn it around," Cindy says, gets up and paces over to the mantel where she touches that picture of Raymond when he was Lion of the Year. Madge would like to burn that picture, and when she's alone she turns it face down so that he can't see what she's doing. "What's Ginny Sue's problem anyway? I saw her earlier and she's huge; she's just pregnant."

"The doctor said toxemia."

"Oh, toxemia," Cindy says, still staring hard into that picture, probably angling the glass so she can see her own face. "All that means is she gets to lay around flat on her back for awhile and have somebody wait on her. I should have toxemia."

"It can be serious," Madge says. "Hannah said she'd never seen anybody so sick. Ben had to come and carry Ginny Sue to the commode that's how sick she's been."

"Well, I hope he didn't strain himself," she says. "People, civilians, get so upset over medical matters and it's because they don't know any better. Ignorance is why doctors can charge an arm and a leg for services rendered."

"You are not a doctor," Madge says and lays out what she's hoping will be a winning board. She sure could use it.

"But I might as well be." Cindy stands there with her purse over her arm and her car keys in her hand. "I'll go by there. I'll go because Ginny Sue will need me to set her straight on toxemia before she has to go back in for therapy. I'll do it but Hannah better go to Hardees and get back fast. If I'm late getting to the Ramada Inn I will never forgive you."

"Thank you, Cindy," Madge says and finally turns up an ace. "I'll take good care of Chuckie while you're out on the town."

"Chuckie will be just fine if you leave him alone." Cindy opens the front door after stopping by Madge's candy dish and filling that suitcase purse of hers full of peppermints. "He says that's what he can't stand about coming over here, the way that you cling so to him and watch everything he does."

"That is not . . ." Cindy slams the door before her mama can launch into something else. If she is late to Ramada, she will never forgive any of them.

When Cindy gets to the duplex, Lena is out pacing up and down the sidewalk, that thin hair of hers looking far worse than the hat she's holding and wringing in her hands. "It's about time!" Lena yells when Cindy comes up the walk. "We have been waiting for hours and I've got to get home. I've got to get to Hardee's and get Roy's dinner."

"Roy is in a box and in a hole," she snaps and turns when Hannah comes out the front door. "Hey Aunt Hannah. I'm sorry Ginny Sue has had such a spell of toxemia."

"Well, thanks for helping out," Hannah says and takes hold of Lena's arm. "I hate to call on Felicia again and I don't want to leave Ginny and Mama all by themselves."

"I know what you mean," Cindy says and stares up at the telephone pole there on the corner. Looking Hannah in the eye sometimes is like having to look at God; it's like that woman can see to your bone. "I don't mind a bit. Mama was fussing and saying how she knew it would be a hassle for me since I've got a date meeting me at the Ramada Inn at 6:30 sharp, but I said, no, no man is more important than my cousin Ginny Sue and her bout with toxemia, poisons there in her blood, fever, vomiting, diarrhea, legs swollen like she might have elephantiasis.''

"I'll be back well before 6:30,'' Hannah says before Cindy even gets to speak of the fear of eclampsia. "I'm just going to take Lena home and pick Ben up a burger.''

"You are so good to him, Aunt Hannah,'' she says.

"I was good to Roy, too.'' Lena shakes her finger at Cindy and then looks at Hannah. "She told me that Roy is in a box and in the ground.''

"Lena,'' Cindy says, feeling Hannah's stare the whole time. "I told you that he is deceased.''

"Diseased,'' Lena puffs. "I'll tell who's diseased.'' Hannah pulls that old bag along and Cindy doesn't even wait for them to pull away before she goes into that duplex to find Ginny Sue perched on that daybed like the Queen of Sheba with pillows underneath her feet, sleeping away and Emily over there with snuff dust all over the front of her gown. Emily is just staring at the news on the TV without one sound coming from it.

"Don't you wake Ginny Sue,'' Emily says in a harsh whisper. That woman could scare the devil with those sharp uppity looks of hers. Cindy tips over and lifts those blankets around Ginny Sue's feet just so she can see how big her legs really look.

"Umm,'' Ginny Sue grunts, that head going from side to side.

"I'll not tell you again!'' Emily says. "Sit down and try to be quiet.''

"I don't have to,'' Cindy says and shakes Ginny Sue's shoulder. "Hey girl,'' she whispers when Ginny Sue's eyes squint open. "Hear you been regurgitating to beat the band.''

"Please,'' Ginny Sue says, and widens her eyes, blinks a few times. She doesn't have on any makeup, not a trace. Cindy has tried to tell her, tried to tell her that getting furniture down to bare wood, painting up pictures and learning how to make food like people might eat in India is not how you can keep a man, but to look sexy at all times of the day and night is how. She read in a book once, "If you've got butter in the fridge he won't look for margarine on the street,'' and she herself knows that it works. That's why Charles Snipes has never gotten over her.

Ginny Sue better wise up. Cindy read that in a book of her mama's, so as she figured, most of the book was horseshit; it was kind of Christian-related, kind of like the woman who is close to God behind the man, but it did have a few good tips in it like that butter thing and like how you might get him to do it under the dining room table or dress up in boots and Saran Wrap.

"You want me to put some makeup on you?" Cindy asks and Ginny Sue just rolls her eyes back.

"I told her not to wake you," Emily says.

"It's okay." Ginny Sue sits up a little and pulls on the strap of that yellow sack that she has worn just about since the day of conception.

"Well, then I'll just turn up the TV a little." Emily aims her remote and the sound goes real loud, so loud Cindy has to close her eyes, then down, up and down, up and down, until that crazy old woman gets it right. "I can't bear to hear that racket on the front porch, those banjos, I'll not have it."

"There is not a front porch." Cindy says. "There are not any banjos." Deception and hallucination, both common to Alzheimer's disease.

"Don't," Ginny Sue presses Cindy's arm and shakes her head like Cindy might be the baby she hasn't had. That child is going to be nervous as a cat by the time it gets in this world, if it does. Things can happen right there during birth, freak knottings of the umbilical or such but Cindy is not about to tell Ginny Sue of the trauma she might have to face. "It's okay, Gram," Ginny Sue says and turns her head so that she can smile at Emily. "They'll go on home soon."

"I hope so," Emily says. "It's hard for me to bear."

"It's all hard for me to bear." Cindy laughs and looks at Ginny Sue so she won't have to see Emily with her chin thrust out and those sharp beady eyes. "Honey, I'm going to Ramada Inn and have a high old time. Randy Skinner is like the man I have searched for and as we know, have yet to find. He's big, tall and built, and he doesn't look like what you think of when you hear 'pharmaceutical sales.' Uh uh. Oh no, he's got a decent job being a pharmaceutical salesman but he looks more like one who would sell real drugs you know? He's got a beard, not long, but a beard and hair that bushes around his head like he just rolled from the sack, big brown eyes." Cindy looks back down at Ginny Sue whose eyes are closed again. You'd think she'd be interested, since Cindy has, after all, always been there to give her support when she needed it. "Ginny Sue?"

"Hmm?"

"Will you leave her alone?" Emily aims the remote and turns the TV off now that the weather report is over. God, that's all that woman does, dip snuff and watch the weather. "You could drive a sane person to do himself in."

"Don't you talk about my daddy!"

"Daddy, foot," Emily says and cleans down in her gum with a Kleenex. "Who said 'Daddy' anything. You pick on Ginny Sue like she's a chicken with a sore."

"That is not true."

"Ginny Sue has already bled today." She clicks the TV back on and of all things it's the new "Newlywed Game." If Cindy had gone on that show with Charles Snipes or Buzz Biggers either one they would have lost and she wouldn't have cared because they give shitty prizes; matching Lazy Boys and who wants them? Lazy Boys are for the sick and the old.

"Bled?" Cindy shakes Ginny Sue's shoulder again. "Mama didn't tell me you had bled. Was it a hemorrhage? Have you been hemorrhaging?"

"God," Ginny Sue mumbles.

"That's right," Emily says. "Talk to him and ignore her. You'll be better off."

"I'm back." Hannah steps in the front door in a different outfit from when she left and a little overnight bag with her. It's not a piece of Samsonite, either; Cindy can tell from one glance. "Is everything okay?"

"The patients are just fine," Cindy says, ready to get the hell on to Ramada. She has got ten minutes to get there and find a parking space, which isn't always easy on a Friday night. "Ginny Sue, I'll talk to you tomorrow. I'll tell you all about my date." Cindy squeezes that damp puffy hand and pulls her bag up on her shoulder. "That'll perk you up."

"I'm sure it will," Hannah says and laughs and Cindy can't tell what kind of a laugh it is, if it's laughing *with* or *at* her. "Thank you so much, Cindy." Hannah follows her to the front door so she can put on a few hundred dead bolts. Those people are scared of their shadows.

Cindy hates that it's daylight savings; she hates that she and Randy Skinner have to wait until practically nine o'clock for it to be dark enough that they can go and sit in her car. Tonight, she's not going to wait. Tonight, she's going to suggest that they go to her house and just order a pizza.

She pulls into Ramada and she has to drive around for five minutes at least looking for a place to park. She has to park at the far end of the lot near that lot of woods, which is fine. Randy Skinner will walk her to her car.

She goes in and there's a woman who looks like she's on MAO inhibitors playing the piano and singing. Cindy doesn't know what MAO stands for; she just knows that shrink was wanting to give her some and telling how she couldn't eat cheese with that drug, but that she wouldn't be depressed. "Nobody says I am but you," she told him. "How in the hell can you eat a nacho without cheese?" But that woman, with her veiny neck straining on every note looks like that's what she'd be taking; she looks like she has the major side effects what with wearing a turquoise shirt with brown slacks. And she's singing of all things, Blue Moon. That broad is depressed and Cindy is glad when she gets past that woman and can look for Randy Skinner. He is over in a far corner where it's good and dark and he lifts his hand when he catches sight of her. But Lord God, Charles Snipes is sitting right there at a table that she's got to walk past. She has never seen him here before and there he sits with a stiff-looking broad, her hair all neat and fixed, boring. She has teeny little flashes at her ears which must be minute earrings and nobody wears little dainty earrings except people like her mama and on occasion Ginny Sue who has never really taken an interest in style.

She keeps walking with her eyes straight ahead, eyes on Randy Skinner. "Hello Cindy," Charles says, halfway smiling, in that dull quiet way of his. "This is Nancy Price."

"Hi," Nancy Price says and smiles. Nancy Price is drinking a pina colada, a pink pina colada like she's somebody she's not. "I've heard so much about you," Nancy Price says and Cindy can just hear it, just hear all that Charles Snipes has told of her. "Chuckie is a wonderful child."

"Chuckie's twelve," she says and looks at Charles, the tips of those Prince Charles looking ears turning red. Prince Charles—imagine that she used to actually call him that. "Remember?"

"Of course I do," Charles says but looks at Nancy Price when he says it and lowers those cow eyes of his.

"I hear matrimony is in the air," she says and stares hard at Nancy Price who doesn't wear much makeup and should.

"Yes," Nancy Price says like she's voting on something, picks at that pineapple sitting on top of that drink.

"I'm sorry that I didn't tell you first," Charles says, those ears like they're about to ignite and hemorrhage at the same time. "I wanted to be the one to tell Chuckie." Fly to Disneyland, Dumbo!

"What? And not let us have the fun of hearing it through the grapevine?" She waves to Randy to let him know she's coming just as soon as they'll stop talking and let her. "I wish I could chat a little more," she says and smiles. "But my date is so jealous. He has watched every move I've made since I passed that MOA-inhibitor-popping lard-ass over there who made Blue Moon sound like two dying alley cats screwing in a brush fire."

"That's my baby sister," Nancy Price says.

"That's the only reason we're here," Charles says, reaching his hand across the table to take hold of Nancy Price's hand which has a diamond on it like he sure can't afford, probably a zircon.

"Well," Cindy says. "I hear those drugs will do wonders if you stay off the dairy stuff."

"I don't know what . . ." Nancy Price is saying when Cindy turns her back and twists her fanny the way Charles used to think was so cute all the way over to the table.

"I ordered you two kamikazes for the price of one," Randy Skinner says and she is so glad. She could drink a kamikaze for every one there ever was. "That woman sure is bad isn't she?" he asks. "I'd rather have the piped-in stuff."

"She is going to be my ex-husband's sister-in-law," Cindy says and bites into a pretzel.

"I'm sure glad she's not my sister-in-law," he says. "My sister-in-law may be fat but she can sing." Cindy stops midchew and looks at the three empty glasses in front of Randy Skinner. He must have meant ex-sister-in-law; Cindy knows that he's an only child.

"How fat is your ex-sister-in-law," Cindy says. "Could be a thyroid."

"Oh," he says and just stares into that bowl of pretzels.

"I guess I had to tell you sooner or later," he says, "I mean you strike me as somebody real open, you know?"

Cindy watches Charles and Nancy Price go over and hug that girl by the piano. And when the three of them are safely outside of the lounge, she turns to Randy Skinner and takes a big swallow of her kamikaze. "Separated?" she asks and he hangs his head and shakes it no.

"Gonna be separated?"

"I might," he says and takes her hand. "Whenever I'm with you, I really start thinking that I might." He is staring at Cindy's boobs and then slowly back up to her face.

"Well, let me know when you do." She finishes that first kamikaze and takes a big gulp of the second before she pulls her bag out from under the table. She starts to tell him what she had planned for the night just so he'd get all erect and couldn't follow her out to the parking lot, but she doesn't. She'd rather get to the parking lot in time to see Charles and that Nancy Price and Nancy Price's sister getting into that new Toyota Camry that he just recently bought with what the God Jesus holy ghost only knows.

"Oh Cindy, Cindy," Randy Skinner says and rubs his hand over that beard like he might be a man that studies the comets and the stars. "Just stay until dark, you know, dark when we can go to your car. One last time to remember."

"Suffer, baby," she says just like in that old joke where that mosquito is trying to screw a elephant. "Just suffer yourself unto me," she says, relying on what she has always known to work. If you quote a little scripture it will usually shut somebody right up. A little scripture will go a long way, and with that she walks right out of the Ramada Inn and into the lobby where Charles and Nancy Price and Nancy Price's sister are waiting while the man behind the counter writes out a check and gives it to that sister. Two cents is what she was worth, if that much.

"Good-bye, Cindy," Charles says, the three of them standing there like they might be posing for Olan Mills. Snap Snap.

"Have a hematoma of a wedding," she says and walks as fast as she can so that she doesn't start to cry and make her makeup run. She is not going to go and get Chuckie; God no, 'cause she can't take him and his bump mashing and her mama's card shuffling tonight. She drives straight home and

calls Constance Ann on the phone. "I'm right in the middle
of a show," Constance Ann whines, her mouth full of something like potato chips it sounds like.

"If you are my friend, you'll come over here, and you'll
come ready to spend the night if I feel I can't make it through
the night," Cindy says. It's not the nicest thing in the world
to make a person feel guilty but it works. "Even my best
friend has turned against me—a woman I completely trusted;
how often we ate together. Psalms 41:9"

"Okay, I'm coming," Constance Ann says, though Cindy
knows she'll watch that show till it's over. Cindy unplugs the
TV and binds the end of that cord in electrical tape; she'll
tell Constance Ann it has a short. Constance Ann will pout
and threaten to go home to watch "Dallas," but Cindy can
handle that. "Be ye not selfish." If she's feeling better by
nine, she'll pull off the tape and plug the set in. You can't
tell what will happen. Randy Skinner might leave his wife;
he might sit at Ramada, drink about four more drinks and
have a head-on collision. You just can't ever know for sure
what will happen, from Friday to Friday, from man to man.

* * *

Virginia wakes to the absence of the window where the
streetlight shines through; she turns to feel for Mark and instead there is a wall, hollow-feeling plasterboard.

"Ginny Sue?" A lamp goes on and she squints to see her
mother standing by Gram's dining room table, her nylon gown
a filmy pink shimmer. "Honey, you're to lie quietly."

She watches her mother cross the room, quietly, ghostlike,
and sit on the floor where she has made a pallet of quilts and
blankets. Gram used to make pallets like that when Virginia
pretended to be camping out; she would hide there with the
stuffed clown that Gram had made. She could close her eyes
tightly and see all the colors on her eyelids; she could think
of a picture and it would form like a movie: Lena and Roy
in New York City, Gramps walking home from work. Now,
she is on the daybed, her legs lifted with a mass of pillows,
a trashcan on the floor right beside her head. "You have been
so sick," her mama says. "There's the trashcan and you call
if you need me. Don't try to get up." Her mother looks so
young sitting there in that short gown, her hair in loose curls

pushed back from her face, just a few shimmering strands of gray.

"It's the baby isn't it?" Virginia asks, suddenly remembering Felicia's friend gripping her wrist, looking at her watch. "Sky high," the woman said when she took her blood pressure.

"You're going to be fine," her mama says. "You've just got to stay in bed awhile, at least a week, maybe longer."

"Here?" Virginia asks and she feels a second of relief, relief to be home, a reason to stay without telling the truth.

"Yes. They said I can take you to our house later in the week if you're feeling better." Her mother stretches her legs out and leans back on her elbows. "Mark was so upset when I called him."

"What did he say?" Virginia asks, trying to picture his expression, upset, the phone cord twisted around his hand with those long legs swung up on the coffee table. His face is white, guilty, under those bright overhead lights, the glaring freak-show lights that he always switches on instead of a lamp where the light is soft, filtered by a shade. His face is white, tennis shoe going back and forth like a windshield wiper.

"He said he was afraid something like this was going to happen. He said that you've been feeling awful lately." Her mother stares at her now, eyebrows lifted and waiting for the confession.

"He wasn't," she mumbles. "He feels guilty is all."

"For?" Again the eyebrows, but Virginia doesn't answer, just shakes her head. If she didn't feel so sleepy, so fuzzy, she'd tell everything.

"You've just been sick," her mama says. "Your hormones can do all kinds of things to you."

"Hormones," Virginia repeats; her mother has always relied on hormones, irritability, sudden tears, lack of energy, full of energy.

"Well, it's true," her mother says. "Mine are doing strange things right now, hot, cold, and hot, cold. They talked about PMS on Donahue the other morning and I knew just what those women meant; I believe in PMS." Virginia wants to smile, to nod, I believe in PMS, but she pictures Mark standing in front of her Animal Kingdom. If she died right now, that's what he'd have to remember her, snarls and death and a fat pregnant monkey; and if Sheila had wanted that baby, if Sheila had wanted things to work, then Mark would already be living in some city, some condo-miniblinds-art deco-thank you for not using that lucite ashtray-living room. And he would be snuggled under some satiny comforter-covered waterbed with the long and lithe Sheila stretched out beside him, her long blonde hair falling in sparkly webs onto a satin pillowcase, and Sheila's long slender fingers would squeeze his thigh and he would say all of the things to Sheila that he has said to her. She feels herself sinking slowly onto that waterbed, ghostlike, while he lies there with Sheila.

"I'm going to turn the light out now," her mama whispers. "I don't want Mama to get back up. She was so confused when she went to bed; Lena always gets her confused." She hears the lamp click off and her mama tiptoeing through the darkness back to the pallet. "Of course, Lena confuses me," she whispers and laughs. Virginia wants to say "me too" but the words will not come, only Sheila with her blonde hair on his pillow, his mouth moving down Sheila's sleek ivory throat. "If I'm ever that way," her mother whispers. "You and Robert don't worry about it. I hope I never am."

"You won't," Virginia tries to say, hoping her mother will not talk about all of that again, wills and funerals, and how she likes Lena's idea of being buried in pajamas, plant a dogwood. Her mother has always talked about these things as easily as she would say how she wanted her hair fixed. "I think it's nature's way of helping people to let go." Her mother's voice is low and whispery now, far away like a whippoorwill song. "Don't let go, Ginny Sue," Gram says. "Hold tight now."

"God has his way," her mother whispers. That could be Gram saying those words, the thunder and lightning, death and illness all figuring into the grand scheme of things. "God has taken my child and my husband," Gram said. "And I am not to question why." And Virginia had stood at the kitchen window and watched while the ambulance took Gramps away, her mama and Gram clutching one another and sobbing like children. "Think about it," her mama whispers, her voice getting slower and slower. "If you hadn't come home today, I'd be worried sick over you flat on your back and alone in that house. Mark's got his studies and those big tests coming up. It's a blessing that you came today." The thought of being alone in that house, in any house, sends a chill over her scalp and she pulls Gram's quilt up close around her face and breathes in the heavy old smell. "You know who is with you always?" Gram had asked that night that Uncle Raymond took her to Gram's house to spend the night. "God is always there with you, no reason to be afraid."

"But what if somebody else is there, too?" she asked, still clutching her Barbie overnight case. "What if there's a man coming to get you?"

"No man will get you," Gram said and the nightlight burned while they lay on that featherbed, the lights from cars passing on Carver Street circling the room, the clock ticking. She focuses on the ticking of the clock, the ticks in rhythm with Sheila's heartbeats as Mark's mouth moves down her body, so pale in the glow of the streetlight, her breasts and stomach, eyes closed, lips parted, her breath rising and falling, slight and then quickened.

"Mama?" Virginia calls, her eyes focused on the heavy outline of Gram's highboy. "I've come home to stay. I made a mistake and I've come back." She waits, the outline of the highboy becoming clearer and sharper, the quiet answer of her mother's steady breathing, broken only by the ticking. "I've always had a feeling when the time was right," Gram said and stared into the sky, her face held back, turning slowly to face the wind, her pockets filled with seeds and a tin of snuff. "I've just always known."

* * *

Cindy wishes that Constance Ann would just go on home with her potato chip-stuffed self. How can you talk to someone that if she's not asleep and snoring her ass off, is matching every story that you've got to tell? Cindy told about the trauma at Ramada and Constance Ann said she has a cousin from somewhere that's going through the exact same thing except the cousin *also* has to have a hysterectomy.

"Now, she's got it bad," Constance Ann said, her hair pulled up in a high ponytail and rolled over three juice cans. Nobody has done their hair in juice cans for years. Everybody stopped using juice cans when Cindy was in high school. Orange juice cans went out with sanitary belts and vanilla Cokes.

"*I've* got it bad," Cindy screamed. "I still . . ." and she

caught herself. Constance Ann is a talker; besides Constance
Ann doesn't listen to anybody but herself. All she's done all
night is stuff herself and stare into a *Cosmopolitan* or walk
around looking for the TV. "I thought you were my friend,"
Cindy screamed and Constance Ann said that she was, that
she had recently taken a friendship test for feminists and that
their friendship came out to be slightly above mediocre.

"I am not a feminist," Cindy screamed. "I'm liberated,
though. You can just look at me and know I'm liberated but
when you get right down to it, every woman whose hormones
are in drive instead of reverse or neutral wants herself a man."

"But I can live without one," Constance Ann had said,
those juice cans rocking on her head. Constance Ann could
lose about twenty pounds and cut that hair and she'd look
fine. Constance Ann has always looked this way, though, just
like she does right now with that big ass facing Cindy. It's
her home training. Constance Ann was never taught the things
about being attractive and seductive, never taught what men
like and what men might mean when they say something like,
"Haven't I seen you somewhere before?" Some women think
that's a stupid line but it's more than that. When a man says
that, what he really means is "Hey chick, I wanna jump your
bones." And when a man says, "let's meet for coffee," that
means that he is all tied up but wants to get something sim-
mering on the back burner. If he says, "What a lovely sweater
or blouse," then he means, "good boobs." She knows all of
that and thank God, her daddy cared enough to tell her the
things that she would need to know. All her mama said was,
"Don't show the merchandise if you ain't selling."

"You can live without one," Cindy said, her voice suddenly filled with sympathy, more than that, downright gut-
wrenching depression. "Because you've never really had one.
An alcoholic who's never had booze, ain't an alcoholic." And
Cindy had watched Constance Ann smile that twisted smile
that halfway said, "I hurt" and halfway said "You don't read
enough, Cindy." Constance Ann put down her magazine and
stared at Cindy, those pale eyes filming behind her polo
glasses that Cindy talked her into buying, telling Constance
Ann that if what she wanted to be was an egghead glued to
magazines and sex books then she should look the part and
they are an improvement over what Cindy called the cat
glasses. God helps those that help themselves. "And you'll

find somebody, Constance Ann,'' Cindy said. ''Somewhere in this world there is a man for you.'' And Cindy smiled even though she doesn't believe that. It was hard as hell for her to get the two that she did. Buzz Biggers not fit for anything short of a Hefty trashbag and Charles Snipes; Charles Snipes might not have even married her if she hadn't been pregnant. His mama didn't want him to marry Cindy and just who did they think they were? Cindy's house was bigger and her daddy made more money and she had her own car which Charles did not. ''He will never measure up, Little Goldilocks,'' her daddy said and gave her a hundred dollars to go buy some lingerie she had seen in Belk's, safari gown with matching robe, wild, like Charles said he liked her. ''Take a walk on the wild side,'' she yelled at him and jumped from the bathroom, her stomach then looking like Ginny Sue's does now and she was never sick with Chuckie, not a day, sex like clockwork and no busted up veins. Ginny Sue might be faking a little, wanting some attention and God knows she doesn't have to beg for it; she can walk in that old duplex and sugar drips from every old sapless tree in the joint.

''I sure will,'' Charles said to her and got up from the couch where he was reading a plumbing book, his face so red, those Prince Charles ears so red, just like tonight at Ramada.

''You said 'I still' and then stopped,'' Constance Ann said, mind like a steel trap that girl, doesn't forget a thing, and Cindy just told her that she was so upset over their friendship that she completely forgot what was on her mind. ''I still feel something for Charles Snipes,'' is what she wanted to say.

She does feel something but she can't figure out what it is. ''Always want what you don't have,'' she can hear her mama saying, her mama always bending forward a little so she doesn't look so big, not fat, but big, big boned. It's pitiful when her mama stands next to Hannah.

''That shit about the apple don't fall far from the tree doesn't apply to me,'' Cindy had told Charles way back. ''I'm my daddy's child and so look at him, lean and still good-looking.''

''I like your mama,'' Charles said and when Cindy told her daddy that, he laughed, threw back his head with those lifeless paralyzed arms clutching the Lazy Boy and laughed.

"Learn from that, Goldilocks," he said. "Your mama has never attracted men."

"But she got you."

"I felt sorry for her," he said slowly, shook his head and then burst into laughter which made Cindy laugh, too. Laughter is contagious, everybody knows that. "And, it was a way for me to redeem myself after all of my wild years. But you, my baby girl," and he paused and stared at her with love in his eyes. "You haven't had your wild years, yet."

"Your old man is trying to bust us up," Charles had said and made her look at him. She was rinsing out Coke bottles and Chuckie was asleep. "Please don't let him," Charles said, that same look of love in his eyes, the water running, her hands dripping with water until Charles pulled them up and kissed that water away. It makes her chest pound to think of it, makes her wish that was Charles Snipes over there snoring instead of Constance Ann. Charles is probably right this minute with Nancy Price; he doesn't have to worry about where Chuckie is spending the night. There's no way that Nancy Price could ever look as good as Cindy there naked in a bed.

"My daddy just wants what's best for me," she had told Charles. "If you really loved me, you'd just live with it."

"If he really loves you," Charles said and looked at her in a way that went clear to the bone just like Hannah can do, making you feel like you need to confess something, "he would let you go."

"Let me go? You make it sound like I'm tied up and in a closet." And he just stood there and looked at her with a look that said "maybe you are, Cindy" or "maybe you need therapy, Cindy" or "maybe you need to read more books."

"He is my daddy and you are my husband," she said, Chuckie screaming his ass off from the other room. "I don't have to make a choice do I? Nobody on God's green earth has to make a choice like that. It's sick. That's a sick thought."

"I'm not saying make a choice," Charles said, stopping in the doorway on his way to Chuckie's room. "Just figure out which is which."

"Are you gonna sit up all night?" Constance Ann asks now and reaches for her glasses on the table beside her. "I mean really, Cindy, what do you care if he remarries. You did."

"I don't. I don't care," Cindy says and takes off her nylon leopard robe that she bought when she burned a hole in the safari one. "It's more than that, Constance Ann. You might know what I'm feeling one day if you find yourself married and then divorced."

"I'll never get divorced," Constance Ann says. "I've read enough to recognize all the warning signs and know what to do if I see them."

"It doesn't work that way," Cindy says and gets under the cover without even taking off her makeup. Never say never. When the Lord slams a door, a window flies open. She gets so sick of the way people act about divorce; even Ginny Sue can't see beyond that bloated-up belly that things change, sometimes so suddenlike, like the weather. Nobody says, oh it's never gonna rain, never gonna snow. But they think my house will never get uprooted from the dirt by a tornado and I will never get VD or cancer or tetanus or hardening of the arteries. Just look around and know that ain't so. Just put your quarter in one of those machines and get what you never in your life wanted but take it and live with it. Bodies are like that, those little clear plastic eggs, and you take what's good out of it, a red rubber worm or a fake diamond ring and then throw that little egg in the trash. Her daddy gave her all that he had that was good. "Take what you can get," he told her. "Get all that you can get and take it with you."

"Are you crying?" Constance Ann asks and sits on the edge of the bed. Constance Ann wears men's pajamas; Cindy has never known a man that wore pajamas, not even her daddy. "I've never seen you crying."

"Well, I don't do it often," Cindy sits up and pulls the covers close to her neck. She ain't used to sporting her lingerie in front of women, not even Constance Ann. It's okay with Ginny Sue because she's related and doesn't seem to check you out like Constance Ann does behind those polo glasses.

"Your period must be coming," Constance Ann says. "Sometimes ovulation will do it, too."

"Do what?"

"Make you cry," Constance Ann says. "A woman's body

is much more complicated than a man's. You should read *Our Bodies, Ourselves*, Cindy.''

"My body is going to sleep," Cindy says and slides back down against her pillow, thinks about all the nights she had with Charles Snipes, nights when she'd reach over and grab him, move her hand back and forth and say, "this is why women like to drive straight drives." Nancy Price will never get him so excited, make him laugh so. "Close your eyes and think about what I've told you," her daddy would say. "Your body is sleepy, sleepy . . ."

"I can't believe it," Constance Ann says. "Ask me over here to talk and then you don't talk. Wake me up and now you go to sleep. No telling what J.R. did tonight that I missed."

No telling what Charles Snipes did tonight that she missed. "God, you're the cutest, sexiest, wildest thing on earth," Charles used to say, and she'd shift down to second, then back up to third. "I'm going to strip your gears," she'd whisper and watch those cute Prince Charles ears turn bright pink.

* * *

Madge sets her coffee cup beside the deck of cards and begins to write. "Dear Hannah, Raymond was so crazy that he made me kill him." She has already won back a hundred dollars this morning which doesn't put a dent in what she owes. Now is probably not the time to write to Hannah with Ginny Sue so sick. Still, it makes Madge feel better to do it. She will confess first to Hannah and then to the police and then to the preacher and then they'll put her in handcuffs and drag her off. Just drag her away like they had to do her mama that time.

"Treat me like a mad dog then!" Madge's mama had screamed. "Call somebody to carry me off. They can't carry my mind away, no, can't carry what's in my head. Emily knows; Emily will keep a secret."

"I just want you to get some help now," Madge said, those two Mormon boys still standing across the street in their little black suits, their faces so pale like they had seen a ghost. "I'm not working against you, Mama."

"You have worked against me since the day you took root," and her mama's face was all twisted and screwed up like a shriveled little crazy mouse, those lace-up boots bigger than she was.

"You don't mean that Aunt Tessy," Hannah said and kissed Madge's mama on the cheek. "Madge loves you, I love you." Thank God that Hannah had come when she called, stopped her sewing and rushed right out in the country where the houses were so far apart. "I don't know why those boys chose this area in the first place," Hannah said. "I guess so they'd have less houses."

"Mighty long bike ride," Madge said, feeling sorry for those boys. "But they're doing God's will."

"A lot is done in God's name," her mama said and shook her head. "Bad things have been done in God's name. I don't mess with nobody. I keep to myself and they come messing. I said 'get away from my door, alley cats' but they kept right on knocking. I had no choice but to get the gun."

"I've wanted to get her into town," Madge had told Hannah later. "I want her to live with me, to let me just once in her life do something for her."

"She'd get used to it I'll bet," Hannah said. "I'll help you, Madge. We can take her to visit Mama more often and it would be good for both of them."

"But," Madge whispered, watching Raymond from the corner of her eye wrap a dead bird round and round in toilet paper, little Cindy watching every move of his while Catherine walked through her mama's house knocking on walls and looking in closets, telling Madge later that she never realized her grandmother lived in such a dump. "Raymond won't let me take her. Raymond says I cannot bring Mama home to live."

"I'm sorry," Hannah whispered back and Madge was hoping that Hannah would offer for her mama to go and live with Emily which she didn't.

"Hannah doesn't think of anyone but herself," Raymond told Madge. "Hannah and Ben are stingy. Poor people have to be I guess."

"They are not poor," Madge said, one of the few times that she ever spoke up to him.

"Well, lower class then, like you were before I rescued you." He poured himself a shot of bourbon and drank it.

"It's because Mama and Lena don't get along," Madge said. "I know that's what Hannah's thinking. Lena and Roy are retiring in Saxapaw and I know Hannah's thinking that they'll be at her mama's most of the time.''

"Lena and Roy," he said and drank another shot. "Rolling in money, but it doesn't change their class. And you're no better, Madge. You believe all those tall tales about how perfect their life is, a romance made in heaven, about Lena being a star on Broadway, hah!'' He carried the bottle and shot glass over to his chair and opened his book on Egypt, glossy pictures of tombs and mummies. Lena and Roy did seem to have a perfect romance, an almost famous one because Hannah had shown her the picture of Lena and Roy in a New York paper, and Madge had also seen the Broadway program that had Lena's name listed as understudy to the star. Madge's mama never liked Lena but Madge did; Madge thought she was beautiful way back and wished that Lena had just once given her the attention that went to Hannah.

"What about your family?'' she asked and Raymond looked up from that book and glared at her in a way that made her blood feel like it was freezing.

"You will never know my family," he said. "I have nothing to do with my family and haven't for years.''

"I think the children have a right to know about their relatives,'' she said. "Catherine and Cindy got a right to at least see some pictures.''

"No pictures," he said. "They're all dead.'' That's all Madge knows about the Sinclairs, no pictures, all dead, buried somewhere in Oklahoma.

"You don't know nothing of his people,'' Madge's mama had said and lit her pipe. "I didn't come from the best stock but I knew what to expect. As for your daddy; well, I knew Mrs. Virginia Pearson and I knew she was fine, Emily, too, so I had some hope in me.''

"But you can't go by things like that,'' Madge told her mother. "It's not fair.''

"Things have a way of coming down the pipes, '' she said. "All comes out in the wash.'' And her mama turned on her almost like she did that day with the Mormon boys. "Is it fair Emily's boy got killed in the war? A boy so fine? The world ain't fair. God ain't fair. You remember that.''

"But the work of God can't be questioned,'' Madge said, hoping to break through those tough old bones.

"That's what Emily believes,'' her mama said and shook

her head. "But what kind of God takes a young man who's got a whole good life ahead of him? What kind of God makes a woman live like me?"

"What do you mean?" Madge asked but her mama moved right off of that and back to Raymond Sinclair, back to how she didn't like his big-talking ways. Madge didn't want to hear any of it. For the first time in her life she was feeling like she really loved somebody, that somebody really loved her.

* * *

"Dear Hannah," she starts again, takes a sip of that cold coffee. "Why has God punished me? I believe, but I wonder why God has given me this very life." She marks through all the words now, a heavy dark line through all of those words.

"Hey Grandma," Chuckie says and she balls up that paper and puts it in her purse. He is at the bottom of the stairs, already dressed in a tee shirt that says, "Miami Vice," his face with red blotches where he's been messing with it.

"Hey Honey," she says. "Don't pick at your face so. It'll leave scars."

"Yeah," he says and sits on the edge of a chair, his sandy colored hair cut close on the sides with some curly little bit in the front. She doesn't say a word about that hairdo. Cindy let him get it cut that way; Cindy said, "don't you say one word about his hair like you used to do me, STILL do me; he's in style." His legs are going back and forth, too long for the rest of him. "My dad has scars," he says. "Mama said his face was messed up all the way through high school."

"Well, I know," Madge says, remembering how Charles looked the first time that Cindy ever brought him home. Madge thought he was so fine, nice parents and well-mannered and she was surprised at how well him and Cindy got along. Surprised that Charles put up with her breaking up and getting back together and surprised that Cindy would give somebody a chance with such a skin problems. "God, he's ugly," Raymond had said and Catherine agreed with him. "You can do better than that, Goldilocks."

"I like him, though, " Cindy said and leaned over and spit

a mouthful of milk onto Catherine's plate. Dinner was always that way.

"Take what you want then," Raymond said and winked at her. And Cindy never said a word back to him, only apologized for Charles's skin troubles.

"There's more that can be done about the skin these days," Madge says. She'd like to get Chuckie in braces too, to correct that overbite, but she is not even going to mention that. "I told your mama that I'd like to do that for you."

"I'm gonna be this way all through high school," he says and goes to the kitchen and stands there with the refrigerator door wide open. He gets that from Cindy. "But Mom said that if Dad could get her with his face that way, that I can get girlfriends, too. Mom says I just got to live with it."

"It wouldn't hurt to try to do something about it," Madge says, feeling herself about to cry, wishing she could take all of his worries and heap them right onto her long list of debts to pay; she's got so much that what difference would it make. "I'm gonna do that for you Chuckie," she says and smiles. "Because I love you." The words are hard getting out but she does and he rolls his eyes and drinks straight from the milk carton. He got that from Cindy, too. She wishes so bad that he'd say it back to her but you can't expect much from children. It has been years since she said those words to Cindy or to Catherine and she can't remember that Cindy has ever said the words to her. Cindy would call out "I love you, Daddy," after Raymond would tuck her in and walk back to their room.

"And me?" Madge would call out in the darkness.

"Yes." That's all Cindy had said, yes, and by then Raymond never said anything close to those words. "You're too big to be a woman" he'd say. "You should have been a man," and he'd yank those covers to his side of the bed, leaving her big bones halfway covered and her feeling like the Amazon women like what he showed her in *National Geographic*.

* * *

Virginia wakes, startled to see Mark, too startled to ask him what he's doing here, in Gram's house. He doesn't belong here; he is out of place, sitting in a straight-back chair with a stack of law books beside him, his hand writing busily on a legal pad. "Awake?" he asks now and his cool hand moves over her hot forehead and then back around her neck.

"Where is everybody?" she asks when she opens her eyes and sees the Lazy Boy empty, the sofa, no sounds in the kitchen, no sound other than the ticking of Gram's clock muffled like a faint heartbeat beneath the rumbling of the air-conditioner. It is late afternoon; she can tell by the dry white light out the window, bright and heavy at a slant showing every particle of dust, void of the screen of smoke that would hit the light and spread like paint on a flat surface were Lena here. "What time is it?"

"It's four o'clock," he whispers, quietly, emotionless, unlike the students when it's two-thirty. "It's two-thirty!" they scream and run and push and fall like a band of demons, no thoughts of what they were doing at noon and no thoughts of what they'll be doing at nine. Two-thirty, that's all. That's all they need to know. Why didn't they tell her Mark was coming? Why didn't he call on the phone?

"Your grandmother is in bed," he continues, which isn't like Gram. She likes to watch TV in the afternoons, always has, and Virginia knows that if Mark weren't here that's what Gram would be doing. He has overstepped his boundaries, invaded her territory, changed everything. "Your mom will be back soon. She and your dad went to an estate auction."

"Whose?" she asks and he shakes his head, holds a glass of water to her lips—good, so good against her rough, dry throat. She is sure that she would at least recognize the name—the front doors of a home swung open for strangers to pick and choose, sift through books and sheet music, the secret passions of someone dead; take the paintings off the walls leaving a clean-painted image like a shadow of what had been there, and you would never know that the wall has, over the years, gotten so dirty if the picture were left in place. Take the tiny silver spoons from the rack, the colander from the kitchen; take the door knocker if your initial is the same. It has been this way in this place for years but take it, its life, the scents of a family, a home; the scents that it will carry with it across town to another house to start all over. Where are the family members? Where are the people who know the scent that is there, the scent that is home, and how can they let it be split and divided and separated? Lena's big two-story house is just as it was, wide spacious rooms, formal Queen Anne, tea set, Roy's stack of *Architectural Digest* that continued to come months after he died and her mom went and carried in the mail, placed the magazines on his large mahogany desk as if he could enter from the dusk and sit there at night with the lamp turned low. And he would say, "Lena? Lena?" and she would shuffle into the room, her lifeless eyes once again filled, her gray hair darkening to auburn, and she would sling her arms around his neck, her cheeks so wet, and say, "Roy, oh God, Roy, I thought I had lost you."

"Virginia?" Mark asks. "Are you feeling okay?" But her mind is on Lena as she left behind that house and furniture, carrying the scent in her Samsonite bag and pasteboard box, never to see it all again. "I think it's best not to take her back," Virginia's mama said. "I think it would be cruel to do that if she can't stay. And she can't. Nursing care. Eventually we'll have to sell it, sell the furniture." And that's why her mother has started going to estate sales, how is it all done? How do you sell a life? "Maybe you and Mark can buy most of the furniture?" her mother asked, hope in her voice.

"I want to buy Lena and Roy's house," she murmurs now. "I want to live there." And she imagines walking through that Victorian house, sitting in the gazebo.

"Oh." That's all he says, the smooth rubbing of his hand stopping suddenly, dead weight pressing on her forehead. "Look, maybe we won't move so soon," he says, a forced falseness in his voice, a forced everything-will-be-okay optimism. "Maybe Richmond's not the place. We can talk about it. What's important right now is the baby, you getting well."

What's important if I lose it, she thinks. Nothing, nothing at all. His hand is on her arm when she tries to sit up.

"You're not supposed to move," he says.

"I have to use the bathroom, though," and she realizes that she sounds just like Lena, an independent adult suddenly reduced to a child's mother may I? May I pee, please? Yes you may. Take one giant step, one baby step, one june bug twirl around.

"I'll carry you," he says and she is amazed at how easily he can lift and carry her, cradling, her long legs swinging lifelessly as if they don't even belong to her, rubbery, when he places her feet in front of the toilet and holds her up, the oozy dots that come and go when she looks at herself in the mirror. Someone at a pajama party once told her that if you close your eyes tightly and say in your head "I believe in Mary Weather, I believe in Mary Weather" fifty times and then open your eyes real fast, that you will see the old woman, see Mary Weather in the mirror where your own face should be.

"Well, what happened to privacy?" she asks now and Mark kisses her lightly on the forehead.

"I believe I've seen it all before," he says and carefully lifts that potato sack dress, slowly pulls down her underwear and helps her to sit, places her hands on the bars that were put there for Gram. She blinks, eyelids so heavy, I believe in Mary Weather, and he looks so much older that way.

"Turn on the faucet 'cause I can't seem to go," she mumbles. He does and she waits, the simplest of all activities becoming an event that she will tell Gram and her mama about when they are the only ones here.

He carries her back but when he places her down, she feels her fingers intertwine, lock behind his neck and hold him there. She stares at him, the slow way his head bends closer, his lips lightly brushing hers, Dentyne, her own mouth like dust, while he kisses her nose, forehead. She is Sheila, long and lithe with her long silky blonde hair fanned on the waterbed, a sparkly net made golden by the slats of light from the miniblinds. "I love you," he whispers. "I was so afraid you had run away from home or something." He kneels beside the daybed, tries to loosen her grip on his neck but she doesn't let him.

* * *

"I have run away from home and I am never coming back," Robert had told her once, his young face so adultlike. "You may visit but this is my permanent home," and he had pointed behind the ligustrums in the side yard where he had his canteen and sleeping bag and she had asked him what "permanent" meant and he had to think a minute before he said, "forever." She had packed her own bag once, stopped on the corner and stood on the manhole cover, trying not to cry when the street looked so long and it was getting dark. She would have to walk all the way to the end, cut behind the shopping center and then walk another long road to the end, turn at the big warehouse near the hardware store and go all the way, following the railroad track to Carver Street where Gram would take her in. "Don't ride with strangers," her mama called out to her, her mama in jeans and sneakers and a flannel shirt as she edged around the sidewalk. "Write me a letter some time. We will miss you Ginny Sue, but I guess you know what's best."

"It's just been a rough week," Mark whispers, his voice this time with sincere optimism, the same way her dad says at the beginning of each summer that he's going to grow a giant squash, the same way her mama had stopped midway to the trash pile with weeds in her arms and said, "I knew you'd come home. We all missed you terribly."

"I wasn't gone long enough to be missed," she had said, picking up a weed that her mother had dropped.

"Oh yes you were."

"I miss you," Mark is saying now. "Last night is the first night we've been apart."

"But I'm glad to be home," she says and watches the confused look on his face. Now is not the time, not the time to say that she doesn't want to go back there. He has boards to take. Now is not the time. "There is never a good time for something hard to do," Gram says. "You think you're ready to handle a loss but there is never a good time. You just do what you have to do."

Virginia feels her cheek wet against his now and she can't tell where it's coming from. She thinks of the small pale girl at the back of the first grade class, eyes wide and damp, her seat wet. "I didn't do it," she told Virginia. "I didn't." And she thinks of Lena on her way to the nursing home, her hand on the car handle as if she were about to jump. "Somebody spilt something back here on this seat," she told Virginia's mother. "It's soggy wet and I didn't do it."

"Just sleep," Mark whispers. "You've still got a fever," and she closes her eyes against that tired Mary Weather face, circles and lines that were not there the first time that she ever saw him, a party, Plexiglass living room; every time she looked his way, a corner of men, he was looking back, and how long ago was that? Two years? Three years? It all happened so fast, too fast to think. "Your mom said I could stay here," he says, hand so cool on her forehead. "Or, I could go on home and try to study. Hannah said there's really nothing that I can do but I brought my books in case you want me to stay."

"Do you want me to stay or go?" he had asked, well after midnight, the TV a dim gray flicker in the dark room where she lay on the couch facing him, an awkward jumble of arms and legs, and she felt like she just wanted to fall asleep that way, but there was the thought of morning, going to work, needing to brush her teeth, and things were going so fast.

"I think maybe you should go," she said, says now.

"Are you sure?" he asks and for a moment she feels so powerful. What does he want her to say? He wants to go home, she knows he does, doesn't sleep well when he's away, doesn't study well; and yet, she has the authority, she can say "stay" and he will. And then what? Stay and be a martyr and resent it for the rest of your life.

"Yes, I'm sure," she says and feels his beard, one-day stubbles, rough against her cheek. And even with his body so close, she feels him slipping away, hears his key turn the lock of that small rented house, his footsteps echo down the hall to find dishes in the sink, the bed twisted and rumpled, creaking with his weight as he stretches there and stares at the small cobweb in the corner. "He's been here so long you might as well let him stay," he had said one night, laughed when she pretended that she had never seen it, stood on the bed and waved a magazine at the web, catching and wrapping it like a strand of cotton candy. She sees him stretching on the bed and staring into that corner and what is on his mind, the spider, baby, her, Sheila?

"I sure will be glad to get you . . ." he pauses, "home" on his tongue and changed to "back." I sure will be glad to get you back. "I don't look forward to another night without you."

Another night. She has only been gone one day. It is only Saturday and it seems like years, stretching like that late afternoon light, measured by the gentle rhythm of Gram's clock.

"I don't look forward to the rest of this party," he had whispered, cocktail glasses clinking. "Want to go to the movies?" She looked at this person, a stranger who had talked for fifteen minutes without introducing himself, this stranger who was now asking her to go out with him. She could have eaten a cigarette but no one there was smoking. "We can catch the seven-thirty if we leave right now," he said and looked at his watch, not Rolex or sport digital, a generic watch that told her nothing about him, just like his clothes, white shirt and striped tie, socks that didn't match, generic shoes. "Then we can go get dinner," he said. "What are you in the mood for? Yuppie burgers? Italian? Chinese? Mexican? I'll eat all but Soul Food."

"I don't even know you," she said. "I really don't know anybody here." And she felt herself wanting to run from the Plexiglass living room, to run to the safety of her car, FM radio and cigarette lighter.

"So, how'd you get invited?" he asked so seriously that she caught herself looking at him with a mixture of "are you crazy?" and amusement.

"I know the hostess," she said, staring at her flat leather moccasins and realizing suddenly that every other woman in the room was in pumps or sexy strapped sandals. "She teaches at the elementary school where I give art lessons."

"Oh," he nodded, one of the front pockets of his pants pulled up empty and hanging out. "I know a friend of a friend of the host," he said, no information in that. "Small world, huh?" he laughed and looked around, probably looking for another woman standing off by herself who would talk to him, and she wanted to say something that could keep him there a little longer so that she *wouldn't* be the single woman standing all by herself but she couldn't think of anything. "I think I saw some of your art work in the Trucker's Diner when I was in Clemmonsville," he said, struck a pensive pose, no smile, sarcastically serious with that voice that clearly said he was a transplant. "I told the waitress, *'ya'll* got some good art here' and I asked her what your name was and she told me and I wrote it down on a napkin and now I can't remember and don't have the napkin on me, must be in my other pair of pants."

"I see," she said, deciding not to give any more information about herself, trying to figure out if he was flirting or making fun of her. I see, a careful enunciation of each word, cut the "I" off quickly, no ahh.

"I told the waitress that I could tell you were a regional

artist and sure enough, went in the bathroom and there was
an ad for your work, had your picture, name, phone number,
place and date of birth.''

"Who are you?'' she asked.

"Mark Williams Ballard,'' he said and extended his hand.
"But my friends call me Mark.''

"And so what should I call you?'' she asked without smiling, a slight flush behind his ears.

"Honey will be fine for starters,'' he said. "You don't
want to get all carried away in front of all these strangers.
You have a reputation to maintain.''

She focused again on her moccasins, again on the first grade
teacher, a different person with white wine instead of chalk
in her hand. He was looking around again, hands deep in his
pockets, "What's playing?'' she finally asked and watched
his shoulders relax.

"I've met someone really nice,'' she had told Gram two
weeks later. "He makes me think of things you've said about
Gramps. He has blue eyes like Gramps.''

"Where's he from?'' Gram asked. "Right close by so he
can drive out here in the country to get you? James would
come down that road in his buggy and somehow I knew he
was close before I even saw him. I wasn't hanging on the
porch post or peeking out a window either because nice people don't do such. Except Lena. Lena would peek out the
windows all the time no matter how many times my mama
told her that good people don't go peeking, but not me. I
didn't have to look out to know he was coming. It was just
something we had with one another. I just always knew he'd
be there, always knew he'd never carry me too far from my
home.''

* * *

"Should I stay here or go home?'' he had asked, again
lying on the couch, the TV station going off the air. It had
become a joke of sorts. He would say, "What if I get in a
wreck on the way home and here it is the middle of the night
and my clothes are all wrinkled and my hair all messed up?
I have a reputation,'' and he would say the word "reputation'' with lengthy slow pronunciation in response to her
voiced wonderings of what her neighbors might say should

they see him leave the next morning in the same clothes that he had worn to pick her up the night before.

"Stay," she had said that night, the warm gray flicker of the TV, his long legs thrown over the arm of the couch, making her feel like she didn't give a damn about anybody or anything right then, except being with him. "Stay," she said, says, but he is gone, and it has gotten darker outside, the light on in the kitchen where she hears her mother's voice, singing quietly, her dad sitting in Gram's Lazy Boy.

"About time you came to, Ginny," he says. "Your mama is fixing a good dinner."

"Where's Gram?" she asks and follows her dad's pointed finger to the doorway of the kitchen where Gram is sitting in her wheelchair with her glasses on the end of her nose and a Bisquik coupon in her hand.

"She's overseeing," he says and laughs.

"I thought I was going to have to wake you," her mama says, standing in the doorway, Gram thrusting the coupon into her hand. "I asked Mark to stay for dinner but he said he better get back before too late."

"Nobody should ever be late," Gram says. "I'm not used to eating so late. Eat early, go to bed early, and wake up early. That's the way we do it here."

It seems so late when Virginia feels her dad bend and kiss her forehead and then the room is dark and quiet, her mother again on the pallet beside her, and she thinks of those Sunday dinners on Carver Street, with Gram in the kitchen, polka-dot apron and hands covered in flour while Virginia licked the cake batter from the large mixing bowl; she thinks of Mark opening a can of tuna and walking down the hall to her bed where Sheila hovers like the cobweb in the corner, ready to wrap and twist and strangle their life like a cord around a neck.

* * *

Emily is tired of her house being a rest stop for every Tom, Dick, or Harry that gets tired of walking the streets and decides to stop by. Lena and Roy have that great big house all to themselves, or so they say, and why don't they just stay in it once in awhile and give her some peace. "You got to make time for yourself," her mama always said. "You got to be a wife as well as a mother no matter how hard it might be."

Yes Lord, her mama believed that you have to tend to the living, tend to your husband and children and brothers and sisters. Her mama had told of that clap of thunder that sent her to her knees right there atop of the grave of Emily's older sister who got so thin with the pneumonia and died. "I learned you can't spend all your time with the dead when there's the living to tend to," her mama said.

People come and people go. Ask that man who was here yesterday who he might be and he said "Mark" like she might believe that old Mark McIntosh is still with the living. "Mark McIntosh is dead and buried," she had told him and he said that he's married to Virginia. "Virginia is my mama," she told him. "And you are not my daddy. My mama and daddy are both dead."

"Ginny Sue's husband," he said and laughed; Ginny Sue is her grand baby, pretty little thing with that dark curly hair and them ways of hers, that way of wanting her hands to do whatever yours are doing. "You can paint that porch for me," she can tell Ginny Sue and send her off with a pail of water and a paint brush and that child will paint all day long; porch dries and she wets it down again. A good child. A good good child who don't need to be worried for some old hog that's got his eyes took out, a hog long ago slaughtered and not feeling pained. A child who don't need to be worried over this dry spell that's ruined the crops near about. There's no need in a child worrying over no money. No crop of tobacco to take to the market, no money come fall and school time, but a child needn't know of it. A child will know of it all soon enough, money and clothes to wash and a husband to feed.

"Ginny Sue is a little girl with no need of a man," she told that one that called himself Mark. It's not right for a grown man to take some young child from her home. She loved her brother Harv Pearson, yes she did, but he never should have took Tessy Brock from her home so young. Tessy didn't have time to be a child before she had a whole flock of her own. Mark, he couldn't fool her with that fancy way of talking. No sir, he was just like the rest, come into her house just waiting for her to leave the room so he could pull out that banjo and commence to playing them old senseless songs and to take a clean towel smelling of the good country air to wipe off himself. She can just see Mag Sykes gathering those towels and sheets in from the line. "I got to admit it, Miss Emily," Mag had said, her chin filled up with some dusty snuff. "I can't hardly bear to see no white sheets strung across a line." She stared down at them worn shoes of hers. "I can glance at it kind of quicklike, sideways, and it looks to me like them bad men coming with they torches and hoods and words of hate like them that killed my daddy."

"You ain't got to worry Mag," she said, thinking of Mag's daddy Curie Sykes. God, she loved old Curie too good. "I'd have it in my mind to kill one that set a foot in my yard."

"I ain't never heard you say such strongness." Mag turned her back on those sheets and towels blowing there against that wide blue sky, pecans soon to fall, put 'em in a tow sack.

"I ain't never felt such strongness," she said. "My James feels it, too."

Mag Sykes is welcome in her house but the others is not, them that come and take in their heads to mow through her shrubbery and to pile groceries all there through her house, pile fruits up there on the bed and swing some hams there in the bathroom where she bathed the children, where James would be bright and early with his face covered in lather and ready to shave while she was in that dark bed watching every move he made. They had no right to bring all that into her house. *It's not yours anymore*, they all say, *it's the Piggly Wiggly. Try to forget.* And how can somebody forget that? How can somebody forget that she had those violets there in the kitchen window where she washed umpteen dishes and her grandbabies, too? How can she forget that her mama is buried out there where people come and park cars and blow horns when there used to be nothing but a still breeze up in the branches.

She clicks on the TV and watches those gray people moving back and forth, a preacher carrying on with hellfire talk when she'd rather hear the talk of heaven, the talk of James and David and Tessy and her mama. She turns the sound down so that she can't hear it. Nobody can say a thing that interests her except them and the weatherman and Mag Sykes. But none of them are here, don't come too often, just that woman stretched out there on the sofa with her stomach all in that way that a woman ought not to show.

"Who are you?" she asks now and watches that woman,

her hair not even brushed out good, sit up a little and look at her. Finally the weatherman is on and she turns up the sound and watches every move of his little stick. There's a storm on the TV there, way down past Florida where Lena used to live. The man says that rain is likely to come but it'll be a few days. No sir, a few more days of dry hot sunshine, that corn stunted and burned, river bank dry and dusty as a bone.

* * *

"We got to have some rain," Curie had told her all those years ago, his big strong arms wrapped around her as he lifted her off the front porch and set her on the ground. "I'm praying for some rain, yes Lord, but if I had the power, I'd get out in that yard and dance a jig, do a rain dance."

"Do it, Curie," she told him and looked out over the yard where Lena was trying to pump water from that dried up well and Lena was going to get herself whipped good, there in the center of the yard and stripped down to her underwear. And Emily would've liked to be in her underwear but she was almost seven years old, too old for such. "Do a rain dance," she said again and laughed when Curie took off his old straw hat and lifted his knees up high like he was marching, raised his arms up and said, "Rain, rain, rain."

"Now, it's your turn," he said and winked at her, and she looked behind her through that front door to make sure her mama wasn't standing there, and she looked at Lena with her hands stuck up in the mouth of that pump, and she turned slowly at first, staring at the sky and then faster and faster, arms lifted, rain, rain, rain. "Dance yourself a jig, Miss Emily," Curie said. "Dance us up a storm."

And it rained. She can't remember if it was that day or the next, or the next week, but there came a storm that set the windows rattling, and lightning that filled the sky. "We might have to build us a ark," Curie said. "We all gonna float on down the Saxapaw whichever way it might go." And her mama came in soaked to the bone and her eyes wild as a trapped dog and her mama ran through the house and knelt there by the bed, shaking her head and looking at the ceiling.

"It's raining 'cause me and Curie did a dance," she told

her mother later when the thunder had stopped and there was just the steady sound of rain on that tin roof.

"It's raining because God means to make me tend to the living," her mother said. "You know better than to dance and carry on, Emily. The Lord's work is serious." And she nodded her head yes to her mother's words while she stood at the window and stared out at that front yard, the dusty dirt that she had swept clean now muddy; she watched Curie hurry down the road, his hands holding his hat on his head while he ran through that cool rain to his own home. "Last time I ask you to dance a jig," he had whispered to her before leaving, his dark face so warm next to hers.

* * *

"It's me, Gram," that woman says and Emily has to stare hard at her, think like she might be in school. "It's me, Gram. It's Ginny Sue."

"Well precious," she whispers. "I knew that was you."

"Gram? Gram?" Ginny Sue whispers now. "Tell me about Gramps, when you first married him, or when you had mama. Tell me about it."

"Well, I married him," she says. "And I had two babies. I had Hannah and then I had David and they both went through all the classes at school. I didn't get but to six."

"Were you ever unhappy?" Ginny Sue asks. "Were you ever sorry that you married Gramps?" That Ginny Sue, questions heaped on questions, why is the sky blue and the grass green and why do you like to make hogshead cheese and why did God make Gramps die and how could she have a Uncle David that she never even knew, and why can't I live in a big house like where Cindy lives and why can't I be a movie star like Lena and why can't I stay here with you, Gram, forever? And she has always had to tell that child that she just don't know all the answers, that she didn't get but to sixth, and she just doesn't know anything beyond what is in her heart and that God knows why and when he takes you to your home, it will all come clear to your mind or if it don't come clear it won't even matter because you will be able to walk on your legs that can't move and you will hear words spoken as clear as a bell on a still windless day and that river will never run dry, and the fields will stretch as far out as a body can see, and nobody will be able to hide his ugly face under a sheet and kill those that are good at heart, those that can call up a storm with a little dance. If it don't come clear, it won't matter none because you'll be at home where you belong.

"Gram? Were you ever unhappy?"

"No," she says. "James never caused me to hurt and I knew I had found the best, found the best this world could offer out to me."

"Always? You knew that always?"

"Always," she says and turns down the sound of the TV, the storm pictures gone now, just some man talking. Always, she repeats in her head. That's the song that Hannah had played on the piano and sang there after her high school graduation after Ben Turner went home. And David gave Hannah the prettiest picture he had painted of the Saxapaw River and had framed. He didn't like nobody outside of the family knowing he could do that, sing either, but the two of them sat there side by side on that piano bench, singing while she and James sat here on the sofa and listened. "I'll be loving you always," Hannah sang and Emily stared down at that fine diploma that James was still holding on his lap. "With a love that's true, always."

"James never made me unhappy," she says and changes the channel, then turns the set off. Perry Mason has got old, too old to walk.

"You are breaking my heart, James," she had told him and he let go of that leather belt there in his hand and let it slip to the floor, the buckle making a noise like a bucket in a dry well there on the kitchen floor. "David is a grown man now. He's just graduated high school and he can make his own decisions."

"I wasn't going to hit him," James said and tried to hand her his handkerchief that Mag had bleached out so white. "Why is it that white sounds so clean and colored don't," Mag had asked her and they laughed. There was no soul on earth cleaner than Mag Sykes, her face scrubbed shiny clean with soap, her heart pure as heaven. She didn't take his handkerchief but put her face in her hands.

"I just want to talk some sense into him is all," James said. "I'm all for him joining the service, but why can't he do like Ben? Why can't he join in a way that'll keep him right here in the country? Why does he want to be such a daredevil? Doesn't know the first thing about flying." James tried to pull her hands away from her face but she turned away. "He's being foolish, Emily. Tell him. Tell him that you think he's a fool."

"He wants to learn to fly," Emily said. "He wants to learn so when he gets out he can go to school and be an engineer."

"Like Roy Carter," James said, staring down at that belt. "Roy has filled his head up with all this, with words that nobody else knows, so let Roy send him to school. He's already had twelve years."

"Things are different now," she said and she wanted to hug him, to pull him close but she felt her backbone go stiff as a board. Things are different; those were David's words. "Why can't he just accept that I want something else?" David had asked her, his bare arms so tan and muscled. "I don't want to follow in his footsteps. I don't want my whole life riding on a crop of tobacco, riding on the wind and weather."

"What's different," James said, "is he's ashamed of me, ashamed and determined to be anything except like me." And she rinsed that sink full of bitter tomatoes like there was no tomorrow, like she couldn't get that shiny red skin clean enough of garden dust. "I think he's ashamed of both of us." James turned off the faucet and gripped her wet hands. "He probably wishes you were Lena," he said. "But he does seem to listen to what you say." He pressed her hands harder between his own. "Why won't you tell him? Why are you afraid to tell him that he's making a mistake?"

"How do I know?" she screamed, staring at her hands pressed between his, her hands so small next to his. "You are killing me, both of you," she sobbed, dropped her chin, determined not to look at him until he let her go. "This arguing. You are killing me piece by piece." He let go of her hands and she stepped back and faced him. "He's smart, James, smarter than me. You could have done as good as Roy if you had had the chance. Look how much further you've come than your own daddy."

"I only picked up where my daddy left it all," he said. "I have never felt ashamed of him."

"He's not ashamed."

"I don't care what he is, Emily. I've had it," he said and left the room while she arranged the tomatoes carefully on the drain board. "I don't care what he says," David had said. "It's my life!" They might as well have roped her legs and taken off in different directions.

"Gram?" Ginny Sue is asking now. "Did you always feel close to Gramps?"

"Oh yes," she says and turns the set back on. "I always did."

* * *

"Get Billy! Get Billy!" that old woman screams and it doesn't matter how many times Lena tells her to shut the hell up, she doesn't and the nurse teacher calls Lena down for that.

"We don't fight with children here at school, Lena Pearson," the third-year teacher had said and sent her to sit in the corner and that was fine, she'd sit in the corner until she dropped dead; she'd sit in a corner until a big old black snake came up from the floor and choked her and then that teacher would have to call Lena's mama and tell that she had killed Lena.

"Mama is going to be so upset," Emily said when she stopped by Lena's chair on her way to recess. "You are not taught fighting at home."

"Don't tell," Lena begged. "I'll never fight here in the school house again if you won't tell Mama." And she knew Emily wouldn't tell, and she knew that she'd catch up with that Lily Moore one afternoon after school was let out and whip her good. She did. Whipped Lily Moore good, slapped her face and left a print. "Call my daddy a nigger-lover again," Lena said, her dress hiked up so she could straddle Lily Moore's stomach. "I'll whip you every day for the rest of your life."

* * *

"She wants Billy and not this doll," Lena tells the nurse teacher. "I can have this baby. I can."

"We'll get you one," nurse teacher says. "I'll tell your niece that you want a baby of your own."

"Oh no," she whispers. "You can't ever tell I want a baby." And she lets nurse teacher take her over by the Pepsi-Cola machine and sit down. All she wants is to care for that baby, clean them dirty panties, nice dry panties. She just

wants to hold that baby up there to her bosom like she held
Pooh and felt that growl there against her chest. You a sweet
kitty Pooh kitty, oh poor poor Pooh baby.

* * *

"You can't tell that I can't have a baby," she had told Roy
and they were in the side yard there in Florida and feeling
that ocean breeze, looking at her name there in that worn out
Broadway program. Her name on that piece of paper didn't
make her laugh like it used to. "Don't tell that I can't have
babies."

"You can't help it," Roy said and those frogs were croak-
ing and carrying on like the world was coming to an end.
"We could adopt a child."

"No," she shook her head. "Then they'd know. They'd
know that I can't." She fanned herself with the program, her
body still young and smooth-looking, and no reason, no reason as to why she'd be all dried up with nothing there where
it was supposed to be. "Tessy would love hearing that I can't
have a baby, love the fact that she's got a yardful of dirty
children and I can't even have one."

"What about Emily?" he asked. "You can tell her."

"No, no, I can't," she said. "Emily'd think less of me."
She leaned forward with her head on her knees and cried.
"It's like I'm not even a woman."

"No, no that's not true," he said. "You're more of a
woman than any of the others."

"Don't tell," she whispered and waited for him to nod.
"Promise me, and don't you stay here with me if you take
in your mind to find yourself a young woman."

"Lena, baby," he said and walked over, sat on the end of
her lawn chair, reached his hands out to her, hands she had
imagined building her a fine crib, a little playhouse that other
children would turn green over when they saw it. "I just want
you," he said but she could see behind all of that, see the
disappointment there. He was going to leave her; she knew
he was going to leave her.

"Don't touch me there, Roy," she said and cried. "I just
can't bear to be touched." She was so afraid that he was
going to leave her. Any woman with any sense would want
him and she'd have to let him go, let those baby kittens go to
good homes 'cause they've got so many cats living up there

under the house to meow so loud and to drink up all the milk.

* * *

"Roy's gonna leave me," she tells nurse teacher who is there now, making her pull herself up straight; nurse gives her that doll to hold. "Is this my baby now?"

"For a little while," nurse teacher says. "You can share it."

"Can't share a baby," she says and laughs, pulls its little face up against her breast. "King Solomon done that to find the mama. He said 'well sir, we'll just saw this baby in half' and the real mama, she said 'oh no, let her take him then' and that's how they know the real mama. The real mama don't let no flea stay there in the fur." Nurse teacher smiles at her now, pretty woman if she was smaller and would buy herself some little red shoes. She names the baby Cord Pearson Carter after her daddy and she rocks him there. He's a tired little baby, a sweet baby, oh poor little tired baby. "Oh no," she says, "Let her take him then." And she points to that old woman down the hall. "She can take him if it'll keep him from being sawed in half. I'm the real mama."

* * *

Cindy goes to work early on Monday morning just so she'll have a little time to herself before Constance Ann and everybody else gets there. Now she's sorry that she had Constance Ann over to spend the night, sorry that Constance Ann saw her cry, afraid that Constance Ann is going to think she was crying over Charles Snipes and now will ask a million and one questions. The Charles Snipeses of this world are a dime a dozen and so are the Buzz Biggerses and the Randy Skinners.

She sits down at her VDT and calls up that little secret file of hers that she keeps hidden, a file that she named "AB" because Constance Ann is squeamish about blood and therefore, wouldn't bother herself to look. Even if anybody did, it wouldn't matter, because Cindy has put all kinds of little signs and symbols at the beginning of the file there and then has a long list of big medical blood words. She runs the screen past all of that, past all of her book titles, past the list of addresses and phone numbers of men that she thinks are right cute. She doesn't do anything with those numbers, of course, because most of those men are married; still you never know when one will divorce, happens all the time. She runs past the addresses, down and past her period chart that she set up for herself so she'll always know when she's due.

When she gets past that, she makes a new heading: REASONS WHY CHARLES SNIPES SHOULD NOT MARRY NANCY PRICE. She has been thinking of these reasons all weekend:

1. Nancy Price wears her hair like an old woman.
2. If they have a child, it will have great big ears.
3. Nancy Price is way out of style.
4. Nancy Price has a sister that does drugs.
5. Nancy Price has a sister that can't sing.
6. Charles Snipes needs a woman in step with the world because he is not.
7. Nancy Price is not in step with the world.

"You're here early," Constance Ann says and Cindy zooms that file up to the top where she has all of her blood words. "What are you working on?"

"The blood data," Cindy says. "Sometimes I don't think I'll ever finish it. I could use some help but I know how you feel about blood words."

"Can't stand to even type them out," Constance Ann says and bites into a huge apple fritter that she has wrapped in a napkin. "It makes me sick to hear those words."

"Words like coagulate?"

"Stop!" Constance Ann looks at her, that big fritter an inch from her mouth. "I'm trying to eat a little breakfast."

"Is that what that is?" Cindy asks. "I thought it was a frisbee."

"Oh ha ha." Constance Ann walks around to her desk. "You're one to be talking after the way you were falling apart the other night."

"Constance Ann, let's drop it. I don't ask you to help with the blood data, do I?" Cindy stands up and leans over her desk so Constance Ann will have to look at her. "I have seniority and I could make you type some blood data but I don't because you are my friend."

"Well, the quiz did say . . ."

"And the quiz was exactly right," Cindy says, Constance Ann with her mouth dropped open, ready for some more fritter but too surprised to bite it. "I always take the quizzes and I believe they tell the truth."

"Why didn't you say that the other night, then?"

"I had a bad night is all and I took it out on you because you are my friend."

"Thanks, Cindy," Constance Ann says and looks like she might cry. "And thanks for not making me type all that stuff."

"You're welcome," Cindy says and sits back down. "Just so you never accidentally have to see those words, the blood data file is named AB."

"Well, I'll never open that one," Constance Ann says, her words mumbled up with fritter.

"You can if you want, but you know I thought I'd warn you." Cindy zooms back to the end of the file when she hears Constance Ann typing.

8. Nancy Price probably takes quizzes which is stupid.
9. Charles Snipes is used to better.
10. Charles Snipes has a son with acne who needs his father to spend time with him.

By the end of the day, Cindy has a list as long as her leg, and is tired of staring at the VDT and listening to Constance Ann. Thank God she doesn't have some man expecting her to get home and cook dinner because she is too tired; she'll swing by Kentucky Fried and get her and Chuckie some snak paks, but first she stops at old Emily's to check on Ginny Sue.

Ginny Sue is still all propped up and looking out of it, Emily watching that damned TV with no sound and that hick woman Esther in the kitchen.

"Hey girl," Cindy says and squats on the floor beside Ginny Sue. Ginny Sue turns and opens her eyes, asks what time it is. "Monday," Cindy says. "The day is Monday and the month is July. You'd have a shitload of trouble if you had to talk to a shrink right now."

"I'm tired," Ginny says.

"I know you are, baby," Emily whispers and then turns

on Cindy. "Why don't you walk on to where you're walking?"

"I came to ask Ginny Sue a question is all," Cindy says and now she doesn't even feel like talking to Ginny Sue, doesn't even feel like telling how Charles Snipes is planning to get married. Nobody cares. Nobody gives a damn what is going on in her life. Ginny Sue has been a touch sick and you'd think it was Armageddon.

"What do you want to ask me?"

"I want to ask you why you don't wake up and prop yourself up a little, brush your hair and put on some cheek color?"

"Because she has good sense," Emily says and points that remote at Cindy like it might be a laserbeam gun.

"I haven't felt like fixing up," Ginny Sue says. "They told me to lie flat."

"Well, then tell me this." Cindy pauses, jingling her car keys. "Why is it that you see couples who look like they don't go together? You know what I mean and you say, 'what is that Don Johnson hunk doing with *her*' because she is not as attractive as he could do."

"Because pretty is as pretty does," Emily says and turns the set on and up loud. Cindy wishes somebody would take that damn gadget away from her.

"You never know what that person is really like," Ginny Sue mumbles. "You might think you know somebody and then you don't. You don't know them at all."

"Well, I do," Cindy says, meaning that she does know Charles Snipes; she knows him better than Nancy Price, knows him better than anybody, but all this mumbling is getting her nowhere. It's just making her more depressed and thank God it's a good TV show night. This place, Ginny Sue included, is as depressing as her mama's house. Cindy sees Hannah drive up and decides to go ahead and leave so that she doesn't get stuck talking to her. "I'll see you," she says and heads to the door.

"Thanks for stopping by, Cindy," Ginny Sue says. "Sorry I wasn't good company."

"Oh now, you're good company," Emily says. "I've always said that you were good company to have."

"And what about me?" Cindy asks and looks right at Emily.

"You need to press your slacks," that old biddy says and

Cindy slams the door behind her, tells Hannah she'd love to stay and talk but that she has a million things to do.

She gets in her car and heads to Kentucky Fried, feeling so mad. Nobody ever says anything that's nice to her. Her daddy is the only family member who ever called attention to how good-looking she is. "Your mother's family is queer," he had told her. "They are the strangest people you'll ever meet and you're better off without them." He was probably right about that, probably right about Charles Snipes. She could do better. She will do better, but it still pisses her off that everywhere she goes people are coupled up. There's a couple of teenagers hanging out in the parking lot and they are all smooched up like she used to do with Charles Snipes. The boy is in a KFC suit and the girl is wearing a miniskirt which she's too big to wear. Cindy could wear it.

Tables for two all over that Kentucky Fried place and it pisses her off. Just once she'd like to see a table for one. "Two Snaks, white meat," she says and stands there waiting, listens to the couple in line behind her, a kiss on the cheek, the little gasp of a hug. She hears the man whisper something that sounds like "cooter clam" in the woman's ear and Cindy turns around and stares at them. Now, they look like they belong together. He's big and burly and she's got all this wild frosted hair.

"You'll have to forgive what he said," the woman tells Cindy. "We are on kind of a holiday for the night. It's our anniversary."

"That's nice," Cindy says, wondering why in the hell anybody on a holiday would come to Saxapaw and eat at KFC.

"You have got the prettiest headful of hair," the woman says and smiles at Cindy. "Hair is my business and I'll swan if you don't have a nice headful."

"Thanks," Cindy says, and she feels like she'd like to stay and talk to them, be on a holiday with them, but her chicken is up and she knows Chuckie is sitting at home waiting. She gives the girl her money and turns back around. "You know I was scared to try this hairdo but I'm glad I did."

"Oh yes," the woman says and squeezes that man tight. "You're little enough to carry it off. That's natural blonde too, isn't it?"

"She's a bottle blonde," the man says and squeezes back on his "cooter clam."

"Well, have fun," Cindy says and leaves, watching them in the reflection of the door. She envies them and it pisses her off. The woman says, "I love thighs" and he says, "I love breasts" and the two fall together and laugh like they might be in high school. God, Cindy wishes she was back in high school.

PART IV

Virginia's hours are all confused; when it's dark and still, she is wide awake tossing, turning; and when daylight appears in Gram's window, she is too tired to open her eyes. The days seem to bleed and run, meals and game shows, cramps and weather reports and tick after tick of the clock. It is morning, Thursday morning, but when she tries to put the days in order, when Mark came, when he called, it seems like one long day with bright hot light through the window and no rain.

She concentrates on the ticking, the clock, so out of place in the duplex. It used to be in the wide hallway of the house on Carver Street, there by the stairs on the pine floors that Gram painted brown every other spring. Gram would hide presents and snacks on top of the clock where Virginia and Robert couldn't reach them.

"If that clock ever stops," Cindy had told her once, Virginia only six, "Aunt Emily will die just like on 'The Twilight Zone.' "

"No." Virginia shook her head. "Stop it!"

* * *

"What honey?" Esther peeks around the corner from the kitchen and Virginia shakes her head. "You're starting to act like her," Esther says and points to Gram who is dozing in the Lazy Boy.

* * *

"It's just a TV show," her brother, Robert, had told her after Cindy left and he found her sitting there in front of the clock, watching the pendulum, thinking if it started to slow down that she would very quickly turn the little key, open that glass door and push it back and forth, back and forth until someone came to fix it. Robert had sat beside her, his long legs tan and skinny, the Saxapaw Junior Baseball jersey that it seems he wore for years. "I mean it Ginny Sue," he said, those clear brown eyes squinting with his smile. "You've got to learn to fight back. I'm not always gonna be around to take up for you."

"I know." She nodded but it seemed that he would always be there; it seemed that they would always eat Sunday dinner with Gram in the house on Carver Street. It seemed she would always be able to run into his room if she got scared at night, that they would always race to see who could get to the bathroom first when they got up in the mornings. They would always sit in those same chairs at the kitchen table and read the backs of the cereal boxes while their mother packed school lunches. They would sit on his bed those rare nights it snowed, the drapes pulled back so they could see by the streetlight while the flakes got bigger and bigger, the yard finally covered in a film of white. "No school tomorrow," he'd say, hope in his voice. And they would get up the next morning, tired from no sleep but urged by the slight flakes still falling. She would sit with her knees pulled up under that long flannel gown while her mother scrambled eggs or pressed seams, and they listened to the radio, listened for cancellations, Saxapaw Schools.

"I just can't stay around here, Ginny," he had told her years later, his legs filled out, a fraternity sweatshirt on, as he sat in a lawn chair, frayed green and white webbing, and twirled a long-handled fork while the steaks dripped into the fire, sizzling and flaming, her dad in the garden, cap pulled low, Mama on the screened porch smocking the tops of tiny christening gowns that people ordered from her as soon as they got home from that first doctor visit. It seemed there would always be steaks on Saturday nights and Sundays on Carver Street with Gram, family vacations to the beach when they returned salty and sunburned, a present of peanut brittle for Gram. "Now how did you know just what I wanted?" Gram asked while she rubbed Virginia's sunburned back with Jergens.

"Take good care of her," Robert said, shook Mark's hand,

the wedding cake looming in the background like a miniature castle. "It's not such a hard job; I've had it for twenty-five years." Susie was hugging Virginia, the two of them laughing, Cindy off to the side sipping champagne, mimicking Susie whenever she could catch Virginia's eye. "She's real gullible," Robert was saying, Mark laughing and acting like he was taking notes. "She won't go to the bathroom by herself at night; you have to go with her and turn on all the lights, stand outside the door until she's through."

"Not true!" Virginia screamed while Robert wrapped his big arms around her and hugged.

* * *

Water runs in the kitchen, glasses clinking into the drain board, clock ticking, Gram breathing. All the movements, every little sound so clear. If Virginia closes her eyes, she could be anywhere, anywhere at all. It is inertia that makes Gram's mind wander, roaming back and forth, up and down the streets of the country before they were paved, before Virginia was born. It isn't age that makes it all confusing but inertia.

"You could go home," her mother had said. "To our house I mean."

"Easier here," she mumbled and dozed, comfortably surrounded by the heavy dark furniture, faint mothball smells from the closets where quilts are piled like a mountain, the sounds, Gram's whispered words, so soothing like the house on Carver Street, making Mark and the rented house seem so far away.

* * *

"Bad, bad old dreams," Gram had said and lifted her up, hugged her close. "You're right here with Gram, sweets," and the cars on Carver Street passed and turned, circles of light and she listened to the clock while Gram lay beside her and whispered a prayer, all of the words to all of the prayers. "You needn't worry, Ginny Sue. Gram's right here."

* * *

"I can't stay," she had told Bryan Parker. "I'm sorry but it would be a mistake."

"How long have you felt this way?" Bryan Parker asked,

with the stunned expression that she can't forget. "Why didn't you tell me sooner?" *Why did you wait until now to tell me?* She rode on the bus until Atlanta was just a sign by the side of the road.

* * *

"Put your little bag there on the seat beside you," Gram had said when she was leaving for Camp Tonawanda. She didn't want to go to Camp Tonawanda but her parents wanted her to, her parents had all the pictures from Cindy's brochure, horses and nature trails and a clear mountain lake. "Then nobody will sit beside you."

"It's a rainy night in Georgia," the bus driver sang and laughed. *Carolina moon keep shining.* "Sit there behind the driver, baby," Gram said. "Don't take candy from strangers," Lena said. "Have a wonderful, wonderful time," and her mother pulled Virginia's hair up and out of the collar of her new go-to-camp outfit, pastel plaid seersucker shorts with a bib and a pink tee shirt.

* * *

The ride from Georgia took hours and Cindy was in the Saxapaw station waiting under the glare of those bright fluorescent lights. "Look at you now," Cindy said. "The bride of whatever fallen. Isn't that a book?"

* * *

If you mess up you can paint right over it, or you can strip it away, coat by coat, dissolving, diluting; you can vacuum that mess. She had painted the same canvas over and over, kept messing up, had to start over. Bryan Parker went to work and she painted a bride from behind, the church doors opened outward, looming large and heavy in the foreground, the bride a fuzzy blur of white midway on that narrowing aisle, blurred faces in bright summer colors filling the pews like dots. But when that was all dry, she painted condos, rigid brick structures with a yardful of dirt, no trees, miniblinds and a fierce dark sky. Then she left and she painted a night sky, no stars, the glare of a Trailways bus sign, small brick building, a Coke machine glaring red beside a woman dressed in brown sitting on a bench, her legs splayed, face lifeless. She was at home then, back in her childhood room, easel by the window, and she painted an old establishment that then was long deserted; something she remembered from going to Gram's old house as a child, a little cinderblock building at the far end of Pecan Avenue right near the tracks, where people had gone for years to get bootleg liquor and various other things. There were two black men that were always out front in straight-back chairs, their feet propped up on old washtubs; one picked a banjo. "Cutty's Place" was spray painted on the front of the building and Cutty, though long dead, was the big black woman who owned the house and kept her liquor hidden somewhere while there were always baskets of butterbeans out front in the summer with a for sale sign and dolls with dresses made of bits of pastel foam so that they'd sit on a bed like a pillow.

Virginia always wanted one of those dolls. She always wanted her mother to stop at Cutty's and let her go up and touch those dolls, pink and white like a birthday cake doll. "Lock your door," her mother would say and drive by without once turning her head towards Cutty's Place.

Virginia had seen Cutty out there once, a large black woman in a faded pink floral dress that looked like it was a real expensive church dress at one time. Her hair was pulled back and she was fanning herself with one of those oriental fans like they used to have at the dime store and she was arranging those dolls on a card table out front. Men were playing horseshoes under a large pecan tree. That's how she painted Cutty's, from memory, the large black woman arranging those dolls, a horseshoe in midpitch, a pale summer sky, the bare dusty dirt beneath the pecan tree, a blue Mercedes parked on the corner, so out of place, the timing all wrong and it seemed that the painting should be split down the middle, the same way that Saxapaw could have been split down the middle at one time, the old part and the new part, until the old finally fell away. The old family farms, fields and sky, distorted by a bright red and yellow Burger King sign.

* * *

That's what the canvas looked like when Virginia had a small showing of her work at the Saxapaw YMCA. "It would do you good to get out of the house," her mother had said. "It would be a good reason for you to shave your legs."

"Why did you put my car in the picture?" a woman that Virginia didn't even know had asked. "I am the only person in Saxapaw that drives a Mercedes and I *never* went to Cutty's Place. I never even drove down that street if I could help it."

"I don't even know you," Virginia said.

"Well, you must." The woman pulled ten dollars out of her billfold and held it there, shook it. "Here, I'll buy it. I don't want anybody else to see it."

"This one isn't for sale," Virginia said and pointed to her smaller paintings, floral watercolors and ink-sketched farmhouses. "But those are."

"Why are you doing this to me?" the woman persisted, her face so red against her dark Joan of Arc haircut.

"It has nothing to do with you." Virginia looked away from those hard blue eyes, glanced over to where Cindy was sitting on the floor, listening and laughing. "It's representative," Virginia continued, feeling that she owed an explanation. "It's a kind of place, a kind of car, each dating the other."

"Well, it isn't any good."

Cindy stepped up, her hands in the back pockets of her cutoffs. "It's better than those country chickens that you crossstitch and sell for an arm and a leg."

"Who are you?" The woman turns and stares at Cindy.

"Never mind who I am," Cindy said. "My mama bought one of your cross-stitched robins, though, and I had to ask what it was. I mean who do you think you are, that man, Ginny Sue, what's the bird man's name?"

"Audubon."

"Yeah, who do you think you are, him?" Cindy rubbed her finger over the wheel of the Mercedes. "This is art. Your birds are arts and crafts and not good ones at that." The woman turned and hurried off, her canvas bag swinging behind here, and Virginia sat down on the floor beside the painting. She didn't know whether to laugh or cry.

"Thanks Cindy," she said. "I needed some help."

"Aw, you could've just told her where to go. She thinks she's hot shit because she used to live somewhere like Idaho. She probably used to cross-stitch potatoes." Cindy had rubbed her fingers over the letters of Cutty's Place and laughed. "That robin Mama bought really doesn't look like a robin. I don't know what it looks like but not a robin. I do have to tell you though," Cindy paused, her face serious. "I don't see why you paint such sights as this. I mean I don't want a retarded-looking robin on my wall but I don't want black men pitching horseshoes, either." She paused again and stared at Virginia. "I mean no offense but a picture ought to make you feel good."

"Why?" Virginia asked and leaned her head against the easel.

"I don't know." Cindy shrugged. "I'd like to see you paint the ocean with lots of shells around and me and Buzz stretched out on a big Budweiser towel there by the water."

"I don't know if I can do that."

"Sure you can! You're getting better and better all the time."

"Well."

"Really, I do have faith in what you do," Cindy said and helped her pick up the other paintings and wrap them up. "Didn't sell a one did you?" Virginia shook her head. "Well, don't feel bad. I mean as soon as you work up to fruit and bottles and religious stuff, you'll sell them faster than hotcakes."

* * *

Virginia opens her eyes to see Esther standing there with a spatula. "I said do you want some hotcakes?" Esther asks and places her other hand, grease-coated, against Virginia's forehead. "Still got a fever and I never can remember if you're to feed or starve the fever."

"Starve, I think," Virginia says, the thought of pancakes and butter and syrup making her sick.

"My daddy died of fever," Gram says. "And I had a sister that starved right in front of my mama's eyes; she got the pneumonia she was so thin. 'Eat just a taste,' Mama would say and leave a tray of food there by her bed and not a bite touched."

"Better speak up," Esther says over Gram's story. "The kitchen is gonna be closed real soon now," and Virginia shakes her head. Now, Esther is back in the kitchen, radio tuned to country, Dolly Parton, Mama's run off with my traveling man.

* * *

"Hurry up," her daddy had yelled, sitting in front of the TV on a Sunday afternoon. "Dolly's gonna sing one without Porter." And Virginia had come over to watch, her Barbie all dressed up to go to the prom with Ken. Cindy said her Barbie with the twist 'n turn waist was going to a shindig and wasn't going to take a thing to put over her bathing suit.

"Dolly sure is cute, isn't she?" her daddy asked and Virginia didn't like for him to say that people other than her mama were cute.

"Not as cute as mama," she said and Cindy laughed great big and then covered her mouth. Dolly was singing "Coat of Many Colors."

"I gave you that shirt you're wearing, Ginny Sue," Cindy said and her Barbie doll did a split. "My daddy says that this kind of music is for the simple-minded," and she crawled back over to where she had her shindig all set up, a background of Coke bottles.

"Lord, this is a tearjerker," her mama said and wiped her eyes, looked at Virginia's daddy and they laughed.

"The shindig is starting up," Cindy had called, flat on her stomach with her knees bent up and her feet going back and forth. "I want your Barbie to come and sell the hot dogs." You'll sell 'em faster than hotcakes. Hot cakes and syrup and butter; the tigers run faster and faster around that tree, Little Black Sambo way up there in the limbs and the tigers run until they turn to butter and Little Black Sambo's mama gets that butter and puts it on the pancakes. Run run fast as you can, tiger tiger burning bright. Nothing was loud enough or fast enough, not Roses, not the shindig, way down yonder in New Orleans wild cats jump on the sewing machines, sew so fast, so so fast, couldn't get on that bus in Georgia fast enough, driver couldn't drive fast enough. Her chest was tight, so tight the heartbeats couldn't get through and she wanted it to beat, she wanted that sucker to beat like insanity so loud it rang in her ears, she wanted music, music so loud it made her chest hurt, vibrate and her head—goddamn, she wanted her whole body to pulse and throb and spin around and around in a circle, whirring and whirring, fly away home—she wanted to be on a subway nonstop express, faster and faster, so fast that the speed holds you upright, inert while the world flies by, bobbling, bumping, blending, graffiti and lights so fast that it blurs, it's all a blur. Run like hell for miles and miles,

run fast fly home, fly north, fly south for winter spring summer and fall, but don't fall, just don't fall till your legs get
heavy numb like rubber and your heart beats till you can't
breathe, sand that wood, sand it hard and feel it when it digs
in your hands; the shindig has started and you ain't here 'cause
you ain't the first, just ain't the first; you'd run if you could
move your legs, slow and then fast fast spinning, spin goddamnit before it all stops and cry if you have to, cry, you can
cry if you try, you can cry.

* * *

"I have never seen such a to-do over a period," Gram says
now and Virginia opens her eyes, those heavy yellow shades
over there too big for the duplex window, overlapping the
sill.

"Period," Esther laughs, her face like it's in the frame of
the mirror over Gram's buffet. "Honey, she's pregnant. I wish
Hannah would hurry up because I need to get home."

It feels better if Virginia closes her eyes, sick and dizzy,
round and round, lips clamped against that spoonful of pancakes and syrup that Esther is holding.

"She's got to eat more," Gram says. "Might need some
fluids." Gram has stories about starving, the one that she
would always tell if Virginia and Robert weren't eating their
meal.

"I had a sister who starved," Gram would say. "Wasted
away. My mama said it started real slowlike the way she
wouldn't eat but would pick little meat scraps from somebody
else's plate when she cleaned the table. Then, she stopped
altogether, stopped eating and died, wasn't but thirteen. She
had pneumonia."

"Sounds like anorexia nervosa," Cindy had said once when
the story was told. "I have to type that all the time and so I
know all about it."

* * *

"I never missed my time of the month," Gram says and
Virginia opens her eyes to see her mother there, a glass of
water in her hand. And she lifts Virginia's head and puts the
cool glass against her lips.

"I told Esther not to feed you anything rich," her mama

says. "You were doing so much better yesterday. I think I'll call the doctor."

"I only missed my time when I was carrying," Gram says. "We never discussed such. I told Esther to fix up some hotcakes. I told her that whenever Ginny Sue comes out here to spend the night with me that's what she wants for breakfast before we walk to the store."

"This is different now, Mama," Virginia's mother says, slowly, patiently. "Ginny is pregnant."

"I wouldn't discuss it," Gram says.

"I know." Virginia's mama holds the glass while she drinks, so good and cool against her throat. "Madge is the one that told me about everything and she didn't know much."

"Madge shouldn't have told," Gram says. "Tessy would whip her good if she knew."

"It's a good thing she did tell me something or I'd have been scared to death of a period."

"Hush now, I would've told you when the time was right."

"When?" her mama asks and places a cool wet cloth on Virginia's forehead. "After the fact, like Lena?" Her mama laughs; Virginia knows that story, that story of how Lena thought she was dying, the way Lena flung herself down on the bed and screamed that she was dying, call a doctor, call a preacher, pray to God because she was bleeding to death.

"Gram asked Felicia for a Kotex," Virginia whispers, feels her lips spreading into a smile when she thinks of it. "She told Felicia that she didn't know if she had ever needed one because of what people say about her."

"Mama, did you? Ginny Sue, why didn't you tell me that before now?"

"I didn't think of it," she says. "It was just earlier."

"Today? Mama did that today?" her mother asks, the daybed sloping when her mama sits down.

"Right before Felicia came and brought the nurse," she says, no noises from the kitchen. "I told Felicia I was sorry."

"Today is Thursday," her mama says, "That was Friday, almost a week ago. Now, I've got to call and apologize to her for that."

"A week?" Virginia asks. Yes, a week. She left that rented house almost a week ago and she hasn't even missed it. Her mama smells like Prell and Spic 'n Span.

"I'm going to call Felicia," her mama says. "I'm going to call her right now. And when you're feeling better, I think you should write her a thank-you card for coming over here and helping you. She's the one that brought dinner over here last night, too."

"She's that way but she's good," Gram says. "Another woman that way will be lucky to marry her."

"She is good," Virginia's mama says. "And it's nobody's business what way she might be."

* * *

"You should write those thank-you cards just as soon as you receive the gift," her mama had said when presents started arriving for Virginia and Bryan Parker. "Some people go off on a long honeymoon and you don't find out until six or seven months later that they even got what you sent."

It was only May then but it seemed like dog days, the sun searing that asphalt that surrounded the condos, the heavy lifeless air hanging like a blanket of stillness, stifling stagnated stillness. The wedding was only three weeks away and it was the heat that brought the realization; it would catch her off guard and make her shake her head reproachfully, then leave her as limp and lifeless as the air.

The afternoon light came through those miniblinded-will-not-open-modern windows in a thin dust-flecked plane and cast distorted images of the window on that brand new plastic-smelling simulated brick congoleum. A stack of unwritten thank-you notes were beside the empty coffee cups where she had put them early that morning, the classified section of the paper, a big big paper, *The Atlanta Constitution*, fine newsprint that says no word of how the folks are doing in Saxapaw, if it has rained in Saxapaw. "That newsprint is getting all over the counter," Bryan Parker had said, tall as a mountain with that thick straight hair, bushy eyebrows. Newsprint is sterile, you can have a baby in a piece of it, wrap it up and put it in the bullrushes. "You'd do better to go to a job agency," he told her. "Call the school board," and he had nuzzled her neck in a way that made her feel like she was standing in the doorway watching it all.

Don't put off till tomorrow what you can do today. And the power saw that was leveling all of the trees across the asphalt was saying "for the rest of your life, for the rest of your life."

* * *

"Today is the first day of the rest of your life," that girl with straight orange hair had said in the school cafeteria.

"Who the shit cares?" Cindy asked while that girl's face turned the same shade as her hair.

"Jesus loves you," the girl said.

"Everybody does." Cindy twisted her hips, carried her tray down the line to desserts. "When you are a child, you speak like a child and now it's time to put those toys away. That's in the Bible and you should listen to it."

"I will fear no evil," the girl said and followed Cindy.

"Psalm 23. You can't say a verse I don't know," Cindy said and put her tray on the table. "You act like you're the first to ever hear of Jesus."

"I'm only trying to save you," the girl said and looked at Virginia. It sent a chill down her spine the way that girl's eyes were so hard. "One way," she said, still looking at Virginia, one finger pointed upward.

"Jesus wept!" Cindy yelled when the girl had gone and sat down by herself at a table in the corner. "Swaddling clothes! Saw that baby in half! Daniel in the lion's den! A camel in the eye of a needle! You take the high road and I'll take the low road and I'll be in heaven before you." All the people around their table laughed and after Cindy had twisted around and nodded to everybody, she turned to Virginia. "Thanks a lot, Ginny Sue," she said. "You really helped me a lot. Thank you so much from the very bottom of my heart."

* * *

"One way," Virginia had said when she bought that bus ticket from Atlanta. But that was after the thank-you notes, a week after she wrote the notes. "Dear Mrs. Jones," she wrote. "Thank you for the tupperware tumblers that you were so kind to give me along with the shower." It made her cringe to think of the shower, the advice: how to fix a peanut butter and jelly sandwich, how to boil water, "if he has butter in the fridge, he won't look for margarine on the street," can't get pregnant? get him to wear boxers. She wanted to tell a Tarzan/Jane/Cheetah/banana joke. Cindy would have done that. Cindy would have said, "What's gray and comes in quarts? Give up? Do you give up? An elephant. Ha Ha Ha.''

"Dear Mrs. Jones," she wrote, that power saw like it was drilling a hole in her head. "I had a horrible time; I hate these tumblers. My butter is in the fridge and it might stay there till it curdles.''

"Dear friends of Bryan Parker's mama's second cousin by divorce, thank you for the bottle of Blue Nun, a bit too sweet for my palate, but sweet is as sweet does and you were *so sweet*! I'm going to drink it all right now as it is feverishly hot outside and chillingly cool in my condo. My thermostat is busted.''

"I can't believe you'd sit here in the middle of the day and get drunk," Bryan Parker had said, but that was before he knew the truth. *I can't believe you waited this long to tell me*. Mark will shake his head and stare at the floor.

"What is wrong?" Bryan Parker had asked and she shook her head, stared at the floor.

"I'll be fine once I throw up," she told him and made her way to the bathroom.

"Vomit will rot your teeth," Cindy had told her once. "I figure Jane Fonda must have gotten hers capped because she used to be bulemic. I know all about it.''

* * *

"I just Fonda-ed," Cindy says. "That's why I'm running around in tights, okay?" Virginia opens her eyes to see Cindy there with her hair pulled up in a high ponytail and a purple leotard cut low. "I was hoping you'd wake up," she says. "I've been scared you were going to get as boring as the rest.''

"She's sick," Madge says from the other side of the room, a white uniform, hot pink can of Tab in her hand. "Been over there sweating and kicking; Hannah said she was sick to her stomach earlier.''

"Don't surprise me," Gram says. "The TV says those things that young women are sticking into themselves during that time can cause a fever that can kill.''

"Toxic shock," Cindy says. "I once thought I had a touch of the toxic shock only to find out that I had a touch of salmonella. It was right after I ate a piece of chicken at Mama's house.''

"Blackberries will cure the diarrhea," Gram says. "And a slice of onion under your arm will cure the vomiting."

"Lord, the medical community would laugh you into tomorrow," Cindy says. "Eternal B.O. That's what somebody with onions in their pits would have."

"You can laugh all you want," Gram says. "I could have helped Ginny Sue with those onions and Hannah wouldn't let me. I can regulate the bleeding, too. Cayenne pepper will regulate a period."

"My cycle was never regular," Madge says and opens a magazine.

"Nothing about you is," Cindy said and it makes Virginia laugh. She can't help it. She looks over there and sees Madge with her face so tight and serious, and she can't help but laugh.

"Laughter is the best medicine," Gram says. "If you ain't over bleeding."

"I'm not bleeding, Gram," she says. "I just spotted that one time."

"Then why do you put those fever sticks inside yourself?" Gram asks and Cindy stretches out on the floor laughing. Virginia is laughing now, too, laughing until her stomach aches more than it already did. She looks at Cindy stretched out on that floor and cannot keep from laughing. Just like that time at Cindy's house, she could not help laughing.

* * *

"I can't find it," Cindy had wailed and run to the door of the kitchen where Virginia and Madge were sitting at the table. She had stood there, a jar of Vaseline in one hand, the other hand held way out to the side and her underwear around her knees.

"What are you talking about?" Madge asked. "You put your pants on before your daddy comes in here."

"What am I gonna do?" Cindy pulled up her underwear and squatted down in the doorway.

"Cindy Sinclair, what on earth is wrong with you?" Madge asked and Virginia had to turn her head to the side to keep from laughing though it didn't work.

"It's not funny, Ginny!" Cindy's face was fire-red and tears were welling up in her eyes. "I've got a tampon up me and I can't find it!"

"How on earth?" Madge got a fixed look on her face, a blend of shock and disgust with her eyebrows raised and nostrils flared.

"I squatted over the mirror and I couldn't see it, not a bit of it and then the mirror fogged all up and I'm scared to go up there and see."

"Hush. I never heard of such in my life. And which mirror did you use?"

Virginia could not control herself then and had to run to the sink to spit out a mouthful of Coke.

"Goddamnit, Ginny Sue!" Cindy screamed and stretched out full length on the kitchen floor, her hands clasped on her abdomen like she was dying of pain.

"Do you want your mouth washed out with soap?" Madge asked.

"Somebody tell me what to do!"

"I told you what to do a long time ago," Madge said. "I told you not to wear those things, it's not natural to wear those things. It's just not right what you girls do, swimming and carrying on during that time."

"That time, that time," Cindy mimicked and sat up. "If I did like you say and did nothing at 'that time' then I'd be sitting in a chair for close to twelve weeks out of the year. That's close to," Cindy looked away for a minute.

"Three months," Virginia said and Cindy made a face back.

"I can add, Ginny Sue," she blared. "You didn't think it was all so funny that time you fell on that boy's bike now did you?"

"God, that hurts me to think of it," Madge said. "I've never felt so sorry 'cause I can't even imagine how that must have hurt." It made Virginia cross her legs tightly, just the thought of when she straddled that bar.

"Well hurt now!" Cindy wailed. "Imagine this! Imagine what I am feeling right now!"

"Why don't you try to find it," Virginia said and came back to the table.

"I don't understand how it happened in the first place," Madge said. "I've never in my life used one."

"There's a lot you've never in your life done!" Cindy stretched back out and pressed all around her abdomen like she could find it that way. "I had one in and I accidentally put one on top of it."

"Well, there's no place for it to go really," Virginia said, legs crossed tightly as she tried not to laugh.

"My stomach! It can go right up in my stomach!"

"Well, I've heard enough and I'm calling a doctor," Madge said and went over to the phone. "I have never been so embarrassed. What on earth can I say?"

"You're embarrassed? I'm the one with it wedged way up in me somewhere!"

"I have gone to Dr. Wilson my whole life near abouts," Madge said and looked at Virginia. "He delivered Cindy. My face turns red as a tomato every time that I have to go. I think it's the worse thing in the world to have to go." She flipped through the phone book and ran her finger down the page. "He's busy, too, and I don't know if this is an emergency or not." She dialed six numbers and then held her finger on that last number before releasing it. "I'm going to say that Cindy is going through that time of the month and that she does not use sanitary napkins like I suggested and as a result has lost one of the others in herself and needs it extracted."

Cindy had walked in front of Virginia, up the stairs, stomping her feet with every step, and flopped down on her bed. "If you ever tell this," Cindy said, "if you ever tell Aunt Hannah or Lena or Emily, I will never speak to you again."

"Oh Cindy, I'm not going to tell."

"I mean it," Cindy sat up straight and looked Virginia square in the eye. "If you do, I'll tell what you did down at the beach with that dumb boy." Virginia felt her face flush and Cindy laughed, those blue eyes in a devilish squint. "I'll tell how first you tongue-kissed and then about how he felt you off and did all *but*."

"I never said that!" Virginia raised her voice a little. "I didn't!"

"But that's what I'll tell." Cindy put on her jeans, the ones that Virginia had embroidered for her. She hadn't wanted to embroider them but Cindy had used that same story to blackmail her. And then Cindy had told her exactly what to embroider, tacky things, loud colored peace signs and "Twist and Shout" across the butt. "I'll tell that and I'll tell that you designed what's embroidered on my jeans."

"Cindy!"

"I will and I'll tell about that funny feeling you got *you know where* when you were with that boy."

"I'm never going to tell you anything as long as I live!" Virginia said. "I never would have told you if you hadn't talked about how *you* felt."

"So?" Cindy smoothed her finger up and down that hideous chartreuse peace sign just above her knee. "We're talking about what you said, though. I remember just how you said it, too."

"Please stop," Virginia begged. "I've never told anything on you."

"You said, 'Cindy, I felt so funny inside, kind of fluttery. . . .' "

"Stop!" Virginia held her hands over her ears and closed her eyes.

"Cindy?" Madge came into the room, her hands on her hips, face still red. "Dr. Wilson has squeezed you in and we've got to hurry. Now, you go wash and put on clean underwear."

"I took a shower when I got up."

"I don't care. Now, that man's got a hard job and I think people ought to be clean when they go."

"I'm clean I tell you!"

"Well, too clean doesn't hurt." Madge turned to leave the room. "Ginny Sue, we'll take you home on the way. Cindy, try to use the bathroom good before you wash so you won't have to go again."

Cindy took her jeans back off and pulled a pair of underwear from her drawer. It was underwear that looked like camouflage and said U.S. Marine Corp. on the back. "It was a flutter, just a flutter," she said lifting her hands to the ceiling.

"I hope he can't find it!" Virginia said. "I hope that one day you're all old and it comes up and out of your ear!"

"It made my legs feel real funny, kind of wobbly." Cindy took her Arrid Extra Dry off the top of her dresser and sprayed the underwear before she put it on. Cindy always talked about things like Arrid Extra Dry like it was the best deodorant and just because it was more expensive and had that picture of a man and a woman's shadows on the front. "Secret's just as good," Virginia had told her one day and Cindy had just rolled her eyes. "And I know you're still using Prell, too," Cindy had said. "Prell and Crest like you've done your whole life, just like your parents. I have my own. I have Close-Up and Pearl Drops and Protein 21.''

Cindy sprayed deodorant into her jeans and buttoned them back up. "When I flutter," she continued. "I flutter like a leaf in a warm breeze."

"I never said that!"

"I believe you did."

Virginia did not say one word the whole way home. She sat in the backseat while Cindy and Madge bickered in the front about what Cindy was going to say to Dr. Wilson.

"Ginny Sue, don't ever tell *anything* that goes on at our house," Madge said and her words sent a chill over Virginia's scalp.

"I won't," Virginia said and looked at Cindy.

"I won't tell either," Cindy finally said and smiled that certain way that let Virginia know that she had been teasing, that she wouldn't *really* tell.

"I hope everything's okay," Virginia had whispered and stepped up on the curb.

"I'll let you know how it comes out." Cindy grinned and turned around in the front seat while Madge sat gripping that steering wheel.

"It's the craziest thing," Cindy said when she called Virginia late that afternoon. "I would've sworn there was something up me and we had to pay fifteen dollars to find out there wasn't. I told him I use 'em all the time, ride horses and do splits, too, just in case he could tell things about me."

"Aren't you glad?"

"No, no I'm not. Mama blessed me out so bad when we got back in the car and she made me go in the Kroger's and buy a box of those big old things. She made me buy the biggest box that was in the store. She said, 'your daddy likes for me to buy the biggest size because it's a better buy.' My mama is crazy, certified and bona fide. You know my daddy don't give a damn about what size box of Kotex I have. He could care less."

"Where are you, Mars?" Cindy asks now and Virginia opens her eyes. "God, try to stay with it." Cindy walks over and stands in front of Gram, her hands on her waist where she has a hot pink string tied around the leotard. "Doctors say there's not a thing wrong with tampons as long as you don't leave them in forever."

"Or lose it," Virginia says and laughs, wanting to stay awake but feeling so sleepy.

"Like losing virginity?" Cindy asks and sits practically on top of her on the daybed. "Like being a teenager down at the beach like a missionary." She raises her eyebrows at Virginia and Virginia knows it's no use, Cindy is going to hold things over her the rest of her life. Now Cindy laughs and pats her hand. "I'm glad you're not regurgitating so. I need to be getting home. A man that I've been seeing is supposed to call so that we can work out a difficulty of our relationship."

"Is he a doctor?" Madge asks and sits up straight.

"No, but he could be. He knows as much if not more than they do." Cindy reaches in her bag for her car keys and Virginia wishes that she could get off the daybed and go somewhere other than the bathroom. "He's the one that sells them the medicine."

"I thought when you got that job that maybe you'd meet a doctor," Madge says and leans back in her chair. "That would be something if Ginny Sue had the lawyer and you had the doctor."

"And you had the Indian chief," Cindy says. "I know those doctors, know every one of them but most of them are married so somebody can wash those white coats. Do you want me to go out with a married?"

"Hush your mouth," Gram says. "You should do nothing of the kind. Madge? Madge did you hear that?"

"She's not going with a married man," Madge says and Cindy turns and winks at Virginia, mouths a "yes." Oh God, Virginia does not even want to know about it if that's the truth. "She said most of the doctors she knows are married."

"Most of the doctors I know are dead," Gram says. "Just about everybody I know is dead."

"We're here," Virginia says and Gram nods, flips on the TV by remote but keeps the sound down.

"Where's Chuckie?" Madge asks and Cindy turns back around.

"He had baseball. I got to run some errands, might get a little something to perk Ginny Sue up. I told Chuckie just to let himself in your house between school and baseball since you live right there. I told him where you keep the key."

"Where?" Madge asks now, glancing at her watch.

"The side yard for godssakes, now let me go so I can get something done."

"Cindy, I haven't left that key out in that side yard in a year."

"Well, he probably figured that out. See ya Ginny Sue," she says and the door slams shut.

"She ought to keep up with him better than that," Madge says but Virginia just keeps her eyes closed because it seems Madge is talking to herself more than anyone else. She does that, talks to herself, has as long as Virginia can remember. "I don't care if he is twelve, children have to be watched. Anything can happen to them, anything."

"I always watched my children," Gram says and turns up the volume, game show music and Madge flipping pages, page after page after page.

"No sir, a child's got no business by himself," Madge says. Yes, that's true but Virginia was at Madge's house by herself that one time, her parents at the beach, Robert at a friend's house, Gram at home.

Virginia had lifted the rock in the side yard and there in a little case surrounded by granddaddy longlegs and roly-polies was the key. Already it was getting dark and she stood on the steps another minute, looking up and down the street, hoping to see Madge's car, her breath visible as she stood and waited. "We're having a wonderful time," her mother had said on the phone and she had felt so jealous of her mother's laugher, her father's voice in the background calling out "we love you." Virginia had imagined them all bundled up and sitting on the pier, waves breaking. She imagined them saying "we sure wish Ginny and Robert were here" and she imagined huge conch shells, skyrockets, a strand of shells like she and her mama always strung in the summer.

The house was quiet and dark and she had flipped on the switch beside the front door and walked up the stairs to Cindy's room. She raised the blinds and sat on the bed where she could see the street, could see when Madge's car turned the corner. It was a pretty room, the French provincial canopy bed, pink walls and hot pink shag carpet, the glass case filled with Madame Alexander dolls, more dolls on the cornice.

"Don't cross this line," Cindy had said the first night, two nights ago, and she had run her finger down the middle of the bed. "And don't you EVER open this up," and she had pulled a diary out of the bedside table and sat there writing. She would laugh and write a little more and then look over at where Virginia was sitting in the chair and reading *Old Yeller*, and laugh again. "I mean it. This is personal," Cindy had said. "You wouldn't understand the first word. I mean you're into dogs, you know?"

"It's a good book," Virginia had said.

"Who cares?" Cindy asked. "I saw the movie. They kill a mad dog, big deal."

Virginia's impulse was to open that drawer and just see what Cindy had written in that book, but instead, she went to the cabinet and pulled out her favorite doll, a doll with a rose velvet dress and a little parasol with lace, dark hair pulled up in a twist with a loose feather hat. Virginia was feeling the feathered hat when she heard something in the kitchen; Sparkie, a Pekinese that was almost blind and as old as Cindy.

"Sparkie?" She had stood in the doorway and waited, the doll in one hand. "Here Sparkie," and she thought she heard him stirring, thought she heard him in the kitchen, and then he barked and whined, outside; she looked out the window at the top of the stairs where there was an old trunk filled with dress-up clothes and she saw Sparkie out there chained to the clothesline where he could run up and down. She heard the dull ticking of a clock somewhere upstairs, probably in Madge's room and the sounds again in the kitchen, a glass clinking, silverware shuffled through. "Catherine has a school meeting and Cindy has tap," Madge had said. "Just go on in and I'll be there soon. Lock the door and you'll be fine there by yourself." She turned on the light in the stairwell. "Catherine?" she called.

"Catherine?" came a high mimicked voice from below and she froze, her hand on the stair rail, dusk outside the window.

"Catherine?" she called again softly and stepped back from the top of the stairs. Nothing, and then footsteps, a closet door opening, closing. "Uncle Raymond?"

"Uncle Raymond?" came the mimic again, and she just stood, her breath held, ready to run into Cindy's room, slam and lock the door; she could call Gram, open a window and scream, climb out Cindy's window and onto the roof like they did last summer. It was dark at the bottom of the stairs, faint

gray light through the venetian blinds in the dining room.
"Hickory dickory dock," came a deep throaty whisper. "The
mouse ran up the clock." Jingling, pockets jingling, footsteps. "Please stop, now, please stop," she said. "I know
it's you Catherine, or Uncle Raymond. It's one of you." And
a hand, black glove, a long silver knife reached around the
corner of the stairwell, a wingtip shoe on that bottom step.

* * *

"No," she says and sits up, Gram in the Lazy Boy, Madge
with her magazine.

"What is it?" Madge asks and puts down her magazine.
"Are you hurting?"

"No, nothing." She lies back down, her hands on her
stomach. "A dream, just a dream."

* * *

"What is it?" Madge had asked, turning from that vanity
top where the mirror was cracked, Cindy's cologne bottles
turned and spilled. "I can't believe you're going to sit right
there and not admit you did this. This isn't like you Ginny
Sue. I'm going to have to tell Hannah how you've behaved."

"I want to go to Gram's," she whispered. "Please call
Gram."

"I hate you," Cindy had said. "Just look at what you've
done. Look at my doll."

"She broke a mirror and wouldn't admit it," Uncle Raymond told Gram. "And then she turned on all of us like we
were the ones who had done something."

"Ginny Sue," Gram had said and hugged her close, the
tears coming so fast by then. "That's not like you, baby,"
she said and stroked Virginia's hair.

"I didn't want to. I didn't want to, Gram."

"Didn't want to admit it, you mean," he said.

"I didn't mean to."

* * *

"Didn't mean to what?" Madge asks now. "Are you awake
or asleep, Ginny Sue?"

"I didn't break the mirror," Virginia says.

"No, you didn't break a mirror," Gram says. "You have

worried your whole life over a mirror you didn't break. Now forget it.''

"What mirror?" Madge asks. "Ginny Sue?" Madge is there now, leaning over her. "What mirror, honey?"

"I was dreaming. I dreamed I broke a mirror.''

"Well," Madge sighs and goes over to the window. "Don't worry over a dream. No sense in worrying over that.''

"It was scary," she says, her eyes so heavy, Madge a blur of white there by the window.

"I know, I know," Madge says. "I've had some scary ones myself. Seemed so real. But at least you can wake up and find they aren't real?''

"Yes, yes," she nods, a car door slamming outside.

"Your mama's back, right on time," Madge says and goes to the front door. "Hannah's so dependable, always right on time.''

* * *

"She'll be here," the patrolwoman at school had said and patted Virginia's shoulder. "Your mama is always here to get you, must be running a little late is all.''

"I thought you had forgotten me," she sobbed all the way home. "I didn't know what to do.''

"Ginny Sue, now you know better. When have I ever left you alone?" her mama asked, and Virginia sat staring down at her bluehorse notebook, her name and little pictures that she had drawn on it during class. "I got tied up taking some drape measurements and didn't notice how late it was. Now what is the matter?''

* * *

"I'm here," Hannah says, the front door closing, the rustling of grocery bags. "We're going to have a good dinner. Madge, won't you stay?''

"Thank you, I believe I will," Madge says. "Sometimes I can't stand going into an empty house.''

* * *

"What are you doing standing here in the parking lot?" Bryan Parker had asked.

"I got tired of being inside," she told him, and it all slapped her in the face, the heat, the neutrality of his face staring at her, a feeling like she could mold his features and face like clay, smooth them all into a flat neutral surface and she thought why am I here? Why am I here this way? It wasn't Bryan Parker's fault; it was hers—scared to be alone, in a room, condo, house. It was nothing more than loneliness, nothing more than the fear of waking up one day to an empty house.

* * *

"What are you doing?" Mark had asked and squatted down beside where she was digging little holes, planting marigolds. "I thought you said you had planted all you were going to plant." And his hand was on her waist, a firm grasp that made her want to pull away.

"I got tired of being inside," she told him. "I don't like being alone."

"You're not alone," he whispered. "Come on," and she had moved away from him, felt her throat go dry, wanting to scream again with no reason whatsoever coming to her mind and his features too strong to blend and mash together so she had to stare into those holes, a slimy worm living off dirt, marigold roots and marigolds stink; she hates marigolds but they're cheap, a cheap thrill. Get out of the house, buy some marigolds, get your fingernails dirty, rub a little dirt on your face so no one wants to touch.

"You're never alone, Ginny Sue," Gram had said. "When you're lying in your bed at night, God is there with you. God is always with you."

"But I'm scared to be alone," she said. "I want somebody with me."

"It's not so bad being alone," Gram had said and ran her finger down that hull, the peas plopping into the tin pan. "I've got things to think on, things I didn't have time to think on before," and Virginia sat there beside her, reaching her small bare foot to the porch bannister to push the swing while they sat there and waited for dark. "Your granddaddy and me had too many good years for me to question why I'm left here alone."

"But I'm with you."

"Yes, you are," Gram said, her hair just starting to gray then.

"So, you're not alone. You're not by yourself because

you've got me and Mama and Daddy and Robert and Lena and Roy.''

"You're right," Gram said. "And it fills up the ways that I am alone."

"But then, you're not alone," she had insisted and Gram stopped her shelling and stared out in the yard like she might have seen something or was listening to something.

"There are many ways a person can be alone," Gram whispered. "One day, you'll understand that. Sometimes I feel so alone and what I'm lonely for is my mother. There's a kind of day that makes me lonely for her, winter days mostly, winter days when it's a bit cloudy because those are the days we'd be sitting there in the house. She'd say, 'You'll take a cold out there on a day like today,' and so we'd just sit there indoors, her rocking in that chair and knitting and teaching me and Lena." She laughed and went back to her shelling. "Lena couldn't knit. She'd make her yarn into a mess and then throw it outside for some old cat to play with."

* * *

"These cats keep me so much company," Lena had said. "Roy's got to work, work, work, go, go, go and as soon as that car cranks, that's an invitation for all the carts to come on in. I let 'em in and they are such good company."

"I'm so lonely here," she had told Bryan Parker, for the first time really wanting to hug him but he moved away. "I'm so sorry."

"I thought this was what you wanted," he said. "You acted so sure this was what you wanted."

* * *

"I know it isn't exactly what you'd want," Mark had said when they were standing in that rented kitchen with the sink backed up and boxes to unpack. "But we won't be here forever."

* * *

"You ain't ever gonna find what you want," Cindy had said. "You're looking for a brain like what's his name, you know the Jew with the bushy hair."

"Einstein?"

"Yeah, you know you're looking for a brain like his, and a bod like Rocky."

"I don't like Rocky."

"Well who then? Whose body do you want?"

"Borg, lean and graceful like Borg," she had said, laughing. "Or maybe Nureyev when he was younger."

"Shit, I don't know who they are," Cindy said. "And whose face? Huh? Paul Newman? Al Pacino? Richard Gere?"

"Or William Hurt."

"God, you see?" Cindy asked. "Honey, they ain't out there. Believe me if they were, I would've found 'em. And you probably want poetic too, don't you?" Cindy had poured herself another drink. "You want Joyce Kilmer," she said and Virginia laughed until she ached. "Or is Joyce a woman?" Virginia held her sides while Cindy continued, a straight face while she drank her rum and Coke. "Oh yeah, and your man can't think of sex as anything but a moment out of space and time, a union of love." And Cindy had reached her arms to the ceiling and hummed "Trees." "Like that boy at the beach made you float."

"No, no, no," is all Virginia could say.

"Admit it, Ginny Sue," Cindy said. "You are never gonna find all that you're looking for so you might as well just spin around and pin the tail on the donkey. Pick a jackass and ride. I mean that's what I did. I did that and now I've got Buzz Biggers, and he is something to ride let me tell you. If you fall off that horse, just get back up and ride like hell. It's better than being alone."

* * *

"God is always here," Gram had said. "You are not alone."

But God doesn't say, "scrooch up sweets," and God doesn't change the washcloth when your head is so hot and God doesn't pick you up and carry you to the commode if you are too sick to stand. God doesn't brush back your hair and tell you that you are not alone; he doesn't squat close to you when you smell like marigolds and have dirt under your nails, doesn't call on the phone to ask how you are, doesn't make things familiar when a long-distance call comes, the lonely sad news, and you turn to face rooms and windows and faces so unfamiliar that it makes you ask why am I here this way? He does not step in and tell you that you are about to make a mistake, that you've made a big mistake because you are moving far from your home and will always be lonesome when the winter sky is gray and cloudy and when Sunday afternoon comes and nobody goes to Carver Street and Roy Carter does not step from that maroon Lincoln and say "Do unto others before they do it to you," and if the clock stops, it will stop and if the baby dies, it will die, and if those shoes are on the step, they do not go away but come closer and closer and closer.

* * *

"Where's Esther?" Gram asks.

"She wanted the night off." Virginia's mama comes into the room. "She was all dressed up, too. I wonder if she's got a date."

"Date. Pshhh," Gram says. "Esther needs a man like a hole in the head."

"She might be happy," Madge says. "She might be happy for the first time in her life and she deserves it if it's the truth."

"That's true," Virginia says and looks over at Gram who nods with her.

"I think you're so lucky, Ginny Sue," Madge says. "I wish Cindy could find herself a nice man like Mark. What kind of law is Mark going to do?"

"Mostly business stuff," she says. "Contracts, wills, divorces, I don't know."

"So, he's not going to be like Perry Mason and solve the murders?"

"If he was," Virginia's mama calls from the kitchen, "he couldn't have more to solve than right here in Saxapaw."

"I love Perry Mason," Gram says. "Now he goes by the name of Ironside because he's old and on wheels like me." Gram laughs until the tears run down her cheeks and she pulls a Kleenex from her robe pocket. "Sometimes I laugh till I weep," Gram says. "I don't know why I do that but it's something I've always done."

"These Pearson girls," Roy Carter used to say. "Cry at the drop of a hat, happy, sad, monthlies or no reason at all."

* * *

Gram had stood by the kitchen table and cried like she was the child instead of Virginia. And Virginia saw the ambulance on the street below, the red light flashing around and around as she stood on a stool and looked out the kitchen window. Gramps was in the bedroom, silence behind that closed door, and her mama sat there at the table with Gram and watched that door as if she were afraid to open it. Virginia had a stuffed clown that Gram had made. His ruffled yellow suit had patches. "I made his hat out of one of your Uncle David's favorite shirts that he had as a child, and I made his suit out of some of James's old pajamas." The clown had brown buttons for eyes and Virginia wanted them to be blue. Blue, she mouthed, her breath fogging the window over the sink where she sat on the counter. They should have been blue and Gram should have known that she'd want him to have blue eyes. She felt she could not give the clown a name until the eyes were right. She had found the ones she wanted, shiny pale blue buttons, and she had them there in the pocket of her corduroy pants. Those buttons did not have holes in them like the brown ones, but small silver hooks on the back so the eyes would be smooth and all blue.

"These are the right eyes," she had told Gram and showed her the buttons but Gram just rubbed her head and nodded.

"I'll do it later, Sweets," Gram said. "Why don't you and that clown take a little nap?" But Virginia couldn't sleep. There was an ambulance on the street and men were coming up to the house with a stretcher and she couldn't sleep at all. The men came in when Gram opened the door and they followed her to the bedroom where Gram showed them the way in but stayed outside herself, her eyes on the edge of the rug in front of her.

"Don't leave. Please don't leave," Virginia had screamed when they brought him through the kitchen, and she jumped from the counter and ran over to Gramps. "Please finish the story," she said but his blue eyes were closed and he did not reach up and catch her nose between his fingers like he usually did. "Got your nose," he would say and hold up his hand, thumb pressed between fingers to look like the stolen nose. "Please?" she asked. "Brer Rabbit?"

"I'm going to miss you," Gram said and traced her fingers down his nose, around his lips, lightly over his closed eyes. "There will never be another," she whispered, and Gram's lips quivered like she was freezing cold. "I will do right by you. I love you," she said and then looked at Virginia's mama, at Virginia. "We all do."

And Virginia's mama and Gram had followed the men outside, leaving her there in the house by herself and she got back on the counter, her feet in the sink, and watched. Gram's African violets were blooming there on the windowsill, purple, pink, white, and they put Gramps into the ambulance and the men got in and started it up. It moved from the curb and Gram and her mama stood there on the sidewalk with their heads pressed together and arms wrapped around each other. Gram started walking back in, bending to pick up a piece of old newspaper blowing in the yard, but her mother still stood there. She looked up and saw Virginia there in the window and lifted her hand, that brown sweater buttoned close and her mama's hair blown back from her face, Gram in her gardening dress, the piece of paper in her hand while she stared in the other direction, stared out at the garden.

Virginia did not leave the window until they were back inside and Gram pulled down her sewing basket and fixed the blue eyes while Virginia's mother made telephone calls, her back turned to them and shaking, while Gram sewed the eyes and made a little pompom for the hat. "And he needs a mouth," Gram said and cut what looked like a valentine from a scrap of red velvet. "This old clown can talk and talk," Gram had said and pressed it under Virginia's neck, moved him back and forth. "He'll tell you every story he knows." And then people started coming and when Virginia went to sleep late that night, it was on a pallet on the floor near Gram's bed, and when she woke up and everything was dark, she saw that Gram's bed was empty and then she heard the glider moving back and forth on the porch. The front door was open and she stood there in the darkness, the clown clutched in her arms, and watched Gram swaying back and forth. "Gram?" she had called, and when the glider stopped and Gram turned to face her, she opened the door and stepped onto the porch. "Are you waiting for Gramps?"

"I guess I am," she said and pulled Virginia up beside her, hugged her close, so close that Gram's face felt wet against her neck. "But it'll be a long time before we see Gramps again," and Gram pushed off the floor and they rocked slowly, and Gram lifted the clown and made him dance a little in the air, back and forth, back and forth. "Do anything, *any*thing," she said and laughed. "Just don't throw me in the brier patch." And Virginia felt herself lean closer and closer into Gram and never remembered being carried back to bed, only remembered staring down the road in the direction that the ambulance had gone and there was nothing there except sparse streetlights and the smell of smoke from some chimney way on down the road.

PART V

VIRGINIA OPENS HER EYES TO DAYLIGHT, A GRAY HAZY SKY
out Gram's window. It is Saturday, and for the first time in a
week, Virginia really feels awake. It is Saturday, the day of
Mark's tests, the day to tell the truth. She will give him time
to get home, time to open a beer and sit down, and then
she'll call. *It's over* she will say.

"Well, I thought you were going to sleep the day away,"
Madge says, glancing up from her cards. "Cindy has been
wanting to wake you up." Madge takes a sip of her iced tea
and shuffles.

"Where's Mama?" she asks, suddenly aware of the con-
gregation. Gram is in the Lazy Boy, Lena stretched out on
the sofa, sounds in the kitchen where Esther must be. "And
what time is it?"

"Hannah had to run to the Piggly Wiggly," Madge says
and looks toward the bathroom door. "She's awake now,
Cindy, so you can stop pouting."

"I've told her not to go to the Piggly Wiggly," Gram says.
"That is still my house."

"No, Aunt Emily," Madge says, pity in her voice. "It's
the Piggly Wiggly now."

"Roy and me have been." Lena opens her eyes and sits
up. "Roy says they've got the seafood there where you used
to sleep."

"Well I wouldn't have it," Gram says and puts a little snuff
in her gum.

"Where's Chuckie?" Virginia asks, hoping to take the focus off the Piggly Wiggly.

"He's swimming and I hope the rain holds off until late

185

tonight so he can stay all day." Cindy moves from the doorway and sits on the floor, flexes her feet out in front of her; her toenails are painted the same shade of blue as her eyeshadow. "He's getting to be a real pain in the rectum."

"Cindy," Madge says. "He is going through a difficult age."

"Tell me about it!" Cindy snaps. "He stays in the bathroom forever; I'm beginning to think he's you know whatting."

"What?" Lena asks and now she and Gram turn to Cindy with a dull blank stare.

"God," Cindy shakes her head and laughs. "I don't know, probably in there squeezing pimples or something. He needs a man to talk to him but Charles doesn't have a thing to do with him, ever."

"He does when you let him," Madge says.

"Oh, right," Cindy snaps. "He only wants Chuckie to do *fun* things. Charles is never around to see Chuckie when he looks so awkward and gawky; Charles doesn't see him look like that when some sleezy little girl calls on the phone and he turns red as a beet, and Charles doesn't have to stand outside that bathroom door about to pee in his pants while Chuckie's in there you know whatting."

"What?" Lena asks again, her voice so slow now, eyes so dull.

"Mashing bumps, I said!"

"Then why don't you say that?" Gram asks. "Why don't you take him to a doctor?"

"I would take him but it costs a hell of a lot. Phisoderm is cheap and if he'd use it like I tell him to, those bumps would probably go away. If Charles Snipes can afford to remarry, he can afford dermatology."

"You haven't told me Charles is getting married," Virginia says.

"Good God, Ginny Sue," Cindy says and waves her hand. "You been laid out like a dead whale for a week. How could I tell you?"

"Your skin was never really bad, Cindy," Madge says and Virginia listens to every word, her face still flushed by the words "dead whale." "Chuckie got his skin troubles from Charles."

"God, you're telling me," Cindy says. "Daddy warned

me, told me that Charles would always have a scarred-up face, and I should have listened to him. God, to think I ever kissed Charles Snipes.''

"Cindy, I'll help you with that, you know, money-wise. Chuckie is so self-conscious about it," Madge says, her forehead wrinkled. "Bless his heart. He asked me if I thought it would go away before long."

"Roy went away," Lena says, her eyes closed.

"Bless his heart," Cindy mimics. "I know you'd pay for it because Chuckie is your little ray of sunshine like I never was. Charles Snipes should have to pay."

"No sunshine today," Gram says. "Weatherman says rain."

"I just wanted to help is all." Madge stacks her deck of cards and wipes the sweat that has gathered around her hairline. "I *know* it's not easy raising a child alone." Madge stops and stares at Cindy, the words, the tension between their stares so strong that it make Virginia's whole body tighten.

"A child is a big responsibility," Gram says.

"Lord God, tell me about it." Now Cindy laughs, her back turned to Madge. "You'll know soon enough, Ginny Sue. Of course you'll have a man there to help you. Everybody really does need a man there to help them."

"Yeah, when I fall asleep there on the sofa watching TV that Roy will pick me right up and put me in my bed."

"Well, that must have been a hundred years ago," Cindy says.

"No sassy messy mouth, it wasn't," Lena says, but Cindy ignores her.

"If we can ever have a little privacy, Ginny Sue," Cindy says. "I'll tell you all about my latest."

"This is my house and if anybody gets privacy, it's me," Gram says.

"Oh, Ginny Sue," Madge says suddenly. "Mark called you bright and early today, said he was going to take his test and would call back later."

"Why didn't you wake me?" she asks, an accusing tone that makes Madge's eyebrows go up. Her heart quickens with the thought of what he's going to say.

"It isn't her fault," Cindy says. "Your mama, St. Peter,

has told us all not to disturb you.'' Cindy sits forward with her feet pressed together like she's doing yoga.

Esther goes and opens the front door. ''Thank God, Hannah's here. Maybe I can get out and do a few things myself. I have a life, too, you know?'' Esther faces them all now and Virginia lies back down, closes her eyes, thinks about what she will say. A baby cannot hold a marriage together. It's hard to raise a child alone but it can be done.

''I could use a little help,'' Hannah comes through the front door with a bag under each arm, her hair all blown every which way and there they all sit.

Cindy does not make one move from her spot on the floor to help. Madge follows Hannah into the kitchen and sits down to watch.

''I see you still buy Crisco in the can,'' Madge says and Hannah just bites her tongue and nods, keeps unloading the groceries. ''Hannah, let's me and you go down to the beach one weekend. Let's go sit and talk.'' Hannah stops unloading for a minute and stares at Madge. How in tarnation does she think Hannah can just drop it all and go to the beach? ''I'll pay for the room,'' Madge says.

''Money is no issue,'' Hannah says now, determined to make a point. ''I sold the shop for a large sum; I have money. Time, time is the issue.''

''Esther could stay here,'' Madge says, her words picking up speed. ''I mean after Ginny's well, of course. Just a day and night, you know, to talk.''

''You might ask Esther,'' Esther says and steps into the room.

Hannah looks at Madge. ''I'll have to see.'' Lena's hat is cocked off to one side and Hannah goes over to straighten it, though God knows it won't stay straight. ''Roy's dead, isn't he?'' Lena asks slowly and Hannah nods. ''Hannah, you are a good child, sweet; you look just like me,'' and Lena reaches out and touches Hannah's hair. All through childhood, Hannah imagined looking just like Aunt Lena, the flashy clothes and dangling earrings, and now, all of that time has passed and it is like seeing what she will be in twenty years, thin little vein-streaked wrists and tired dull eyes.

''If I should suddenly get quiet and not have anything to say,'' Emily says, her hands gripping the edge of her lap robe and holding it up to her neck. ''I don't want any of you to bother me, I don't want anybody trying to get me back.'' She looks around the room, Lena with that fake fur cocked to one side. They just come in and make themselves right at home when there's so much to be done to get ready.

"Are you fixing to die?'' Lena asks and hands the filter of her burned-out cigarette to Hannah. '' 'Cause I am. I'm fixing to die.''

"Now you two stop it.'' Madge drains the last of her iced tea and goes in Emily's kitchen.

"I get so tired of this,'' that sassy Cindy says to Ginny Sue like she might own this house and they are the only two in it. "I wish you could get out and do something.''

"Well, there's a plenty to be done right here,'' Emily says. "The wedding is today and there's plenty to do.''

"What wedding is that?'' Hannah asks and Emily laughs, turns the TV up louder with her remote control. She'd rather listen to what they're saying on TV anyway. Hannah wasn't even at the wedding, wasn't even born, so how would she know about it? It makes Emily laugh until tears come to her eyes.

"Let's talk about getting your hair fixed.'' Hannah gets up and turns off the TV.

"Before the wedding?'' Emily waits, green eyes staring, until Hannah nods.

"God, it's always a wedding or a funeral,'' Cindy says. "They don't even know they're on this earth, Alzheimer's, and it really pisses me off the way everybody goes along with them.''

"You talk so filthy,'' Emily says, shaking her finger, so thin beneath that gnarled knuckle. "What I don't know is how you all found me here and some not even born or invited.''

"I said who's getting married?'' Lena tugs on her hat. "I thought we were at Emily's house.''

"No, we're way up North at the Kennedy wedding,'' Cindy says. "And then we might go to England for the royal wedding.''

"We are at Mama's house,'' Hannah says over Cindy and Lena lies down, lights a cigarette.

"I know where I am,'' Emily says. "It was James's idea that we marry here.''

"Where are we then?" Cindy asks. "I just want to hear it."

"Tessy ought to wear you out for that sharp tongue," Emily says and shakes her finger again. "And for painting your face."

"My grandmother is dead!"

"So is Roy," Lena says and puffs out a cloud of smoke. "I wish I was."

"James said South Carolina is a nice place to marry," Emily says. "So here we are."

"South Carolina?" Lena sits back up.

"You heard it. South Carolina, Boston, England, all at the same time." Cindy goes in the kitchen and opens the refrigerator and just stands there looking in.

"Don't let all the cold out," Madge says and fans herself with one of Emily's old paper fans like the funeral homes used to give out.

"Don't, don't, don't!" Cindy yells. "Here I am with a child, two husbands under my belt and all I ever get is *don't*."

"I don't remember coming to South Carolina," Lena says.

"You didn't." Emily pulls out her tin of snuff. "Me and James didn't tell you where we were going because we eloped and you stood there at the edge of the yard and pitched a fit because you didn't want to stay home with Mama."

"Well, you must have brought me with you, else why am I here?" Lena drops her cigarette in the ashtray and just lets it burn. "Wedding," she sighs. "I ain't about to put on a pair of hose." Lena sits up straight and looks at Hannah. "I remember coming by car. We all must have come by car, Roy's Lincoln."

"I flew," Cindy says. "My lover rented a jet and flew me here and Ginny Sue came by Trailways and Mama got brought by some men from another planet."

Madge is too tired to say anything, just looks out the window where Felicia is standing in her half of the yard, folding a yard chair and looking up at the sky. Sometimes, Madge can almost see why Felicia chose her way, life without men, and Felicia is not even a big woman.

"Cindy is teasing," Hannah says to Emily and Lena. "She made all that up."

"I haven't made a thing since I tried to make a purse at the hotel school," Lena says. "I didn't want to make a purse.

Straw shit, cheap straw and so Roy said don't make a purse, Lena, for godssakes don't make a purse; I'll buy you a purse when we go to Chicago.''

"I'll not go to Chicago with anyone,'' Emily says.

"It's not Chi*car*go, even I know that.''

"Cindy,'' Madge says, still watching Felicia who is now pulling some weeds from around her shrubs. Felicia has probably never had a man that made her do something she didn't want to do. Felicia has never had a child. Madge looks away from the window when it looks like Felicia is looking in her direction. Madge tries to focus on her card game but she can't help but wonder what Felicia would think of her, if a woman interested in other woman would find her just as unattractive as Raymond had. And what becomes of people who are so unattractive that nobody, not man nor woman, wants them?

* * *

"Don't marry anybody unless it's really for love,'' Madge's mama had told her. "You'd be better off right by yourself. A person might as well be right by herself and all alone than to live a life that's nothing but a lie.'' And her mama was so rough-looking, even then; she looked like those pictures of old rough farm women with her worn out high-tops and little pipe. That was a mouthful for her mama to say because she rarely talked at all except to tell Madge to do something, feed the chickens or go get a bucket of water.

"Tessy knows what she's talking about.'' Madge's daddy was in the doorway and she hadn't even heard him come in. Her mama didn't even flinch with his voice but set her mouth straight and tight with a determined look while she licked the end of a thread and guided it through the needle. Madge waited for her mama to say something but she didn't and he just stood there, a big man with wild gray hair that he didn't even cut in those later years. Her mama just kept right on quilting, staring down at those tough old hands. And Madge felt the tension there between them, her daddy's hard stare and her mama's spine rigid as a post.

"What did he mean?'' she had asked when her father went out the side door and let it slam behind him.

"Nothing. Didn't mean nothing,'' her mama said without even looking up. "I'm just saying you'd be better off alone

than with a man you don't love and got no hopes of loving."
And she had wanted to ask her mama questions but those
dark brown eyes silenced her.

"Come live with me and be my love," Raymond had said.
He had a car, an old Bel Air, and when they'd drive down
that filthy dusty road into town to go to the movies, he'd put
his arm around her and pull her close on that seat. "No wife
of mine will ever have to work in a field like a nigger," he
told her.

"I hear he's fast," Hannah had said one day at school.
"And he's a lot older."

"Just eight years," Madge said. "Daddy is ten years older
than Mama."

"Find yourself a younger man," her mama had said.

Raymond had taught Ben how to drive, all of them laughing at the way Ben was so stiff and nervous behind the wheel,
couldn't even put his arm around Hannah or smoke a cigarette while he drove he was so nervous.

"I like it when you drive, Ben," Raymond said, those
wingtips propped on the front seat between Hannah and Ben.
"I like having Madge back in this backseat all to myself."
She had to fight that man every inch of the way, fought him
right up to their wedding night when she stood in the bathroom in a motel in Florence, South Carolina.

"I'm ready," Raymond had called through that closed door.
And she had brushed her hair down around her shoulders,
taken off the locket her mama had given her, a locket that
Madge didn't even know her mama had. "Just take it," her
mama said. "And don't tell nobody I gave it to you."

"Hope you come with a guarantee little country mouse,"
Raymond called and when she opened the bathroom door, he
was sitting in the bed with the sheet pulled up to his hips,
that blonde hair combed up off his forehead; his large blue
eyes were taking in every inch of her. "I'm ready," he said
and lifted a shot glass. Madge would not want to go back;
she would not want to relive one minute. She watches Felicia
pulling weeds and she is relieved that it's all over Now all
she has to do is tell Hannah.

* * *

"You could pick the time and place, Hannah," Madge says.
"You know if you feel like you can get away for a day."

Hannah steps in from the bathroom, wiping her hands on a towel. Lena is pacing and muttering now, a towel wrapped around her head.

"I'll talk to Ben," Hannah says and follows Lena. Madge turns back to the window, feeling more hopeful every time she asks Hannah. Soon she will say yes; she will have to say yes. Madge can't carry it any longer. She is thinking about the words, her letters, when a car pulls up to the curb and stops. Madge sits and waits to see who will get out. Felicia has turned from her weeding and is watching, too.

"Roy and I used to go to the beach," Lena makes a face and says, "sh sh shit," when Hannah starts combing out her hair, her head jerking forward with each sh. "They had sand fleas where we stayed. Roy said he liked the way I hopped around."

"Nobody wants to hear of it," Emily says. "Somebody go to the door. There's a man on the porch."

"Yeah, boy, banjos and all," Cindy says.

"There really is a man," Madge says. "It's a black man with a Bible."

"It's the nigger that stole the car!" Lena gasps when Hannah goes to the door. "I'd know him anywhere. Come back to finish poisoning me with that gum."

"I'm looking for Miss Emily Roberts," he says when Hannah opens the door. He takes off his hat. "I'm Buddy Sharpey from Little Swamp Baptist Church. I'm the preacher there and Mag Sykes asked me to come." He nods his head with each word.

"Mag?" Emily calls, leaning forward in her chair. "Did you bring Mag?"

"Mama speaks of Mag often," Hannah says and shows him in. "Mama, this is Buddy Sharpey. He knows Mag Sykes."

"Tell him I'll chew it," Lena says and Hannah shakes her head, shushes her.

"Hope I'm not interrupting," he takes Emily's hand. "Mag Sykes asked that I come by." Emily nods with every word. "She told me to tell you that she has missed you. Said to say that Curie loved you, too."

"I knew Curie," Lena says like a left-out child. "He loved me, too. I'm the one that found him that time." The man turns and smiles at Lena, nods. He looks just like that one that stole the car; oh boy, you can tell when they're up to something.

"I miss Mag," Emily says, tears coming to her eyes, her voice trembling while she squeezes his hand. "Tell her to come sit a spell."

"Miss Mag has passed on," he says. "Miss Mag has gone home to the Lord." Emily takes a Kleenex from her pocket and holds it against her cheek. "She asked me a good month ago to come find you but she couldn't remember your last name."

"I'm a Pearson," she says. "I'm Emily Pearson."

"And I'm a Pearson," Lena says. "I married a Carter and Emily married a Roberts." Lena pulls away from Hannah and that comb as long as she can. "Have you ever stolen a car?"

"Of course he hasn't," Hannah says and pulls Lena back, looks over at her mama who is staring down at her hands and sniffing. "He's a preacher."

"I didn't know Roberts," he says. "Mag just called you Miss Emily and I had to ask around until one of Mag's children remembered your married name." Emily just nods without looking at him, smiles when she thinks of that Mag with her hair all braided up under that scarf while she stirred the washtub; Emily would be there beside her adding twigs to the fire and clothes to the water. "I guess I should go," the man says now. "Got a wedding today. I just couldn't rest till I had done as Mag asked."

"Mag is a good fine soul," Emily says and watches Hannah lead the man back to the front door. "Curie worked for my daddy," Emily whispers, ignoring Lena when Lena says it was her daddy, too. "He'd stay there with us sometimes at night. He'd tell mama, he'd say, 'Miss Virginia, I can't sleep with your children. They likes to sleep with they feets covered and they heads out and I'm just the different. I likes to sleep with my head covered and my feets out in the air.'" Emily laughs, shakes her head and laughs.

"I've never even heard that one," Hannah says and clamps the last curler on Lena's head.

"I have," Lena says. "I'm the one that found him there dead."

"Bad men." Emily shakes her head. "My daddy said they were nothing but bad trashy men that done that."

"What happened?" Madge asks. She's tired of playing solitaire, tired.

"The Klan," Hannah says. "I guess they were called the Klan then, were they Mama?"

"Trash," Emily says and shakes her head. "It was close to dark. My daddy said he was worried. 'It ain't like Curie to be so late,' he said and so he decided he'd ride a piece down the road to look for him."

"I went," Lena says and lights a cigarette. "Me and Roy went in the Lincoln."

"You went because nobody could leave that house without you," Emily says. "Daddy said, 'I'll be right back. Curie might have forgot he was supposed to help me put up that meat tonight.' And when my daddy come back, he looked like he had seen a ghost and he sent me and Lena to the kitchen while he told my mama of how he'd found Curie not but about a half a mile from his own house, tied to a tree and dead, murdered."

"Whoever did it, should have been hung," Hannah says and Madge goes to the kitchen to put up her glass, turns on the faucet and listens to the water while she rinses and rinses that glass. "It's still going on," Hannah is saying. "I saw the president of that mess on TV." Madge takes a deep breath and goes back in. "My daddy never even told me that story," she says.

"Harv was too busy tending to Messy," Lena says and is about to say more but Emily interrupts.

"Nobody knew who done that to Curie," she whispers, "and years later when I come to meet up with Mag Sykes, I learned that she was Curie's baby girl and I hadn't even known it, hadn't even remembered Curie's last name. I mentioned him one day and Mag's face lit into a smile, said her daddy talked of some children he knew, clean white children that had doll babies like what he wanted Mag to have. Mag even remembered that doll baby that Mama asked me to give to Curie; I didn't want to give up that baby, didn't have but two and they weren't nothing but rags." She stops and laughs. "Lena cried and said she couldn't have just one doll because who would that other doll sleep with if she was scared at night."

"It was the truth," Lena says and nods, though now she is as calm and quiet as Emily.

"My mama said, 'Emily, you are the oldest and I don't ask much of you' and she sent me out to the edge of the road where Curie was waiting and I said, 'this is for you, Curie,' and he bent down and kissed my face. He said, 'my baby girl is going to take good care of your baby, now. You a good child.'

"Mag Sykes remembered. 'I loved that baby, Lord yes I did,' she said to me that day we remembered it all. Mag could work circles around anybody. She said, 'Miss Emily, them people had they faces covered up, and my whole life I have stared at white faces, wondering, just wondering if they a part of such bastards.' I said, 'Mag, you got every right to say what you say. Filthy, my daddy said they were nothing but filth' and I told Mag she ought to be afraid, there was reason. I said she ought to be afraid of those that show their faces, too. I said, 'They are everywhere, Mag, they are everywhere and they will always be there.' I said, 'Them that cover their faces and ignorance is bad and the Lord will not have them, but them that show their faces and act proud of their ignorance is worse.' "

"They murdered him," Virginia says, the story that Gram has only mentioned in the past becoming so clear and sharp in her mind. "Did your daddy know who any of the men were?"

"He did," she nods and wipes the edges of her mouth. "He said he felt sorry for their wives and sorry for their children. He said if we knew that we'd act different to those children at the school and at church, and that their lives was already so bent to misery and ignorance."

"Didn't you have any ideas who?" Hannah asks. "Ever?"

"I was not a questioning child," she says. "I did as I was told. I was told that children should be seen and not heard, shouldn't speak unless spoken to."

"I have always hated that saying," Cindy says. "Everytime I come over here, ya'll start on those old depressing stories. This family is full of death."

"Just hush," Madge says suddenly. "You should follow that rule."

"Amen, tell it, sister," Lena says and Hannah can't help but laugh; she knows that's a rule that Lena never followed.

"You know Buzz Biggers went to some of those meetings," Cindy says to Ginny Sue and shakes her head. "I

wasn't ever going to tell it but I can say whatever I please
about him now that we're divorced.''

"Well I wouldn't say it too loud," Madge says. "You might
say it to the wrong person." Good God, that sends a chill
through Cindy.

"That doesn't surprise me," Ginny Sue says. "He made
me sick with all of his 'nigger' talk. He was such a redneck.''

"It made me mad, too, okay?" Cindy says. "I left him,
okay? I didn't know he was such a piece of shit until I had
him, okay?''

"All right. All right," Hannah says and it is like God has
spoken.

"Cindy, why didn't you ever tell me Buzz Biggers was that
way?" Madge asks, staring down at that diamond on her
hand.

"You? Why would I have told you? You're the one that
snatched Catherine right out of public school when we inte-
grated.''

"Your daddy did that," Madge says, twists a strand of her
hair. "He wanted you to go there, too, when you were high
school age but I talked him out of it.''

"Yeah sure," Cindy says. "You can say anything you want
since he's dead.''

"It's the truth," Madge says and looks around but nobody
knows, nobody knows about those years consumed in baggies
and King Tut. Madge takes a deep breath and sits forward in
her chair. "He said, 'If Cindy marries a nigger, it's your
fault.' '' She pauses while Cindy smirks, stares down at her
toes and shakes her head back and forth. "He said, 'Hannah
and Ben can raise their children like niggers if they want
to.' ''

"What?" Hannah faces Madge, her mouth open and face
red.

"She's lying," Cindy says. "You know that's a lie!''

"Messy was a liar," Lena says.

"Get off my grandma, okay?" Cindy beats her hand on
the floor with every word. "I'm real goddamned tired of it.''

"She didn't mean . . .''

"And you take up for her." Cindy stares at Ginny Sue and
toxemia or epilepsy, right this minute, she doesn't give a
damn, and nobody in this room is even thinking to defend
her daddy. Blessed are the sick she wants to tell them but she

doesn't because Ginny Sue and Emily and Lena and probably even her mama and St. Peter standing there with her face still red would take it to mean them.

"It's true," Madge says. "I feel like most of my life is buried with him, all the things I never told."

"Like what, Madge?" Hannah goes over now and touches Madge on the shoulder and though Madge tries to keep herself from shaking and letting it all out, she can't control herself and just sits there and cries while the sky gets darker outside and the trees blow back and forth with the wind.

"The weatherman was right," Emily says. "Showers by afternoon. Thunderstorms today and tomorrow."

"Well, I need to get Chuckie before it starts. He's supposed to spend the night at a friend's and I'll just see if he can go on over there." Cindy stands and speaks only to Ginny Sue. "I'll come back later when it's cooled off," and she walks out of the duplex without once looking back.

"Is it going to cool off?" Lena asks.

"Weatherman says not." Emily cannot understand why Madge doesn't go on home if she's to behave this way. A person ought not to show herself to others. Mag Sykes has passed on. "I believe the Lord will see me through," Mag had said. "This life is nothing but a pathway." Yes, Emily knows that; this life is nothing but a pathway.

* * *

Emily was in the kitchen when James died. She was standing at that sink washing dishes and looking out the window at all the leaves blowing from her trees. She had just finished making a little clown doll for Ginny Sue and had him propped up in a chair at the kitchen table so that Ginny Sue would be surprised when Emily called the two of them in to lunch. They were in the bedroom, the big stuffed chair over near the window where James liked to sit and read to Ginny Sue. He didn't know how to read too well, but he didn't need to; he knew those Brer Rabbit stories by heart and she loved to hear him making his voice go different for each character, loved to hear Ginny Sue squeal with laughter and beg him for more stories.

She thought so often then that she didn't know what the two of them would have done without Ginny Sue and Robert to fill up their days. James had given up his farming not long after David died, had men that moved onto all that farmland down where James came from, and he gave them most of the profit when the tobacco was sold. He'd walk down to the warehouses every now and then or get Hannah and Ben to drive him out past his land, but that was all. They didn't talk about David too much because it didn't even seem real that he was dead; there was no body to bury down where she and James had a plot not far from where his parents were buried. There was just a piece of paper signed by the president and she didn't even have that anymore because James tore it up and threw it in the fire. It was always on the tip of her tongue to say, "David would have done this" or "David would have said that" but she'd see Ginny Sue sitting there on his lap, making him laugh and there was no cause to upset him, no cause for a child to hear of such sad things that young.

For years James had gotten up early and crept behind her where she was building a fire in the living room, or washing up breakfast dishes, wrapped his arms around her waist and squeezed; she would squeal out in alarm and then press her face into his dark neck, the thick black hair, the oils of his face carrying the faint trace of the cigars that he smoked. For years now, she has felt that bare emptiness of her shoulder and waist, as she sat on the porch or when she pressed her face into her pillow pretending that it was the tight weathered skin of his neck and face, the sparse gray hair of his old age.

"If anything ever happened to me," he had asked, the first time when they were so young, when it was a cold winter morning and she had not even gotten up to light the fire, David just a little baby in a cradle, Hannah barely walking and talking. "Would you marry someone else?"

"Never," she told him that morning and all the other times over the years, the last being the day before he died, his face as weathered as that pecan tree, hit by lightning and split in two.

"I will never marry again," she told him. "I will never love anybody like I love you." And she had hugged him so close, not wanting to think of anything happening. She had already lost David and she couldn't stand to think of losing him. She would tell herself that she would still have Hannah and Hannah's children.

She looks over at Hannah, now, sitting there holding Madge's hand just like they did when they were children out skipping rope. Lena's got her head back and her mouth dropped open like she might be dead and she might as well be. Lena wants to die and the Lord is making her wait until he feels she's ready. And the Lord is sending rain; the rain is falling and the river's gonna rise, gonna rise, gonna rise, and she feels so excited when she thinks of standing out in that yard, Curie telling her to dance a jig, dance yourself a rain dance, and she had felt so free right that second with her skirt lifted and her feet turning her around and around in a circle, slow at first and then faster, with Curie just a dark blur off to the side as she spun around. "Just let go and dance, Miss Emily," he called out, and she did; she danced herself a rain dance and she felt like nobody had ever felt so free, just a child letting go, her hair falling out of the neatly pinned bun, her white apron dusty from the dirt she was kicking up, pantaloons showing, and sweat trickling down her neck, until she finally got tired and sprawled out flat on her back on a grassy spot and laughed until her stomach ached, laughed until she heard her mama come out that front door. The river's gonna rise now and Ginny Sue is lying there with her eyes closed. "Sweet dreams," she has always said to Ginny Sue and James would say, "don't let the bed bugs bite."

* * *

She was right there in the kitchen when he died, right there at the sink when Ginny Sue came in and told her that he fell asleep right in the middle of The Tar Baby.

"Do I have to take a nap, too?" Ginny Sue had asked and she took that child by the hand and led her over to the chair where the clown was sitting.

"I'll go check on Gramps," she told Ginny Sue and she had known, she had known with each and every one of her steps on that floor that sounded so loud to her ears. She knew as soon as she walked into the room and saw his head turned to one side, the direction of the window, the book opened on his lap with his still hand marking the place. "I'm going to miss you so bad," she whispered and leaned close to his face, the breathless mouth. Hannah came within minutes of her call, her face so small and pale-looking. And then the ambulance came and then others started coming so by late afternoon her house was full of people. Tessy came, her eyes swollen and she made her way across that crowded living room so slowly.

"Why you?" she had asked and squeezed Emily so tightly. "First your son and now your husband, why you?" And later, Tessy stood on that back porch and stomped her feet and cursed, looked up in the sky and cursed until Emily went and got her, pulled her back inside where it was warm, and Emily didn't care what any of those other women might think, didn't care what Lena said about Tessy.

* * *

"Tessy didn't mean to cut a shine when James died," she says now. She doesn't care what they think, these women here to cry and say they're sorry that James is dead.

"Mama, we know that." It is Hannah, Hannah.

"Tessy didn't mean those curses," she says and shakes her head.

"We know," Hannah whispers and takes her hand.

"I told James I'd never have another man," she says. "I loved James and I told him that I'd do right by him."

"And you have," Hannah says. "Now dry those tears and let's talk about something happy. You too, Madge." And Madge nods, smiles a weak smile.

"Happy," Lena mumbles and lights a cigarette. "I used to be happy. I used to stroll down Park Avenue happy as a lark. I used to sunbathe down in Florida, me and Roy, and I was never so happy as then. I was happy."

"Well, be happy right now," Hannah says, looks at the daybed where Ginny Sue is just staring out the window like she's not even listening.

"How?" Lena asks. "How can I be happy while Roy's dead?" Roy never should have died; he wasn't even sick. He had never been sick, full of energy, do this, do that. She should have died. After all those years for him to up and leave her so fast. It makes her so damn mad.

* * *

"Roy? Roy, lunch is ready," she had called out the back door. He was under the house messing with the plumbing, fixing, always fixing something, wires and pipes, or sitting at that kitchen table with all those rulers and pencils, drawing up something that would need wires and pipes. "I'm an engineer,'' he had told her the first time they met and he was driving around in that car with a rumble seat, his pants cut short with bright argyle socks and that light brown hair parted down the middle. She had been in New York then, working and modeling a little; she worked in cosmetics, spent her day taking simple-looking women and doing something with them.

"Guess you get to travel a lot," she said. "But I'd get tired if all I did was sit on a train." And he had laughed great big, offered her a cigarette from the little gold case he kept in his coat pocket.

"A mechanical engineer," he told her. "I build things." They were at a party, sipping champagne and eating shrimp, and she was wearing a skirt that showed her knees. Emily would have turned purple and dropped dead if she had seen Lena at that party; her mama would have let her have it, but they weren't there to see. They were way out in the country, out in Saxapaw with chickens and pole beans and slop jars and she was at a party in a swanky hotel in New York City. She wore a red silky dress and beads that hung near about to her knees and Roy Carter pulled her onto that dance floor and she twirled until everybody else backed off and watched; just she and Roy Carter cutting a rug. "But I am going places," he had told her later. "I go all the time, Washington, Chicago, you name it. But if I'm on a train, I'm going first class, not the clown tooting the whistle."

* * *

"Roy?" she had leaned out that back door and yelled again, rang that little bell that he had put on the back porch for her to ring for the cats. The turnips were getting cold and all those cats sitting there rubbing on her legs but not a word from him. That was so like him, get off with some machine or pipes that he could take apart and put back together, and never pay her a bit of attention.

She had finally had to put on her housecoat and go out there herself. Her whole life she felt like she had to go after that man. He'd talk to this person or that person for as long as they'd listen, would talk to that Mrs. Simms across the street some afternoons and it would make Lena so mad that she couldn't see straight. "What have you got to say to that ugly old widow anyway?"

"She's not ugly and she's not old," Roy had said time and time again, then patted her on the fanny and kissed her cheek. "You just get a little jealous, that's all."

"Jealous?" Lena had asked time and time again. "Why in the hell would I get jealous of that?" But she had gotten jealous, had always been jealous. God, she loved him, would have done anything for him. But she never would have died and left him all alone; and she couldn't have a child. It wasn't her fault that she couldn't. She didn't make him stay. But she always knew he was wishing for somebody that could have children.

* * *

"That's ridiculous, Lena," he had said once when he had found her crying. They were in Florida then and it was so damn hot; it was so damn hot and she told him that that was why she was crying.

"I don't want a baby," she had said. "I've seen what Emily went through. I was right in her kitchen watching after Hannah when she had David and I heard what she went through."

"I don't want a child either," he said. "Having you is like having both, a wife and a child."

"Go on to hell," she had said and pushed him away, then quickly pulled him to her with those old tree frogs making so much noise she thought her head would split wide open.

* * *

"Go on to hell then," she had said and looked through the opening to the cool, damp darkness under the house. "Just go on to hell." And somebody called the police, the ambulance, probably old lady Simms with her ugly self, still interested in Roy and him under the house dead as a doornail.

But she saw him after that; she saw him in their house having a party, women half-naked chasing after him. He stopped by her bed and asked her if she wanted to go see the royal wedding over in England and she said, "I am tired, Roy, tired." But he wouldn't leave her alone, wanted her to party, and a policeman was at that front door and she yelled for Roy to open it up but he didn't, too busy entertaining himself, so she did it herself, embarrassed that anybody should see such goings-on in her house, but thinking maybe he could get it to stop.

"One of your neighbors reported that you were screaming," he had said and she asked him in.

"Who wouldn't? Just look around here." She had gone and sat on the sofa with all that noise coming from the kitchen. "They're the ones."

"Who?" he had asked, walked around her house and then came and sat down beside her. "Is there someone that I can call for you? A friend? A relative?"

"Emily can't go nowhere," she had said. "I never had a child." Finally she had given him Hannah's name and then Hannah had come and taken her to their house to spend the night and neither of them, that policeman or Hannah, let on like they had seen what Roy was up to.

She saw him the next day as well; he was up on the roof of that house that he loved more than her, and he wouldn't come when she called him. He just stood there and opened that raccoon coat to show that he wasn't wearing any clothes. "Get the hell down, Roy," she screamed, so embarrassed because old lady Simms was in her yard watching. Roy wouldn't even look at her. "I can't get him to come inside," she told Hannah. "First he was on the house and now he's under it."

Hannah took her to the doctor and she left Roy a note on the table in case he should come home. "Don't leave me, Roy," she had written and the doctor gave her a shot and he was a nice doctor, handsome. "I know your wife's proud," she said, feeling so tired, that room so cool with those white sheets. "I bet your mama is, too," and she could barely see Hannah standing there, barely feel that nice man's hand on her arm.

"Roy's dead," the man said. "You were dreaming, bad dreams, and we'll take care of you now." Roy's dead and they wouldn't let her stay at home. She should have died; she should have been the one up under that house dead.

* * *

It is raining hard now and Madge watches the drops collecting on the window, moving together, rolling down. "Feeling better?" Hannah asks her and she nods as she watches Cindy park in front of the duplex and run through the rain.

"Whew!" Cindy says when she comes through the door, her hair wet and stringy. "I hope you've decided to stop talking about Daddy," she says and looks at Madge. Madge feels like she could bust wide open, like she could grab Cindy's tiny little body and shake some sense into her.

"Cindy, what I said was the truth," Madge says, swallows hard, and stares back.

"Oh yeah, I know. I know how much you loved him and all." Cindy sits on the floor facing Ginny Sue, her back to Madge. "She didn't even cry at his funeral," she says to Ginny Sue.

"I did," Madge says. "I had already cried for years."

* * *

Madge's house had been full of people the day of the funeral. Cindy was at the kitchen table with Raymond's necktie clutched in her hands. "I couldn't let him wear it," Cindy wailed. "He looked like he would choke." Cindy picked up a napkin and blew her nose, wiped away those flakes of blue mascara that had fallen to her cheeks. Cindy looked more like Raymond than she ever had, that little thin nose, her blue eyes too large for her thin face.

"I want to keep this tie," Cindy had sobbed while she pulled a thin strip of hot pink polish from her thumbnail. "I want to save this tie because he wore it to my sophomore dance when ya'll chaperoned. I might frame this tie. I might hang it out in the hallway near little Chuckie's bedroom just so I can think of Daddy whenever I tell my little baby goodnight."

"Keep it," Madge said and went to stand by the window, the sky so blue, the limbs of the pecan tree rattling against the house. She couldn't wait for that day to be over, couldn't wait to get back to the dental office, to wash those ashtrays that were filled to the brim and put them away forever.

"Charles stopped by this morning." Cindy got a glass of water and popped something into her mouth. "Can you believe that?"

"Well, that was nice," she said and sat at the table, wondering why Ginny Sue or somebody didn't come and do something with Cindy. Catherine was in the other room talking about selling houses and Roy Carter talking about building houses and Lena talking about cleaning house. She had never felt so all alone in her whole life. Hannah would whip past every few minutes with another dish that somebody had brought, or she'd be over at the sink washing dishes, but nobody, nobody sat down at that table and took hold of her hands and said, "Tell me about it, Madge."

"Nice? Nice? Some whore woman was out in the car. He had a date. And there he was in my house, in my room with me in nothing but a robe and do you know that he hugged me? He hugged me with me in nothing but a thin silky Vanity Fair robe and I hope he remembered that he gave me that robe. I hope he remembered it all and that his you-know-what aches for having thought of it."

"That's enough," Madge had said.

"Yeah, tell me." Cindy shook her head back and forth and paced. "He was making a move on me with that woman sitting right out there in the car, said they would take care of Chuckie for me. That wasn't what he was thinking of taking care of right that minute, no sir, he had other thoughts in that skull of his."

"Cindy, could you please be a little quieter." Catherine came into the kitchen and sat down beside Madge, a *Southern Living* in her hand. "This is a funeral."

"What in the hell would I do without you to inform me of what's going on," Cindy said. "Since when have you decided to talk to me, breaking your oath of the King James Bible."

"I think we should try to get along," Catherine had said. "For mother," and she patted Madge's hand like Madge might have been a dog. How? How did she get two children like that? Then Catherine waved and went into the other room to speak to somebody who was talking to Brent. Madge had never cared for Brent; all he did was sip liquor and talk big, like Raymond.

"It probably would have been a good thing for Charles to keep Chuckie today," Madge had said and watched Cindy pace back and forth.

"Chuckie needs to be exposed to things like this. God knows I'm the only person to teach him what's going on in the world." Cindy twisted the necktie round and round her hands. "Daddy is dead," she sobbed. "I don't know if I can stand it. I fainted while Charles was there and next thing I knew, I was laid out on the bed with my robe all loosened up. He could have done anything to me with me in that state."

"You'd know if he had," Madge said and got up from the table. "I'm sure he didn't. Charles isn't that kind."

"Oh you have always taken up for Charles. You like Charles more than you've ever liked me or ever liked Daddy."

"You know that's not true."

"I haven't seen you shed one tear, not one." Cindy's eyes were twitching back and forth so fast they looked like they might fall out. "I keep expecting to see him," Cindy said, her words slowing down. "I saw him this morning. I was sure of it. He was right in front of Rexall when I went to fill my prescription. I ran up to the door and he was gone."

"Lay off the Valium, Cindy," Madge said. Just the thought of Raymond suddenly appearing anywhere gave her goose-flesh. She was relieved when Hannah came into the room with Chuckie.

"I want some candy," Chuckie said and in no time at all, Cindy was squatted down with half her slip showing and her arms wrapped around him.

"Bless your heart," Cindy said and kissed all over the top of that child's head. "I know you're having a hard time understanding that Granddaddy has passed on. It's a trauma you will remember your whole life."

"I want some candy," Chuckie said again and looked at Madge. She got him a Hershey's kiss out of the cabinet.

"He wanted his mama," Hannah had whispered and gripped Madge's arm. "Ginny Sue is on her way over and maybe it'll do Cindy good to see her." Hannah, still watching Cindy squatted there, leaned closer to Madge. "Are you okay?" Madge nodded and couldn't help but smile when she saw Chuckie put that kiss in his mouth and roll it all around. It wouldn't be a trauma for him unless Cindy turned it into one.

"Granddaddy is up in heaven," Cindy continued. "Heaven is up there with the clouds and God and Jesus." She pointed upwards. "When people die, especially people with long incurable diseases," she glanced up at Madge and Hannah looked at her as well; she knew Hannah was wondering what in the hell Cindy was talking about. "These people with rare cancers go and live with God and they watch over us just like Jesus does and sometimes they take a little trip back to earth

to let us know how much they care like when we saw Granddaddy at the Rexall today.''

"Cindy?'' Madge whispered but it did no good.

"Your body is only a shell, baby,'' Cindy said and hugged
Chuckie closer. He had chocolate all over his mouth and it
got on the front of Cindy's dress. Cindy still sometimes
blames Chuckie's acne on the chocolate that he ate at Madge's
house during the funeral. "Your body is like a pecan,'' Cindy
had said, except she said it like "pee-can'' and Madge had
to bite her tongue near about off to keep from correcting. "A
pee can is what people used to keep under their beds,'' she
had told Cindy once and that made Cindy say it twice as
much.

"You know the pee-cans that are out in this yard?'' Cindy
asked and looked at Chuckie who was eyeing the cabinet that
had the kisses. "And you crack the shell and take out the
good part.''

"Eat the good part,'' Chuckie said. "I want more candy.''

"Our bodies are the shells and inside of us where we have
souls is the good part and that's the part that lives with Jesus.
Do you see?'' Cindy shook him and Chuckie twisted to get
away. "I know it's hard to take, but life is hard. It's damn
hard for me and the worst of it all is the way that good for
nothing daddy of yours tried to take me.'' Cindy leaned back
and sat straddle-legged on the floor and Madge took Chuckie's hand and pulled him over to her. He needed to be told
that what he just heard about his daddy was not true. Hannah
was washing glasses in the sink and Madge knew, was trying
to pretend that she had heard none of Cindy's mess.

"How about a little lunch, Cindy?'' Hannah asked. "It
might help.'' Cindy rolled her head from side to side, kneecap to kneecap. "Ginny Sue will be here soon.''

"So?'' Cindy asked. "What good can she do me at a time
like this? Her daddy isn't dead. Her husband didn't leave her
only to come back and try to get it.''

"Where's Jesus?'' Chuckie asked and Madge took his hand
and walked out on the back porch. It was crisp and cold
outside and Madge walked Chuckie over to the pecan tree
where the nuts had fallen. She stood and watched him running around, first chasing a frightened squirrel and then picking up the nuts. She waved when Ginny Sue pulled up and
parked, but Madge stayed out there in the yard with Chuckie;

Ginny Sue would have to understand, they all would, that she needed some fresh air.

"Jesus is in here," Chuckie said and handed her a nut. "Jesus stays in this pee-can."

"It's a pecan," Madge corrected. "And Jesus is in heaven."

"My mommy says it's a pee-can. Mommy says Jesus stays in it." Madge just smiled at him and let it go at that.

* * *

"You're not thinking of me," she had said to Raymond. "You're not thinking of us. You've got to help yourself get better."

"I'm thinking of the future," he said and grinned, his teeth unbrushed, graying hair disheveled. "I bought a cemetery plot didn't I? That's thinking of us." He pulled the receipt from his shirt pocket. "One of the nicest spots there is, little stream nearby, shrubbery, so quiet you can hear acorns thump the ground."

"But you won't be hearing it," she had said, crying. There had been so many times when she *was* crying.

"Who's to say?" he asked. "The Egyptians believed that life went on. They took it all with them, valuables, food. Some of them had their wives put in the tomb." He looked at her and she felt her spine freeze, a split second of fear that she knew he saw before she responded.

"It's not right to spend your life getting ready to die," she said.

"I bet people didn't think King Tut was crazy. I think it was right, and I'll be ready, oh yeah, I'll be all ready." Then he laughed and went back to his book, the pictures of tombs and mummies. Cindy never saw what was happening; Cindy said that her father was "cultural," an artist of the mind. Cindy bought him that King Tut record that Steve Martin did and though Madge tried to talk Cindy out of giving it to him, and tried to explain, Cindy would not hear of it. He got out the hammer after Cindy left and cracked that record into hundreds of pieces there on the living room floor. "You shouldn't make fun. You shouldn't make fun," he had said over and over, eyeing Madge while he beat that record.

* * *

"I can't believe that we're not having a church service," Cindy had said when Madge and Chuckie came back into the kitchen. Cindy's words were so slow, like she had a mouthful of cotton and Ginny Sue was trying to get her to drink coffee. "And a song or two. We need for somebody to sing 'Love Lifted Me' or 'Take Me in Your Arms, Sweet Jesus, I'm Ready.' "

"I've never heard of that one," Hannah said and it was one of those strange moments when in the midst of a serious time, something becomes hilarious. Madge could tell that Ginny Sue was trying not to laugh and once she and Hannah had let go, she joined right in, the kind of laughter that brings tears. It made Cindy furious.

* * *

The sunlight had been warm, sinking through Madge's dark coat as they'd walked from the small dirt road to the grave-side. There were flowers everywhere, straight metal chairs. Cindy was sobbing uncontrollably before anything even started so Madge pulled Chuckie closer. Before the service was over, Madge had to turn and motion to Ginny Sue to come get Cindy, and during the silent prayer, she watched Ginny Sue halfway carrying Cindy over to that funeral home limousine. And then there was a silent prayer and yes, she could hear the stream, and yes, she thought she heard an acorn. People began walking towards her at the end but she stepped away a minute so that she could see what Raymond had done, all of the plans that had occupied all those years. There was concrete like a vault, a room, a picture of a pyramid on one wall, a TV stand that she had never seen before with that brand new widescreen color set, books, and a huge metal grate off to one side of the grave that she knew was meant to cover the top, to seal the tomb. It sent a chill through her body to watch them lower that casket onto a small bed-frame, her Raymond, that Raymond, both gone. And again, there was that slight shiver when she realized that there was no room for her, no way for that seal to be broken once the concrete was poured over the top. He had never intended for her to be with him.

"That wasn't granddaddy," Cindy was whispering to Chuckie when Madge got back in the car. "It was a shell of a man."

"You're right," Madge had said and watched Catherine and Brent lingering to talk to people. Madge thought about cleaning her house from floor to ceiling. She would take Chuckie to a Walt Disney movie or to the zoo. Or maybe, she'd just go right back to work and keep right on playing solitaire.

"Jesus is in the pee can," Chuckie said and Madge couldn't help but laugh, hurting her cheeks, tears springing to her eyes.

* * *

"What's so funny?" Cindy asks now and Madge shakes her head, looks at Hannah.

"I was thinking of how Chuckie said Jesus lived in a pee can," she says, the tears coming to her eyes. "At the funeral, that's what Chuckie said."

"That's not funny," Cindy says. "Chuckie was a baby and that's how I happened to explain death to him."

"A pee can?" Virginia asks now, only for Cindy to sigh out loud like she could pop.

"Oh I'm sorry. All of you speak such good English. Pecan, okay? Pecan! I mean I'm the only one that gets corrected, right? Nobody says a word when Emily says Chi*cargo* or Lena says ain't or the way Mama calls Thalhimers with a Th. She says Thall like shall, thallhimers."

"I do not," Madge says but Cindy is determined to go right on and right on and drive her out of her mind.

"Mama says purrio, too, instead of perio when she does all of her teeth talk."

"I do not." Madge is blushing and has put her cards aside. "And there's no such song as 'Take Me in Your Arms Sweet Jesus, I'm Ready,' and it's not natural to wear blue nail polish."

"Well, I see," Cindy says. "You got an audience now so let's hear it. Just go right on and say what about me you hate, and Daddy, go right ahead and talk about him, too."

"He was crazy," Lena says and Hannah tried to Shh her now, the wind whistling outside, rain pelting against that window. "Roy said he knew that man was crazy as hell when we saw him there atop the hardware store acting like a woman."

"It was a campaign for Chevrolet," Cindy snaps and looks

around the room. "Everybody knows that!" She looks at her mama but she's staring out at that rain like a zombie. "Will you tell them the truth?" she asks and her mama turns and looks at her with those eyes all teared up again; her mama is diseased, disease of the mind, and the rest of them here are diseased in the brain, won't even listen, won't even talk. "Will you tell them that Daddy was not crazy!"

"He was, though," Emily says. "Me and Ginny Sue know. Me and Ginny Sue and God. I said, 'Ginny Sue, me and you and God, that's all that needs to know.' "

"Gram," Virginia says, everyone looking at her.

"What?" Cindy asks. "Just tell me what. Go ahead and make up some story. Great weather for it. Thunder and lightning so go right ahead and tell some ghost story."

"He just scared me one time," Virginia says, staring back at Gram, nodding until Gram nods with her.

"Who hasn't scared you?" Cindy asks. "All you got to do is say 'boo' and it scares you."

"When?" Hannah asks, remembering all those times Ginny Sue flung herself down on the floor, begging not to go to Madge's house.

"Years ago," she says, shakes her head but her mother and Madge are still staring at her. "I was there and he came up the steps with a mask on and it scared me."

"That was a game," Cindy says. "My daddy liked to have fun. My daddy did things other than grow squash and pump gas."

"Yes, he did," Madge says. "He did things like dress like a woman and climb on top of the hardware store."

"It was funny when he did that," Cindy says, her hair drying in frizzy little wisps. "It was a creative thing."

"Well, it wasn't a campaign for Chevrolet," Madge says, gaining strength as she looks around the room. "We all remember it; people have been nice about acting like they don't remember but we all do."

"I remember," Lena says and laughs, stands by her chair and twists one arm out behind her, the other out front in an Egyptian pose. It tickled Roy so when she'd strike that pose.

* * *

"He's crazy as hell," Roy had said and parked the Lincoln there in front of the hardware store. Lena could see him up there big as Ike, dressed like a woman with his eyes all made up and everybody in town coming out to see. "I got to tell him a thing or two before he gets arrested."

"Well, you can try," Lena said and lit a cigarette, that sweet little Pooh Kitty stretched out on the backseat in the sunshine. "But me and Pooh are going to sit here in the car where it's cool."

She had sat there and watched it all, pure tee embarrassment. Madge was all slumped over on that slut-looking Cindy with shorts so tight they rode into her crack, and people, good decent people taking the time out of a hot as hell busy day to just pull up a yard chair and sit and watch like they might be in New York preparing for a Broadway play. God, she had missed the city, missed the walking and bumping and horn blowing, flashing blinking lights and mannequins in windows dressed in pure gold, while she held that cigarette lighter out to Roy, and swayed back and forth there on the street corner with that colored man playing the sax while Roy whistled for a taxi and they flew through the streets from place to place. There are things in this world to see, and there all those people had sat and watched Raymond Sinclair on top of Kinglee Hardware. Lena wished he'd just jump if that's what was on his mind so she and Roy could get on home and have a little time to themselves.

Pooh had stretched and growled, tiptoed right into the front seat and sprawled out on her lap. She saw Roy walk out on that rooftop and shake his finger at Raymond, shake his head, throw his arms up in the air and let them slap to his sides like he always did when she got the last word in an argument. "Sheesh, Lena," he'd say and those hands would slap his sides, "I give," and she'd say, "I take," and wrap her arms around him and they'd flop down in a chair or on the sofa, bed, floor, whatever was closest and stay that way till he felt the urge to tinker with a pipe or draw some lines on a piece of paper.

"I see you couldn't talk him down," she had said when Roy got back in the car, those eyebrows arched and eyes like hard round pebbles, just like when he always got agitated. He was something else when he looked like that. "You do better talking Pooh from a tree."

"Pooh ain't crazy as hell," he said and patted Pooh on the head. Pooh craned his neck, and his little cat eyes squinted like he always did when he wanted a little loving. That Pooh was a love, yes Jesus, loved her so. "I told Raymond he was making a big fool of himself."

"And?" she asked, spotting several women that she knew and turning her head so she wouldn't have to wave to them as they passed.

"He said, 'Fuck you Roy.' Can you believe he said that?"

"He's trash," Lena said and pulled Pooh up to her face so she could hear his motor. "Right Pooh? Pooh knows he's a trashy trashy man, yeah, pooh, little pooh pooh knows. Raymond Sinclair is shit. Right little pooh?"

* * *

"Pooh knew he was crazy," Lena says. "Yessir, we all knew."

"I knew," Emily says. "You and Roy told me he was on the hardware store." It didn't surprise Emily a bit when she heard what he did. No sir, he had scared Ginny Sue that time and she knew that man couldn't do a thing that would surprise her. Dressed like a woman and why did he marry if that's what interested him? Felicia is a good woman and she is that way but Felicia doesn't show herself on top of a hardware store and Felicia doesn't scare children. She wasn't surprised; she isn't surprised at what they've got on TV. People walking down beaches with near to nothing on sipping a soda like there aren't peas to shell and get to boiling and corn to shuck and clothes to wash. Emily was so glad that Tessy didn't have to hear of her son-in-law on top of the hardware store, 'cause Tessy would have lit into that man like a fevered dog, the same as she done that time them young Mormon boys come to her screen door that time. Tessy shot 'em with that BB gun of hers, put a blister on one of those boy's faces, told Emily all about it over the telephone.

"I'm glad Tessy didn't have to hear of it," Emily says. It makes her laugh to think of Lena striking that pose with her hands all crooked. Lena has always been able to strike a pose that way. Lena is striking one now with her mouth dropped open and that skint animal hat pulled to one side. Lena looks old and bad but she can strike a pose like nobody's business.

* * *

"My God, it was no big deal," Cindy says now and fluffs

her hair. She hates when it goes flat. "Your hair looks nice," Randy Skinner had said just last night and nuzzled up to her in the parking lot of Ramada. She knew she shouldn't have gone at all, but she told herself well, if she'd had something better to do, she would have done it. "Play with fire, you get burned," Constance Ann had said late yesterday afternoon. "Don't call me to come spend the night again, because I'm warning you now. Besides, I can't stand to miss 'Dallas' two weeks in a row." And Cindy didn't call her last night after making out with Randy Skinner; she didn't need to call anybody because Randy Skinner meant nothing to her except a way to kill a little time. Charles and Nancy Price weren't there even though Nancy's sister was singing again.

"Don't go, Cindy," Constance Ann had turned right around and called on the phone to say. "Really, I'll come spend the night. We could pop some popcorn."

"Thanks, but it's something I've got to do," Cindy told her and even though the whole night was boring, two kamikazes and kissing on an old married nothing, it was something Cindy had to do. Constance Ann does not understand desperation; Constance Ann does not understand what a difference a little manly attention can make in this otherwise suck hole world. If Cindy's going to make a mistake, then it's her mistake, her business and the fact that Ginny Sue is sitting over there pregnant as a horse with a lawyer husband does not take back the mistakes that she has made. Give somebody a marriage certificate and suddenly they're the born again virgin, like the honeymoon opened that door for the first time. Everybody knows that when the Lord slams a door, he tries to crack a window and all she's doing is just as he would have her to do, sniff down that window with a crack and fling it to the roof, let the world in. Anybody that looks hard enough can find a crack in this world, it might not be the one they've always dreamed up like Ginny Sue wanting to be Barbie and live in the dream house or like Constance Ann thinking a man is going to come along and find her there in her bathrobe watching TV and fall madly in love with her. The Lord helps them that helps themselves. "His cancer was a big deal," Cindy says. "But not the hardware store."

"It was all a big deal," Madge says. "I tried to get him to the doctor."

"Doctor, smoctor." Cindy waves her hand. "What Daddy

had hasn't even been discovered, yet. They'll probably name it after Daddy when it's discovered.''

"He was crazy," Lena says. "Yes Jesus, tell it 'cause he was. Roy said it and Roy knows."

"Say 'Alzheimer's,' " Cindy says to Lena in a way she hopes that bitch can hear. "Alls Hiii Merrs!"

"I was so embarrassed," Madge says and looks at Hannah. "I was."

"I know you were," Hannah says. "I wish somebody had called me."

"I called you," Virginia says. "Remember? I called from school because I had seen Betsy Peterson and her mama had been downtown and seen it all."

"Seen it all," Cindy says. "You make it sound like my daddy hung his pecker in the wind or something."

"Cindy!" Madge gasps but Emily thinks its funny. Lord to picture that pose like Lena showed with *that* hung out. A man is nothing to see unless you love that man. That's what she told Hannah before she married; it ain't much to see.

"Oh pardon me," Cindy says. "Now what should I have said instead of pecker, since we're all so pure and holy."

"You coulda said dick," Lena says and laughs.

"Or peter." Emily has to reach for another tissue. "Heeee," she laughs in a high wheeze.

"One-eyed trouser snake," Cindy says and even Hannah has to laugh at that one.

"God, I'd hate to get bit," Emily says and grips the arms of her chair. "Pssssh Heeee," snuff dust spraying. "I told Hannah just before she married that it was not much to see." She wipes her eyes.

"You told me nothing of the kind," Hannah says. "You never told me a thing about anything."

"You weren't even at the hardware store," Cindy says to Ginny Sue. "You were off with your nose in a book and then gossiped about it."

"I did not gossip!"

"Shit!" Cindy says and leans back on her elbows. "You probably told all your snotty college friends and made it sound like my daddy was crazy."

"Heeee, she's said another word that makes me laugh," Emily says and never in Hannah's life would she have thought her mama would laugh over ugly words. Her mama had once made Hannah lick a bar of soap for saying "pee."

"And she coulda said B.M.," Lena says. "Couldn't she Hannah?" Lena is laughing now too, shaking those curlers right out of her thin hair.

"It would have been nicer," Hannah says.

"Or job," Emily says and sprays snuff all over herself. "Business. Heeee."

"Roy worked at his job," Lena says. "Roy was into big business" and now Hannah cannot control her laugher; she just lets go and joins in, God knows, better the laugher than tears for a change.

"Roy got a watch when he retired," Lena says. "That man he worked for said, 'you've done a fine job, Roy,' " and she barely gets that out of her mouth but what they all fall to one side and laugh like they might be retarded when there's not a damn thing funny about it. "Don't laugh at Roy!" she yells. "He was into big business," and there they go again, just laugh and laugh and laugh till you drop dead. Roy worked hard and Roy played hard and he'd get that way better than any man that any of these sitting here will ever know. Let 'em laugh and laugh and laugh. They'll be sorry when her and Roy are dead and there's no laughing to be done. Jealous. Her and Roy had everything and they're jealous and Ginny Sue sitting there with her legs straddled about to give birth ain't got a reason to be jealous just because her and Roy had them happy times; Lord yes, tell it, New York, Chicago, Key West, you name it and she could fish like a man if she took a notion. "If you wanted our car you should have bought it before the nigger stole it," she says now and they finally get quiet. Yeah boy, Roy could pick a good car. He told her getting a new car was like winning the New York lottery. "But you're the real prize, you beautiful bitch, you," he'd always say.

* * *

"It's a prize all right," Roy had said and gingerly rubbed his fingertip along the hood ornament of that great maroon Lincoln. And it was, a surprise, her birthday present though she never drove it. Roy told her over and over how he had gone and picked it out. He'd just walked on that lot and he said, "Give me your flashiest and most well-built model with lots of pep, full of gas and fast, 'cause that's who it's for."

He had stood there, so tall and handsome, that little cap tilted on his head while he squinted against that summer sun and ran his finger up and down the ornament. He had already blown the horn five times. "Surprise!" he yelled when she came out on the porch.

"What is going on out here?" she asked, still in a fury over a big old chunk of ice she couldn't get loose from the Frigidaire. She hated to defrost. She hated any kind of household chore. "I hate that damn color," she said when he pointed to the car. "Looks like blood. Whose is it?"

"It's yours," he said, the keys dangling from his fingers, glittering in the sun like golden carrots while she made her way down the steps. "And what's yours is mine, right?" he asked and hugged her close, whispered "Happy Birthday, Miss Rolena, love of my life and beautiful bitch."

All the times over the years that he had told the story, he put in the part where her eyes lit up like Christmas and how she couldn't get inside that house and into some different clothes fast enough. She wasn't about to ride around town in those pedal pushers and plaid shirt. She put on her gold threaded shell top and some black pants, gold shoes, teased her hair a speck and she was ready. She intended to get out and stand by that car every chance she got so people would know it was hers. He bought some little gold letters and put "Queen B.B." on her car door, "Boss" on his; he bought sheepskin seat covers even though they were in Florida and a pair of leather gloves. She filled the backseat with gold velvet pillows so that Trickie would have a place to sit, and Trickie would stretch and meow so sweetlike. Trickie loved that car as good as her. Everything she had pulled out of the Frigidaire that morning went bad and they went to the grocery store and filled that big trunk full of grocery bags.

"I feel like a queen," she had told him when they were on the highway, heading home to see Emily, her right index finger fiddling with the electric window, a quick spurt of air and then the quiet ticking of the little clock that came with the car and was deep in the dash, all padded like velvet.

"I'd not have such written there on the door," Emily said when they finally got to Saxapaw, poor Trickie with a little upset stomach. "What does that mean anyway, Queen B.B. ?"

"It's mine and Roy's secret," Lena said. "You want to know?"

"Queen Beautiful Bitch," Roy said from across the hood, sexy, he looked so sexy there leaning over that hood. "That's what I call Lena."

* * *

Lena had stood and watched that car pull away when it was sold, her hand firmly holding the porch post, her eyes getting all filmed over like she might have had some Sominex. That niggra man leaned his arm out the window and tooted the horn, waved until he was hidden by the Piggly Wiggly. "I rode by here last night to show my wife the car," he had said, said he taught school, liked to fix up cars. "I hope you don't mind, the lights were off and I didn't want to disturb you."

"Disturb? What the hell difference would it have made with all that took place here last night?" He just looked at her, nice of him, acting like he didn't notice the wild party. "I hate your wife had to see all that." He just looked at her like he was confused. Well, good enough. He could pretend that he didn't notice. She'd have rather had that man and his niggra wife in her house over them tramps and wild-acting men that Roy had invited over and him dead under that house with a piece of pipe clutched to his chest like he loved it, loved a piece of pipe and a set of blueprints better than he loved her.

"But you and your wife can't have Trickie," she had told that man, shaking her finger to let him know that she meant business and he acted like he hadn't even seen Trickie. You can tell when one's up to something, yeah boy, you can tell it. And Hannah said, "Come on now and let's go to the doctor." And that man that stole her birthday car rode by later, a woman in the front seat, a herd of little colored children in the backseat playing with the windows, and he beeped that horn and waved, those children turned around backwards and grinning at her.

Lena had held onto the porch post and waved back; "Bring your children to see me," she called and then she remembered that was her car they were driving, the new car, the prize, and it made her mad as sin. "Stop it you colored thieves!" she screamed. "Stop!" but they had rounded the corner again, rounded the Piggly Wiggly and Emily's house should have been there. "Trickie?" she called and he was rubbing up on her leg, purring, but he was old and thin and blind, his long hair all short and pulled out in places.

"Leave him alone, now," Hannah had said. "That cat just about tore your leg up last week," and she looked down at those red scratches on her ankle.

"Trickie wouldn't hurt me," she said and laughed. "No sir, me and Trickie have been together here in Florida for years now."

"That's not Trickie," Hannah had whispered and hugged her hard, too hard, 'cause it made Trickie scoot away and under the house where they all lived. "It's just an old stray."

* * *

"It's not your business!" she says now and they laugh again. "Just laugh. Laugh like you get paid for it. You don't have to live under the house!" She feels herself ready to cry and she doesn't give a damn if she does 'cause they've got no right to laugh at Roy. "I'm tired of it, now, I am tired."

"Oh, we're not laughing at you," Hannah says and is there with her arms around Lena's neck. "What you said was funny, Lena. That's all. You know we love you."

"She knows it," Emily says. "She has pulled this stunt her whole life."

"I have never pulled a stunt," Lena says and wipes her eyes on her shirt. She doesn't care, doesn't wear makeup anymore, not like floozie Cindy sitting there with her legs straddled. "All I ever wanted was Roy Carter."

"And you had him," Madge says. "Aren't too many that get just what they want."

"No." Lena shakes her head. "But I want him now." She bangs her fist on the arm of the chair with each word.

"Then behave so you'll end up where he is," Emily says. "I'd think Roy made it to heaven."

"Of course he did," Hannah says. "He's probably driving around in a big car right now, probably has already built a city of his own."

"I hope Daddy's riding around with him," Cindy says.

"Of course Daddy probably has a whole lot full of Chevrolets."

"Um," Emily shakes her head. "Jesus will not have one that takes his own life."

"Yes, he will," Cindy says. "Jesus counts in rare diseases and such."

"No, Jesus will not have one that takes hisself off earth," Lena says. " 'Cause if he would then I'd get me some Sominex and go on out right now."

"You would not," Emily says and stares hard at Lena. "Don't say such."

"It's true. Sominex can kill." Lena sits up straight. "I lived in New York and I lived in Chicago and when I had my part on Broadway, it was the popular way to leave this earth."

"God, not again," Cindy says. "You had one little part. Big deal."

"Shhh," Madge says and she makes Cindy so sick. They can say that her daddy is burning in hell like a giant french fry and her mama doesn't open her mouth, but God, don't admit that Lena has spent her life acting like Miss Hollywood when she had one little part on one little night when somebody else had taken a few too many Sominex.

"I came out in a little black suit with a ruffly white blouse," Lena says and stands, her hands on those polyester hips. "I said, 'I'm back. I think you always knew I'd be back.' " She trails her finger along the coffee table while she speaks with a slight British accent, turns her head from side to side and smiles. "Roy was front row, center, and tossed a rose up on the stage and it made the man in charge so mad that I had to choose between my part and Roy Carter, so I chose Roy and that's why I only did it one night."

"I've never heard that part," Ginny Sue says, and acts like she believes it. Ginny Sue has always believed any and everything. Cindy could say, "Your epidermis is showing" and Ginny Sue would look down at the crotch of her pants and say, "isn't."

"She just made it up," Cindy says and looks around the room. They all know it but they won't admit it.

"That was so good, Lena," Emily says and wipes her eyes. "Me and James were so proud when Roy called us long distance to say you were going on the stage."

"Roy stood up and he said, 'More, more you beautiful bitch you!' "

"I'd leave that out of the telling," Emily says and turns to Madge. "You can pray Raymond out if you try. If you know a Catholic they could help you better than me."

"She doesn't have to," Cindy says. "My daddy is in heaven. He was not well and killed himself so we wouldn't have to watch him wither up into an old senile nothing."

"Crazy," Lena says with her accent, still trailing her finger.

"What he did is no worse than killing somebody else," Cindy says. "I think it'd be better to kill yourself than somebody else. I bet your son, David, killed somebody in the war." She looks at Emily.

"Cindy, don't," Ginny Sue says as if she's coming out of a daze.

"David did what the service ordered," Emily says. "I don't know that he ever killed a person. The telegram said he was good and brave."

"My daddy was brave," Cindy says. "Makes no difference. Murder is murder and I say it's better to kill yourself than somebody else."

"It makes no difference," Madge says, again feeling the tears coming to her eyes. She would like to get up and leave, to let the wind and the rain push her through the street, to feel a bolt of lightning go right into her head. "Either way, you're hurting others."

"David was defending himself, this country," Hannah says and rubs her mama's back. "I think the Lord understands that."

"I think the Lord knows that if I had kept my part, that I would've been famous forever but that I chose Roy Carter because he is all I ever wanted." Lena stares hard at a smudge on the coffee table that somebody needs to take some Pledge to and says her line again. All these years and she hasn't forgotten a thing. "I never wanted another man."

"I'm with you." Madge forces a laugh. "And all I've got to choose over a man is my job."

"But," Lena says and turns to Madge. "Your mama would've had another. Your mama was crazy over that stray fiddler that took up here for awhile."

"Lena," Hannah says and leads her back to the sofa like she can't walk.

"He was a handsome man," Emily says and takes out her snuff. "And a good nice man."

"Well, let's hear it all," Cindy says. "I'm so tired of ya'll bringing this up and never telling it."

"Nothing to it," Emily says.

"What do *you* know about it?" Cindy turns to Madge.

"About what?" Madge turns suddenly from the window, her heart beating so fast.

"About what? About Grandma Tessy and her boyfriend?"

"His name was Jake," Emily says. "He could play a violin, taught music."

"It was a fiddle," Lena says. "Messy was fiddling with her beau." She laughs. "Roy made that up, fiddling with her beau."

"She did no such thing," Emily says. "Tessy Brock couldn't even sing a note, but she could quilt."

"What did Jake look like?" Virginia asks. She barely remembers Tessy, only remembers a woman with long gray hair screaming and cursing the day Gramps died. Gram had told her that sometimes people couldn't control themselves, that sometimes people do things without thinking.

"He was right handsome," Gram says. "He looked like his people." Virginia tries to focus on Gram, the story, the words. Mark is probably through with his test by now, probably on his way home, or already there.

"His people," Cindy says. "Well that tells all doesn't it? That's like saying I look like my people and there's not a one of you that I resemble."

"He looked like a Jew," Lena says. "And you're the spitting image of Messy Brock."

"Oh, I get you," Cindy says. "He looked like Jesus. He had long silky hair and big brown eyes and a straight nose." She stretches her legs out and laughs. "And he wore a robe, too, a long white robe."

"Not in public he didn't," Emily says. "I don't know what he wore in that room he rented."

"Bet Messy Brock knew," Lena says. "And he looked nothing like Jesus."

"He had dark curly hair and dark eyes and a dark tan," Emily says. "He looked nothing like the Lord."

"He could've been black from that description," Cindy says.

"No," Lena says. "It wouldn't have surprised me if Messy had got herself a niggra but this one wasn't. There might have been a niggra but this one looked like a fiddling monkey."

"He looked like a person," Emily says and glares at Lena. "And Tessy never did anything with him or nobody else, white or colored." Emily looks at Madge. "Him and your mama were friends 'cause Tessy liked the music that he played there in front of the dry goods store."

"Mess took to more than the music," Lena says. "And he was married. Married to one of his own kind. We didn't have many of his kind in these parts."

"What *kind* are you?" Cindy asks and Lena just stops and stares at her.

"Where was his wife?" Madge asks, feeling so uncomfortable that she never knew her mother at all. Her mama wouldn't let her get close, and that's why she married Raymond; that's why she let Raymond make his promises and carry her away from the dull silence of a house she had always hated.

"She lived over in Spottsville," Emily says. "He come by train ever so often to teach some music lessons. Tessy told me he was a sad sweet man; him and Tessy were the same age."

"Harv said he was a freeloader," Lena says. "Harv said he was a bum."

"My parents never agreed," Madge says. "If they talked at all, it was to disagree." She feels them all staring at her, and that rain pounding the ground outside, the street steaming, and she'd like to go right on, tell how her daddy had slapped her mama's face and how her mama picked up the gun. "I've had enough now, Harv," she said and Madge was crouched in her nightgown behind a chair, her feet so cold on that old cracked floor, and her daddy said, "I give up, Tessy. Just go right on hating me for the rest of your life. I'm sorry I took you from that shack where you lived, sorry I've given you a home and a family. Sorry that I'm not what you want. But as long as you stay here, you'll do as I say." And she had seen her daddy crying when he was out in that clearing, blasting those bottles and she had seen her mama's cheeks glisten while she sat by the window and sewed, humming tunes that Madge had never heard before. That's why Madge never wanted to sew; it was sad and lonely and that's all sewing meant. Madge didn't want to be like her mother; she didn't want a life like her mother's and that's why she had married Raymond.

* * *

"I never noticed them arguing," Hannah says, watching Madge stare out the window. "I loved Aunt Tessy and nobody on this earth will ever sew like she could."

"She was lucky to get Harv," Lena says. "And look how she said thank-you."

"But she was too young to marry," Emily says, remembering Tessy clutching her hand. Tessy was not but thirteen with eyes like saucers, knowing she was going to have to climb in bed with a man she barely knew when the sun went down and Harv come up from that field. "I'm so scared," she had whispered to Emily. "I know there ain't a God for this to happen to me." Emily squeezed Tessy's hand, scared to even imagine what goes on in a bed. She told Tessy that now they were like sisters and all her secrets were safe. She wanted Tessy to believe that there is a God, even though she could see why Tessy felt like there wasn't. "Tessy wasn't but thirteen when they married and Harv was already thirty," she says.

"I never knew she was that young," Hannah says. "I thought she was at least sixteen when she married and I had no idea he was that much older."

"Neither did I," Madge says and turns from the window. "You see how much I know."

"Tessy had herself a hard time," Emily says. "Tessy lost two babies right early on."

Virginia instinctively clasps her hands over her stomach and presses until she feels a little kick, a little knee or elbow. Then she lies back, eyes closed, imagines that she can hear the heartbeat.

"Thirteen," Cindy says. "Good God, that sounds like," Cindy pauses. "Ginny Sue, what's that book about that child screwing that old man? I saw the movie."

"*Lolita*," Virginia says and opens her eyes, the heartbeats disappearing.

"Honestly, the way you choose to say something," Madge says to Cindy.

"She could've said the *F* word," Lena says but nobody laughs. They'll laugh at Roy though. Yeah, they'll laugh when it isn't funny.

"Oh I'm sorry," Cindy says. "Let's see Miss Purrio, that child that was engaging in relations."

"Tessy didn't want to marry," Emily says. "She had no choice about it."

"I didn't know that either," Madge says. "I was never told anything."

"And I'm never told anything," Cindy says, and Madge catches herself feeling like she'd like to go and wrap her arms around Cindy and hold her so close like she did when Cindy was a tiny baby. That's why she loved being in a dark room when she nursed her babies. It felt so good to have that warm little body there. "First sign of a tooth and I'm done," Hannah had told her right after Robert was born. And when Ginny Sue came, Hannah said, "I can't work and nurse, too. Ginny Sue's on the bottle." But, it was the happiest part of Madge's life when she was nursing, those helpless babies, her ignorance that they were gonna grow up and be so indifferent to her.

"You were such a pretty baby," Madge says to Cindy, the words rolling from her tongue before she can stop them.

"And now I'm not? Is that what you mean?" Cindy asks and watches her mama sigh one of those long pitiful sighs.

"That's what Tessy and Jake had in common together," Emily says. "They were both told to marry the people they married."

"That's why she didn't want me to marry Raymond," Madge whispers. "But she should have told me the truth. She should have told me that she never loved my daddy!"

"And you should have told me that you never loved mine!" Cindy says.

"But I did love Raymond," Madge says, the rain hitting the sidewalk, rushing from the gutters over the duplex stoop. "When I married Raymond, I loved him very much." There is a flash of lightning, low rumbling thunder.

"And I loved Charles Snipes," Cindy says. "I get so damned tired of everybody acting like I'm so terrible for being married two times when the truth is that I loved Charles

Snipes and he walked out on me.'' Cindy feels herself wanting to cry and that's the last goddamned thing she wants to do in this creepy place. Whoever thinks of her feelings? Who? Name one.

"I loved Roy," Lena says. "But he's dead isn't he?" She looks around the room and they all nod, and they're not laughing this time. No sir, they learned a lesson.

"Divorce is worse than death." Now, Cindy walks over near where her mama is sitting and watches the rain, listens to the slow rumbling of the thunder. "At least when somebody dies you can cover him up and forget it. You don't have to see him out places."

"Have you seen Charles?" Ginny Sue asks, her voice a whisper, the kind of kindness that has always made Cindy nervous. Relative, good friend, it doesn't matter, they will yank out your gut and smear it from here to tomorrow if you care enough to let them. "Your body is a tomb," her daddy had told her once. "And there you must hide all that is bad, all the secrets of all your life."

"Roy's dead you know," Lena tells Emily and Virginia watches Gram's eyebrows go up in surprise and then the recognition on her face as she nods that she remembers. "James, too," she says.

"But ya'll had years together," Cindy says quietly and Virginia is almost holding her breath, so rare to see Cindy so serious; Cindy is framed by the window, that dark black sky, her face pale. "You don't have to sit around and wonder if he's gone because of you." Cindy faces Madge now, her hands clutching her necklace. "And the same for you," she says. "Daddy took his own life because he was sick and Roy had a stroke and James . . ."

"Heart attack," Hannah whispers as she feels herself calling the roll of the others; Tessy, so old and pitiful; David, burned in the helicopter so far from his home, his body destroyed; Curie, murdered. And her mother is so old and helpless, and Lena.

"Anyway," Cindy continues. "They are dead, but I tell you, every time I lay my eyes on Charles Snipes, I have to ask myself why? Why didn't it work?"

* * *

"It's just never going to work," Charles Snipes had said

that day, early morning, Chuckie not even awake yet, Fisher Price people without arms and legs strung across the hallway, and he put those greasy plumber's hands up to his face while she slowly filled a Coke bottle with water and put an African violet leaf in it to root. She loved to see his hands that way, loved to smell those old blue shirts that had "Charles" written up on the pocket. She must have used a ton of laundry powder during those first three years and she always bought the big size just like her mama always did. She'd use extra-strength whatever on Charles's and use Snowy Bleach for Chuckie, and there were times when she was happy, really happy. "I'll never be able to satisfy you," he had said. "I'm a plumber, okay?" He wrapped his arms around her from behind, squeezed, and then walked away. "I asked you not to ask your daddy for money. I told you we didn't have to have a new car, that stereo, the TV."

"I thought you'd be happy," she told him, spitting the words with an anger that she really didn't even feel. "I can't sit around here and never try to improve when my sister is flying to Aruba with likoor-sucker to get a tan."

"You knew it was going to be hard when you married me," he said.

"And why did I marry you? Why?" she yelled and turned to see Chuckie in the doorway in his little sleeper pajamas. "That's why," she said, and she watched Charles squat there and hug Chuckie. "It's somebody else, isn't it?" she asked. "It's not exciting for you now that I've shown all that I have to show."

"No, no, you need more," he said. "You and your dad need more." And she had spent that whole day crying before she pulled herself right together. "It was mutual," she had told everybody. "He doesn't try, will never get ahead because he is lazy and is not good in business. He beat me up a couple of times," she told a few but none of that was true.

* * *

"Sometimes I ask myself why it didn't work," Cindy says now. "Ginny Sue made a fool of herself that time she called off her engagement, but at least she didn't marry somebody who would leave her."

Virginia just listens now; the words, the rain. *Why didn't it work?*

"I'm sure you thought it would work," Hannah says, the nicest that Cindy has ever heard her be. "You wouldn't have married him if you had thought otherwise."

"She had to get married," Lena says. "Everybody knows she had to. Roy said it didn't surprise him one bit."

"But I didn't have to," Cindy says. "I could have got an abortion!"

"Don't you say such with Ginny Sue about to give birth," Emily says, her eyebrows raised and lips pursed.

"Chuckie is a blessing," Madge says. "Don't you ever say that in front of that child."

"I just said I could've," Cindy says, sits in a chair and pulls her knees up to her chest. "I didn't say I would've. It's the wondering about it all which is why I say that divorce is worse than a death."

"Death sounds pretty good to me," Lena says and lights a cigarette. Cindy points out to Madge a card that she can play up on the board.

"I didn't love Buzz Biggers, though," Cindy whispers. "I know that I didn't."

"Then why did you marry him?" Hannah asks and Cindy just shrugs and pulls on those wisps of hair near her face.

* * *

Cindy had known in the first week that she and Buzz Biggers would never share a double monument, no way would they die together; they couldn't even live together. He'd say, "I'm a steak and potatoes man—a man's man." He'd say all those "man" things that in the beginning turned her on, and he'd tell crude jokes that made even Cindy blush. All those things that she liked about him were all those things that made him so different from Charles Snipes. "The niggers and women are taking over the world," Buzz had told her. "They got a place and they ought to stay there." And he made fun of Jane Fonda, too, knowing full well that Jane Fonda is one of Cindy's very favorite people in the world. Jane looked up to and took after her daddy the same way that Cindy looked up to hers. "Liberals," Buzz Biggers would say and crush a beer can on the side of his head which Cindy had grown tired of; it didn't make her laugh anymore to see him do that. "There's no place in this world for liberals."

"I like Jane Fonda," Cindy had said.

"I don't," he said, his cap pulled low, a little Skoals in his gum, a Confederate flag patch on his army jacket. "I'd fuck her, though."

"You'd fuck a whale," she said and he grabbed her arm tight and twisted it. "I'd fuck your cousin, too," he said and grinned. "I think that's what she needs, too. I'd love to fuck those long lean bones."

"Don't you talk about Ginny Sue," she said and it made her feel sick. She didn't even want Ginny Sue around because of the things Buzz Biggers would say about her after she left.

"Jane Fonda sucks," is what he had said when he saw Cindy all dressed up in new leotards that she had gotten on sale at Belk's. Magenta tights, a magenta and black striped leotard with a low "V" cut in the back. She thought he'd like it; she thought he'd get off his talk about Ginny Sue, thought he'd like the fact that she and Constance Ann were going to the Saxapaw YMCA three nights a week so that when she hit forty, she'd look like Jane. "That's a bunch of shit," he said and grabbed her suit by the "V," near about stretched it all out of shape.

"It makes me feel good to Fonda," she said and took off her outfit before he could stretch it any more. "Where's Chuckie?" she asked and before she could get those tights from around her ankles he had pushed her back on the bed and had her feet pulled up just below his belt buckle. "I'll show you what feels good," he said and forced her legs back, knees bending, and leaned over her. "I like this little fleshy part here," he said and pinched up the soft white skin around her navel.

* * *

"Don't worry about it," Charles Snipes had told her and rubbed his hand over her navel where Chuckie had stretched her all out of shape. It was her first night home from the hospital, Chuckie finally asleep. "Who's gonna see but me and I think you look beautiful," Charles said and he was so gentle with her like she might have been a virgin; it was just like the first time they were ever together, both of them virgins, up in her bedroom on a Saturday afternoon while her parents were at a doctor appointment. And then, who fucking saw but that wide-assed redneck mobile home salesman, Buzz Biggers.

* * *

"Think about it," Buzz had told her the night they were sitting in the Bonanza steak house and decided to get married. "You've come up a notch or two, come from the sewer up to a home." If Charles Snipes hadn't been sitting in the corner of Bonanza with grease under his nails and a copy of *Popular Mechanics* spread out in front of him, she might not have even married Buzz Biggers. And if Charles Snipes hadn't been at the Ramada the other night with what's her name, Cindy probably never would have gone back to see Randy Skinner again.

"Oh, oh, oh," Buzz Biggers had said, digging into her like a fence post digger and it didn't sound like a thing but divorce, loud and clear, it said divorce, and Cindy hopes that her Grandma Tessy at some point in her life did get what she wanted. She hopes there was some moment when that old spooky woman was everything all at the same time, that she was a child and a virgin, and a whore all rolled into one.

* * *

"I didn't love Buzz Biggers," Cindy says. "It was a mistake. I made a mistake. I got left the first time and the second time I made a mistake."

"Well, just don't make another," Madge says.

"Just don't make another," Cindy mimics. "Like a person knows when he's making one." Cindy sits up straight and looks at Madge. "Only one of those was my mistake so you might as well say I was only divorced once."

"It doesn't work that way," Madge says.

"Well, ya'll think Mark is so great," she says, glances at Ginny Sue who is rising up on her elbows like a ghost from a coffin. "And Ginny Sue is his second."

"Cindy," Virginia says but with one glance around the room, she sees that no one is surprised.

"Oh I told them ages ago," Cindy says and waves her hand. "I told them before you told me not to tell."

"I told you not to tell before I told you," Virginia says, the blood rushing to her face.

"Now, don't get upset," her mama says and pushes her back down flat on her back. "You are in no condition to get upset."

"You knew?" she asks her mother. "All this time you knew he was divorced and you never mentioned it?"

"I told Ben," her mama says, sits down on the daybed and toys with the top of Virginia's sock where the yarn is pulled. "I don't know why you felt you couldn't tell me. You must think I have no sense of what goes on in this world."

"It's not that," Virginia says. "I was just scared of what you'd think."

"What?" her mother asks, still staring at the pulled sock, her eyebrows raised. "That he made a mistake? You think I wouldn't forgive someone a mistake?"

"Tessy knew she made a mistake," Gram says.

"By marrying my daddy or with that other man?" Madge asks but Emily just shakes her head.

"But it's the same difference," Cindy continues. "If Ginny Sue ever leaves Mark then that man will be divorced two times and only one will be his fault and he'll have to carry his mistake and Ginny Sue's mistake right on with him forever."

"The first wasn't Mark's mistake," Virginia says and raises to her elbows. "You know that. Why didn't you tell everything you know?"

"You told me it was mutual," Cindy says. "You said that Mark said it never would've worked."

"That's what he says now," Virginia says, feeling her mother's stare, so she concentrates on Gram who is staring into the blank TV. "He got left. *She* made a mistake. She left him just like Charles Snipes left you and what happened? What happened?" Virginia feels her heart beating faster, face flush. "Buzz Biggers, that's what. *Your* mistake!"

"It's not the same," Cindy says. "Good God, I just used you as an example."

"It is the same, it is." Virginia lies back down and stares at the ceiling, her mother's hand as heavy as a stone on her foot. "You didn't know what was going to happen or you wouldn't have married him; nobody knows."

"Harv sure didn't know," Lena says and fans herself with her hat. "I think he come to know but there was awhile there that Messy was standing in front of that store showing herself and he didn't know."

"She did not show herself," Emily says. "They didn't even talk to one another if others were around."

"You know something," Madge says suddenly, looking at Emily who stares up at the ceiling and shakes her head. "You know all about it."

"Tessy said, 'Emily, I got no one to tell but you,' and I said, 'you can pray over it.' " Those banjos are starting up again and Emily leans forward so she can see just which one of them is making the most racket. "Tessy said, 'throw some boiling water out there on the porch and that'll get rid of them.' "

"She was so hateful," Lena says. "She hated cats and I hated her."

"Well, I loved her!" Emily says to Lena but Lena ain't going to pay any mind. Mama says "Lena, go get the water from the pump" and Lena is gone running across that field like a squirrel, ain't about to do as she's told, argue with a fence post and that Roy just like her.

"Why did she leave him?" Virginia's mama asks, and Virginia looks past her, out the window where a large tree across the street is rocking and swaying against that dark sky. "He's a fine person," her mother continues. "I'm sure it wasn't his *fault*."

"Let Cindy tell you," Virginia says. "Or has she already?"

"No, I haven't." Cindy leans back on her elbows, crosses her feet. "It's no big deal."

"No, no," Virginia says. "It's no big deal. His wife got pregnant and didn't want it so she just left and had an abortion."

"Poor Mark," her mother says. "That must have been hard for him."

"It really isn't a big deal," Cindy says. "Good God, Ginny Sue, every event of your life has been so BIG, so COMPLICATED, a major secret."

"Better than a soap opera," Virginia says and stares at the cheap square tiles of the ceiling. She wishes she was in her room at Gram's old house, the bead board ceiling, venetian blinds raised while the rain hit that tin awning, slow and then fast, rising, falling.

"Soap opera?" Cindy asks and Virginia just wishes she would drop it and leave. *Poor Mark, that must have been hard for him.* Gram flips on the TV, changes channels, static and noise, and then cuts it back off. "I don't think I should play this during a storm,'' Gram says and Virginia's mama agrees, goes and unplugs the set.

"You're the soap opera,'' Cindy continues, ignoring Madge's Shh. "Your first period was like the Red Sea had parted, and my God, what a scene when you lost your virginity.'' Cindy pauses, Virginia's mama's eyebrows go up. "And no, I haven't told about that if you're wondering. You break off an engagement after I've spent a fortune on a dress that I've got no place to wear and you act like you're the first to ever get hurt over something or be a little upset and then you marry Mark and it's like the first wedding, like you might be Lady Di and now you're pregnant and getting all of the attention for that.'' Cindy is all red in the face, her blue eye shadow showing up like sparkly clouds above her eyes. "That's the soap opera, As Ginny Sue Turner Turns, like you might be the world.''

"That's a lie,'' Virginia says, feeling too tired to argue.

"We sent you to summer camp and we never even told about how you broke my vanity mirror.''

"Ginny Sue did not break that mirror,'' Emily says. "She told me she didn't and I believed her in spite of what Raymond Sinclair said. I never believed all he had to say.''

"He got his seven bad years,'' Lena says.

"What?'' Madge and Hannah ask at the same time but Cindy jumps in.

"Talk about a lie!'' Cindy shakes her head back and forth. "You have always been jealous of my daddy, Ginny Sue. I remember when you said he was crazy. Don't worry, I've never forgotten.''

"Raymond said Ginny Sue broke it,'' Madge says and looks at Hannah. "We never told you and Ben because I didn't want you to feel like you had to replace it.''

"Well, for God's sake,'' Hannah says and pulls some darning out of her purse. "We surely could have bought a mirror. I get so tired of everybody acting like we don't have a pot to pee in or a window to throw it out of.'' She bites off some thread and knots one end. "I'll still buy a mirror if all this nonsense can stop.'' She turns suddenly to Virginia. "Why didn't you tell me about it? Who have I been all these years that you can't seem to tell me anything?'' Virginia watches her mother's mouth moving with the words and she'd like to be in one of Gram's closets right now with a quilt pulled up around her while it thunders and lightnings; she'd like to be on the feather bed lying so still just the way that Gram had always made her do during a storm. "It's the Lord speaking," Gram had said. "It's a disrespect to talk and be loud during it," and Gram would tell the story of how her sister perished and how her mother, the other Virginia Suzanne, went to the grave every afternoon for four months to sit there and cry and to beg that child to forgive her because she hadn't known what else to do. She'd put food on top of the grave, things that deer and birds could come and eat and she'd stay there for hours, until one day a storm came up and lightning struck right near her feet, and she told of how it was like the sky had opened up and was threatening to take her too if she didn't get back home and tend to her business, tend to the living. "Virginia? Just tell me why you've kept things from me?" her mother asks now.

"She told me about it," Gram says. "She told me that she didn't break that mirror and she told me that she didn't want to stay over at that house no more because it scared her and I didn't blame her. A grown man creeping around to jump out and say boo at a child when he should've had better sense."

"What happened?" Hannah asks, Ginny not looking at her.

"He scared her with his silliness," Gram says. "And then he tried to blame that broken mirror on her when it was probably Cindy that done it."

"He did it," Virginia says before Cindy can speak.

"What happened?" Madge asks. "*How* did he break the mirror?"

"He didn't," Cindy says and flops back down in her chair. "God, I wish it would stop raining so I could get the hell out of here."

"Ginny Sue cried so that night," Gram says and Virginia turns and tries to catch Gram's eye, tries to get her to stop. "I told her that he wasn't worth the worry and for her just not to go over there anymore."

"See? See?" Cindy screams. "A soap opera! Poor little Ginny Sue, can't even take a joke. My daddy tried to make your life a little bit fun and you couldn't take it."

"He said he'd kill me if I ever told." Virginia sits up, her eyes still on Gram. "I couldn't even tell Gram the whole story because he said he'd kill me."

"What?" Hannah stands, her hands clasped together while she turns first to Madge and then to Virginia. "What did he do to you?" she asks and Virginia shakes her head, closes her eyes tightly and keeps them closed. She hears Madge breathe out "Oh my God" and she hears Cindy rummaging in the closet to find an umbrella and she hears the sound of those wingtip shoes coming up the steps. "Did he touch you?" Virginia hears her mother, shudders with the thought of what she's really asking, shakes her head.

"That's sick!" Cindy screams, still rummaging.

"I can't believe you didn't tell me that Ginny got scared like that," Hannah says and stares at Gram. "I know you didn't know the whole story but you knew she was scared and you should have told me. I am her mother."

"And I am your mother," Emily says and stares at Hannah until she looks away. They might think that living in a wheel-chair means you can't take care of your business and tend to the living, but they are wrong. It is her house and she is in charge and if she wants to throw scalding water to stop that alley cat banjo picking then she will and if she wants nobody to keep her company but Tessy and Mag Sykes then that's who she'll invite the next time and they'll split themselves a little glass of beer and they'll make a quilt that God hisself would not dare to sit upon.

"I never knew what he might do," Madge says. "From day to day, I never knew."

"I want to hear exactly what happened," Hannah says, lowering her voice, her needle frozen in midair. Cindy is standing at the front door staring out, her car keys clenched in her fist but Virginia knows she is listening. "Virginia, I am your mother!" Virginia, it has an odd sound coming from her mother.

"I was a mother," Lena whispers. "That woman gave me the baby and I called him Cord after my daddy."

Hannah turns now and stares at Lena sitting there with a pillow clutched up to her chest. "You never had a child, Lena," she says slowly.

"Yes she did," Emily says. "I said, 'don't you cry now, Lena. My babies are like your babies.' Lena had my babies like her own."

"I had you for a baby, Hannah," Lena says now, her eyes so tired and dull. "You are my baby and Ginny Sue is my grandbaby."

"I guess you don't want us," Cindy says. "Come on, Mama. I don't know how you can sit there and hear all this craziness. It's the Twilight Zone."

"Lena wasn't big enough to have herself a baby," Emily says. "Besides, she didn't want one."

"That's a lie," Cindy says and turns. She is ready to jump on anything or anybody. "Look at me, I'm smaller than she's ever been."

"The doctor said I was not to have children and he fixed me," Lena says. "I was fixed like a give-out cat."

"God, it scares me for Ginny Sue," Emily says. "I know what it's like to be a child and be scared. It can be a sheet in the wind but if it scares you, then you're scared and nothing's gonna change it. I knew just how she felt that night Raymond left her here. I know fear."

"Raymond was not himself those last ten years," Madge says, still staring down at the floor. "He was a very sick man."

"I never wanted a child was all!" Lena yells and nobody questions her.

"He told me that I'd look nice in a tomb," Virginia whispers. "He said he could just see me wrapped up in a pure white sheet, my body oiled and perfumed, and he made me tell him that he was the king, that he was beautiful and that I worshipped him, and he said that I better never tell that I said all of those things to him because everyone would hate me, that you and Cindy would hate me." She looks at Cindy, her jaw clenched and face red, while she toys with her key chain. "And I loved you and Cindy, Aunt Madge."

"It was just a game," Cindy says slowly, her chin quivering. "I played it. It was like playing King on the Mountain. Sometimes he'd tell me to be real still and he'd wrap me in a sheet and I'd start laughing because it was like any other game where you scare yourself. I knew it was just a *game*!"

"A game?" Hannah asks, her voice so clear that it seems to echo. "So do you play this *game* with Chuckie?"

Cindy freezes, glares at Hannah with all the hatred she can feel; her mama is on the edge of her chair waiting for the answer, and Cindy feels herself breaking, her throat closing.

He had told her it was *their* game, *their* secret. She stays in the darkness by the front door, the sound of rain still running through the gutters. But it wasn't just a game and she had believed him. She had believed him when he said that he loved her and she had believed him when he said that Charles would never be good enough for her, that Charles was a nothing. But Charles is not a nothing, and now she doesn't have anybody. Cindy leans her back against the wall and slides down, pulls her knees up to her chest and rolls her head from side to side. She hears her father, over and over, telling her how she is his child; "Your mama prefers Catherine and I prefer you," he had said. "You are just like me and I'd never let Catherine be Queen in the Tomb." But, he let Ginny Sue; no, no, he *made* Ginny Sue.

Cindy looks up and shakes her head back and forth; they are in that gray light of the window, the lamp behind Emily's chair and she can see pale white faces, silent faces except for Lena who is bent over the pillow she cradles. "Oh, baby, baby," Lena whispers.

"I do not play the game with Chuckie," Cindy says slowly, trying to meet eyes with Hannah. "My daddy never hurt me. He loved me. I know that he really did love me. He was the only person that loved me."

"Oh God," Madge breathes and rises from her chair, awkwardly makes her way over to Cindy. "What about me?" she whispers and she feels like she did when she walked through that hallway, leaving Raymond there behind her on the floor, and even though he was dead, there was the fear that he would suddenly spring up and grab her by the ankle, suddenly spring up and drag her down with him. She was relieved; she was glad he was dead. Now, she squats and nervously wraps her arms around Cindy, expecting her daughter to change suddenly as she usually does, to spit harsh words, blame her for everything that's ever happened. "It's okay Little Goldilocks," she whispers and Cindy stares at her with dull surprise. "I'm the one that gave you that name, you know. That's what I called you when you were a tiny baby and nursing."

Hannah goes now and squats beside Lena's chair and Lena stares down at her, whispers, "I wanted you for my baby. I wanted you to be right here," and she takes Hannah's hand and presses it into her stomach, and Virginia presses her own as she watches, and waits, movement, a flutter of arms and

legs like a swimmer trying to reach the surface. "That ex-
plains a whole lot," her mother whispers, voice shaking as
she stares over at Virginia. "All those times you were so
scared, times you thought there was a man in the closet, the
way it would frighten you so to break something."

Madge comes back into the room now, Cindy behind her
and they both sit back down at the table and turn their backs
to the pouring rain. The lamp behind Emily's chair flickers
when there is a loud peal of thunder. "We ought to be on a
bed and quiet," Emily whispers. That's what her mama always said. She had made Emily get on the bed that day after
Curie left and the rain was pouring down. "Lie quiet, now,
and say your prayers," her mama said, and Emily tried to
pray but her mind kept wandering to that day that she stood
out there and danced and laughed herself tired and the harder
the rain fell, the faster she turned in her mind, Curie off to
the side while she spun around like she owned the whole sky.

"I think God has already spoken," Hannah says, glancing
around the room and trying to pull it all together, this simple
simple life, suddenly grown so huge. How can you live all
these years without knowing?

"Yeah," Cindy says, her voice so low and serious. "But
he *did* love me. He didn't mean to scare Ginny Sue." She
looks at Virginia, but then has to look away, all the hatred
and anger that she had felt, leaving her numb. Everyone gets
quiet when the lights flicker off and the rain is like an endless
drone. Cindy fumbles in her purse and clicks a lighter, goes
to the mantel where there is a candle and lights it.

"I wasn't even there for you, Madge," Hannah says after
awhile. "If I had only known how bad it was."

"I didn't even know myself," Madge says. "It was all so
slowlike." And she feels her chest tighten as the words start
coming, Crisco cans and that anniversary night, her mama's
funeral. Her voice never breaks and she keeps expecting that
one will interrupt, that one will suddenly stand and point her
finger at her. It is the last game, win or lose, spin the barrel
and shoot; and it really doesn't matter anymore.

"Raymond made me kill him," she whispers and rises to
her feet as if she expects that they will lunge on her hair tooth
and nail. "I didn't want to kill him but I did it. I killed
Raymond." She is crying now, twisting her hands and they
are all staring at her as if they'd seen a ghost. Hannah takes

one step forward but stops when Cindy jumps from her chair and runs to the phone.

"Who are you calling?" Hannah asks and Cindy shrugs, sobbing now and shaking her head back and forth. "There's nobody to call. We're all here. It's all over," and with Hannah's words, Madge sinks to the floor and curls up with her back to them, the candle flickering there in front of the window. Madge feels Hannah's hand on her shoulder, feels Hannah lift her up and dab a Kleenex under her eyes.

"Mama said it was a sign from God not to sit before a grave," Emily says. "He was letting her know that she had business of the living to tend to."

"That's what you told me," Lena says and nods. "My business was with Roy, mine and Roy's business; now y'all laugh over business if you please. Just laugh, just goddamn laugh." She looks around the room but they ain't laughing; no sir, they learned not to laugh over Roy Carter just like she learned not to cry over a baby, because she took good care of those cats, yeah Jesus she did and Roy said he could fire a gun and scare them cats but they were too smart for that, yeah boy, stay up there under the house where it's cool and shady and come morning you can have some milk.

"I can't believe I've told it," Madge says and wipes her eyes. "I can't believe after all these years."

"Neither can I," Cindy whispers and Madge feels a chill up her neck; she can't believe what? that Madge killed him? that he was out of his mind? She has said the words and can't take them back, words hanging, words that can be repeated and why should she trust them? Why should she trust anybody? "You can't sink your trust or faith into nothing," her mama had said, that long gray hair hanging to her waist while she puffed that pipe.

"What's going to happen to me?" Madge asks suddenly. "What are you going to do with me?"

"Keep you I reckon," Emily says and laughs. That's what she used to tell David when he was a child. She'd catch him using her good scissors to cut out pictures of all the places he was going, cars he'd drive, the big house where he'd live with a pretty young wife. She'd say, "David Roberts, what am I going to do with you?" and he'd look at her with those big brown eyes, shrug his shoulders and she'd hug him so tight. "I'll keep you I reckon," she'd say and laugh, feeling his childhood squeal vibrating there against her chest.

"That's right," Hannah says. "We'll keep you. You did what you had to do, Madge." Hannah says the words and watches Madge start to cry again but she is wondering why Madge hadn't run from the house, why Madge hadn't called the police, why Madge hadn't packed a bag years before and left that man with his crazy ways. That's what Hannah would have done; she would have felt that instinct that she has always known, like an animal she would have fought to protect her children and herself.

"What about Catherine?" Cindy asks slowly, unable to look at her mother, unable to shake the horrible pictures of her father that have formed in her mind. But her mother could be lying; she could have made it all up.

"I don't know," Madge murmurs. "He never spent much time with Catherine, not like he did with you." Madge releases her grip on the arms of the chair. "I tried to tell Catherine once how bad it had gotten and she said that Raymond was just going through the change, that men go through the change just like a woman."

"She's so stupid," Cindy spits and shakes her head. "At least I knew he was sick. I mean you don't get paralyzed if you aren't sick." She looks at her mother now, hunched forward like there's not a bone in her back. No, she never would have taken it upon herself to kill him.

"That is stupid," Lena says, her shape in the darkened corner marked by the glow of her cigarette. "If you've never bled then you don't up and stop doing it. I haven't had the curse since I was thirty-three years old."

"Do we have to tell Catherine?" Cindy asks. "Because she'll blame me. It'll just be one more thing she can say about me, one more reason to hate me."

"Ginny Sue got the curse," Emily says. "I called Felicia and I said, 'Now, I know you probably can't help me because I know of what people say about you but Ginny Sue is in need of a Kotex.' "

"You did that?" Cindy turns now and watches old Emily nod her head. Cindy feels herself nodding with her, slowly, and she feels now like she might have taken a bottle of Sominex herself, her eyes heavy, her whole body numb and tired, unable to move.

"This is what men and women do," her daddy told her once and opened a magazine to a big colored picture. "You're starting to grow now," he whispered. "Has your mother told you what will happen to you?" She nodded, thinking of her mother's explanation of breasts and ovaries, Kotex and elastic belt. "It's a discomfort but it's something you've got to live with," her mother had said and left her in her room with a little pamphlet.

"You are sprouting like a little bud," her daddy said and pointed to her breasts, her nipples small hard bumps beneath her tee shirt. "Very soon, you'll look like this," and he turned to another picture, a woman with her legs spread and she shook her head. "You will," he whispered. "You'll probably be blonde and fair like me. Your mother is so dark and coarse but you are like me. See?" and he turned back to the other picture. "It is best when the people are alike because you can't tell which part belongs to who. It is like they are one part; like they are both man and woman. That's how it should be."

"Like you and mama?" she asked, but he shook his head, laughed.

"Your mama doesn't know how to feel," he had said. "Do you feel anything at all when you see this picture?" and he turned to one, tracing down the page with his finger to the man's tongue, then all around it. "Does seeing this make you feel something? Do you feel something pulsing and beating like your heart, except there," and he pointed to the buttons on her shorts; he glanced at her crotch and she nodded. "You see? You're fine, healthy, alive. As long as you have these feelings, you will be okay. It's healthy to have these feelings, healthy to think of things that make you feel this way. You should never marry a man who cannot keep you feeling this way." And Charles Snipes had made her feel that way, way back. But whenever he did, she thought of the pictures, heard her father's voice. It was like her father was always watching her; she never got to have Charles, all by himself, and that's what she wanted. Cindy feels her stomach churning, the cool sweat on her face, and she runs to the bathroom where she kneels in the dark over the toilet.

"Are you okay?" Her mama is standing there with the candle. "I'll wet you a cloth," and Cindy watches her, still so gray and dull looking, as if she's the one who has been drained of blood.

"It's his fault I lost Charles," Cindy cries and grabs hold of her mama's white dental pants. "Why did he do that to me?" she screams and holds onto her mama's tightly clenched legs, so tight, Cindy feels like that leg could snap off like a rotten piece of timber and that there would be nothing left inside of her mother that he hadn't sucked away. "I thought he loved me. He always told me how he was the one that loved me and you never seemed to. You never seemed to love me."

"Oh but I did," Madge says and squats beside her. "I did and I do. He was so sick, Cindy." Madge swallows hard. "I think he did love you. You are probably the one person he loved, but he was sick."

"But why didn't you do something? When Charles left me, why didn't you step in and do something? All you did was cry and I felt like you blamed me."

"I'm sorry," Madge whispers. "All I can say is that I'm sorry. I guess I'm as weak as he was in a different way. I gave up." Madge squeezes Cindy's arm until Cindy looks at her, "I think I gave up so long ago that for awhile I forgot there was anything different. For eight years now, I've been telling myself how what I lived was not right, and sometimes I catch myself wishing that I'd taken things into my own hands years before. I'd read things in the paper of women who waited until their husband was asleep and then killed them, women who were so desperate they couldn't face another day, and I felt for them, God knows I did, and I also understood why they did it." Madge takes a deep breath, again waiting for a blow that doesn't come. Cindy squeezes her hand back. "It's a little late for me," Madge says. "But you're young, Cindy. You're young and pretty with a good job and cute little figure and a fine son. You can make something of your life."

"It's not too late," Cindy whispers, wipes her face with that cool washcloth. "You've got that man in Clemmonsville."

"I made that up," Madge whispers. "I felt Hannah wanting to step in and try to take care of my life and I figured she had enough to take care of." Madge leans against the cold side of the tub, the rain still pouring outside of that bathroom window. "You know my mama had a sad life, too," Madge says. "God only knows how sad. She never talked to me about anything except how to sew something. Maybe if she had talked to me, I would have been different. Maybe I wouldn't have been so taken with Raymond and what he had to offer me."

"But then I wouldn't be here," Cindy says. "And Chuckie."

"Or Catherine," Madge says.

"Slutbucket," Cindy mumbles and turns to hug her mother the same way that she had always hugged her daddy, with her face turned into his neck so that she could whisper secrets, so that she could say the secret "I love you" without anyone knowing. God, if she could just forget it all.

"She's still my daughter," Madge says, squeezing Cindy's back three hard times to give the message of those words that she realizes she hasn't said to anybody in years, only written them to Hannah and never given them to her. "But you are my daughter, too," Madge says. "And I love you and Chuckie. You are my entire life. That's what I always wanted to hear your Grandma Tessy say to me and I'd think that it could make all the difference in the world. The day she died I guess I was still waiting to hear it."

"Lena has to tee tee," Emily is trying to roll herself down the hallway but Hannah is behind her, holding the chair in place.

"Lena really does have to go," Hannah says. "I'm sorry to interrupt. Is everything okay?"

"Yes," Madge says. "We're going to be okay, aren't we?" Cindy nods and Madge helps her to her feet. "I'm thinking we might call Catherine later today and see if she has macraméd her tubes." Madge waits for somebody to laugh but they are too shocked. She hasn't said anything funny in years and it will take time.

"No Madge," Hannah says when she steps back in the room, Lena right behind her. "I don't blame you a bit. I just wish I'd known." Hannah watches Madge inch towards her now, her eyes cast down like a mistreated puppy, and Hannah reaches out her arms, hugs so tight, her arms squeezing Madge's back; Hannah wishes she could squeeze it all away.

"But now what, Hannah?" Madge whispers and then pulls away. "What now that everybody knows about Raymond?"

"He was crazy," Lena says. "Imagine saying the *F* word

to Roy Carter. I wish Roy had knocked him off that building. Roy said Raymond was bad business.''

"Heee eee eee, bad business," Emily wheezes and puts a hand up to her chest. "He took hisself off this earth and the Lord won't have him.''

"But," Madge says and looks at the two of them.

"I think the Lord will have him," Cindy interrupts. "He killed himself but I think the Lord will still have him.''

"Cindy," Madge starts.

"That's what I believe," Cindy says. "I believe he shot himself and now he's up in heaven, without the gun wound of course.''

"Of course," Virginia says and lies back, stares at the dark sky. She wants to erase all pictures of Uncle Raymond, erase all memory of being trapped in that room, trapped in a room that didn't belong to her, trapped and unable to get home with no knowledge of what he was planning to do to her, of what was going to happen. She hears his footsteps, the doorway, the hall, making his way to the bedroom, shadows at the foot of her bed, a faceless creature hovering in the corner, coming closer and closer and there is nowhere to go and she can't make it stop; she has no control. "He's dead," Virginia says and sits up. "He killed himself.''

"Yes, he killed himself," Hannah says and pulls Madge close. She looks at Virginia, tearful eyes so wide and frightened, and she feels Madge's heart racing, racing, and she holds her, rocks her, until it slows.

PART VI

IT IS MIDAFTERNOON AND THE RAIN HAS SLOWED, THE DARK sky lightened to a strange yellow that seems to fill the room, makes the candle only a small light to itself like the glow of Cindy's and Lena's cigarettes. Gram is dozing now, her hands calmly crossed on her lap; Lena is smiling to herself; Cindy, peeling the last of the blue polish from her toenails. Madge is staring out the window, her murmurs of "I'm sorry" dwindled to periodic sighs. Madge has yet to look Virginia in the eye, as if by looking she will have to hear every word that Raymond said that day. It is the same fear Virginia would have if she had to look Sheila in the eye. It is one thing to imagine, another to know. Virginia's mama is for once sitting calmly, her sewing put away, hand protectively rubbing up and down the arch of Virginia's foot.

The silence, Madge's confession, has left them all so quiet as if they will sit like this forever, that it will rain forever and they will sink deeper and deeper, closer and closer, leaving no room for anyone else. "A tornado hit Clemmonsville," her dad had called to say, his call an interruption to the odd calm that follows pain, like crawling into a bed and letting sleep dissolve all the worries; Virginia thinks dying must be like that, a simple numbness that makes it all go away. "You girls stay put," her dad had said. "Just let it all blow over."

"Oh sweet Jesus," Gram had said with the news. "We must be very quiet while the Lord has his way," and Virginia had seen in Gram's eyes a childlike fear, a fear that she recognized, though Gram also had a calming sense of faith which

Virginia could not feel. "Everything will be okay," Gram said.

"I'm afraid," Virginia whispered, the yellow sky, but more so what has happened, a fear of what will happen.

"No reason to be afraid, Ginny Sue," Gram whispered. "Ain't no reason."

Now Virginia feels the same fear as she looks at all of the faces, waxy and pale in the strange yellow glow.

"Here comes Felicia," Madge whispers, her low voice seeming to echo in the stillness and Hannah goes to the front door and holds it open for Felicia to run inside. Cindy is on the phone making sure that Chuckie is at his friend's house, her face relaxing as she fusses at him, tells him not to fill himself up on chocolate.

"My goodness," Felicia whispers. "I hope you all weren't napping." She sets a box of candles on the table and takes off her bright red slicker. "I heard on the radio that we'd be without power for a bit so I brought you some candles."

"Thank you, Felicia," Madge says and smiles, her hand self-consciously smoothing her puffy eyes. "That is so kind of you," and Madge realizes that she has said the words that Hannah would normally say and Hannah doesn't seem to mind at all, just nods.

"Well, I wasn't sure who-all was over here and you know I worry over Miss Emily like she is my own."

Emily opens her eyes now and looks around the room. She had told them to be quiet. "I just came to give you a check, Miss Emily," Felicia says and goes over and pats her hand.

"Well, you needn't pay me for that dab of work I done," Emily says and laughs. "That was years ago that I patched that quilt, Miss Walker."

"No, honey, I'm Felicia, your neighbor, came to check on you," Felicia says and looks at Hannah. "She's a sweetie."

"Uh huh," Lena says. "Told you."

"Hush up," Emily shakes her finger and turns back to Felicia. "I was going to phone you after the storm passed us," Emily says. "I've a secret to tell."

"Okay," Felicia says and Madge feels herself rising from her chair. "You want to say it in my ear?"

"No." Emily laughs and waves her hand. "They all know the secret."

"This is a bargain for all these candles," Madge says, but Felicia doesn't turn away from Emily.

"They have all gotten after me for asking you for a Kotex," Emily says.

"Don't you worry a second," Felicia laughs. "And you just call me the next time you need one."

"I'll never need another," Emily says, "not for myself anyways."

"We have not gotten on her about it," Hannah says and Felicia turns, still smiling, her cheeks flushed. "It was the way she said it."

"Oh, a Kotex is a Kotex no matter how you ask for it." Felicia waves her hand. "Miss Emily and I are good friends, aren't we?"

"What about me?" Lena asks. "Everybody always said I was the prettiest."

"And you are pretty." Felicia laughs, looks around the room. "You all are lucky to have these two." Felicia points to Emily and Lena and puts back on her slicker. "And how *is* the mama?" she asks and turns to Virginia.

"She's so much better," Madge says. "I don't know what we'd have done if you hadn't helped her the other day." Again she has taken the words right out of Hannah's mouth.

"You folks beat on the wall if you need anything," Felicia says and goes to the front door.

"Won't you stay with us?" Emily asks. "Mag Sykes brung me a big pot of butterbeans."

"I would," she says. "But I'm having cramps myself and think I'll just go stretch out and take a nap. I'm lost without electricity."

"Yes, they say in some cities they got lights," Emily says and laughs, "My mama says it will be a long time coming to fangle up any wires out this way. Lord, yes. Gotta live by the God-given light of day. Eat yourself some garlic," she says. "Garlic will cure the cramps," and Lena just stares in disbelief as Felicia goes out the front door.

"Everybody knows," Lena says. "That if I don't have the cramps and me being the woman that I am that she doesn't have cramps being not a woman. And did you hear her? She stood right there and called me pretty."

Madge turns back to the window and watches Felicia run

to her side of the duplex and who would have ever thought? Who'd've thought just from looking at Madge and Felicia, that Madge was the one with a life to feel ashamed over. Madge hears Felicia's door slam right when the rain picks back up, heavy, and that wind blowing the trees against that strange-looking sky.

Ben calls Hannah again to say that another twister has touched down between here and Clemmonsville and for Hannah not to think she can get out and drive in this weather, hailing at their house, tomatoes ruined. Hannah repeats it all to them while she stands with the receiver pressed to her ear and Madge cannot help but wonder what it would feel like to be like Hannah, to stand so little and straight with a firm hand on the hip that says, "you all can relax; I got it under control," to have a man telling you to do something because he loves you and not because he's so taken with himself.

"You guess Catherine and likoor-sucker have blown off the earth?" Cindy asks.

"Lord, where is my mind?" Madge asks. "Cindy, call and check."

"Me?" Cindy asks, but decides to do it anyway. Would Hannah do it? Ginny Sue? Yes. Cindy dials while Madge calls out the number, then waits for an answer. She starts to hang up when Catherine answers but something about her mama's face makes her ask just as nice as possible if their house has blown off. "Mama's with me," Cindy says, then holds the receiver away from her ear while she laughs. "A condo for me?" Another pause but this time Cindy is listening, her face serious. "Does it have a Jacuzzi?"

* * *

Cindy has plaited all the hair around Virginia's face in what she calls "an almost Bo Derek" style. She will do anything to forget, plait hair, talk about Jacuzzis, anything to keep those pictures out of her mind. Hannah and Madge have played hand after hand of honeymoon bridge just like they used to at the beach. Traveler's advisory until seven o'clock, Gram's radio weatherman says, if you spot a tornado open all windows and doors and get in a hallway windowless area protect your head those with cellars . . . again seven P.M. stay where you are unless an emergency . . .

A key turns in the lock and before they can all look up, Esther has rushed into the room with a paper sack torn and spread over her head. "I been in the Piggly Wiggly for hours," Esther says. "Lights never came on and they finally let us go by checking us out one by one with a flashlight to make sure we hadn't taken anything." Esther flops down in a chair and shakes her head back and forth. "God knows," she sighs."I got to get home and make sure my house hasn't floated off. I bet my man can't even come tonight."

"I think you should stay here," Hannah says but Esther shakes her head. "No sir, I gotta get home. I want to be there if things start floating." Esther stares hard at Hannah and then the rest of them. "Ya'll gals been crying?"

"I don't cry before others," Emily says. "Tears is personal."

"I cry at the drop of a hat," Lena says. "That's what Roy says."

"I was telling everybody about a sad old movie," Cindy says, her mind shifting up to fourth gear. "I told about this moved called *An Unmarried Woman* and when I got to the part about that fool traipsing down the street with a picture and leaving Alan Bates right by himself, everybody cried."

"I didn't care for that show myself," Esther says. "But I do like a movie that can make you cry. I like *Madam X* Lord, yes, now that's a tearjerker, and *Imitation of Life*."

"I wish David would come on home," Emily says, the lamp behind her flickering back on. She looks at all of them with their eyes swoll up like they've been stung by a bee, except Lena. Lena looks as pretty as ever with that fur cap tilted on her head.

"So do I," Lena says. "Roy, too." She fumbles in her purse until she finds cigarettes and some matches. "They say don't keep no matches at the school but I do," she laughs and waves the little book back and forth. "I stole these matches."

"From where," Hannah asks.

"When me and you went in that store," Lena says and opens her purse out toward Hannah. "Got me two packs of cigarettes and four books of matches."

"Do hush your mouth," Emily says. "You know better than to steal."

"You got to go after what you want is what Roy always said," Lena says and laughs, holds those two packs up for Hannah to see. Yeah Lord, she and Roy went after what they wanted, they went like wildcats. "I want so many cats there will always be a motor running," she told Roy and he said he wanted so many cars that there'd always be a motor running. Lord, yeah, tell it. She had stopped saying she wanted a baby by then. "Shit, I'll smoke right there in the school yard. I'm too old to be paddled."

"You needed paddling long ago," Emily says. "You needed your fanny smacked that time you stole candy from the store. Just walk in and take something like it's your own."

"Your children are like my own," Lena says and puts the packs back in her purse, zips it up tight so that nurse teacher with them barrel legs won't find them. If that woman takes those cigarettes, she will arch her back and hiss real loud and scratch that woman's eyeballs out.

"But you didn't take my children," Emily says. "You didn't." She shakes her finger and watches that Lena blow some smoke out into the room. "The Lord took David and Hannah's right here."

"Well," Lena says and shakes her head, her face primping. "I use an ashtray." Now she points her finger, her voice loud and defensive. "I have smoked my whole life and ain't St. Peter or nobody gonna tell me to quit."

"Told you," Cindy says to Virginia and lights a cigarette herself. "You ain't gonna drop dead from smoking a cigarette." Virginia looks at the window where the sky is a little lighter, late afternoon, a fine drizzle of rain still coming down.

"I thought you quit," Virginia's mama says. "You told me you had."

"I have," Virginia says and then catches herself, continues. "But I've slipped a couple here and there." She feels suddenly like making a confession. It's why people trapped in elevators of burning buildings spill their guts, trapped; it's why people remain friends or remain married. "I have smoked and Mark doesn't know. There's a lot he doesn't know and I'm glad because there's a lot that I don't know about him. He has a whole life that I don't know a thing about."

"What, his past?" Cindy asks, her eyes wide, mascara on her cheeks. "We all have one. I do, you do, Mama does." Cindy glances at Madge and then turns back to Virginia. "It's better to forget, just pretend nothing happened."

"But I haven't kept mine a secret," Virginia says. "I have told him everything. I wanted him to know everything about me *before* he married me. I wanted him to know who I was."

"It's not good to tell everything," Gram whispers. "You got to have something that you keep for yourself. That's what I told Tessy."

"But I didn't have anything big or important enough to keep it to myself," Virginia says, irritated when Madge mumbles, "be glad" and Cindy nods.

"Did you tell him what Daddy did?" Cindy asks slowly, glancing away.

"No." Virginia shakes her head and sits up. "But that's different. I never told anyone; I couldn't." Virginia doesn't even look at her mother; she knows that eventually her mother will want to hear the whole story, every detail and she can't stand to think about it. "But I told him about Bryan Parker. I told him because it didn't matter to me and I didn't want him to hear years from now that I lived with someone and wonder *why* I hadn't told."

"You never even told me that you lived with him," Cindy says, and Virginia feels her face burn with her mother's stare.

"No. Mark is the only person that I told," Virginia says. "I made a mistake and I wanted him to know it. And if his marriage and Sheila were all behind him then he would've told me everything in the beginning."

"Maybe he knew you well enough not to," Cindy says now, eyebrows lifted, nothing funny coming out of her mouth. "Maybe he was afraid he'd lose you, maybe he was afraid that you'd act like you're acting right now."

"Well I wouldn't have," Virginia says and has to look away from Cindy, that face so calm and serious like she has never seen it before. "He could have told me, could have told me that he was hurt. At least I would have felt like he had gotten over it."

"Well maybe there are some things you don't get over," Cindy says. "Part of me will probably always love Charles

Snipes but am I supposed to tell that? It's something I can't help. I can't help what happened to my daddy.''

"Part of me will always love Raymond," Madge whispers. "The Raymond I knew in those early years."

"But you didn't love him later," Cindy says and turns to Madge. "Tell the truth. Even though you had loved him, you didn't in the end did you?" Madge sits, her face twisting like she's not sure what to say, and then she sighs and shakes her head. "And I bet sometimes you think about when you did love him don't you?" Cindy asks and Madge nods, mouths a yes. "But that doesn't mean you want to go back does it?"

"God no."

"But you would go back," Virginia says to Cindy. "You'd go back to Charles."

"Yes, yes, I would," Cindy says. "I will if I have the chance, too. But it would be different. I'm different."

"Some people never get a chance," Gram says. "Tessy never really had a chance. Her life would've been so different if she'd had her way."

"You mean she never would have married my daddy," Madge says. "Or if she had married him, that she would have left him later on to be with that fiddler."

"Fiddler," Lena says and nods her head. "He was a fiddler!"

"I never would have been born," Madge says, her voice speeding up. "If my mama had had her way I never would've been born. If my mama had lived right now when everybody and his brother gets a divorce, then I wouldn't even be here. I'm on this earth and it has nothing to do with love." Madge looks at Emily but she is looking away, toward the front door. "She never loved my daddy. Not even in the beginning did she love him."

"I think she grew to love Harv," Emily says slowly. "I do."

"But did she ever tell you that?" Madge asks. "Did you ever hear her say that she loved my daddy?" Madge waits but Emily isn't talking, and why? Why does she even care if they ever loved each other? It has all been one big miserable mistake.

"If I had lived when Grandma Tessy did," Cindy says,

"then Charles and I would've stayed together. We would have made it work."

"And Sheila would have stayed with Mark," Virginia says.

"And you wouldn't have lived with a man, either," her mama says, but Virginia doesn't look at her. Her mother will want to know all about that, too. "And I don't see what good any of this is doing anybody," her mother continues. "I think it's all gone far enough. We're here right now. It is 1986. And what's gone is gone. Mark is a human." She stares hard at Virginia. "He made a mistake and you made a mistake. God knows we've all made mistakes."

"That's right," Cindy says. "You can't hold Mark's past against him."

"It's not his past that I hold against him," Virginia says. God knows, where have they all been? It's not the past, it's now. He called her Sheila once, right after they were married, in his sleep, in a dream, he called her Sheila and she had not even told him. She had tried to overlook it, overlooked the time before they got married when she saw that envelope with Sheila's return address in a stack of letters on his bedside table. "Do you ever hear from her?" she had asked, and he told her not really, that occasionally he'd get a change of address card. And there were all those times that the phone would ring and Virginia would answer to silence and then a click, the time a woman asked to speak to Mark and then left no message. And she took it, took all of that, rationalized it away until that night a month ago when for some God only knows reason, he decided to tell her everything, all of these things that he has thought about in secret.

"Then what do you hold against him?" Madge asks. "Does he make you buy the biggest box of Kotex in the world?" She has done it; they smile and she doesn't even have to lay out a solitaire board. She's done it and to quote Cindy, though the Lord'll have to pardon her, fuck solitaire.

"No," Virginia shakes her head, crying again. "I just feel so out of place sometimes. I get homesick."

"For this?" Cindy asks. "You get homesick for True Confessions in the Twilight Zone?" Cindy laughs, her mind speeding. "That would make a fine title of a book now wouldn't it?"

"I get homesick for ya'll." Virginia nods, focuses on Gram who is clicking the TV on, the volume turned down.

"I got so homesick," Gram says. "I'd go to my mama's during the day I'd get so homesick. I never would have married a man who would carry me from my home."

"I know," Virginia says, speaking only to Gram now, wanting so much to be told that everything's okay. "But I have married somebody who's going to take me from my home. He already has and I don't know what it is but sometimes I feel like I'm going to lose everything, that bit by bit everything that I love is going to be taken away from me." She looks at her mother now. "I have always wanted to be like Gram. And I'm not, look at me. I have never been like I want to be."

"Yes, you always said you wanted to be like me," Gram says. "And I always said 'yes Sweets, I know, but you'll have to be more than me; the world will change.'"

"You never said that," she says and shakes her head. "How could I be more when I can't even be like you? I'll never be like you."

"Then be like me," Lena says and smiles, adjusts her hat.

"That's who I wanted to be like," Hannah says and points to Lena. "I dreamed of being just like Lena, so funny and exciting."

"I wanted to be like Emily," Madge says and drops her deck of cards into the trashcan. "Or you, Hannah."

"Better watch it, Ginny Sue," Cindy says and laughs dramatically, trying so hard to act normal. "I bet your baby will want to be just like me."

"Oh God," Lena says and shakes her head.

"That baby will be fine if it takes after me," Cindy says. She feels the life coming back into her body, the sun after the storm and all that kind of shit that people will say to make you feel better. This has all gone far enough. "Ginny Sue? You know your idea about me finding a hobby?" Cindy stands in the center of the room, her hands on her hips. "Well, you were exactly right. I have found that I'm good at putting words together in a funny way. I make up titles for books and I make up lines to country songs. I've even been thinking I might take me a poetry class at Saxon Tech 'cause I've got it in my mind that I could write some funny greeting cards." Her mind is flying; it has to. There's no other way to go.

"Good," Virginia says and grips her stomach like she

might be dying, probably had a little kick and she better get used to it. Children, parents, men, and life will kick you right in the teeth and you best get used to it, learn to live with it. Cindy feels better, stronger, lightheaded; she knows she is never going to see Randy Skinner again; she is going to try to get Charles back, make it all up to him before it's too late. "I'll show you," she says now, Ginny Sue still so pale and long-faced. "Here's one thing I came up with just off the top of my head." Cindy tilts her head to one side and laughs. "My name's not Merle, but I am Haggard. My name's not Charlie but I got some Pride. My name's not Tanya, but I am Tuckered so Parton me, 'cause your Dolly's got to ride." Cindy bows and Madge and Hannah clap, Ginny Sue smiling a weak smile. "That's as far as I got. I was at work and you know my job is complicated, serious and complicated, everything from cardiac arrest to anorexia nervosa, to the major depression."

"Oregano is good for the melancholy," Emily says.

"Well I need to eat spaghetti every day," Madge eyes the trashcan but decides to forget that deck of cards. She has carried that dog-eared deck around for eight years and it's time to say good-bye.

"We can have spaghetti tonight," Hannah says. "I think Mama's got all we need right there in the kitchen and ya'll can stay."

"I might have plans," Cindy says, still wondering if she's got the nerve to get on her knees and tell Charles how she knows that she fucked up. No, no, that's not her style. He loved her for being wild and so that's how she'll be. He'll open that front door and she'll say "I'm a doctor I'm a lawyer I'm a movie star; I'm an astronaut and I own this bar. I'd lie to you for your love," and she'll grin and he'll let her in because Charles Snipes loves the Bellamy Brothers and then she'll start singing what was their first song that they had together, Grass Roots, "Sooner or Later," and then Don McLean's "American Pie," and then a little of Paul Anka's "You're Having My Baby." Faster, go faster. She turns to Emily. "I don't think doctors would agree about oregano."

"Makes no difference if they agree or disagree," Emily says. "It's true."

"Well, listen to this then," Cindy says and waits until she has Ginny Sue's attention. "I also make up songs about Jane Fonda and they're all to the tune of hymns." Cindy waits, her palms held out while she turns around to make sure everybody is paying attention; you can't really expect Lena and Emily to pay attention but she still waits until they're looking at her. She clears her throat. "What a friend we have in Jayyyne, all our cellulite to spare. It's a privilege to Fonda, all it takes is tights and air." Emily's eyebrows go up, Hannah's too, but it looks like Ginny Sue might laugh any minute now. "Praise Jane when you ain't got cellulite, praise Jane when you can touch your feet. Praise Jane when your butt don't shake. Praise Jane when you feel your muscles ache."

"Hush now," Emily says and finally Ginny Sue smiles; Ginny Sue is about to laugh and then the phone rings and everything stops.

Emily has the receiver pressed against her ear before it even rings the second time. "Ginny Sue," she whispers. "It's a man calling for you. I think it's James or Raymond."

"God, I hope not," Cindy says and forces a laugh. It makes her scalp ache to think of such a thing for real, to imagine her daddy's voice coming through a wire. "God," she shakes her head from side to side. "Let the dead stay where they are," and she sinks to her knees, runs her hand through her hair.

"Hello?" At first Virginia cannot focus on Mark's voice, Gram and Lena saying how they wish they'd get long-distance calls, the static on the wire. "Thank God," he says. "I've been calling for two hours and couldn't get through. I was about to drive down there but the radio said there were some lines down on the highway, that the traffic is backed up." Virginia twists the cord, listening, his voice so strange and distant. "I want you home, really, I called your doctor here and he said that it would probably be okay if I come and get you this weekend. Virginia? Are you still there?"

"Yes." They are all watching her, listening, so she turns and faces the wall. "How were the tests?"

"I don't know," his voice comes through in sketchy breaks. "I think I did okay but right now I really don't care. God, they said on the news that two tobacco warehouses down there were blown away." His voice quickens. "Look, I'm coming tomorrow, okay? Virginia?"

"I'm not ready," she says. "I don't want to go back." She concentrates on the faces around her, shapes and shades of mouths and eyes that know everything there is to know about her life. He is talking now, his voice cracking in her ear, cracking like plaster where she could reach her fingers and strip away, layers at a time.

"You really meant to leave, didn't you?" he asks, crackling static. "When you told me that you wanted me to leave, you really meant it didn't you?" She sees him standing there, pacing, that beige phone cord stretching as he moves from the door to the bathroom back over to the edge of the bed, his face gone pale, circles under his eyes as the bed creaks with his weight and he stares at that cobweb in the corner, weaving, netting, tighter and tighter, and she feels as cold and distant as that overhead bulb that she knows he has switched on.

"Yes," she says, her voice so clear and cold. "I don't have a life with you." She holds the receiver tightly, the silence on his end, and he might be on the phone in the kitchen and she sees his back as he stares out that kitchen window where the wisteria vines wrap and squeeze, choking that maple tree that has shaded that rented piece of land longer than she's been alive. "You don't mean that," he says, the same way that Bryan Parker said it, the same way that he must have said it to Sheila. "We have so much," he says to Sheila but Sheila had a mind of her own, a life of her own.

"The only reason that you are with me," she says, everyone watching her with frozen sketchy faces, her voice slow and deliberate, "is because it didn't work with Sheila. If Sheila had been like me, if she had been passive and malleable and willing to put her life on hold . . ." she stops with the pressure of her mother's hand on her arm, the frightened look on her mother's face.

"But that's not true," he says and she can't stand hearing him for another second, can't stand the thought of all that there is to face. She hands the receiver to her mother who refuses at first, but takes it when Virginia drops it to the floor and rolls back to face the cheap prefab wall, that yellow light from the window forming a distorted square.

"Tell him Ginny Sue needs some nicotine," Cindy says. "Tell him it's withdrawals."

"She's had a rather upsetting day," her mother says. "We've all been talking over sad old things that we should have left alone." Her mother pauses and Virginia can hear her sighs, hear her comforting words to Mark, Lena shuffling to the bathroom, Madge going through the trashcan. "I know that, honey," her mother says and Virginia imagines what his words must have been. "I am her husband! Virginia is acting crazy!"

"I'll see you tomorrow," her mother says. "Ben and I can follow and take the other car home." Another pause and then, "Okay, yes I will" and then "You know that we love you, Mark."

"Don't do this to me," Virginia says when Hannah hangs up. "Please. Don't make me go." And Hannah just wants to shake her, to tell her to grow up; but all Hannah can think about now are all those times that Ginny begged not to stay at Madge's house. She thinks of when she had stood on the curb of Carver Street and watched the ambulance pull away with her daddy in the back, the sheet over his head. Ginny Sue was just a tiny thing, peeping out the kitchen window, waving her small hand when Hannah looked up. "Please don't go," Ginny had said, "Please," when they carried that stretcher through the kitchen, Hannah and her mama following to the street, a child saying "please don't." Hannah had watched her mama roaming over toward the garden, litter that she had collected clutched in her hand; she watched Ginny pressing her forehead against that window, the glass fogging with her breath. And in that moment, Hannah felt all alone, the ambulance gone and all alone, straining to keep an eye on both mother and child, and then she had felt herself moving, acting, telephoning and cooking and washing dishes and straightening the house before people began to come while her mama sat and sewed a clown for Ginny Sue, all of her attention seemingly focused on a child who didn't really know what was going on.

"You're not thinking about your child," Hannah says now. "You are thinking of no one but yourself."

"Myself, that's right," Virginia says and sits up. "I'm thinking of myself like Madge should have done, thinking of myself like Cindy did when she left Buzz. Cindy and Chuckie are fine all by themselves." She looks at Cindy who is shaking her head back and forth. Cindy takes the deck of cards from Madge's hand and puts it back in the trashcan, then walks towards Virginia as if she's in slow motion.

"Don't blow it, Ginny Sue," Cindy whispers. "You don't know how lucky you are." Cindy squeezes her hand. "You are lucky, lucky. Your whole life has been lucky. I can't count the times that Mama has looked at me and said, 'why can't you be more like Ginny Sue?' "

"Oh Cindy, I'm sorry," Madge says but Cindy just shrugs, smiles at Madge.

"I guess even my daddy felt that way," Cindy whispers, her face turning pink. "I know Buzz Biggers did. Honey, if he could have had you, he wouldn't have looked twice at me."

"Cindy," Virginia says, repulsed by the very thought of Buzz Biggers, but held fast by Cindy's watery gaze.

"No, it's true," Cindy says. "You were two years behind me in high school and I always knew that whoever I dated would have chosen you over me if he could've, and I also knew that anybody you went out with wouldn't have wanted to go out with me."

"That's not true," Virginia says. "You are so much prettier, and look at your figure and you're exciting. You were always so popular."

"That's what Charles said," Cindy says, the tears coming to her eyes. "I guess Charles is the one person who I felt would have chosen me first; mainly because I asked him one time. I asked him if he wished I was more like you."

"Oh Cindy."

"No, let me finish." Cindy leans back, her legs crossed Indian style on the daybed. "Charles felt that way about me and I blew it. I've always made fun of you and stuff but it's because I was jealous. I was jealous of everything you had and it was easier to just do everything opposite from you than to compete."

"Maybe you should tell Charles how you feel." Virginia sits up, looks at Madge. "Don't you think she should tell him?"

"And you should think about how you feel about Mark," Hannah says. "He's a good person and he loves you."

"Roy was a good person," Lena says.

"Yes," Emily nods. "But Roy Carter would not have had me. No, for I was a lady and Roy would not have had me."

"No, he wouldn't have," Lena says. "And I'd not've had James, as sweet a person as I thought he was." Lena looks around the room and laughs. "James was nice but he was dull. Roy said, 'James is about as funny as a bubblegum machine on a lockjaw ward.' " She laughs and fans her hat back and forth.

"He was never silly," Emily says. "If that's what you mean."

"I can't believe you were ever jealous of me," Virginia says, for the first time noticing the little lines leading from the corners of Cindy's eyes where she used to draw long black eyeliner tails like a cat.

"Yes," Cindy smiles, the lines reaching into her hairline, but she looks pretty this way with her hair in wisps instead of stiff and sprayed. Cindy laughs and slaps Virginia on the leg. "I guess that's why I've always made a soap opera of something. Having people tell me what NOT to do was better than nothing."

"Oh, Cindy," Madge gasps. "You needed attention, and here all this time I've ignored you thinking if I ignored something that it would stop."

"Didn't work with Daddy," Cindy says and catches herself when she sees her mother wince like she might have just sliced a finger. "Oh, don't get yourself all worked up and ready to hemorrhage over it." Cindy waves her hand and Madge is almost relieved to have Cindy talk to her that way. You can't just start your life over and everything be brand new, can't teach an old dog new tricks.

"This has gone on long enough," Hannah says. "I say it's time we all wake up and grow up," she pauses and looks at Ginny Sue. "And get on with it. This kind of talk will get you nowhere." Hannah glances around the room now and they are all silent. Somebody has to do it; somebody has to step in and keep things moving. "I'm going to fix a big pot of spaghetti and hope that Ben will come on over soon. I think the storm has passed."

"It's not but five," Madge says. "The radio says the watch is on until seven."

"The weatherman is not always right," Emily says and shakes her finger at Madge. "God knows better than the weatherman."

"But what am I going to do?" Virginia asks and for the first time other than walking to the bathroom, she gets up off that daybed and starts pacing. She goes over and straightens that hat on Lena's head because it has been about to drive her crazy seeing it tilted that way, and she straightens out Gram's drapes where whoever opened them this morning let them get all twisted. "Just because Cindy is being nice to me doesn't fix everything right up."

"I think somebody that chose to live with a person, chose not to marry that person, decided on a college and a major, chose another person to live with and did marry, ought to be able to think for herself." Her mother is standing in the doorway of the kitchen with a pack of hamburger meat in her hand. "You decided all of those things without any help from me. Why, then, at twenty-eight years old and ready to be a mother yourself are you asking for advice?"

"Because I need it," Virginia says. "You've always given me all kinds of advice that I didn't need, how to spray starch a collar, how to hem a skirt, how to make biscuits like Gram used to make, but now I need some advice and you won't give it to me."

"Well, pardon me," Hannah says and drops the hamburger meat to the floor. "I have done all that I know to do, done and done and done for years and this is the thanks that I get." Her voice shakes and the tears roll from the corners of her eyes. "Why are you coming to me now? Why, after all these other things have gone on in your life and you didn't see reason to tell me."

"You wouldn't have understood," Virginia says, her head light and dizzy. "What would you have said if I had told you that I was living with somebody?"

"I would have told you that I thought you had lost your mind. I would have told you that you were making a big mistake."

"And that's why I didn't ask you," Virginia says and sits on the end of the daybed. "You've always done things exactly right. You wore white when you got married and it meant something. You don't smoke, you had two children, a station wagon, a business that was all your own, and you've never been in therapy.''

"Well, I'm sorry," Hannah says and shakes her head back and forth. "You talk like my life has been easy and perfect, like I've never had a problem."

"You haven't." Virginia shakes her head from side to side.

"Oh, I haven't?" Hannah laughs sarcastically and looks away from Ginny Sue, those eyes too much like her own, this conversation like one that she could've had with her mama years ago. "I've had my share of problems," she says. "Just imagine if you were to lose Robert right now and never have him again. Just think about that. I lost my brother and I was as close to him as you are to Robert, maybe even closer. I don't have my daddy either, Ginny Sue. And, yes, we all lose our parents, people talk about it all the time but it's different when it's yours and there's nothing that anybody on this earth can do to prepare you for it." Hannah pauses and looks over at her mama, feels the dryness of her throat. "And I've made my share of mistakes and don't you ever forget it."

"You have?" Madge asks and Hannah feels like the rug has been pulled out from under her. She hasn't been divorced and hasn't killed anybody but God knows, she's had problems like everybody else.

"Of course I have." Hannah picks up the hamburger from the floor and pulls a piece of dust away from the cellophane. "I left Ben one time," she says which is the truth though Ben never knew of it. She's never been able to figure out if she really at any moment intended to leave him or if it was just a game, a trial to see how she would feel if she really left him, and she drove down to the beach and sat on a towel and watched the ocean and thought about Ben Turner until she cried and got back in the car and drove home, sunburned and sandy and so glad to get there.

"What's wrong?" he had asked and held her so close. "I was afraid you had left me," and he laughed, those rough hand of his cupping her face, and he told her all about a Rolls that had pulled through, stopping for gas, heading to New York, and how he called Roy on the phone and Roy had gotten there just in time to see it pulling off. "Roy wanted to get under that hood so bad," Ben said. "And I wanted him to, kind of to pay him back for all the times he let me look at his Lincoln. I sat down with a piece of paper and drew it all out for him.'' And that's when she made up her mind that this was her life, no make believe and no fairy tales, this was it, and she knew that she'd be a whole lot happier just knowing and accepting; it's been a fine life with Ben Turner.

"You did not," Virginia states in her best school-teacher voice. "You're just saying that to make me feel bad for what I said to Mark."

"Or to make me feel better," Madge says.

"She's saying it because I told her so when she was a child," Emily says and nods her head.

"Maybe I'm saying it because I want to say it and because it doesn't have a thing to do with a one of you here," Hannah says. "I do have some life all my own, you know. My whole life is not tied up to all of you."

"I am your mother," Emily says.

"I am like your mother." Lena stands on her wobbly legs and shakes a finger.

"Yes and Madge is my cousin and Ginny Sue is my daughter and Cindy is some kind of cousin."

"Just say niece," Cindy says. "Really I'm like a niece."

"Yes, a niece," Hannah says so that she can say what she wants before the conversation goes to some other godforbidden secret of death or babies or incest. "But what goes on behind closed doors is my business, a life that has nothing to do with any of you. I'm sorry but that's the truth. Ben is my husband and I love him dearly, but he ain't perfect."

"Does he do funny things with his underwear?" Madge asks.

"Is he a redneck in the Klan?" Cindy asks and Hannah is getting madder by the minute. Not once in her entire life has she been able to have a headache or a sunburn or indigestion that somebody in this family has not had it worse.

"Can't I have a problem of my own?" Hannah asks. "Aren't I a person?"

"I'll give you my problems," Madge says and Lena nods, starts to talk, but Hannah jumps in while she's got the energy.

"I don't want your problems," Hannah says, her voice causing Madge to shrink, causing Cindy to jump right over and put her hand on her mama's shoulder. Good, that's where

Cindy ought to be, where she should have been years ago.
"I've had my own."

"But why would you want to leave Daddy?" Virginia asks.
"How could you have ever thought such a thing?"

"The same way you're thinking it now," Hannah says and
watches that know-it-all look come to Virginia's face.

"You're making this up." Virginia grips her stomach when
it kicks, a hard one, and her mama doesn't even ask if she's
okay; her mama just shakes her head. "Then why did you
leave him?"

"Because it wasn't going like I expected."

"It never does," Gram says and laughs. "I told Hannah
when she got married, I said, 'Now, it ain't always going to
go as you expect and you might from time to time wish that
you weren't there; you might wish that you were here at home
with me and your daddy.' "

"You didn't tell me that," Hannah whispers and goes and
takes her mama's hand, those blue veins so large, the wedding band loose and worn, trapped under that swollen
knuckle. "I wish you had but you didn't."

"That's what Mama told me," Emily says. "I'd go to her
house and James didn't know. I'd say, 'Mama, it ain't like
being at home' and she'd say 'one day it will be though. One
day when I'm dead and buried you'll all of a sudden feel like
you've got a home.' " Emily shakes her head and smiles to
think of her mama so old then and the way her mama took
to roaming the streets, forgetting where and who she was.
God, to be able to walk and to get out on those dusty roads
and walk towards town with nothing on your mind but buying
some calico and hoop cheese. "It comes on you sudden like,"
she whispers. "You get out and start walking and it starts to
get dark and you say to yourself, 'I got to get myself home
before the storm comes' and your feet carry you home but
not way out in the country a piece where your mama still
boils her bath water on the stove. No, you go on home where
you got children wanting their dinner."

"God, I fixed Pooh some good dinners," Lena whispers.
"Sardines."

"Pssshhh," Emily says. "Them cats are better than people."

"Because they're better than most people." Lena rubs the
pillow on her lap.

"But why did you leave Ben?" Cindy asks. "You knew him. You had known him your whole life."

"For the very reason Mama just said," Hannah says. "I was feeling homesick and I was starting to realize that I was never going to live in New York and be a fashion designer like Lena had always said I could be. I realized that I was never going to be a housewife and sip coffee and chat. No, I was going to work; I was going to send my children to school with keys around their necks. I was homesick for all the times that I had been able to sit around and think about what I wanted to be instead of having to get out and be something."

"And you are something, Hannah," Cindy says and Virginia can't help but feel a twinge of jealousy when her mother smiles and nods at Cindy.

"There are choices to make," Gram says. "James said, 'Emily, if you didn't want to get married, you should have just stayed out there in the country with your mama.' And I said 'I can do both just fine, thank you' and when I told my mama that she said 'you got to learn to let go, Emily. God taught me with that thunderstorm that you just got to let go. Your place is with your husband, now.' "

"That's what Charles said to me," Cindy says and goes and sits in front of Emily's chair. "Charles told me I might have to make some choices."

"I sure made a bad one," Madge says.

"So did your mama," Lena says and shuffles over to the window. "I got to get home before dark. Roy can't do a thing without me."

"Please stay, Lena," Virginia begs, her mind still on Gram's words, still trying to form a picture of her mother, much younger, designing clothes in some big store in New York City. And where would she be if that had happened?

"Tessy never had a choice," Emily says and stares down at Cindy, smiles, her eyes widening in surprise. "I declare Tessy, you never had a choice over anything. That's what I tell folks when they ask about the other, even Lena, that's what I say. I'd never tell a word more, Tessy. I'd never tell your secrets."

"And I hope you never do," Cindy whispers and Virginia

cannot believe that's Cindy's sitting there, her legs bent and tucked under her, her hair so soft and natural-looking.

"Tessy," Emily says and clasps Cindy's hands. "I do know that feeling you spoke of that day. At the time I didn't but I come to find it just like you said, and I'd never tell. You know I never would." She squeezes Cindy's hand and giggles in a high girlish way. "I want you to have that green velvet dress so you can dance and laugh and know some happiness in your life. I danced that time, remember? Remember how I told you about the time I danced?"

"Yes, I remember." Cindy pats Emily's hand and then without looking at anyone, dashes into the bathroom, her hands up to her face like blinders on a horse, and she stands in the dark bathroom, splatter of rain on the window while she cries. God, how long will it take for it all to go away?

"I've got to get home now," Lena says.

"Well, you and Roy come again." Emily wipes her eyes. "You and Roy are always welcome here."

"Oh, we'll be back all right." Lena laughs and smooths her hair back behind her ear. "Roy says we'll be back before you can say Frank Lloyd Wright Eiffel Tower Brooklyn Bridge. He's coming to get me in that car with the convertible top."

"James come to get me," Gram says now. "I was at my mama's and he came in that house and said, 'It's time for you to come home' and I said, 'I'll be there directly. I need to stay here with Mama a bit more,' and he said, 'I think you need to come now if you're coming.' He had never spoke to me that way and I got it in my mind that he never would again and I stared right back. I stood there in my mama's front room and I watched him go out that front door and leave. I heard that horse clip-clopping off and my mama come in that room and she said that I best be going, that it was time I went, and I got to the end of the yard and I saw James way down the road. My mama was standing on her front porch waving her hands at me like she might have been shooing an old dog and I felt myself walking faster and faster till soon I was running and the sky looked yellow like there might come a twister and I felt so scared like I needed to run faster." She breathes quickly and closes her eyes.

"No, Mama said you gotta know when to let go a little,

let go and just leave it there behind you and then go make yourself a plate of biscuits and bleach them shirts of your husband's just as white as they can get and then just let go a little.''

PART VII

Virginia is walking down Carver Street, her thick dark hair pulled up and tied with tobacco twine, a sack dress in a faded lavender print pulled across her full belly while she drags an empty burlap bag. "It's for bottles" she will say if anyone asks what she's doing here where the town has fallen apart, freestanding chimneys amidst weeds and brambles like a long line of abandoned tombstones. There is no one else in the street, no Coke bottles in the ditch as she walks along, the concrete burning her feet as she steps over every crack, weblike filaments, tiny veins, silver shimmers where a slug has dragged his tired heavy body and hidden in the cool darkness beneath the cracks. Her back feels like it's breaking, like it could snap like a twig, and the dry hot sun makes everything so white, so sterile. She has the impulse to run, to get away from the emptiness that leaks from the abandoned houses, to get away from the clip clip of those wingtip shoes, but her legs are so heavy, so tired and heavy.

The sky darkens when the wind starts, a fine whistling that makes the dry cornstalks rustle, the leaves whirl in a flash of color. There is one ear of corn in the garden, one perfect ear on an empty stalk, pink silks falling from its crown and the silks would look so pretty in her hair, tied and knotted. Her dress whips faster with the rush of wind, the train with its loud piercing whistle, smoke billowing beyond the tracks, smoke from Cutty's Place, her grandfather's cigar, smoke billowing from a helicopter circling the sky.

"That's your Gram's house right there," a woman with long gray hair tells her, a satchel filled with corn and drink bottles over the woman's arm, and she points to a building

275

that Virginia had not noticed, a flat concrete building rising three stories, gothic columns halved and propped against that flat front, a door that reaches to the second level, heavy and dark, no window. "You ought to let her know you're here, Ginny Sue."

"That's not Gram's house." She turns to ask the woman who she is, what she's doing here where the town has fallen apart. "Are you Tessy?" she thinks but her lips won't move, words won't come.

"You better hurry," she says and bends to pick up a glass milk bottle. "Emily can't wait forever."

The door pushes open easily and everything is dark; she feels her way along the wall for a light switch, her other hand on the chair rail, her fingers slipping below the familiar tongue-and-groove boards there, and there is the rusty smell of country well water, a kerosene stove and the light comes quickly, late afternoon rose light, winter light, that falls in slats from the venetian blinds onto the wallpaper, and her hand finds that cool porcelain switch but there is no need and the light moves in patches from room to room, huge clock ticking, the dark mahogany headboard, soft quilt-covered feather bed, Gram's shape pressed into her side. And the light moves, the breakfast room, kerosene stove, a blue flickering light through that little glass window, her clothes hung on a small rocking chair, because Gram said to dress there where it's warm. A hog head is in the kitchen sink and Gram takes a spoon and scoops the eyes. "Don't you be bothered," Gram says. And Lena and Roy are on the front porch picking up the roses that people throw and David is flying overhead, sounding out a secret signal to Gram and she understands because she looks up and smiles and Gramps is in his stuffed chair with the Brer Rabbit book on his lap.

The African violets are so lush on that windowsill, the blooms reaching and stretching and she is a child at the window and she sees her mother on the street below. There is an ambulance and her mother is young and tiny like a schoolgirl, her auburn hair curling onto her shoulders as she turns slowly, tries to smile when she sees Virginia in the window, and Virginia has buttons deep in the pocket of her corduroy pants, pale blue buttons like pale blue eyes.

Gram steps in from the garden, young, her hair still dark,

tied with a gray scarf, a brooch clamped to her sweater, rolled down support hose, galoshes, the plaid cotton dress.

"Were you looking for this, Sweets?" Gram asks and pulls the ear of corn from her pocket, the pink silks falling over her hand. "Tessy said you wanted this."

"Oh yes," Virginia whispers, never taking her eyes from Gram until she reaches for her own pocket in that faded dress and finds the material so loose and full, her belly flat and empty.

"Gram, where's my baby?" she asks, a dull sickness filling her chest.

"And where's my baby, Ginny Sue?" Gram asks and looks past her to the dark frost-covered kitchen window, rolling her wheelchair closer and closer, her hair so white against that pink bathrobe, blue buttons in her open palm.

"I've lost it, Gram. I'm so afraid I've lost it."

"We all lose things, Ginny Sue. We hold on so tight and we lose them just the same."

* * *

"I sure hope that dogwood tree lives," Tessy whispers and watches Hannah stand there by the bed and cry like a little girl. She can see Hannah's hand there on her arm where there are all kinds of strange tubes, but she can't feel it. It seems like everything worth feeling in this world is leaving her in an easy way, a way much easier than it has all come to her. "Hannah would fill the world up with dogwoods if she could," Emily told Tessy one day when the two of them sat on Tessy's back door stoop, dipping snuff and talking over all that had happened in their lives. "Yes, my children have always had big fine dreams," Emily had said and Tessy realized that day that she didn't know what her children dreamed or if they dreamed at all. And Harv, what kind of dreams did Harv ever have? It seems so long since she's talked to Emily, so long since she felt Emily's warm hand cupped around her own. A world filled with dogwoods, a symbol of resurrection in that cross pattern and little blood-pink marks. Emily told her that and it makes her smile now to think of it, the dogwood blossom that Emily pressed into her hand, a world filled with dogwoods and they aren't even the kind of tree that you have to buy for they spring up and grow wild in the woods. A world filled with them; it makes her laugh but Hannah goes right on crying and Tessy wants Hannah to go get Madge; she wants to see Madge, to talk to her. "You can't do nothing for me," she told Madge once, but that wasn't the truth. No, no, Madge can do something for her. Madge can make herself a better life. If there is any love left, if there ever was any there, that's what Madge can do for her. Madge can hold her hand like Hannah is doing and say "mother, mother," and everything is getting so quietlike just like Emily always said she believed it would, that it all comes so quietlike. Don't fight it. Don't fight any more. Let the world do what's natural for you because you are tired, too tired to fight it and come springtime the world will be filled with dogwoods, pink and white crossed blossoms that Emily will pick and press into her hand, her mind, her heart.

* * *

"Sparkie?" Virginia stands in the doorway and waits, the doll in one hand. "Sparkie, here boy," and she thinks she hears him stirring, the kitchen, but no, he is outside; he is barking and whining, outside. She hears the dull ticking of a clock and then sounds in the kitchen, silverware shuffling. She turns on the light over the stairs. "Catherine?"

"Catherine?" comes a high mimic from below and she freezes, her hand on the railing, dusk outside the window.

"Uncle Raymond?" she calls softly and steps back from the top of the stairs. Nothing, and then footsteps, closet door opens, closes. "Uncle Raymond?"

"Uncle Raymond?" comes the mimic again and she stands, breath held, ready to run into Cindy's room, slam and lock the door. "Hickory dickory dock," comes the throaty whisper. "The mouse ran up the clock."

"Please stop! Please stop!" she cries and a hand, black glove, a long silver knife, reach around the corner of the stairwell, that wingtip shoe on the bottom step.

"Please," he says, his voice high and shrill and she stands in the doorway of Cindy's room where she can see the hand, the shoe. "Who is Uncle Raymond?" And he starts up the stairs, a Halloween mask covering his face, a smiling hobo face with bushy eyebrows. "There's no one here named Raymond."

"I know it's you," she whispers. "I see your Chevrolet

tag.'' She squats in the doorway. ''Please stop,'' and he reaches up and puts his hand over the tag, his other hand clicks the edge of the knife against the bannister. The light over the stairs clicks off and she can see him, a shadow, coming up the steps. She is crying now, crawls into Cindy's room, slams and locks the door. She stands by the window where the streetlight two blocks away is buzzing on, flickering. The door handle jiggles, slow at first and now hard, shaking the door. The edge of the knife is under the door, moving back and forth over the pink shag carpet. ''Hickory dickory dock,'' he whispers and then she hears him walk away, down the hall.

Silence and she turns on the lamp and sits on the edge of the bed so that she can watch the corner where Madge's car should be turning any second now. Then she remembers the phone, Cindy's princess phone, and she rushes over, dials Gram's number but there is no dial tone, just a steady buzzing. The corner is empty, no sign of Madge's car and when the phone rings she jumps, drops the doll to the floor. ''Aunt Madge?'' she screams into the receiver and there is silence. ''Open the door now,'' he whispers. ''It's time to open your little door.''

She places the receiver down quietly and stands in the center of the room, the doll at her feet and she hears him coming back, hears the door handle jiggling again and then it swings open and he is there, a bobby pin held in his hand instead of the knife, his Chevrolet tag on, the mask and gloves gone.

''When I ask you to open a door you should do it,'' he says. ''What's wrong with you?'' He steps closer. ''Why are you crying?''

''You scared me,'' she whispers.

''I scared you?'' he asks and picks up the doll, tosses it on the bed.

''Yes,'' she says, tries to laugh. She wants him to laugh, to say it was all a joke, a very bad joke and he is sorry. ''That mask, and the knife.''

''What mask?'' he asks and stands in front of Cindy's vanity, stooping so that his face appears there. ''My face frightens you?'' He stares at her image in the mirror. ''I see the way you look at me. I know what you're thinking.'' He turns from the mirror and laughs, walks over to her. ''Your mother would be ashamed of you. You worship me. Go ahead, say how you worship me.''

"Aunt Madge will be here any minute.''

He steps closer and she is trapped in the corner, the driveway just below. "When it stops, death comes and hovers, a shadow will carry you away.''

"Please, please.'' She leans against the wall and slides to the floor, her foot near that little lacy parasol that has slipped from the doll's hand.

"Come now,'' he says and reaches his arms to her. "Uncle Raymond didn't mean to scare you.''

"But you did, you did,'' she says. "Aunt Madge should be here soon.''

"But I'm here,'' he whispers, pulls her up from the floor and over beside him on the bed. "See my birdhouse out the window?'' he asks. "Just watch the little birds.''

"There aren't any,'' she says. "I've got to put Cindy's doll up.''

"The birdies are all dead,'' he says, teeth gritted while he holds her there. "Their souls belong to me now. I wrapped them in clean white sheets, so slowly and gently I wrapped them. I fed the birds and they worshipped me and then when they tried to fly away, I killed them. And I see how you look at me.'' He lifts her hair and stares up and down her neck and she doesn't move, barely breathes while she stares down at the corner where she knows Madge's car should be turning. "You are like a little bird,'' he says and lets her go, laughs when she runs to the door. "Oh, you'll never fly away,'' he whispers and is there, his hand on the doorknob and he pushes her back. "I'll wrap you in a sheet,'' he says and steps closer. "But first you must worship me. First you must tell me that you worship me.'' He grabs her arm, twists. "Speak!''

"I worship you,'' she gasps and then she sees Madge's car pulling into the driveway. "Aunt Madge!'' she screams but he pushes her to the floor.

"If you ever tell anyone,'' he says, Cindy's hairbrush in his hand as he slaps his open palm. "Then I will take you. Don't think you can hide, you can't. I'll make you worship me, bathe my feet in oils, dry my feet with your hair and then I'll wrap you in a sheet until you can't breathe.''

"No!'' she screams, the car door slamming below, and he

hurls the hairbrush into the mirror while she runs to the stairs, glass shattering.

"Oh yes," he whispers and the front door opens and Madge is there, Cindy, and Virginia grabs hold of Madge's arm, her sobs uncontrollable.

"Ginny Sue, what on earth is wrong?" Madge asks, Cindy's tap shoes making a light click on the floor.

"She broke Cindy's mirror," he says and she hears his slow steps down the stairs. "She threw a little tantrum when I told her that she shouldn't be going through Cindy's things."

* * *

Tessy Pearson stays busy all day long, working and moving, so that in these late middle years, she looks much older than most women. Her long hair is almost all gray and she keeps it yanked up in a loose bun that by midafternoon has fallen and that's when she sits out on her door stoop and brushes it over one shoulder, stroke after stroke. "What are you thinking Tessy?" folks have always asked and it is as if her mind freezes shut, as if all of her thoughts creep way back up in her mind to hide. And they aren't always big thoughts; she might be thinking about red ripe tomatoes and how she will hold them under the tap, turning them over and over, the bitter earthy smell going down the drain but lingering on her hands. They might not be big thoughts but they are hers and she clings to that one fact like it is the only thing that can keep her alive.

She thinks a lot these days, more and more. She puffs her pipe and watches that smoke go straight up to heaven and it makes her feel warm deep in her body. She wears those little lace-up boots that it seems she has worn her whole life and she'll sit with her feet turned out while she whittles a little or pares apples, shells butterbeans, whatever it takes to help her to rest. Sometimes Hannah and Madge will stop by but it seems they talk mostly to themselves, like they don't know what to say to Tessy. It seems a lot of people feel that way about her; Lena won't even speak her name. It seems a lot of people aside from Emily are scared of her like those school children that creep up to her door like she might be a witch; they say that she is, tell each other that she's a witch. "She hates everybody," a little boy had said just the other day when he brought a whole bunch of young'uns to come and stand at her house. "That's not so," she whispered but they didn't hear her, didn't see her standing there behind the curtain. "I saw her once," the boy said. "Got long gray hair that sticks straight out and no teeth." She had shaken her head from side to side and gone and lain on her bed. More and more that's what she wants to do, lie in the bed and close her eyes to it all. But she has to stay busy, has to keep her mind busy, to concentrate on that ridge of pine trees that have grown so over the years, and how just beyond that line of trees is the Saxapaw River curving and winding way on out of the county where she was born, winding and twisting past Spottsville and on. When she gets in her bed at the end of the day, she wants sleep to come quickly so that she won't lose control of her thoughts.

There was one night way back when she had lain in that bed, Harv there beside her and she had pulled back the sheets and carefully lifted the leg of his pajama pants so that she could see that big scar on his shin, that smooth hairless white crescent that seemed so slick and shiny next to the rest of his leg. It was a mark of sorts, a story that had been told by Emily years ago when Tessy was just a girl. Emily told of that slipped axe and all that blood and Harv back there behind the woodpile trying not to cry. She had never seen Harv cry. She had rubbed her finger over that scar as he stirred in his sleep, head from side to side and then still. Harv's scar and Harv's blood and it seemed to be the first time that Harv's flesh and blood, that Harv, had ever materialized in such a way, the warmth of his skin. The hairs around that scar were gray, on his chest, his head, all of that a part of Harv and a part of her by marriage though she had never felt any claim. All those years and she had never touched the scar, not intentionally, not with the gentleness that she felt that night. She tried to remember if she had ever touched anybody that way, so tenderly and it seemed that she had; it seemed that there had been a moment at least once when her fingers could read it all but she had let herself forget it, worked it clean from her mind. No one had ever read her that way; no one had ever touched her in a way that said they wanted her whole life, wanted to be a part of it, wanted the good and the bad and all that fell between the cracks, all the times they weren't there and the times they were.

And she wanted that; she suddenly wanted that as she

rubbed the scar, that sensitive skin that though toughened, looking so bare and painful like that second before bleeding starts, that second before the blood can surface and spill over. She had wanted it, wanted that feeling, wanted it all, but even more so that night with Harv as if all those years sharing a house and a bed counted for something big that she had spent her life overlooking. She had leaned over and kissed that scar, ran her tongue down it like a cat and then stretched out beside him, tried to understand how it had come so far.

She'd hear bits of music in her mind as she still does and try real hard to think of where it came from; sometimes she thinks it must have come from Harv, that he must have hummed or whistled those slow painful melodies that will come to her with her footsteps or the creak of her rocker or the rain on that tin roof. Even now it makes her want to cry when she pictures in her mind Harv behind that woodpile with his leg bleeding. She would cry those nights that she lifted his pants to see that scar; she'd cry for Harv and herself and that pure white scar. That's what she did every night until Harv died. That's what replaced the prayers that she had mouthed night after night up to the ceiling like Emily had said she should. But bending there in the light of the window, touching Harv's scar gave her a sense of peacefulness that those prayers never had. He never woke to see her there, kneeling over his leg, her lips gently brushing the surface of his scar, and she never even planned what she would say should he wake and see her there. She still wonders what she might have said. She thinks, I love you, Harv, and the sounds lilt and bend in her mind like one of those tunes, rising and falling, like Harv's slow steady breathing on all those nights.

"Harv, I'm sorry," she had said the day the doctor came and said that Harv had no business out in those fields anymore, that Harv probably wouldn't live to see harvest. "I'm sorry," she said and put her arms around his neck and whispered the words up against his rough stubbled cheek, over and over, I'm sorry, and she felt the tears coming to her eyes, startling her as if she had forgotten there was such a thing and he leaned his head against hers for a moment, pressed in and then shook his head from side to side. "Little late for sorry ain't it?" he asked. "It's so late little Messy," and he pinched her cheek and then turned away from her as she backed into the kitchen where there was a whole sinkful of tomatoes to wash and beans to snap and sheets to wash, and she wanted to go back in there and pull up the leg of his pants, to kneel there in front of him and press her mouth against the scar, and say those words over and over until he said that he knew. She wanted him to know that she had done that for months, that she spent her whole day waiting for him to be asleep so that she could do that, could feel some feeling in her fingers. She wanted to tell him that that's what kept her sane but she never did. She lay there night after night, wondering which day or which night that breathing would stop. And when that tender green tobacco broke the soil, she knew that she had seen that scar for the last time. So she has to stay busy now, day after day, those words that she never said keeping her company with their strange little tunes that she hears with every turn and scrape of her knife against a bare piece of wood.

* * *

Emily stands in the doorway and watches James sitting in that overstuffed chair by the window, Ginny Sue curled on his lap like a little kitten while he reads the Uncle Remus stories. He can't really read at all, but it doesn't matter; he knows those stories by heart and Ginny Sue can't read. She doesn't know that he's just looking at the pictures and making up from what he remembers. "Please don't ever let her know that I can't read," he begged Emily and she assured him that she never would. "Though it's nothing to be ashamed of," she told him but he just stared down at his feet and shook his head. Now Ginny Sue is asleep there on his chest, her little mouth dropped open and drooling a little and he just stares out the window at the dog pen that David built when he was a boy. Belle is what David called that dog that Lena and Roy gave him. For years he was looking after Belle till that dog was so old and blind that it was almost a sin to expect her to go on living. That pen is near-about fallen down and she keeps telling James they need to get rid of it, that a child could get hurt on that old rusty wire. He won't have any part of it, won't let her have it torn down. And he won't discuss it with her either. Night after night, she lies in that bed, tries to talk about David, tries to make him feel easy about it all, but he only rolls into her like a child and hushes her words with kisses, hard kisses on her lips until she is silent.

"Whatchoo wanna hear?" he whispers now and Ginny Sue opens her eyes, stretches against him.

"Tar Baby," she says and he flips through the book till he finds the right picture. Emily wants so much to go and sit on the arm of that chair and cuddle up with the two of them, to take the book from his hands and read all the words she can recognize, but he needs the child to himself, he needs to feel that childhood squeal vibrating against his chest.

* * *

Hannah is nursing Robert, just a tiny thing, when the phone rings. She goes quickly and places him in his bed before answering to her mama's short breath and sobs. The telegram. As soon as Hannah hears the word, she knows and she turns to look at the small apartment kitchen and it all looks so strange to her, out of focus, like she might be in a stranger's home instead of hers and Ben's. She calls Ben to come home and be with the baby until a sitter can arrive, and it seems like hours before he walks through that strange doorway and hands her the keys to the car, tells her that he will get there as soon as he can. And the whole town seems silent as if everybody and everything knows what has happened.

Tessy is already there, her hair gray and tangled as she stands with a plate of biscuits like she doesn't know what to do with them. Hannah's mama's eyes are red and puffy but she has stopped crying now; now she is worried about Hannah's dad, the way that he has gone to bed and won't get up. Hannah tiptoes into the room and draws back the cover to find him curled there, his face in the pillow, and when he looks up at Hannah, his eyes so swollen and red, his hair not even combed, Hannah feels a fear that runs down her spine, seeming to freeze her there, her hand just short of rubbing his face. "He's gone," he whispers to Hannah. "He will never be back."

It is late when Hannah finally goes home, her dad asleep and her mother getting ready for bed. "Are you sure you don't want me to stay?" she asks but her mama shakes her head, says Robert will be needing his feeding. Ben is waiting up for her, Robert asleep in his crib and for the first time, she sits down and cries for every second of her life, all of those good times that now will be so hard to look back on. And she goes to get Robert only to find him sleeping so peacefully and she shakes his little leg until he wakes so that she can nurse him. Ben sits in the dark of the bedroom with her, off to the side, the chair at the desk, while Robert nuzzles and roots until he finds her breast, and all she can think about over and over is the time that she saw David and Mary Harper down by the river. They were leaning against the trunk of a tree and drinking moonshine out of Mary's shoe. David lifted that shoe to his mouth and the two of them laughed and hugged, their bodies pressed close together in the way that only lovers know. And now the warmth of this tiny body pressing and sucking her breast is not enough for her. Now, more than she ever has, she wants Ben. She wants to feel his body cover and press against her; she wants to close her eyes and move against him, to feel every motion, and then to open her eyes and see that he is still there.

* * *

When Madge gets to the oak tree midway down the road, she starts running as fast as she can, her heart beating so fast and it feels good just to get out and run. "I'm just going for a walk," she had told her mama and her mama didn't care. Her mama wouldn't notice if Madge took off and never came back. She gets to the end of the road, there at the crossroads where that long dusty road stretches into town, and stops, catches her breath, smooths the skirt of her dress. She waits and she hears his car coming before she sees the cloud of dust when he turns the corner, so good-looking, his blonde hair brushed back high off of his forehead.

"Can I give you a lift?" he asks, smiles at her, and she laughs, climbs in beside him and he pulls her over closer, his arm around her shoulder making her feel so small and protected. "What have you been doing all day?" he asks and it makes her feel so warm inside. She could be toting a sack of potatoes on her back that she had spent the whole day digging and he would still be interested in hearing about it. "Find a man that's interested in you and not what you can give him," her mama had said on one of those rare times that she talked. She has found someone, now, and for the first time in her life, Madge is happy. "I can't stand being away from you,

Raymond,'' she says. "I know I haven't known you long but
I feel that way, I do."

"You know all you'll ever need to know," he says and
kisses her cheek. "This is me and I want to spend the rest
of my life loving you."

* * *

Tessy Pearson would have seven children if she hadn't mis-
carried those two times. Now she's got five and one on the
way, but this new one isn't going to make it, doesn't have a
chance. She doesn't call out for a doctor or Harv or anybody
else; she just lies there in that big iron bed, her knees pulled
up to her chest and waits for it to be over. She can hear leaves
rustling and limbs brushing against the tin roof, wood being
chopped and tossed on that pile outside the kitchen door. She
knows Harv isn't chopping; he has Tom Parker doing it because it is slow and sporadic, unlike the steady mechanical
chop of Harv. She knows Harv probably never chops a piece
of wood that he doesn't think about that accident he had. He
doesn't talk about that accident, never has, but Tessy can
imagine it all from what Emily has said. Now she imagines
the axe slipping from Tom Parker's hand, his thin pale face
twisted in pain; his shoulder blades so sharp they look like
they could pierce his skin as he hunches forward, his leg
covered in blood.

She lifts herself from the bed, pulls the sheet out from
under her and removes her gown. "Tom Parker!" she raps
on the window and he puts down the axe. It makes her hurt
to look at that child, that wood all ragged and splintered in
a pile around him. "Come wait outside my door," she calls.
"I need you a minute." She drops the curtains and puts on
a clean nightgown, bundles up all that other and puts it in a
burlap bag that she uses to tote laundry to the river. "Come
in, son," she calls and gets back in the bed, pulls the quilt
around her. Her fingers are icy cold against her thin ribs and
she breathes a sigh of relief when she runs her hand over her
empty abdomen. "Take this sack to the river."

"It's freezing cold, Mama," he says. "I can't wash those
clothes."

"I said take it to the river." She sits up and pulls the quilt
closer. "Sink it." She waits for him to answer but he only
stares back at her, his dull brown eyes so much like Harv's

she can't bear to look. "That's right," she says. "Just like the doctor done last time."

"Is it dead?" he asks, hands thrust in his pockets.

"It ain't nothing. Never was living so it can't be dead."

"Want me to tell Daddy?" he asks when she motions again for him to come take the bag.

"I'll tell him directly," she says, takes his warm hand into hers and places the end of the bag there, folds his fingers around it. "Don't look like that," she says. "It wasn't meant to be." And she watches him tiptoe from the room and pull the door to behind him. She gets down under the covers and tries to say a prayer for whatever was there in that bag. She tries to sleep but the sound of chopping goes right on and on in her head.

She gets herself up and dresses, warm stockings and a big thick sweater, and she goes out and starts raking leaves up into huge piles around the pecan trees, the whole time sifting through and picking up nuts, filling the pockets of her dress. The light is so strange today, gray and misty, like it might be close to nighttime though it isn't even noon. It might as well be any time and that's what she thinks while she rakes back and forth in long straight strokes while the wind lifts and scatters the neat piles.

"Doctor says you're to stay bedded," Harv says. He is standing over the woodpile and she hadn't even noticed. She bends and sifts through the pile of leaves at her feet. "You don't want to lose another."

"Done lost it," she says, never stopping, reaching and sifting. "I already sent Tom Parker to the river with it."

"What was it?" Harv asks and steps closer, his big hands hanging clumsily like they don't even belong to him.

"It was nothing yet," she says and squeezes two of the nuts together between her palms. "I didn't even look at it." She picks some of the meat from the shell and puts it in her mouth. "It was nothing."

"You been doing too much," he says. "Next time you're gonna stay in the bed like you're supposed to if I have to get me a colored woman to come here and work."

"There ain't gonna be a next time," she says. "It ain't meant for me to have another." She concentrates on picking the bits of meat from the shell.

"You wouldn't get that way if it weren't meant to be." He

takes that nut from her hand and sails it way up high over the woodpile where it hits and bounces into the leaves.

"I wouldn't get that way if . . ." Tessy stops herself and goes back to sifting. "Just let me be." She can hear him now, walking away, up the steps and when the door slams, she bundles up her pile of pecans in the bottom of her dress and goes to sit in the barn to crack and pick them.

She is still sitting there late afternoon while Emily eases open that heavy wooden door and lets the gray cold light come through. "It's getting dark, Tessy," Emily whispers. "And it's getting cold. Me and James stopped by to visit a little."

"I reckon Harv told you," she says and looks up, those green eyes of Emily's just as calm and steady as ever. "I'll send you home some pecans. I got this whole pile right here."

"I'm sorry, Tessy."

"Most of them ain't even broke. I like to put the whole ones on top of a cake and make a little picture."

"Is there anything I can do?" Emily sits there in the straw at Tessy's feet, that old skinny cow wanting to nuzzle Emily's neck.

"I ain't gonna do it again," she says. "I ain't. I'd rather die."

"Don't say things like that," Emily whispers. "You don't mean it."

"Me and you are the same age," Tessy says and toys with the pecans in her lap. "You are just now carrying your first and I have got five living and three that never was. Now that's a plenty. My Tom Parker is nine years old and can chop wood like a man."

"He's a fine son," Emily says. "Looks like he's grown a foot."

"They all have," she says. "They eat and grow and out-grow clothes faster than I can make them." Tessy leans forward and whispers like a child, her eyes clear and young though her hands are as rough as any old farm wife. "When I was fifteen, I was having a baby and your mama was making you a dress to wear to a picnic social, and when I was twenty I was having another baby while you were getting ready for James to come home from the war. Lena was out in the yard playing games and honest to God there was times that I wanted nothing better than to take off my shoes and run through some cornfield with some fool dog. Harv didn't see me that way, though; nobody saw me the way that they saw you and Lena and there I had all those dreams that I'd marry Harv like my daddy said and that it would be like I was one of you, that I'd have sisters and a mama. Harv said he'd take me away from that life I was living with my daddy out in Slade Township and he brought me to a life that's worse. I haven't come to love him like my daddy said I would and I still don't feel like I've got a mama."

"Tessy."

"No listen," she whispers louder. "You are the only good thing to come from me marrying Harv, not Lena, not your mama, just you. There are only two people on this earth that I love; I love you and I love . . ."

"Tessy don't," Emily says and grabs her hand. "They're liable to come looking for us out here."

"I don't have to tell you," she says. "I don't even have to say his name. You're the only person I'll ever tell and that's enough. I know he loves me and I love him. All day long I hear his sad sweet music in my head like a promise." She lies back in the hay and crosses her hands over her stomach. "I'd like to hold onto a green velvet dress, a dress the color of a deep dark forest and I'd fix my hair all up in a twist and then let it down real slow over one shoulder."

"Oh Tessy," Emily shakes her head. "You'd look pretty but where around here would you wear a green velvet dress?"

"I'd wear it right out in the field. I'd wear it into town when I went to the store. I'd wear it at a ball and I'd dance around and around." Tessy stands and holds her dress out to the side, curtsies. "And I'll wear it when . . ." she turns and drops back down in the hay, her cheeks flushed.

"When?" Emily asks, fearing what she knows to be the truth, that Tessy has never given up on her dream that that man will be back for her. Tessy is so pretty here in the dusky light, her thick hair curling and twisting, the color blending with the hay, her thin face filled with color.

"When? When?" Tessy laughs, lies back and laughs such a loud fit of laughter that Emily catches herself laughing even though she's not certain why. "When I'm buried," Tessy sighs. "I'll wear it in the grave." And she laughs until the tears start rolling down her cheeks and Emily leans over to hug her.

"That's a long way off," Emily whispers.

"And a long way down."

"Tessy!" Emily hugs her closer. "You're forgiven all of that. You've asked haven't you?"

"Oh I've asked." Tessy backs away. "But I ain't so sure that'll take care of it. I ain't so sure I want to be forgiven; that's asking forgiveness for the best part of my life."

"You believe don't you?"

"You gotta believe something, I reckon," she says. "I believe I ain't meant to have more babies. I believe I ain't meant to spend my whole life like an old woman." She pauses and stares hard at Emily. "But I believe that if God is good like you say that he wouldn't give me such a bad life, that he'd give me a chance."

"We can't question how things are done," Emily says, tears coming to her eyes.

"Oh, you can't cry enough over it," Tessy says. "It's all so sad. The only thing that keeps me going and working and living this life is that feeling I had that I told you about," Tessy lowers her voice and watches Emily's back go stiff. "Just tell me if you've ever felt something, if you've ever felt like every drop of blood in your body could pump right out, felt your face go hot and felt so funny between the legs like you needed to cross them real tight."

"Tessy," Emily whispers, stares at her hands. "Just hush up."

"No, tell me." Tessy kneels and grips her hands. "Has James ever made you feel that way? Has anybody?"

"James is my husband."

"And Harv is my husband," she says. "But he has never made me feel that way."

"Harv is good to you, a good husband. If a woman's got a good husband who is kind to her then she's got a lot."

"But she doesn't have everything."

"Nobody has everything."

"Oh, I think you do, Emily," Tessy says and stands, brushes off her dress. "I never would have told you how I felt that night and all those afternoons when I'd see him downtown. I wouldn't have told you how he made me feel that way if I hadn't thought that you'd know what I was saying."

"I have never discussed myself with you. It's not to be discussed."

"Why? Why can't we discuss it?" Tessy pulls that barn door open wide and they can see Harv and James standing over by the woodpile, one of Tessy's children chasing after a hound dog with a stick. "But you know what I'm talking about, though. I know you do and I reckon I feel lucky to have felt it once." Tessy steps out into the yard and reaches for Emily's hand. "I think you're lucky 'cause you've got your whole life to feel it." Emily doesn't look at her as they walk side by side, but Tessy feels stronger now; she feels the energy coming back to her, she hears that slow sweet tune with every step of her feet in those dead crackly leaves.

Tessy stands and watches James and Emily get in the buggy and pull away, down the road, a fine slice of that strange gray light between their bodies. She takes a deep breath, that crisp autumn air, feeling like a part of her is in that buggy and gone in a cloud of yellow dust.

"I reckon you needed a woman to talk to," Harv says, his hand clumsily finding hers as they walk up to the house. He has already built a fire and has the lantern on the front porch lit. "I'm sorry for what you went through."

"I know you are," she says. "I'm thinking I might go to town with you tomorrow, thinking I might buy me some cloth. I want to sew some cloth."

By summertime, Emily has herself a baby girl that she calls Hannah Elizabeth, straight from the Bible and Tessy is all swoll up with what she hopes will be her last. If it's a boy, she wants to call him Jacob; if it's a girl she'll just call her something like Madge or Peg and try to get on with her life.

* * *

The silence, the way that his eyes never leave Tessy's face, is comfortable until a large acorn thumps the dusty dirt, reminding her that there are people passing on the street, the iced salted fish that she has just bought leaking through the newspaper onto her hands. She looks briefly away, past the tall oak where a straw-haired child pulls a wagon full of empty bottles, then down at her hands, the black sticky smudges.

"I best be going," she says and takes one step back from

him, his violin in the case beside his feet. "Mighty nice to have seen you again."

"Yes," once again he looks at her and there is that impulsive sense that he might suddenly reach and grab her hands, pull her close in spite of the people, the fish, the child who now is passing, the wagon wheels whining with every bump of the road, bottles clanging. He extends his hand to her and she pauses a minute, realizing her hands are covered in sticky smudges, as calloused as any man's hand. He waits, palm toward her, long smooth fingers with tiny callouses at the tips where he pressed the strings of his violin. "It's always nice when you stop by, Tessy. I hope to see you again."

She nods and turns quickly, hurries down the road, the colors so warm beyond the fields where the sun is setting. Just the sight of it all makes her feel as if she could be swallowed up by the sky; it makes her feel so good, so sad, free, strong, and then weak and tired. She can hear his music, calling her back, or maybe giving her the strength to go on. Just hearing the music, knowing he is there, is going to stay for awhile, is enough to make her keep walking, down the road, past the small row of houses, the large open fields that lead down to where she and Harv live.

She realizes that she is walking faster and faster, ready to run at any moment, the fish clutched so tightly that they are soiling the front of her dress. She must stop, breathe, because Harv will be at home, will see the flush in her cheeks and the slight shaking of her hands. She stops at the curve in the road and relaxes her grip on the fish, turns to look back where he is standing in front of the hardware store, a handful of people stopped there to listen to his music, to toss coins in that open case. She slows her pace to that of the music, steady, sweeping, the whole time that she imagines his smooth lineless face, his young strong body, and at night when there is someone there beside her, she imagines that it's him.

She arranges her days in ways that she has to go to town; she takes her time getting ready, combs her hair down smooth around her shoulder, pinches her cheeks and lips. She does this for weeks, her stops in front of the hardware store sometimes lasting into late afternoon, their stares becoming longer and longer until one day she meets him there by the Saxapaw River, the bend that is always deserted, as he follows the road by the river to his home and his wife and children. The bend

is a shaded area blanketed in moist green moss and hidden
from the ridge of trees that blocks the sight of her own home,
Spanish moss hangs from the trees, grapevines like large
ropes all around. She meets him just that once and soon there
is no reason to go to town, no reason to comb her hair down
around her shoulders. His name repeats itself in her mind,
over and over, like a song of her own until too many weeks
and months and years pass and the tunes that he played only
come to her in odd little bits and pieces.

* * *

Lena thinks she's dying at thirteen. That's all blood can
mean, dying, and she flings herself on top of the bed, pulls
a quilt up over her and rocks back and forth, her hands covering the wounded area while she prays as loud as she can.
She thinks of all the lies she has told, how she told her mama
that the reason she didn't have recess at school was because
the teacher needed a helper when all the time it was because
she slapped a girl upside of her fat head for not letting Lena
use the speller that had bad pictures drawn in it. She thinks
of all the times she had called Curie, "Nigger, nigger black
as tar," and gotten switched for it. She thinks of her sister
way up there in the churchyard "starved like a skeleton" or
so they say. But Lena isn't starving, she is bleeding to death
and it makes her scream louder just to think of it.

"Lena Pearson, what on earth?" her mama asks, standing in the doorway so gray and washed out, always so gray
and washed out like she might not have any blood and
Lena's blood is so red and dark, on her hand and between
her legs. She can't even tell where it's coming from. When
Harv sliced up the front of his leg with that axe, they were
able to get it to stop because they could see where it was
coming from. But when Curie was tied up to that tree, before her daddy took him down and threw his coat over him,
she couldn't tell where the blood was coming from. It
seemed the blood was coming from everywhere like right
now and Curie died.

"I'm hurt," Lena says. "I'm dying," and she is somehow
relieved by the very sound of it, the pronouncement. "I'm
dying."

"What is wrong?" her mama sits down at the end of the
bed.

"I'm bleeding, bleeding to death."

"Where?" Her mama pulls back the quilt.

"Here, down here," she says and holds up her hand for her mama to see. "I'm bleeding from where I pee." Her mama turns away and shakes her head.

"All women bleed that way," her mama whispers as if Lena should have known, as if she's done something wrong in not knowing. "It's how women have babies."

"By bleeding?" Lena sits up and looks at her mother. She suddenly doesn't feel quite as weak as she did before. "But I don't want to have a baby. I want to go to the fair." Her mama goes on and on about how women are put on this earth to suffer, that it is God's will that they suffer, that a lady (if she is a lady) has a hard row to hoe and the earlier that lesson is learned, the better off she will be. Then she takes Lena to the linen closet where she has a stack of diapers there on the bottom shelf and tells her how that's what she'll wear and how she'll need to wash them out and hang them on the line down at the end of the field so that no man will see them hanging there.

"Why didn't you tell me about this?" Lena asks Emily late that night when they are in bed. "I'm so mad that nobody told me this."

"Mama said it needn't be discussed," Emily whispers. "It's personal."

"Well, you still should have told. I thought I was dying, bent over to pick up some chicken feed and caught a glimpse up my dress and thought I was dying."

Emily turns her face to the wall. "You'll get used to it."

"How? How can I get used to something that I'm supposed to keep a secret?" Lena lifts her gown and hikes that diaper back in place. "Mama says it's a sign from God that you can have babies. Mama says that God wants you to cramp up and bleed like a river, that he makes you." Lena watches Emily's back jerk with a loud sigh. "Mary Towney told me that babies are made from pee."

"That's not true."

"What is true then? Tell me what is true." Lena feels so mad she could spit fire. "Do you know?"

"Not completely, no," Emily says and rolls to face her, Emily's eyes so wide and fearful. It seems to take the anger right out of her to see Emily look that way.

"Well, I'm gonna find out all there is to know," Lena whispers. "I am." She nods her head at Emily but now she feels so tired and confused about the whole thing, concentrates on that throbbing she can feel like a tiny heartbeat, dreads that she's going to have to wash that nasty thing out and walk half a mile where nobody will see it drying.

*　*　*

Emily stands in the center of the yard and watches Lena playing there by the pump. Lena is in her underwear, her feet potty black. She glances at the front door to make sure her mama isn't there behind the screen, and Curie is off to the side, waving his hat and grinning at her. "Dance yourself a jig, Miss Emily," he says, "Come on, now" and raises one finger, twirls it as if he has a june bug on a string, and she starts, slow at first and then faster and faster, Lena and the front door and Curie's dark face just a blur beneath that wide blue sky. She laughs and twirls till her head is light and dizzy. "Rain, rain, rain," she cries, her heart beating fast like the word might be magic. She knows the yellow dust of the yard is clouding up and covering her shoes that she just greased to a fine shine with chicken fat, covering the hem of her dress and her ankles. Her hair has come undone and is whirling with her, sweat trickling down her neck, and she has to breath faster and faster to keep up with her feet, the sky spinning, until finally, she flops down on a grassy spot and stares open-eyed at the spinning trees and clouds, Curie's face spinning as he gets closer. "That was a fine dance now," he says. "Don't it make your heart feel good?"

"Yes, yes," she whispers and closes her eyes to the spinning, her arms and legs so tired in a good way. "I'm going to dance every day."

"Emily Pearson? What are you doing?" Her mama is on the porch, the screen door creaking shut, and she bolts up and brushes off her dress, searches through the yellow dust for her hair pins. "You are too old for such."

"Last time I ask you to dance a rain dance," Curie whispers the next day when the sky is so black and stormy. "And you just a child." His warm face is right next to hers so her mama who is kneeling by the bed won't hear. "I guess children got the power," and he grins and heads down the road through the pouring rain, and she stands at the window and watches, thinks about Curie's girl that he speaks of so often, the girl that has one of Emily's doll babies, a girl that Emily bets gets to spin and dance and feel that good feeling every day. Her mama tells her to kneel down and pray, that God has the power and that Emily must believe that God has the power. And yes, she does believe in the power but it has nothing to do with her mama's ways.

*　*　*

Virginia Suzanne Pearson wakes to see her mother standing at the end of the bed, a slight shadow, white bony hands clutching the neck of her robe made visible by the glow of the kerosene lamp that Curie had hung from a porch rafter. "I gotta see my way from the house to the barn or back," he had told her. "I can't stand no pitch black darkness."

"All right, Curie," she told him, recalling with amusement the last time he stayed overnight. It was the middle of the night and he made his way to the end of their bed and stood there reeling off all the chores that he had in mind for the next day. Cord had not even awakened until she returned to bed after walking Curie back to the door. "It was so awful," he finally confessed as he stood in the darkness on the other side of the screened door. "I dreamed I come into this house and you was all ghosts, white and still with glassy eyes and not a breath I tell you. I called out and nobody said nothin', I was the only one of us livin'. I says 'Miss Virginia, I's scared' and your head turned so slowlike, them eyes still glassy and you says, 'Curie, ain't no reason,' and I says 'but I am, why ain't you in the bed, why're them children setting up and it way in the night' and you says, 'Curie, ain't no reason' just that same way. You said it over and over and then little Lena she said it too, and Emily and on and on till I woke up in a sweat like I've never in my life had." His eyes were wide and frightened as he told the dream and she felt a chill go through her scalp just listening, the same chill that comes now with Mother's voice.

"I've come to tell you something," her mother says and though Virginia cannot distinguish her mother's mouth in the darkness, there is a difference in her voice, her teeth clenched. "You have to listen," she whispers and steps closer to the bed. "I've come to tell you that if any of those children of yours ever run wild, if you let them grow up to be hateful or cheap, if you ever let them go without food and clothes and knowledge of the Lord, I'll come and stand here every night after I'm gone. I'll stand right here and I'll never let you rest."

"Mother," she begs. "Please don't say things like that. You know I'll take care of my babies." But her mother turns and leaves the room as quietly as she had come in. In the days that follow when Virginia's mama sits out on the porch and waves a straw broom back and forth, Virginia tries to ask her about what she said, ask her why she did that, but her mama's stare is foggy and distant. It is as if that night never happened, as if Virginia dreamed it all. Even after her mother's death, she catches herself wondering about those words, if they were real, or if they were like the words "ain't no reason" that Curie's dream had given to her, words so foreign to her mouth and yet so real for him. And Curie did have a reason to be afraid, and now she has a child who is dead, a child who went without food and starved.

* * *

It is 1897, mid-December, and Virginia Suzanne Pearson is sitting by the fire, her cherry rocker moving back and forth, a worn woolen quilt pulled up over her full abdomen, her hands clasped under her stomach to support the weight. Just a few minutes ago, she had looked out that frosted kitchen window and studied the thick gray clouds in the sky. This area rarely gets snow, but this night, Virginia has a feeling that it is coming, the clouds, the crisp sharp smell, the frozen rattling of the limbs of the pecan tree outside the window. She had stood, watching and waiting, as if there would come a sign, but then she had been distracted by a kick, a tiny unknown elbow trying to make room. She had held her breath but had not moved for fear that the moment would end too quickly as it had the other times. It is time, yes, and it will snow before morning, she had thought and pressed her heart-shaped face against the frozen window, her thick curly hair pulled up away from her face. She watched Cord brush down that old mule and lead it into the barn and now she is waiting for him to come in from the cold, the fear that the pneumonia that has taken so many could take him.

It is like a secret that she has, this knowledge that the time has come and she will enjoy it, enjoy when Cord sits beside her and speaks of the fields and what he did today. She will hold this secret like she might be a child herself, until she can hold it no longer and needs to let go. She will rise so early, all the feelings that she has felt before and she will concentrate on a smudge on the ceiling, her hands gripping that bed and she will not concentrate on the pain for good can come from pain. This pain will bring her so much good and when the sun is there within her sight out that window, it will all be over and she will cradle that warm little body beneath the quilt and Cord's eyes will say how he's glad that part is over and her breath on that little neck will say Emily Suzanne Pearson. Yes, she will know when the time has come and she will just let go.

*   *   *

"Were you looking for this?" Gram asks and pulls an ear of corn from her pocket, the pink silks falling over her hand. "Tessy said you wanted this."

"Oh yes," Virginia whispers, and reaches her hand, closer and closer, until it is there, the silks falling onto her own hand while Gram's hair grows darker in the faint light, her face gets younger.

"A person's got to know when to let go," Gram says. "You can hold on tight but it don't change the fact that sooner or later you've got to let go."

*   *   *

Virginia wakes late, radio alarm still playing, the sky through the bedroom windows still overcast, bathroom light on and towels strewn across the floor but Mark has already left. She gets up switching the orange nightshirt for the lavender sack dress that her mother made for her while she was there. Things are coming to her so clearly now, so many things that she had forgotten. She remembers the house on Carver Street so vividly, the windows, the way the light fell, and sees now what she wants to paint, from the back door as though you just stepped in, standing in that doorway and looking into the breakfast room as Gram had done so many times, kerosene stove to the left, the table, venetian blinds, china cupboard on the right with that pink china bowl on the second shelf, the same bowl that Virginia accidentally dropped and broke when she was ten, the hat box filled with buttons in the center of the table, a coffee cup, the white oilcloth, red and white woven placemats, rice in the salt shaker, through to the kitchen, the outside rim of the sink and counter showing through the doorway, the little step stool in front of the window, violets on the sill.

She sees it now, sees it so clearly, the colors and shadows, and then she will paint what it looked like to sit on that counter and look out the window, the huge brick warehouses down the street, smoke from what used to be Cutty's Place, the pecan tree just outside the window where her mother stands with that brown sweater drawn close around her shoulders, standing on the sidewalk with its bumps and cracks, her mother's hair brown black, so young-looking; and then she will paint it from her mother's eyes as she looked up at that window and saw Virginia standing there, face pressed against the glass, her breath forming a circle, and her mother sees the leaves tumbling from those gutters over the back porch, the white wooden siding, gray shutters; and she will paint that same day from Gram's eyes, staring down that hall to the bedroom, chair railing and bead boards narrowing like a railroad track to that closed bedroom door, a dim filtered light coming from the crack below the door, slants of light from the venetian blinds falling on the wall to the left; and she will paint it from Gramp's eyes, those large blue eyes as he sat in his chair and looked over the backyard to that chicken-wire dog pen, the Uncle Remus book that he had read so many times he knew it by heart, held on his lap.

Mark has left a note pinned to the lavender dress, "the new uniform" as he called it while she shredded up the yellow one and used it to clean the drops of paint from the floor in the baby's room. He has gone to the library and then to mail the lease on the house in Richmond that they are going to rent, a small house with hardwood floors and dormer windows upstairs. He had brought her detailed floor plans and photos, which direction every wall and window faced and then he sat there like he was holding his breath. "What? Am I a difficult person?" she asked.

She goes into the spare room where she has already started

packing some boxes and put them in the closet, all law books
cleared away, replaced with toys and a new painting, painted
on top of the old, this time friendly animals, zoo animals in
their bright colors, Tony the Tiger and Peppi Le Peu. The
phone rings and Virginia goes to the kitchen to answer, no
dishes in the sink, windows still smelling of Windex.

"Hey girl," Cindy says. "Just checking to see if you've
dropped it yet."

"Not yet."

"You haven't been back in three weeks," Cindy says. "Of
course it's probably good; you might get stuck again and
wasn't that a trip?"

"Quite a trip," Virginia says, stretching the cord to reach
the Mr. Coffee that Mark had left turned on. "I must have
been going through something psychological, you know?"

"Shit," Cindy's laugh comes through the receiver so loud.
"Why do you always have to have some smart sounding reason for acting like a spoiled bitch?"

"Was I that bad?"

"Oh God, Virginia," Cindy says. "You have acted that
way your whole life. And yes, I called you Virginia. Mama
said if you wanted to be called Virginia that we should call
you Virginia because you're grown up now."

"Madge said all that?"

"Oh man, she's been saying all kinds of things," Cindy
says and laughs again. "But, I do think Hannah coached her
on that one."

"You can still call me Ginny Sue," she says. "Really, it
sounds funny for you *not* to call me Ginny Sue. Tell everybody just to stick with the way it's been."

"Well, the leopard has changed its damn spots," Cindy
says. "Listen, I got to tell you my news. I've decided me and
Chuckie are gonna buy one of those solar condos that my
sister has been pushing on me forever."

"You are?"

"Yeah, and what's more, I took Mama to Merle Norman's
like what Hannah did, and I left her there, wasn't about to
let them mess with my face. But, when I picked Mama up, I
couldn't believe it, night and day, and then she went and got
her hair frosted so it looks kind of blonde instead of gray and
then we drove over to Ivey's in Clemmonsville and Mama

bought herself a whole new wardrobe. I even picked out some of it. I got me some black leather pants for the fall.''

"I'm glad ya'll are getting along.'' Virginia is staring at the phone now, wondering if this is really Cindy on the line.

"Well, she gets on my nerves so bad still, but we're trying,'' Cindy says. "And I got no choice but to be nice to slutbucket and likoor-sucker if I'm buying a condo through her.''

"Now you sound normal,'' Virginia says. "Have you seen Charles?''

"Yes.'' There is a stillness at the other end. "Got hitched, ah, I guess about an hour ago. Mama bought Chuckie a new suit and he looked real cute when I dropped him off at the church, face is getting better since he went to the dermatologist. Charles is paying for it.'' Cindy pauses again, sounds like she moves away from the receiver for a second. "Charles saw me when I pulled into the parking lot there. He waved and I tooted the horn, made him laugh. You know he probably needed to laugh, probably was scared and I know how his neck will start to sweat if he's scared.''

"I'm sorry, Cindy.''

"Yeah, well, I had my turn. Now it's his turn, and who knows what'll ever happen,'' Cindy whispers. "I wanted to tell you that and too, shit, honey, I met the cutest doctor and he ain't married; he's so cute, too, and cute like I like it, a little rough-looking but clean. He's so cute that I don't say 'ain't' in front of him, told that drug pusher to fuck off. I said 'fuck your wife, buddy. That's what she's for.' ''

"Cindy!''

"Now, don't climb on my ass over liberation. I mean you can look in my wallet and know that I am, look at me, but he probably has the kind of mind that that's what made sense to him. I'm through with him and anybody like him.''

"Good,'' Virginia says, straddling her legs and lifting her skirt a little in front of the floor fan so that the cool air will billow up her dress. "Come see me soon. Please. We'll be moving in five weeks.''

"Hell, I will,'' Cindy says. "But I want you to have that baby and take up smoking again before I do. Good God, I was telling Mama that I never want to sit through such a hellhole time as we all did that day at Emily's house.''

"I know."

"Don't you ever tell all that went on," Cindy says. "I'd be embarrassed for people to know that I come from such."

"Who am I gonna tell?" Virginia asks and laughs. "The old folks? Constance Ann? Earl Conners in front of Endicott Johnson's?"

"Yeah, yeah, make up something of your own for a change," Cindy says and pauses. "But you know, that was something what Emily said to me wasn't it?"

"What?"

"About getting me a green dress and dancing," Cindy says and laughs softly. "It seemed so real, too, didn't it? You might think Grandma Tessy turned into a tree but I think she's off somewhere dancing with that man."

"I never said she turned *into* a tree," Virginia says slowly, though still feeling a prickle over her scalp from Cindy's words.

"I'm still your favorite cousin, though."

Virginia goes out onto the porch, that Virginia Slims still wrapped in a baggie on the rafter. "Sure I saw it," Mark had said and laughed. "But God knows with the way you were acting, I wasn't about to touch it." She takes it down and drops it in the trashcan, walks out into the yard where it seems the weeds have grown a foot overnight.

"Sure is hot isn't it?" Mrs. Short calls from her side of the fence.

"Yes," Virginia nods and bends to pick the wild violets growing there.

"Your husband told me you were sick a while back but I see you ain't had the baby."

"Not yet."

"Well, it'll come when it's ready." Mrs. Short steps close to the fence, her body greased in suntan oil even though there's no sun and her hair pulled up in a blue floral towel. "Husband tells me ya'll are moving North, too."

"Just to Richmond."

"Well, I'm sorry to hear it. I've felt right safe with ya'll here beside me and I was telling my Buddy the other day," she pauses. "You know my boy, Buddy? One that drives the flashy car?"

"Yes." Virginia squats there to pick more violets, pull the milkweeds.

"Well, I told him that I've felt right safe with you two here. I mean you just never know who you're gonna end up living beside." Mrs. Short talks on and on and Virginia smiles and nods but the words all escape her and she concentrates on the way she's feeling, a strange way that takes her breath. She sits and stretches her legs out and watches the gray clouds gathering and she turns until the breeze is blowing into her face.

"Looks like more rain," Mrs. Short says. "First we go on and on without it and now it seems like it's rained for a month." And now Mrs. Short is folding her lawn chair, going inside while Virginia sits and watches the clouds, names coming to her mind. Mark will be home for lunch soon just as he promised when he leaned over her this morning, Colgate and shaving cream. She can't wait for him to get home, now. She holds her breath, waits and it disappears again, leaving her feeling odd and uncertain so she concentrates on names like Emily and Lena, James and David, and the sky is getting darker, so she concentrates on Mark getting home, thinks about how she will arrange the furniture in Richmond.

In just a few minutes the wind has picked up and the umbrella of Mrs. Short's patio table is rocking back and forth. She smells the clear sharp smell of rain; it is coming, she knows and she watches the clouds gathering in the distance like dark swirls and it seems like she should be thinking of something that can slow it all down, some secret that she will remember forever, but all she can think is that she wishes Mark would hurry; all she can think is barefoot and pregnant, drop a rusty nail in a bottle of vinegar. She thinks of that cloud rushing towards her and how right now that cloud is probably over Gram's duplex and her parents' home, and how very soon it will be right here, in her yard. Something is about to happen and she knows it with the first cool drop of rain, that cloud letting go. I've always known when the time was right, Gram says, I've just always known. I would never leave you, she told Mark and buried her face in his warm neck, there is no one who could ever take your place. I've known that river my whole life, Gram says, it'll rise come a rain. And she sees that river so far from its source, growing and rushing as if there are not enough places or hours in the world. Easy does it, Gram says and the june bug twirls faster and faster around her head while she digs her feet into that warm black dirt and Gram stoops and picks her way down that garden row, then disappears in the thick field of corn. I'll always be with you, she says.

About the Author

JILL MCCORKLE, a native of Lumberton, North Carolina, graduated from the University of North Carolina at Chapel Hill and received her M.A. from Hollins College. Until her recent marriage, she lived in Chapel Hill and taught in the writing program at UNC. She and her husband now live in Boston. Her previous books are THE CHEER LEADER and JULY 7TH.

THE
STREET-SMART
WORLD OF
Alice
Hoffman